MURDER
ON
Pratas Reef

A NOVEL

BY
RICK AINSWORTH

By Rick Ainsworth

Thunder and Storm: The Haverfield Incident

National Award Winner
2007 Indie Excellence Award in Historical Fiction

National Award Finalist
2006 Best Books Award in Historical Fiction

This book is a work of fiction. All names, characters, places and incidents portrayed in this novel are the product of the author's imagination or are used fictitiously. Any resemblance to actual events, locales, or persons, living or dead, is coincidental.

Published by VRA Publishing of Las Vegas
www.vrapublishing.com

Cover design and formatting by Matt Mitchell (mattmitchelldesign.com)

Original Cover artwork by Therese Van Rijn
"USS Frank Knox Aground on Pratas Reef", © 2007

Edited by Debbie Hall (hallwayprod@yahoo.com)

ISBN: 978-0-9770376-1-2

Library of Congress control number: 2007933742

This book is dedicated to all the sailors who were with the USS Frank Knox when she hit Pratas Reef, and especially to the brave crewmen, officers and enlisted, who saved their ship by remaining aboard during the dangerous and unpredictable salvage operation. These men, working 18- to 24-hour days, suffering overwhelming humidity, no fresh water, very little hot food, and numbing lack of sleep, demonstrated the dedication and pride that, for almost two hundred years, has forged the United States Navy into the most powerful military force on the face of the Earth.

AMONG THEM ARE:
Bill Dall
Bob Harp
Gary Johnson
Gary Platou
Harry Abbott
Jim Lewis
K.C. Troise
Richard Huehn

WE, WHO SAILED THE BLUE PACIFIC WITH THEM,
ARE PROUD.

AND ALSO TO THERESE:
my 'Split-Apart.'

"...but the Raven, still beguiling all my sad soul into smiling,
Straight I wheeled a cushioned seat in front of bird and bust and door;
Then, upon the velvet sinking, I betook myself to linking
Fancy unto fancy thinking what this ominous bird of yore-
What this grim, ungainly, ghastly, gaunt and ominous bird of yore
Meant in croaking, 'Nevermore.'"

—Edgar Allan Poe
The Raven
1845

PROLOGUE

Press release from CINCPACFLT on 20 July 1965:

"The 2400-ton U.S. Naval destroyer USS FRANK KNOX (DDR-742), while operating in the South China Sea, ran aground on a coral reef seven and one-half miles southwest of Pratas Island Saturday, July 18, at 0300 local time. Pratas Island is located 165 miles south-east of Hong Kong and approximately 240 miles southwest of Taiwan. The auxiliary ships MUNSEE, COCOPA, GRAPPLE and MAHOPAC steamed to the aid of FRANK KNOX and are conducting salvage operations. The exact extent of damage to the KNOX has not been determined. There are no personnel injuries to date. Commanding officer of FRANK KNOX is Commander Gerald Pizzonovich, USN of Muncie, Indiana. FRANK KNOX is a unit of the Seventh Fleet and is home-ported in San Diego, California."

Pratas Reef is located west of the International Date Line, and is, therefore, one day ahead of the United States, or more accurately, sixteen hours ahead of Los Angeles.

Author's Note:

In July, 1965, the USS Frank Knox did, indeed, run aground on Pratas Reef. While this is a work of fiction, the history contained in this volume is reasonably accurate, including the details of some of the salvage operations. These operations, and the men involved, were heroic in nature, and the main reason for putting it all down is to honor the memory of what they accomplished under almost impossible conditions.

The United States Navy was at its best during the Knox crisis. Within hours of the first call for help, rescue and salvage ships arrived on the scene to provide emergency assistance. Within days, the destroyer tender Prairie, the helicopter carrier Iwo Jima, the combat supply ship Mars, and many other assets arrived on the scene. The amassed salvage force, under the command of a rear admiral, toiled 24 hours a day for 37 days to free the Knox from the reef. During that time, thousands of tons of supplies were ferried by helicopter or boat back and forth between the 15 ships in 'Operation Maximum Effort.' Side-by-side underway refueling and personnel transfer (called 'hi-lining') often occurred simultaneously on both port and starboard sides of the Prairie and Mars. Salvage experts from Pearl Harbor and San Diego were flown to the scene. A Navy SEAL team arrived to blow away part of the reef. Innovative procedures such as the use of liquid Styrofoam were tested and employed.

After 37 days of maximum effort, the Knox was freed and towed away, but few really believed she would ever sail again. The damage was too extensive. The only people who thought she could be made seaworthy again were those crazy Navy engineers.

During the salvage operation, there were few injuries and no deaths.

The people, personalities, and locations in this work are fictional, strictly a work of my imagination. Actual people and locations are used in a fictional sense. Certain individuals I knew at the time suggested some of the novel's characters. With permission, I have used the real names of some of the Knox sailors.

I was there. I witnessed 'Operation Maximum Effort' from the USS Prairie's signal bridge.

PART ONE:

THE REEF

CHAPTER ONE

Aboard the USS Frank Knox, (DDR-742)
Southwest of Pratas Island
South China Sea
Sunday, July 18, 1965
0230 Hours

Day 1

The South China Sea lay like a soft, smooth blanket, slowly undulating with gentle swells in the early Sunday morning hours. The mid-watch was more than two hours old, and on the bridge, officers and enlisted men yawned at their stations, lulled nearly to sleep by the hour, by the soft sea and by the easy, rolling movement of the ship. The moon was waning, but still cast a pale light over the sea and over the Frank Knox. In a few short hours the tropical heat would arrive with the rising sun, and sweating, cursing sailors would go about the ship's routine, bitching and griping about anything they could think of, but privately pleased they were headed to a good liberty port. They needed a good liberty, especially after their most recent duty, patrolling Yankee Station off the coast of Viet Nam. The war there was expanding, and President Johnson was committing more and more troops to the conflict. The darkening specter of Viet Nam was becoming more prominent in the minds of all sailors in the Seventh Fleet. The men of the Knox were glad to get away from Yankee Station, and the anticipation of liberty in Hong Kong kept their spirits high.

The OOD, Lieutenant (jg) Medford Prentiss II, sipped coffee and leaned against the chart table, running his hand through his already thinning blond hair, his long, thin nose pointing down at the chart table like a penguin's beak. He examined the area's charts and the course he had plotted earlier that evening. As officer of the deck and assistant navigator, it was Mr. Prentiss' responsibility to monitor the ship's location throughout the night. The plotted course would take them northeast to Taiwan, then southwest to Hong Kong, where the crew would enjoy their first time ashore in over two months.

Mr. Prentiss had been named assistant navigator, a position largely invented by the captain, because Medford was not a very good sailor and not highly thought of by the captain or the crew. He would only allow Lieutenant (jg) Prentiss to be OOD during the mid-watch, where nothing much ever happened. The navigator and executive officer, Lieutenant Lamb, charged with keeping an eye on Medford, had left explicit instructions with Lieutenant (jg) Prentiss before the exec had retired for the evening: "...make hourly course corrections, if necessary, and be sure to use the sextant to plot the course..." It was assumed nothing could go wrong.

Medford Prentiss II had joined the navy after an unspectacular ROTC career at Boston University, because all the Prentisses back to the Revolutionary War had served in the Navy, though none with any distinction. The Navy was to be tolerated, reasoned young Med, until he finished his enlistment and went home to join his father's public relations firm. Med wasn't any more interested in public relations than he was in a Navy career. Medford Prentiss II had only one passion: tsunamis. He read everything he could about them, what caused them, where they occurred and when. It was more than a passion, it was an obsession. Medford had never seen a tsunami, but he had seen pictures of the damage they could do. He fantasized about seeing one at sea, and what it might look like. He had remarked to other officers that he thought a tsunami at sea would look just like a big wave coming in on the beach; and he would, were he the OOD when a tsunami was spotted, head right for it and crash into it. His theory was that he could break up the tsunami by steaming into it. There was no scientific evidence to support this theory, but that didn't discourage Medford. Nor was Lieutenant (jg) Prentiss discouraged by the fact that the U.S. Government might not appreciate his using one of their ships as a tool for his dubious experiment.

Perhaps his preoccupation with the tsunami and his heroic daydreams were the reasons Lt. (jg) Prentiss used the LORAN rather than a sextant to plot his course to Taiwan. The sextant was an instrument of mystery to Medford. He had been trained in its use, but he couldn't muster any enthusiasm for navigating by the stars. Besides, he believed the senior officers insisted on it to keep him busy. He much preferred the LORAN, where everything was pretty much done for you. The LORAN navigates by a series of land-based signal stations. Its accuracy diminishes the farther the ship is from the land-based stations, and the Frank Knox was almost two hundred miles away from any body of land. The sextant navigates by the stars, and while it is a bit more complicated to use, real sailors swore by its accuracy. *Bunch of old farts stuck in their ways,* Medford often thought. He had very little respect for his superiors or the Navy, a fact that was lost on neither, and as a result he stood a lot of midwatches. Had Medford used the sextant, the USS Frank Knox would not have been three degrees off course, leaning toward port. Every knot the ship traveled took it farther and farther away from the base course. Medford did not notice.

Patrolling Yankee Station off South Viet Nam had been a tense and stressful duty. Boarding sampans, searching for weapons and contraband, always knowing one of those obsequious little gooks could pull a gun and shoot your ass was not a pleasant job, particularly not to Medford Prentiss II. He looked at his watch. A little less than two hours to go, then he could climb into his cozy bunk and get some sleep.

"Sir?" The port-side watch leaned down from the 04 level, his binoculars hanging from his neck, swaying gently with the movement of the ship.

"What is it, Pepper?" the OOD asked, looking up.

Seaman Dale Pepper pointed toward the bow. "I think I seen white water ahead, sir," he said sheepishly.

Lieutenant Junior Grade Prentiss felt his heart leap. "White water?" he asked excitedly. "Are you sure, Pepper?" *It had to be a tsunami. They weren't even close to any island or reef.*

"Yessir," the lookout replied. "It looks like we're headed for a reef, sir."

"Don't be absurd," Mr. Prentiss snapped impatiently. He stepped into the pilot house and studied the chart, muttering to himself, "There are no reefs around here." The ship was doing twenty knots, steaming easily and determinedly on course. The OOD moved quickly to the radar scope. The sweeping radar showed nothing. No blips, no bogies, and certainly no reef. Mr. Prentiss pulled on his earlobe, as he did when he was nervous, and smiled to himself. *Finally, a tsunami in the middle of the ocean. A dream come true!*

He hurried out to the flying bridge and trained his binoculars ahead, then swept left and right, trying to locate the white water. There it was, dead ahead! He checked the magnetic compass and then his chart. "Steady on course!"

The helmsman looked around nervously and craned his neck, trying to see out the porthole at the white water. He gripped the helm tightly with both hands and concentrated intently on the gyrocompass, worry etched on his face.

The sound powered phone shrieked and the messenger of the watch plucked it out of its cradle. "Bridge!" he barked into the mouthpiece. "Wait one." He turned to the OOD. "Sir, it's Sonar, they say they're picking up a submerged reef. Suggest course zero-four-five to avoid contact."

"Nonsense!" Mr. Prentiss went out on the port wing and trained his binoculars on the white water. It was definitely a tsunami! It was beautiful, really, the bright white foam glistening in the soft moonlight as it traveled forward, borne from some earthquake deep in the sea. He would hit it straight on and break it up, proving his theory once and for all. He ran into the pilot house and checked the chart again, just in case. Nothing in their path, and they were on course. He was about to suggest the recalibration of the sonar dome when his thoughts were rudely interrupted.

"Reef dead ahead!" The port wing lookout shouted and pointed ahead excitedly. "Dead ahead, sir, dead ahead!"

Lieutenant Prentiss looked up from his chart just as the bow crashed into the reef. The ship skidded up on the coral reef like a boy's winter sled hitting an unexpected patch of bare street. Horrible crunching, grinding and popping sounds came from under the ship's hull and rivets exploded from the bulkheads and decks as 2400 tons of speeding warship smashed into Pratas Reef. The noise was deafening, horrifying. She gouged into the coral, screeching and grinding, and then finally came to a stop. The bridge crew was thrown against bulkheads and bounced off the deck, cursing and yelling. The stern came out of the water, the screws spinning at sixteen knots. Finally, the shrill, insistent, siren-like sound of the spinning screws stopped, and the reef grew quiet. Everything became strangely calm and serene. The smell of the coral reef, mixed with salt spray, blew softly across the decks of the Frank Knox. The only sound that remained was that of the waves slapping angrily against the sides of the ship.

Down in the engine room, Bob Harp had just closed a water valve as part of regular maintenance when the ship hit. He had no idea what had happened, but he thought his action had caused it so he quickly opened the water valve back up and looked around nervously.

In the ship's office, Richard Huehn was knocked off his makeshift bunk; three padded chairs supplemented with pillows and blankets for extra cushioning. He hit the deck hard and swore angrily. The ship's office was the only place he could get any sleep. It was too hot for him below decks, and in the office, he could open the porthole and set up a few fans. It was like having his own private stateroom. He ran out on deck and stared down the starboard side at the reef. *Well,* he thought, realizing it was Sunday, *there goes our eggs-to-order breakfast.*

In the after crew's compartment, K.C. Troise was thrown from his bunk and hit the deck hard. The ship vibrated violently, and as K.C. made it to the fantail, he heard waves lapping up against her sides. *Waves in the middle of the ocean?* he thought. *That doesn't seem...*The ship listed slowly to starboard and K.C. looked over the side. *Uh oh!*

"All stop! All stop!" Mr. Prentiss yelled, pulling himself off the deck. "Sound collision alarm!" He ran out onto the flying bridge, trying to get a better look at what they had hit. "Oh Christ...oh Christ," he moaned as he looked down at the reef. The ship had plowed up onto the reef almost amidships, and was aground, swaying slowly port to starboard. The USS Frank Knox seemed to pause as if she were trying to catch her breath. The waves of the reef continued slapping against her bow, seeming to comprehend, in some instinctive way, that she didn't belong there. They crashed and foamed against her starboard side, expressing their displeasure at her presence on their reef.

Below decks, sailors had been thrown out of their bunks, and scrambled around for their clothes. Harry Abbot rolled out of his top bunk and landed on three other scrambling sailors. They were certain the ship had been torpedoed as they rushed to their stations, hurriedly tucking in shirttails and pulling on boondockers, anticipating the BONG-BONG-BONG of the general alarm. One of them, Charlie 'Pea' Peacock, a third class boatswains' mate, was the first to reach the deck. He looked over the side and was shocked at what he saw.

"Oh, shit," Pea exclaimed.

"What happened?" Pea's friend, Jimmy Dole, ran up behind him. Jimmy was six foot three and towered over Pea who was only five foot five, but like a small dog among big ones, Pea didn't seem to notice the size difference.

"We ran aground, Jimmy!" Pea replied. He leaned over the starboard side and squinted down at the reef. "Shit, man, we are stuck up on a fuckin' reef!" He looked up at his friend and shook his head sadly. "We ran aground, Jimmy, we fuckin' ran aground!"

Up on the bridge, the messenger of the watch pulled the collision alarm and the loud siren whooped shrilly in the early morning air. Below in their compartments, sailors stopped dressing and looked at each other curiously. *Collision?*

"Holy crap," Harry Abbot exclaimed. "We hit another ship!" He hurried up the ladder only to find it blocked by the large rear end of another sailor. Harry pushed as hard as he could, the rotund sailor pulled as hard as he could, and he finally popped out of the hatch, releasing a stream of grateful sailors who scrambled quickly up the ladder and headed to their battle stations.

Captain Gerald Pizzonovich came out of his cabin quickly, glancing around, not quite fully awake, trying to grasp the severity of the situation. Coffee cups, charts, the quartermaster log and various pieces of equipment were strewn on the deck. The bridge crew stood at their stations uneasily with pale, anxious looks on their faces.

"What the hell happened, Medford?" the captain demanded.

Lieutenant Prentiss stood at the chart table, pointing to the chart and pulling at his earlobe nervously. His shirt tail was sticking out of the back of his trousers. "There are no indications of a reef in this area, sir," he pleaded. "Radar didn't pick up anything either. The lookout said he saw white water, but no one else saw it and..." It was obvious the OOD had no idea how far off course he was.

The captain held up his hand for silence. He looked around at the bridge crew and took a deep breath. The men were scared, many sporting bumps and bruises, but they remained at their posts, awaiting orders. Whatever happened, accident or not, the captain knew instinctively his Naval career was over. A U.S. Navy destroyer did not run aground on a coral reef. When he spoke, he spoke in a quiet, but firm voice. "I want damage reports immediately," he ordered, hoping he didn't sound as stressed as he felt. "I want to know if anyone is hurt. Get all department heads in the wardroom to make reports after they have determined the damage." The captain turned back to face Prentiss and scowled. He stared into the OOD's blank eyes, all pretense of sympathy, patience or understanding gone. The OOD shrank under his gaze. "Take the quartermaster log," the captain said tersely. "Go over the entries and write up a report detailing everything that happened prior to hitting the reef."

"Yes sir," the OOD replied meekly. "Sir, I'm sorry. I take full responsibility..."

"Yes, yes," the captain said irritably. "We'll get to all that later." Captain Pizzonovich scowled sadly. "There's only one man who'll be held responsible here." He looked up at the OOD, a weary look on his face. "And it won't be you, will it, Medford?" Prentiss backed away, head down, tugging hard on his ear with his left hand.

The executive officer, Lieutenant Roger Lamb, came rushing into the pilot house. "Captain, are you...?"

The captain held up a hand and nodded solemnly. "Roger, I'm glad you're here. Please get the sextant and take a reading of our position. We need to get a message to CINCPACFLT right away and I want to make sure they know exactly where we are." He glanced over at Lt. Prentiss. "I'm sure we are off course, by how much I don't know. Pinpoint our position and have the radio shack get the message off at once. Then I'm going to need you to supervise the repairs in engineering."

"Aye, sir," the exec replied.

"I'm going below to check things out."

The exec looked at Medford and back at the captain. "Aye, sir," he said quietly, and went into the chart house to retrieve the sextant.

Captain Pizzonovich did not look forward to CINCPACFLT's reply. He headed below decks to try to determine the extent of the damage. *Could they pull off the reef under their own power?* The captain knew that old sailing ships that ran aground were 'sallied' with the crew running port to starboard, making the ship rock until she pulled herself loose.

The forward engine room was in chaos. Several large holes in the hull gaped grotesquely and sea water rushed in to flood the lower compartments. Damage control teams set up pumps to try to stem the flow. They fought for hours in the thick humidity of the below deck compartments, working desperately against the onslaught of the water, but they didn't have enough pumps to do the job and they were losing the fight. It was determined reluctantly that the forward compartments below the water line had to be closed off to prevent further flooding. The forward fire room and engine room were searched quickly and carefully for casualties. There were none, and sailors began dogging down watertight doors to close off the flooded compartments. Once help arrived with more pumps, they could revisit those spaces and pump the water out then.

Meanwhile, the ship rolled a bit and groaned mournfully, settling on the reef. The crew all paused, frozen at their work stations, and listened expectantly. The groaning stopped and the working parties took a collective breath and went back to work. The insistent waves continued breaking over the reef and up against the ship.

Back up on the bridge, the captain determined that the stern had settled and the screws were free and in the water. After examining the damage from the forecastle, the captain decided to try to get the ship off the reef under her own power. But after several attempts to pull her off in reverse or push her off forward, he realized it was futile. He assembled the crew along the starboard side and had them run to the port side and back to starboard several times, trying to 'sally' the ship off the reef like those crews of old used to do, but they could not make the ship roll enough to move it. There was nothing for the crew to do but wait for help. Captain Pizzonovich rubbed his eyes with the heels of his hands. "Christ," he muttered, shaking his head sadly. "Holy Christ." He was suddenly very tired, all the energy drained out of him. He stared catatonically at the chart, where Mr. Lamb had plotted their position before going down to engineering. *Pratas Reef*, the captain thought, but the name did not register. He gazed down at the deck, slowly shaking his head, isolated from the crew, alone with his thoughts. The early morning brightened with the pre-dawn, and cast unforgiving light across Pratas

Reef, illuminating the Frank Knox in the stark dawn. She listed farther to starboard, as if she were shying away from the unflattering light, her imperfections revealed, her bruises apparent. As the cold reality of his ship's dilemma began to sink in, Captain Pizzonovich slipped further into shock, and stared blankly down at the deck, his eyes fixed, as if in a trance.

The crew organized and spread out over the entire ship, looking for injured sailors and gathering up foodstuffs and tools, anything that might come in handy during salvage operations. Amazingly, it seemed no one had been seriously hurt. A few banged heads, skinned knees and bruises were the worst of it. The crew had cleaned up most of the compartments, and were checking the fresh water flow in the after crew's head when they came upon the body. Boatswain's Mate First Class C.C. Green lay face down in the small shower stall, bent at the waist, his hands bound behind him with quarter-inch nylon line, tied expertly in a perfect square knot. A black, wool-knitted watch cap was pulled over his face and under his chin, but it did not cover the large, deep gash in the back of his head. Blood ran from the wound to the shower drain. C.C. Green wore only his skivvy shorts and rubber thong shower shoes, and he was very, very dead.

CHAPTER TWO

Captain Pizzonovich

The nightmare was proving to be real as the cruel and remorseless dawn slowly brought into focus the terrible damage to the ship. It looked so much worse in the daylight. Crewmembers on deck shook their heads sadly, and many wiped at tears. Captain Pizzonovich sat in his cabin with his head in his hands. This was going to be bad. He tried hard to recall from memory other instances of Navy ships running aground, but though he knew there had been others, he couldn't think of a single one. The captain sighed and shook his head. *That moron, Prentiss!*

After almost twenty years in the Navy, enjoying a distinguished career, Gerald Pizzonovich was up for a captaincy. A four-striper! Since graduating from the Naval Academy, he had plotted his course for flag rank, made all the right moves, and was given command of a minesweeper as a lieutenant. Then he commanded a DE as a lieutenant commander and the Frank Knox as a full commander. He had attended all the courses on command and battle tactics and weaponry that the Navy had to offer. Under his command, the USS Frank Knox had served admirably in the West Pacific, earning letters of commendation from his superiors on three different occasions. Captain Pizzonovich had a crack crew on a front line war ship and he was very proud of his command.

With his captaincy looming on the horizon, Commander Pizzonovich had been almost assured of making rear admiral. Now, his career was going down the garbage chute because of Medford Prentiss. The Lieutenant (jg) was one of the worst officers with whom Gerald Pizzonovich had ever served. Prentiss had been transferred from one command to another, spending an average of seven months in six duty stations. His personnel file held unsatisfactory fitness reports from several of his previous commanders. He had arrived on the Knox six months ago, and almost at once had demonstrated his incompetence in every way possible. In a few short months he had become a favorite target of the crew's jokes. Privately, the crew referred to him as 'Tsunami Tsue.' The captain worked and reworked the daily rotation, trying to keep Prentiss away from duties which required a sense of responsibility or even some basic intelligence, knowing he couldn't handle it. He was not a bad guy, just unfit to be an officer in the US Navy. His term of duty would be up in about a year, and Captain Pizzonovich figured he could put up with Prentiss until then. The man was incompetent, but basically harmless. At least that's what the captain thought before all this happened.

Gerald Pizzonovich stood, sighed and made his way to the bridge. He gritted his teeth and fought to steel himself against the days ahead. The on-duty pilot house crew had stayed at their posts, waiting nervously for direction. They brightened when the captain came out of his cabin. Finally, they would be told what to do.

The captain ignored the bridge crew and stepped out on the port wing. The sun was creeping up the eastern horizon, and in the full morning light, the Knox looked like a forlorn beached whale. Waves, breaking over the reef, pummeled the ship along both sides, making her rock gently on the coral. Each movement brought a plaintive groan from the proud ship, as if she were mortally wounded and desperately crying for help. The moaning of the ship drove the captain into a deep sense of sorrow and dread, and he ground his teeth in frustration. Soon, the frustration became anger and slowly built to rage. It was a blinding rage like he had never experienced, and he felt like his life was slipping away from his control. He looked down at the forecastle, and couldn't believe his eyes. Crew members were fishing off the bow. *Fishing!*

At that moment, Captain Pizzonovich snapped. All the emotion, the stress of the situation, the prospect of a long and protracted salvage operation, his anger at Prentiss, his fear of the future, was galvanized by the sight of two of his sailors calmly fishing off the forecastle.

"WHAT IN THE GODDAM HELL ARE YOU PEOPLE DOING DOWN THERE?" he screamed angrily, startling the bridge crew who looked at each other nervously. "I WANT YOU MEN UP HERE NOW!" he screamed. "YOU HEAR ME, GODDAMIT? NOW!"

Turning back to the pilot house, the captain looked around frantically, a furious expression on his face. His composure was gone, his face beet-red, his eyes angry and bloodshot, his entire body shaking. "Where in the hell is the OOD?" he demanded between clenched teeth. "Where is that fucking Prentiss?" Without waiting for an answer, the captain grabbed the microphone on the 1-MC and barked into it.

"PRENTISS, YOU GET YOUR ASS BACK UP ON THIS BRIDGE! NOW, MISTER!" The men in the pilot house looked around at each other with worried expressions but avoided looking at the captain.

All over the ship, crew members stopped what they were doing and looked up, startled at the captain's voice. "Boy, he don't sound right," Jimmy Dole said, matter of factly.

"Yeah, well no shit," Pea replied. "You really can't blame him."

The fishermen from the forecastle finally arrived on the bridge and were being chewed out by the captain when Mr. Prentiss arrived, rubbing sleep from his eyes and looking confused.

"...major crisis on our hands and you people decide to go fishing?" The captain's face was getting even redder and he looked like he was going to explode. Big veins throbbed in his forehead and he stood, fists held together in front of him, shaking uncontrollably. "I ought to bust the both of you right now!" He looked around and noticed Mr. Prentiss on the bridge. He looked back at the two sailors. "Get below and get to work!" he instructed. The two fishermen lowered their heads and scrambled below. Captain Pizzonovich redirected his wrath at Lieutenant Prentiss.

"You half-witted moron!" he yelled. "You still have the duty and you left the bridge! What the hell is wrong with you?"

Prentiss gulped and stammered, "I thought...I figured..."

"You thought what, Medford? We were no longer underway, so you could leave your post? Where the hell were you?" Large, blue veins popped up on the captain's temples, he shook all over, and his eyes danced wildly, trying to focus.

"I was in my bunk asleep, sir," Prentiss replied, self-consciously pulling on his earlobe, looking like a frightened little boy whose father had come home from work to punish him.

The captain stared at Prentiss open-mouthed, like he didn't quite believe what he was hearing. All the anger and frustration, the shame and humiliation, the knowledge that he would never get his fourth stripe bubbled up at once and Captain Pizzonovich stepped forward, cocked his right fist and punched Prentiss on the left eye. Prentiss dropped immediately to the deck, landing on his rear end. The bridge grew quiet; the crew stared down at Mr. Prentiss, shocked at what they had just seen. Outside, the waves continued slapping against the side of the ship, seemingly spanking her for her nautical indiscretion.

The captain curled his lip and looked down at Prentiss. "You run my ship aground on a reef in the middle of the night and your professional reaction is to go below and take a nap?" The captain was shaking angrily. "GET YOUR ASS OFF MY BRIDGE, MISTER," he yelled at the top of his lungs. He stopped and took a deep breath, continuing in a lower, more controlled voice. "You are confined to quarters until further notice. I'm transferring your ass to the first ship on station, and I don't care if it's a CHINESE JUNK!" Prentiss sat on the deck, holding his hand to his eye, weeping like a little girl.

The helmsman and the watch messenger pulled Mr. Prentiss off the deck and led him toward the aft ladder. The captain stood glaring at him, and then turned back to the 1-MC. He wanted an OOD on the bridge he could depend on.

"MR. HOLLIDAY," he barked into the 1-MC. "PLEASE REPORT TO THE BRIDGE!"

CHAPTER THREE

Aboard the USS Prairie (AD-15)
Port of Hong Kong

"How in the hell does a Navy destroyer hit a reef?" R.J. Davis, SM-3 asked irritably. He balanced his lanky frame on the rung of the starboard flag bag on the tender's signal bridge. He was talking to Charlie Mayweather, SM-2 who stood on the port flag bag. They were raising the personnel recall flags on both yardarms, calling crew members who were ashore to return immediately to the ship. They had just been advised about a destroyer's running aground a hundred and sixty miles southeast of Hong Kong. That meant the destroyer tender was being called away from the crew's much anticipated liberty in Hong Kong to assist in the salvage operation.

R.J. hooked up and raised the flag hoist automatically, mindlessly, his thoughts elsewhere. He was in a surly mood, his heavy Irish eyebrows bunched together in a scowl. Millie's letters always pissed him off, always brought on the damned headache just behind his eye, but what pissed him off more was that he never seemed capable of keeping a romantic relationship together. No matter how much he liked her, a girl would always lose her appeal after a few months and R.J. would end up picking a fight just to have an excuse to dump her. *Except for Renee,* he thought. *She dumped me!* He shook his head slowly. *Why is it as much fun to fight with them as it is to...*

"Thing that pisses me off," Charlie interrupted his thought, "is that we were supposed to be here for ten days of R and R." He shook his head disgustedly. "Some dumb shit runs a Navy warship onto a reef? What are the odds of that?" Charlie Mayweather was the self-proclaimed philosopher of the operations division, and eagerly shared his wisdom with those who would listen. Charlie was older, almost thirty, and had been in the Navy long enough to develop the Navy lope, the loose-jointed stroll of the veteran sailor, and along with it, the Navy slouch. He wore his brown hair long and combed straight back, covered in part by his well-seasoned steaming cap. It was said that Charlie's steaming cap had seen more action than a Hong Kong whore.

R.J. fumed. He didn't much care about Hong Kong; *too dirty, too messy, too teeming...that was the term.* The streets gave him the creeps. People were piled up on each other, stacked like cordwood. What he resented was the fact that at sea he couldn't get paid for standing watches for the other signalmen, and the lucrative 'Big Eyes' binoculars were useless. He could charge for a peek into the windows of the Hong Kong Hilton across the harbor, but who was going to pay to look at sea gulls? R.J. shook his head disgustedly, and resigned himself to the fact that he was out a lot of money. He frowned. *Maybe fifty bucks or more!* R.J. tied off the flag hoist. *Oh, well,* he thought, *maybe it won't take long and we can get back to Hong Kong.* His birthday was coming up and he wanted to spend it in a liberty port, even if it was Hong Kong. *At least I'll have time to study,* he mused. He had decided to take on The Raven. He opened his book on Edgar Allan Poe each night when he hit the sack and had almost memorized the entire poem. He kept a dictionary beside him as he read and reread the stanzas. Poe had a way of saying something and meaning something else. Sometimes he just challenged the reader to figure out what it meant. R.J. believed he was up to that challenge. He didn't know why, but reading Poe always eased his headaches. He thought he knew the key to the poem, but...*it's in the Raven's utterance of that one word. I just have to figure out what he means by that one word.*

Ricky Buford, SM-3 and R.J.'s best buddy, slouched against the flag bag, munching on a candy bar, watching as R.J. and Charlie tied off the recall flag hoists. He was as tall as R.J. but even thinner, and when he walked he strolled in a loose and carefree manner, as though he were guided along by a puppet master. He had a long shank of unruly black hair, and was constantly brushing it out of his eyes. Ricky was a Cajun from New Orleans, Louisiana, or as he called it, Nawrlans, Looseyana, and spoke in an accent straight out of the delta. "Mah first time in this here port of Hong Kong and I don't getta go ashore 'cause some dumb sumbitch cain't navigate?" Ricky shook his head in disbelief. "What the hell kinda coon-ass shit is that?"

"Where's Peggy Sue, Rick?" Charlie asked with a mischievous smile.

Ricky blushed and grinned sheepishly. "She's tucked away safely in bed, thank ya'll for askin'," he replied.

Charlie and R.J. winked at each other knowingly. 'Peggy Sue' was Ricky's guitar, and he was rarely seen without 'her.' Chief Benson wouldn't let Ricky play his guitar when he was on watch, but didn't mind if he occasionally serenaded the signal bridge when he was off duty. Everyone agreed that Ricky was a terror on the guitar. He had all the Chuck Berry tunes down pat, and could play them from memory. He was a guitar fiend, and his favorite musician was Les Paul.

"But Rick," Charlie prodded, "How do you know someone's not down there right now, tryin' to strum her or something?"

"Yeah, Ricky," R.J. chimed in. "One of them crazy radiomen is probably down there plucking Peggy Sue's strings."

"Or maybe they're gang-strumming her, Rick," Charlie suggested.

"Okay, okay," Ricky protested. "Leave Peggy Sue alone. She needs her rest. Besides, we was talkin' about that coon-ass destroyer runnin' up on that coon-ass reef."

"I only feel sorry for that crew," R.J. said, straightening out the flags in his flag bag. He turned and looked at Charlie and Ricky. "They got no control over anything."

"I feel sorry for the commanding officer," Charlie replied. "His goose is friggin' cooked. Hell, he might as well join the Army, 'cause his Navy career is in the shitter."

"You think it's gonna be that bad?"

"Lemme tell you somethin', R.J." Charlie got that gleam in his eye, a signal that something irreverent was coming. "Running a US Navy warship up on a reef is akin to sneaking into the admiral's garden and screwing his goat." He grinned. "It just ain't done."

Ricky and R.J. laughed. Good old Charlie. "What ship was it, Charlie, do you know?" R.J. asked, glad the joke had lightened the mood.

Just then Tom Blanchard, RM-2, came up the ladder from the radio shack and greeted the signalmen. "What you guys got goin' up here, a circle jerk?"

"Yeah," Charlie said good-naturedly, "c'mon up, you can be the pivot man."

"You guys wanna see some new card tricks?" Tommy Blanchard was a whiz with a deck of cards. No one trusted him enough to let him play in the ship's pinochle tournament, even though he promised not to cheat.

"Hey, Tommy," R.J. asked, "what ship was it that ran into the reef?"

"It was a DDR," Tom replied. "The USS Frank Knox, DDR-742."

"Oh, crap," R.J. muttered.

"What's wrong?" Charlie asked.

"I got a buddy on the Knox," R.J. replied. "A good buddy. Name's Peacock, but we always called him Pea. We served together on the Haverfield." He chuckled at a private memory and looked up, grinning at Charlie and Ricky. "You guys'll like him. He's a funny little dude." He chewed his lip and added, "Sure hope the little guy is okay."

CHAPTER FOUR

USS Frank Knox
Aground on Pratas Reef

Lieutenant Holliday

Lieutenant William Holliday, ship's operations officer, made his way to the bridge, answering the captain's call. A career naval officer and Annapolis grad, he had only two pet peeves: he could not abide lazy or incompetent people, and he hated it when anyone called him 'Doc.' He therefore had two reasons to dislike Medford Prentiss II. The man was incompetent AND lazy, and, in an attempt at being witty, had addressed the Lieutenant as "Doc Holliday.' It usually only took the one time to straighten out someone who called him 'Doc,' but Medford Prentiss, even after having been warned once, did it again. Bill Holliday had made it very clear that he did not like that nickname, and if Prentiss used it again, he, Lieutenant Holliday, would deck him. At six three and two hundred and twenty pounds, he was capable of it. Mr. Holliday was second string linebacker on the Naval Academy football team in the late fifties. He had played with the great Joe Bellino a few years before the fast little halfback won the Heisman Trophy. Lieutenant (jg) Prentiss finally had gotten the word, and never called him 'Doc' again.

Mr. Holliday had been thrown out of his bunk by the collision and, once he learned what had happened, had spent his time in the Combat Information Center and the radio shack, making certain the operations department could operate. In his usual efficient, professional manner, Mr. Holliday quickly took command of his department and organized his men after the grounding.

On his way to report to the captain on the bridge, Bill Holliday stopped for a moment and looked out across the reef. *This is a beautiful place,* he thought to himself. He shook his head sadly and made his way toward the pilot house. Bad days were clearly ahead, Lieutenant Holliday knew he would be required to assume a leadership role, and he was worried about the captain. He sounded strange over the 1-MC.

The operations department commander stepped into the pilot house and took a quick look around. The bridge crew was cleaning up the mess and brightened at the sight of Mr. Holliday. The captain was on the port wing, staring blankly down at Pratas Reef. He turned when he sensed Mr. Holliday behind him. Captain Pizzonovich's eyes were blank, his face slack. He looked like he could fall asleep at any moment.

"Captain, you wanted to see me?"

"Yes, Bill..." The captain focused on the operations officer with sad eyes. The gravity of his situation was dawning on him and he looked like a man who was waiting for his execution. "That idiot, Prentiss, left the bridge before he was properly relieved and I sent him below. Will you take over the deck for him?"

Mr. Holliday looked around the bridge. "Yes, sir, but what about Roger?"

"I asked him to go down to engineering and get a first hand look. I expect him to be up to his ass by now." The captain stared at his operations officer. "I need you up here, Bill."

"Aye, sir," Mr. Holliday replied. The captain's demeanor concerned him, and the operations officer was genuinely worried about him. Captain Pizzonovich was always confident, sure, and quick decisions came easy to him. He was a natural leader, but now he looked beaten, ready to give up. "Any orders, sir?" Mr. Holliday asked gently.

"Orders?" The captain looked around absently as if he were trying to remember what was happening. "Yes, yes. Keep an eye on things up here, Bill. Those damage reports will be coming in anytime and I want to find out how bad it is." He looked back down at the reef and tears welled up in his eyes. "It's bad," he muttered to himself.

"I've been in the radio shack, sir," Mr. Holliday explained, "monitoring traffic about our situation. There's a typhoon headed this way. It's due to hit in two, three days."

"Great," the captain exclaimed. "More bad news. Anything else?"

"Several ships are en route to assist us."

"Yes," the captain replied blankly, "I know. Have we identified any of them yet?"

Mr. Holliday consulted his notes. "Yessir, a couple of salvage ships are on their way. The Conserver, the Grapple, two or three fleet tugs, and the combat supply ship, Mars." He looked up from his notes and smiled wanly. "The Prairie is being called out of Hong Kong."

"Thank God," Captain Pizzonovich whispered, and he meant it. The destroyer tender Prairie coming to their aid was indeed a God-send. The huge repair ship had on board every type of repair facility imaginable. Wood shops, metal shops, machine shops capable of manufacturing almost anything, the best repair engineers in the fleet. It even had a foundry! The Prairie could provide or manufacture anything a destroyer needed. Unfortunately, the big tender could not repair the damage to the ship's pride, nor could it repair the damage to Gerald Pizzonovich's career. Other ships were speeding to the aid of the Frank Knox. The helicopter carrier Iwo Jima was en route, as well as the destroyer Cogswell, and a few more fleet tugs. Captain Pizzonovich sighed, knowing that he and the crew of the Knox would be humiliated publicly with plenty of witnesses on hand to tell about it. This event would provide stories for sailors to tell for years.

"I'll be in my cabin, Bill," the captain said sadly. "I need to see the exec. Would you send a messenger to Roger and ask him to join me?"

"Yes, sir," Lieutenant Holliday replied. He watched the captain leave the bridge dejectedly, and the lieutenant felt genuine sympathy for him. Mr. Holliday, Mr. Lamb and the captain were good friends, and shared many thoughtful conversations together. They were all Academy men, with a great deal in common, so it was natural that they would gravitate toward one another. Bill Holliday sighed deeply. *I wonder how Roger's doing below,* he thought, worried about his friend. *I wonder if he's seen the way the captain is behaving.* He shook off the thought and looked around at the bridge crew.

"How long have you men been on watch?" he asked.

"All night, sir," the helmsman replied wearily.

"What duty section are you in?" the lieutenant asked. *No one had thought to relieve the watch!*

"Duty section three, sir."

Mr. Holliday picked up the 1-MC and clicked the button. "DUTY SECTION ONE WILL RELIEVE THE WATCH AT ONCE. DUTY SECTION TWO STAND BY!" He turned back to the bridge crew.

"Sorry about that, men." He smiled pleasantly at them and received self conscious smiles in return.

The captain returned to his cabin and tried to organize his thoughts. It was critical, he knew, that he show leadership at this difficult time. He took deep breaths through his nose and exhaled out his mouth, desperately trying to get his emotions in check. He sat at his desk and began making a list of things that would have to be done. First was to determine the exact extent of the damage. The ship's diver was over the side, preparing a report on the condition of the hull. Every department was busy cleaning up and inspecting damage, but Captain Pizzonovich knew the reports would be bad. *Very bad.* Just as he began to think it couldn't possibly get any worse, there was a knock on his cabin door.

CHAPTER FIVE

Pratas

Pratas Island, with its accompanying coral reef, is located along busy shipping routes just southwest of Taiwan and a little southeast of Hong Kong. Its location has long been known because of its proximity to the Philippines, Hong Kong, and Taiwan. Navigators are aware of its location, and know to chart courses around it.

The Frank Knox was not the first ship to run aground on Pratas Reef. It had happened before, many times. West Pacific sailors have become familiar with its location, and it is clearly defined on the navigational charts of the area. Still, ferocious typhoons and severe lapses in judgment can easily misdirect ships and throw them off course. Running a ship aground is one of the biggest sins a sailor can commit, especially a sailor in command of a US Navy warship. The stigma lasts forever, and most sailors would rather die in a burning, sinking ship than run up on a reef, especially a well known reef like Pratas.

Seen from above, the reef forms a circle around a shallow lagoon rich in marine life. To the west of the reef sits Pratas Island, roughly two miles long and a half mile wide. The island's location ensures a great deal of rain and at least two typhoons per season, which provide fresh water in abundance. Pratas Island is almost flat, with no mountains. The vegetation is lush, and many coconut trees flourish on the island. A large community of birds provides a non-stop serenade. Probably because of their presence, there are very few insects and no mosquitoes.

The coral reef sparkles with a deep aqua glow, easily seen from a half mile away at night. Cobalt waves crash over the reef and reduce themselves to white, swirling foam. The purple lagoon is a beautiful sight in the middle of the day. Its dark water is compelling, beckoning to the would-be swimmer. Pratas is truly an idyllic, postcard setting in the middle of the ocean. Paradise! Unless, of course, your ship has just run aground on the reef.

CHAPTER SIX

Lieutenant Lamb

"A dead man!" Captain Pizzonovich jumped to his feet. His executive officer and friend, Lieutenant Roger Lamb, had just informed him of the discovery in the after crew's head. "A dead man?" the captain repeated. "Good Lord." He seemed to deflate as he sat down wearily in his chair and hung his head. It was bad enough to be run up on the damn reef, *but a man got killed?* "Who, Roger, who?"

Lieutenant Lamb frowned and bit his lip. He had delivered the bad news, now he had to tell his captain the really bad news. "It was Boatswain's Mate First Class C.C. Green, sir," he said as soothingly as he could. "New man. Only on board a few months." The exec shuffled his feet nervously and looked around the captain's cabin. It seemed dark and depressing, almost foreboding. "The thing is, Captain," he said slowly.

"What, Roger?" the captain asked irritably. "What?"

"I...*We* think he was...murdered."

Gerald Pizzonovich looked up blankly at his friend. He seemed not to fully understand what the exec was telling him, and he frowned deeply, one eyebrow arched in skepticism. His face became blank for just a moment, not more than a second, and then a small smile appeared at the corners of his mouth. The smile grew larger until his whole face was grinning and his eyes sparkled wildly. He began to laugh, not the laugh of amusement, but a laugh with attitude, like the laugh of a condemned man strutting defiantly down the last mile toward the electric chair, head held high, sneering at the screws who escorted him, cackling insanely like James Fucking Cagney.

The captain laughed hysterically, slapping himself on the knee because he had suddenly figured out he was the butt of some Kafka-inspired joke. He expected to wake up in the morning, like Gregor Samsa, and discover he had been transformed into a giant cockroach. It seemed like that kind of a day.

"Ha Ha Ha Ha Ha!" the captain wailed. He saw the horrified look on Mr. Lamb's face and it made him laugh even harder. He stood, doubled over and began a long coughing spell. The exec began to worry that the captain might never stop coughing. The captain regained his breath, sat back down in his chair and looked at Lieutenant Lamb through wet, bloodshot eyes.

"It just keeps getting better, doesn't it, Roger?" the captain demanded, breathing heavily. "Please tell me the bad news is over."

The exec took a deep breath. "CINCPACFLT is sending a criminal investigator."

"Yeah," the captain nodded, catching his breath. "That is to be expected."

"He's flying from Pearl to Subic and then out here to the Iwo Jima," the exec explained. "He'll be here on the twenty-first." The exec consulted his schedule. "That's when the Prairie is due to get here."

"Well, good!" the captain spat. "We'll have a party. Tell the Prairie to bring the cake." He looked up blankly at the exec, and then his expression turned serious. The stress and strain became etched on his face and he frowned deeply. The change happened so quickly, the exec was not sure he had seen it. "When do we get the damage reports, Roger?" the captain asked. He had switched imperceptibly back to his professional naval officer persona.

"On their way, captain," the exec assured him. "So far it doesn't look good."

"Doesn't look good?" The wild look was back in the captain's eye. "We ran aground on a fucking reef, Roger! I don't expect it to look good." He rubbed his hands together nervously.

The exec took a deep, patient breath. "I'll ask all departments to expedite, sir."

"Ask them to expedite?" the captain roared, standing suddenly. "What the hell have they BEEN doing?" He looked around, exasperated. "This is a major crisis, everyone should already be expediting." He stood and began pacing back and forth, as if in a cage. "I've got people fishing off the friggin' focsul, for chrissakes!"

"Captain?" The exec looked at his commanding officer cautiously, not wanting to send him into another tirade.

"Yes, Roger?" Captain Pizzonovich was irritated, distant.

"I've ordered the body to be moved into sickbay, so the men can use the after crew's head."

"NO, NO, NO!" the captain exploded. "Leave everything right where it is. Nothing is to be moved, do you understand me?"

The exec understood. "Yessir, but the men..."

Captain Pizzonovich grabbed the 1-MC mike and shouted into it. "ATTENTION YOU MEN IN THE AFTER CREW'S HEAD! DO NOT TOUCH THAT BODY! LEAVE THAT BODY WHERE IT IS!"

In the after crew's head, the working party assigned to body removal stopped arguing over who had to do what and when, and stared silently at each other when they heard the captain's orders echo through the ship. The four of them backed off cautiously, staring down at the corpse as if they thought it might wake up.

Throughout the ship, the rest of the crew stopped whatever they were doing and stared nervously at each other with expressions that seemed to ask, "Body? What body?"

The exec shook his head slowly and led the captain to his chair, where he sat down heavily. "Captain, let me get Doc up here to take a look at you." The captain waved him off. "Please, sir," the exec insisted. "You appear to be in shock."

No shit! the captain thought to himself, but he nodded slowly and leaned forward, his elbows on his knees, his head in his hands. The exec picked up the sound powered phone and ordered the messenger to fetch the corpsman. The crew had a big day ahead of them. The exec knew there was much that had to be done to salvage the ship, and now they had a murder investigation to contend with. It was growing more and more apparent that the captain could not command. The exec stepped out of the captain's cabin and on to the starboard wing. The afternoon sun was high and bright in the sky, and Roger Lamb glared down at the reef. *Why the hell did this have to happen to us?* he thought sadly. Up on the focsul, sailors scurried about, gathering any and all items that could be off-loaded. Down on the fantail, sailors were doing the same thing. When the Munsee got there later with the barge, there would be a lot of off-loading to do. *We have to beat the typhoon,* Lieutenant Lamb thought, squinting up at the sky. So far, there was no sign of a storm.

Later that night, down in the engine room, EM-3 Bob Harp began the first letter to his folks informing them of the grounding. He decided to write them every day the Knox was on the reef. He had no way of knowing he would write 37 such letters.

Dear Mom and Dad,
Guess where I am?

CHAPTER SEVEN

Port of Hong Kong
August 19, 1965

The Prairie sat patiently at anchor in Hong Kong harbor. The personnel recall signal had been flying for over twenty-four hours, and the big destroyer tender had retrieved most but not all of her liberty-bound crew. Only a few had missed the personnel recall, but they would be transported to the ship as soon as they were gathered up. The captain had issued orders to get underway before dark, putting the Prairie on station early Wednesday morning, August twenty-first, the same day typhoon Gilda was scheduled to arrive.

R.J. Davis sat in the signal shack and read the reports about the Frank Knox provided him by Tom Blanchard. Ricky Buford sat on the deck in the corner, Peggy Sue cradled in his lap. A cigarette dangled from his mouth and he strummed lovingly on his guitar.

The reports were sparse and contained no important details, like if there had been any injuries. R.J. was worried about his friend, Peacock. He smiled when he thought of Pea. They had shared a lot of happy adventures aboard the Haverfield. The last time he had seen him was almost a year ago, when they visited the Arizona Monument together at Pearl Harbor. *Was that really almost a year ago?* He thought of Guam and of his disastrous affair with Annie and the headache began to seep in, just behind his left eye. He shook his head to exorcise the unwanted memory.

Ricky was playing 'Raunchy,' a Bill Justis song. R.J. had to smile. *Ricky sure was good on that guitar!*

The headache subsided, and R.J. sighed, leaning back in his chair. The sun was dipping slowly into the horizon, announcing the coming of evening. The sky was becoming darker, prompted by the approach of typhoon Gilda, which would make the Knox salvage operations more difficult. R.J. closed his eyes and thought of Pearl Harbor and the last time he had seen Pea. The little guy was standing on the fantail of the Haverfield as she headed out to sea, leaving R.J. on the pier, sadly watching her steam away. He had returned to Longmont, Colorado after that, to attend the wedding of his ex-girlfriend, Renee, to one of his best friends, Chuck Phipps. *Another relationship I managed to screw up,* he thought. Stationed on the Haverfield, home-ported in Guam, he hadn't been home in eighteen months. He had looked forward to seeing his friends, albeit with a bit of trepidation. He smiled when he remembered the reunion. *Hard to believe it was almost a year ago.*

CHAPTER EIGHT

Longmont, Colorado
August, 1964

Millicent

The reunion wasn't as stressful as R.J. had imagined it would be. First, he was truly happy for Chuck and Renee, and he was overjoyed at being home after a year and a half overseas. His father and stepmother picked him up at the Greyhound bus terminal down on Main Street just after midnight, and they drove back to their house on Sunset Road, all talking at once. R.J. took in all the familiar sights on the way home, and Longmont never looked more beautiful to him. They spent the next few hours drinking coffee and catching up. He entertained them with stories about Guam, the Trust Territory, Japan, the Philippines and patrolling the Tonkin Gulf. He deliberately left out the tragic details of the Haverfield incident. He stayed up long after they had gone to bed, standing at his traditional post on the front porch, leaning against the railing, watching the night sky. It felt comfortable and familiar, being home on his front porch again. He looked forward to seeing his friends, but he felt uneasy when he thought about that and he didn't know why. He went inside, sat down on the couch and removed his shoes, then stretched out and quickly fell asleep.

He awoke about ten, his parents gone to work, and read the note his stepmother had left on the table. It was typical 'Granny,' as R.J. had nicknamed her after an unsuccessful attempt at becoming a blonde rendered her hair completely white. She had put out clean towels for him in the bathroom, a box of Cheerios on the table with directions as to where to find the milk, (not surprisingly, it was in the refrigerator), and instructions on how to build a sandwich out of bread and leftover roast beef for lunch. He grinned as he read her note. It always amazed him that any woman could be so considerate, so sweet. Then he saw the postscript and his brow furrowed.

P.S. Chuck called. He and Renee will be here at noon to see you. He smiled and opened the Cheerios.

R.J. ate some Cheerios and drank a hot cup of Granny's coffee, which tasted much better than the Navy coffee he had grown used to drinking. He took a long, hot shower, something else he hadn't done in a year and a half, and shaved closely. He stood under the spray, luxuriating in the warm shower until the water turned cold. He decided to greet Chuck and Renee in his uniform, and spent a half hour pressing his dress blues, even though it was August, and technically whites weather. Then he stepped out on the porch, bare-headed, and leaned forward against the rail, looking up and down Sunset Road, waiting for Chuck, just like he used to do as a teenager when he and his buddy chugged around town on Chuck's Vespa. R.J. smiled happily to himself and took a deep breath of clean Colorado air. It sure felt good to be back. Then his thoughts turned to Denver and his family there. He looked forward to seeing his grandparents again, but thoughts of a reunion with his mother made him anxious and irritable. Very often he wished Granny was his real mother. All his friends in Longmont thought she was.

Interrupting his thoughts, Chuck Phipps' 1954 Ford roared up the street, lowered all around with outside pipes along the sides and tear-drop skirts covering the rear wheel wells. Right behind the Ford were two other customized cars, a 1949 Plymouth owned by Dean Phillips and Benny Ortega's 1953 Oldsmobile. The three cars squealed to a stop in front of the house, horns honking. The doors flew open, and all his childhood friends, male and female, came pouring out and up the hill to the porch. They laughed, waved and yelled his name, creating a clamor that disturbed the peaceful setting of the neighborhood, just as they had always done. Chuck and Renee came up the steps first, hand in hand. Renee's blonde hair had grown quite a bit since R.J. last saw her. She wore it in a pig-tail and her blue eyes sparkled. Chuck, tall, gangly and already sporting a quickly-receding hair line, grinned happily and reached out to be the first to hug R.J.

R.J. felt a lump in his throat. All his uneasiness was swept away with that one hug, and he suddenly felt good to be greeted home by the friends he had grown up with since junior high. He almost pinched himself to make sure it wasn't a dream. It had been a dream very often overseas. Now, they were all together again, and it was better than his imaginings. He embraced everyone warmly, holding Chuck and Renee particularly close as he congratulated them. Benny Ortega had a case of Coors 3.2 beer and they all went into R.J.'s house to celebrate his homecoming.

"You look really good, R.J.," Dean said. He threw his arm around R.J.'s shoulders and walked with him into the house. "Looks like the Navy's been good for you."

"I wish you woulda come with me, Dino," R.J. said, smiling warmly at his friend.

"I guess I shoulda, 'cause me and Maryann broke up about six months ago."

"Lots of fish in the sea, right, buddy?" R.J. was glad Dino wasn't going with Maryann anymore. He had never liked her since he spotted her making out with another guy at the drive-in. He had never told Dino about it. Maryann didn't even know he knew. He hadn't even told Renee, and she had been with him.

"You got that right," Dean agreed, "only I ain't the smooth talkin' sumbitch you are."

Fifteen people crammed into the small living room and Benny began passing out beers, all the time keeping up a running commentary about what had been happening in R.J.'s absence.

"...she broke the window at the Silver Spur last June! Pitched a goddamn ketchup bottle through it and none of us can come back." Benny laughed at the memory. "You shoulda seen Dino trying to sweet-talk old man Cozner. He just told us to get the fuck outta there!"

"Benny!" his girlfriend Karen admonished him. "Watch your language."

"Yeah, Benny," Jim Wallace agreed. "Watch your fuckin' language."

"Who broke the window?" R.J. asked, amused.

"Millie did!" They all turned and pointed at Millicent Brewster, Renee's best friend.

R.J. hadn't noticed Millie yet and when he turned to look at her, his mouth dropped. Millicent Brewster had been a skinny little girl with braces when he'd left a year and a half ago. She had grown up. Her braces were gone, she had filled out nicely, and she wore only a little make-up. She had taken off her glasses, letting them rest in her lap, and her soft brown eyes looked at him with a myopic sweetness that made him gulp.

"Hello, Millie," he said, taking her hand.

"Hello yourself," she replied, looking up coyly. Millie had always had a crush on R.J., but he had been going steady with Renee, so she had kept her distance. Now all bets were off. "I'm glad you're home. I've been wanting to ask you a question." She batted her lashes at him mischievously.

"Yeah, what?" Her soft brown eyes were bugging him, and he felt uneasy, but didn't know why. Still, she was lovely!

"In the ladies' restroom at the Spur, someone wrote on the stall door, 'R.J. Davis is the coolest guy in Longmont.' So, Mr. R.J. Davis, my question is, which one of your many girlfriends wrote that? Do you even know?"

Dean Phillips began choking on his beer, trying not to laugh.

R.J. grinned. He had written it on the stall door, but the girls didn't know that. The only person who knew was Dean, who watched the door while R.J. snuck into the women's restroom late one night. "I heard about that, too," R.J. said, still grinning. "Hell Millie, I always thought you did it."

Everyone laughed and Millie blushed, but she was smiling demurely and batting those lashes.

Renee elbowed Chuck in the ribs and pointed to R.J. and Millie, who were staring dewy-eyed at each other. Chuck winked and grinned.

"Millie's my maid of honor," Renee said. "Maybe you'll escort her to the wedding, R.J."

"Renee!" Millie protested and everyone laughed.

"I would be honored," R.J. grinned at Millie who blushed. "That okay with you, Millie?"

"On one condition," she cautioned, looking him up and down. "You have to wear your uniform."

"I'm the best man!" Benny announced. "In more ways than one!" He gulped his beer and belched loudly.

"Benny!" All the girls admonished him at once.

"What?" he asked, looking around with false innocence. "What?"

R.J. leaned against the kitchen doorjamb and smiled at the scene. They say nothing much ever changes in Longmont, except the weather, and R.J. agreed. It was though he had never left, and the gang was gathering for a night of fun and games at Sunset Park.

"Let's cruise the Johnsons!" Chuck suggested, and everyone piled out the door toward the waiting cars. R.J. wrote a quick note to his folks and locked the front door behind him. Millie was waiting for him halfway down the sidewalk and took his arm when he reached her.

"Well, let's go," she cooed. Her soft brown eyes were mocking him, but she had a sweet smile on her face. He took her hand and led her to Benny's car. They piled into the back seat. R.J. didn't want to ride with Chuck and Renee...yet. The convoy started up loudly and headed down Sunset to Third, pipes rumbling, where they turned left toward Main Street. Millie cuddled up next to R.J. and he put his arm around her shoulders. Benny caught R.J.'s eye in the rear view mirror and winked lewdly. R.J. chuckled and put his nose in Millie's hair, inhaling deeply. She smelled as good as she looked! She peered up at him and smiled sweetly.

South Johnson's Corner, a filling station, garage and snack shop located at First and Main, marked the south end of town. North Johnson's Corner at 17th and Main marked the north side of town. Longmont teenagers had cruised Main Street for years between these two gas stations. R.J. pulled Millie closer, and smiled smugly when she leaned against him. They cruised up and down Main Street most of the afternoon, and R.J. watched the scenery roll past the car windows. Little had changed in eighteen months. His friends had gotten older, and the girls had become more like women, but his male friends did not seem to have grown at all. They were exactly as he had left them. Three years after high school and they hadn't changed a bit! A few short years ago, R.J. had loved cruising the Johnsons, four or more cars in a caravan. It was always the highlight of any evening, but now it seemed somehow...*boring?* R.J. began to feel restless. The connection he thought he felt for Longmont was beginning to fade. He and Longmont were growing apart, distancing him from his youth. He also realized at that moment that Longmont wasn't growing away from him, he was growing away from it. Longmont wasn't growing at all. It was if his friends lived in a perpetual state of adolescent innocence as long as they stayed there in that town.

"Hey, R.J.!" Benny called to him from behind the wheel. He was watching them in the rear-view mirror. "You look like you're in a trance. Did you cast a spell on his ass, Millie?"

She looked up at R.J. and smiled sweetly. "I've been trying to," she whispered.

R.J. leaned over and said something into Millie's ear. She giggled, looked up into his eyes and nodded.

"Let us out here, Benny," R.J. tapped his friend on the shoulder. Benny looked back at R.J. and Millie, shrugged, and pulled over in front of the cemetery, across Main Street from the Silver Spur restaurant. The other two cars had gone ahead, but slowed and waited for Benny. R.J. and Millie got out of the car and waved goodbye. Benny squealed away from the curb and caught up with the others.

"Shall we walk the granite trail?" R.J. grinned, motioning with his head toward the cemetery.

"We only walk the granite trail at midnight, R.J.," Millie replied seriously, but she took his arm, and together they walked into the cemetery. It wasn't nearly as spooky as it was at night. R.J. recalled how several of them, high on 3.2 Coors, would park in the lot of the Silver Spur and run across Main Street en masse to walk the granite trail through the cemetery as close to midnight as they could manage. Once inside, the girls would huddle close to the guys as they walked from grave to grave, reciting the names off the headstones and making up stories about the lives of the deceased. R.J. remembered the cemetery as a great place to cop a feel.

"C'mon," Millie pulled him farther into the cemetery. "I want to show you something." She put on her glasses and marched forward resolutely, looking around with her nose in the air as if she were getting her bearings.

R.J. let Millie lead him by the hand along the narrow path until they were completely out of sight of the street. "Here," she said, stopping at a grave.

What little breeze there was died down, and the cemetery suddenly became very quiet. The leaves hung limp in the humid air, and sunlight slashed down through the trees in bright, bold streams. R.J. looked down at the headstone. It was very old, weathered by years of exposure to the elements. The name was difficult to make out, so R.J. leaned down closer and read the epitaph:

PENELOPE LAINE
Beloved Wife of Jonathan
February 1903 - November 1924
R.I.P.

"She was only twenty one when she died," Millie whispered, running her hand lovingly over the gravestone.

"Was she related to you?" R.J. asked. He eyed the grave suspiciously. *What is this all about?*

Millie took off her glasses and looked up into his eyes. "No, she wasn't." She looked back down at the grave. "But she's my friend," she whispered softly. She dropped down to her knees and began brushing leaves and twigs off the grave of Penelope Laine. "She came here from Wisconsin." Millie's soft voice seemed to echo eerily throughout the graveyard. "Jonathan was a blacksmith and they married against her family's wishes. They disowned her, so she and Jonathan left to find a better life for themselves, and they settled in Longmont because of the beautiful view of the mountains." Millie stood and brushed dirt off her hands. "They were very much in love," she continued. She looked up into the trees surrounding the cemetery. "But in 1924 she caught tuberculosis and died. Jonathan was at her bedside when she passed away, and he vowed he would never marry again." Tears rolled down her cheeks and dropped on the grave. R.J. realized Millie had manufactured the story from her imagination, just as they all had done while walking the granite trail, but this was somehow different. Millie was doing more than dreaming up an imaginary life for a name on a headstone. Penelope Laine seemed to be as much a part of Millie's life as if she were real. R.J. wondered if Millie knew the difference.

"You probably think I'm an ass," she said, wiping her tears away.

Yeah, I do, he thought to himself. "No, I don't," he said aloud. He put his arms around her and lifted her chin so she was looking into his eyes. "I really like the story." He brushed the hair out of her eyes and smiled sympathetically. She looked so lovely, so vulnerable...*So what if she's a little goofy? She's got that perky little butt...*

"She's good luck to me, R.J.," Millie whispered, looking down at the grave. "Last year I really wanted the job at the newspaper. I got an interview and I was really scared, so I came up here to talk to Penelope about it. I swear she spoke to me, R.J." She looked up to see if he was laughing at her. He wasn't. "Not out loud, but in my mind I heard her say something to me."

Oh-kay. "What did she say?"

"She said to stand up straight and answer all questions with a smile, and everything would be okay. You know what? It was. I got the job."

"That's great." *She has really filled out nicely.*

"Oh, you probably think I'm nuts or something."

"No, I don't." *I like that cute little butt. I've always liked cute little...*

"She told me you'd come back here and you'd want to be with me," Millie whispered so softly R.J. could hardly hear her. "You don't believe me, do you?" She looked at him, frowning, her brow furrowed.

R.J. looked at her. He looked at the grave. He looked at the sky and the trees. He couldn't think of anything to say. *How long is this going to take?*

"I told Penelope all about you," she went on in a vacant voice. "I told her I really liked you but you were going with Renee. She told me to be patient; that Renee was not going to wait for you."

R.J. stared at her, unsure of how he was supposed to react, what he was supposed to say.

"So, I guess she was right, huh, R.J.?"

He smiled gently, held her close, and decided to take the light approach. "I'm here, Renee is marrying Chuck, so I guess old Penelope knows her shit."

"Don't make fun of her, R.J." Millie pulled away and her face took on a serious, almost angry look. "She's my one true friend, and I don't think I could stand it if you make fun of her."

Okay, wrong approach. "I...I won't, Millie," he stammered, surprised at her tone.

She relaxed and smiled. The anger quickly evaporated; she took his hand and together they walked through the cemetery toward Main Street. "It's going to be a really nice wedding, don't you think?" She looked up at him and the sweetness returned to her face. She looked as if she had been away, had returned, and was delighted to see him again.

A little voice in the back of his head yelled at him: *Run!* But he held her hand and walked with her through the cemetery. A light breeze wafted high in the trees, softly rustling the leaves. He looked down at Millie and discovered she was watching him intently, a frown wrinkling her brow, her eyes glazed, unfocused, seeming to look beyond him.

"Yes, I think it is," he replied.

Run!

R.J. would come to realize he should have listened to that little voice.

CHAPTER NINE

USS Frank Knox
Aground on Pratas Reef
August 19, 1965

Day 2

Lieutenant Holliday sat with the other officers at the wardroom table and rubbed his hands over his face. The damage was far worse than anyone had imagined, and they had imagined a lot. The hull was shredded from the bow to midships. The sonar dome had been destroyed, leaving a large hole where the sonar array was once deployed. The ship had become impaled on a large outcrop of coral that had imbedded itself in the empty sonar dome.

"Like we're being FUCKED by this goddamn reef!" Captain Pizzonovich spat.

The other officers gathered around the table glanced at each other nervously. The captain's behavior was deteriorating quickly, the strain of losing his ship becoming more evident every hour. Lieutenant Holliday looked at Roger Lamb and frowned. The exec cleared his throat. "Captain?"

The captain was staring out a porthole, his back turned to the wardroom, and did not turn around. "What is it, Roger?" He sounded distant, preoccupied, and a little fearful.

"We've prepared a priority list of tasks we must get done as soon as possible."

"Yes, Roger?" The captain's voice had a strange edge to it. He turned and sat heavily in his chair.

"Well, sir," the exec went on, "first priority is to transfer all ordinance and fuel oil off the ship at once. I'm talking hedgehogs, five inch shells, torpedoes, the entire inventory along with all the fuel oil." Mr. Lamb looked around the table. "We are afraid the whole thing might explode," he said unnecessarily. "Anyway, we've been working all night stacking everything on the fantail. We'll be ready to start the off-loading as soon as the barge gets here."

The captain stared blankly at the table. The officers fidgeted uncomfortably, and many of them looked to the exec with questioning expressions. Just as the exec was going to say something, the captain looked up at him. "Keep all handguns and rifles aboard, Roger," he said quietly, his voice flat. "I want the salvage crew to be armed. I have a feeling we're going to be surrounded by sharks real soon."

"Next," the exec continued, ignoring the worried stares of the other officers, "we must transfer all non-essential personnel as soon as possible. The Prairie will be here soon, and the Iwo Jima is on her way..."

"Okay," the captain interrupted. "Ask for volunteers to stay aboard, and if that doesn't work, assign some volunteers. Transfer the rest of the crew to the first arriving ship big enough to accommodate them." He placed his hands flat on the table and looked at the faces of his officers. "And leave that body where it is. I want a watch on that after crew's head, twenty four hours a day until the investigator gets here." He blinked hard and shook his head, trying to clear his vision. "You take charge, Roger, and keep working down your list. I'm going to lie down." With that he turned and started out of the wardroom. "One more thing," he said, turning back, an angry look on his face. "Get that fucking Prentiss off my ship in the first evacuation. Do you hear me?" He turned and stepped out the door, leaving his officers sitting around the table staring at each other. No one said what was obviously on everyone's mind: the captain was losing his grip.

Lieutenant Lamb took a deep breath and looked around at the other officers. They were watching him intently, looking for him to lead them, to order them, to tell them what the hell to do. "Well, I'm sorry the captain isn't feeling well, but..." he looked at his notes. "We're going to get hit with the ass-end of a typhoon Wednesday morning. It's going to be windy and choppy, and we have to unload that ammunition now."

"The Munsee will be on station with a barge any time," Mr. Holliday said, as if trying to reassure everyone. "We can start offloading right away."

"I don't like that ordinance stacked on the fantail," Lieutenant Thomas McCarthy, weapons officer said. "If we can get that off the ship before the storm hits, I'll be thankful."

"We don't have a lot to do in engineering," ship's engineer Lieutenant Geoff Darby interjected. "We've sealed up the forward engine room, and we've cleaned up all the other spaces. Remaining engines and electrical are fine, but don't count on the evaporators for fresh water." He looked through his notes. "At least for the foreseeable future. Meanwhile, we'll do our best to salvage what we can from the forward engine room."

The exec nodded solemnly. "We have a lot to do, gentlemen." He stood and gathered up his notes. "Let's get started."

Lieutenant Holliday was surprised at the reaction of the crew to the call for volunteers. Of the almost three hundred men aboard the

Knox, all but a handful volunteered to stay on board and help with the salvage operations. Mr. Holliday was in the unenviable position of choosing who would stay and who would be evacuated. He decided every volunteer from engineering, deck and weapons would stay, along with the department heads. Most of the operations people would be evacuated, leaving a skeleton force on the signal bridge and in the radio shack. There was no reason for CIC personnel to stay. When he had finished making up his list, he had seventy men who would remain aboard and salvage the ship.

Lieutenant Tom McCarthy hurried to the fantail and immediately began inventorying the ordinance. Gilda was coming, sucking all the air off the reef, and the water was becoming choppy, forming large, angry whitecaps, the first warning signs of the approaching storm. It was eighteen hours before she was due to hit.

The Munsee arrived on station and quickly eased a barge next to the Knox. The deck crew tethered it to the ship. Mr. McCarthy watched the barge bang firmly against the side of the ship. When the wind picked up, he knew the barge would be banging a lot harder. The weapons officer tried to calculate how long it would take to transfer the ammo to the barge, versus the speed with which Typhoon Gilda was approaching from the south. He was not happy with his conclusions.

Meanwhile, the crew worked feverishly, unloading the ship's ordinance on to the barge as fast as circumstances, and the choppy water, would allow. Gilda was not far off, evidenced by the increasingly choppy water and the fast rising winds. It would be an all-night job, and the weapons officer wasn't sure they could finish before the weather got extremely nasty.

Lieutenant McCarthy had ridden out typhoons before and knew the kind of power they could generate. He stood on the 02 level and watched as sailors swarmed across the fantail, some stacking hedgehogs and five inch shells near the side of the ship so others could offload the ordinance onto the barge. As hard and as fast as they worked, they seemed to be making little headway. The hedgehogs and five inch shells just kept coming.

"Damn, we ain't makin' no progress at all," Jimmy Dole complained. He arched his back, trying to relieve the aching pain, and wiped sweat from his face.

"Just keep goin'," Pea answered. He looked around the fantail. Men were sweating and struggling against the heat and the weight of the ammunition. The pace of the work had slowed as sailors began to react to the stifling heat. The men were sweating profusely in the humidity, and most peeled off their shirts and went hatless. A few of them, exhausted by the work and by the heat, simply slumped down on the deck like wilted flowers and stared straight ahead. The corpsman fed them salt tablets and water until their energy returned, then they pulled themselves up and continued. Mr. McCarthy shook his head sadly. *These men are going through hell,* he thought, tears welling in his eyes. He slid down the ladder to the fantail and joined the line of men passing the ordinance to the barge.

Linc

Up on the Frank Knox's signal bridge, SM-2 Lincoln "Linc" Jones busied himself with tidying up his work station. He was tall and built like a tight end. His cocoa features were smooth, giving him a dark, Caribbean look. He wore his hair natural, and let it grow as long as the Navy allowed, or until his division officer ordered him to cut it. His steaming hat sat perched softly on top of his 'do'. Linc was proud of his hair and spent much time at the mirror, fluffing it, picking it, piling it up.

The signal bridge had survived the grounding intact. There was no damage to either of the signal lights, and Linc had sound-powered phone contact with the rest of the ship. He had volunteered to stay with the rescue crew and handle any and all signal traffic. He had stayed for two reasons: First, he wanted to help salvage his ship, and second, because Lincoln Jones considered himself to be the premier flashing light expert in the seventh fleet. His Morse code was smooth as silk, and he could read as fast as he could send. During the ship's last visit to Yokosuka, Japan, Linc had been invited to visit the signal tower. A signalman was not invited to the tower unless he was pretty damn good, and Linc knew he was pretty damn good. His visit with Chief Carruthers and the retiring Chief Signalman Joe Williams turned bittersweet, however, because while they admitted that Lincoln Jones was great on the flashing light, they told him, to his dismay, that he would always be number two until a certain SM-3 got out of the Navy in September. Linc frowned, recalling the visit, and polished his signal light. He had read the plan of the day. He knew which ships were coming to the aid of the Frank Knox. Among them was the USS Prairie, and on the signal bridge of the Prairie was the signalman third class who was held in such high regard in the Yokosuka signal tower. Linc grinned to himself as he polished the light lovingly. He was finally going to get a chance to trade some code with the guy they thought was the best. Lincoln Jones couldn't wait to meet up with R.J. Davis.

Lieutenant McCarthy

Later that evening, the salvage vessels USS Grapple ARS-7 and the USS Conserver, ARS-9, arrived to assist the fleet ocean tug, USS Munsee ATF-107. The Iwo Jima would arrive soon with a small contingent of Marines to assist with the ammunition transfer, and some hot food for the Knox crew. Both would be welcome.

The Grapple and Conserver sent salvage experts to board the Knox and determine the exact extent of the damage. Everyone voiced optimism that the ship could be salvaged and pulled off the reef in very short order. Once their divers went over the side and they determined the extent to which the Knox was impaled on the reef, their optimism dimmed. They worried that it might be a long, protracted salvage operation. They were right to worry.

With the approaching storm, the salvage engineers decided to try to stabilize the Knox so the storm wouldn't force her farther up on the reef. They laid out a set of beach gear, consisting of a large, heavy anchor attached to wire cable and chain, and secured it to the Knox's stern. They sank the anchor as far seaward from the Knox as they could get it. The anchor settled onto the ocean floor and stabilized the Knox...a little. It was determined that more beach gear would have to be employed.

The mast of the Iwo Jima broke above the horizon just before 1600. A Marine helicopter, carrying a squad of Marines, appeared in the air and made its way to the stranded destroyer. Another helicopter followed close behind, bringing food and as much fresh water as it could carry. The crew of the Knox stood on the fantail and cheered. The sight of the Iwo Jima instilled them with hope, and they sped up their efforts to off-load the ammunition with renewed optimism.

The Marines landed on the small flight deck, filed out of the helicopter and aligned themselves in ranks. A gunnery sergeant came slowly off the copter and looked around. He was about five foot ten and had a strong, stocky physique. He wore a fatigue cap and when he took off his sunglasses he looked at Mr. McCarthy with cold, business-like gray eyes. The gunnery sergeant saluted the lieutenant.

"Permission to come aboard, sir."

Mr. McCarthy returned the salute. "Granted. We are very happy to see you, Gunny." He put out his hand. "I'm Lieutenant McCarthy, weapons officer."

"Terry Davis," the sergeant said, shaking Mr. McCarthy's hand. "What can we do to help?"

"We can use a hand with the ammo transfer," the lieutenant explained. "But, first I'd like to load as many of our crew as possible on these helicopters. We'll retain a salvage crew of about seventy or so."

"No problem." Gunny Davis turned to his squad and barked a few orders. The Marines began organizing the Knox crew for evacuation.

Lieutenant McCarthy watched the operation on the fantail. Most of the crew were being shuttled to the Iwo Jima and Mars, and the rest would be billeted on the Prairie when she arrived. Men were scurrying about the fantail deck, stacking the last rows of hedgehog missiles and five inch shells. Other crew members were handing them down to the men on the barge, who took them and gently stacked them in neat rows. They had worked all day and had transferred most of the ammunition, but there was still quite a bit more to be moved. Mr. McCarthy looked up at the graying sky. "Just give us a little more time," he pleaded. "Just a little more time." The wind was picking up, the sky was darkening, and the barge was banging harder on the ship's starboard quarter. Gilda was promising a rough night.

CHAPTER TEN

Day 2

Gunny Davis

It was a terrible night. Typhoon Gilda's winds were getting closer, and seemed to take delight in slapping away at the stranded ship. At least it seemed that way to the sailors and Marines who struggled all night to off-load the ammunition. Mr. McCarthy figured it would be well into the night before it was all off-loaded, and he knew typhoon Gilda would arrive in full force in the morning. This was cutting it a little thin, but by midnight much of the ordinance had been transferred to the barge. The remaining hedgehogs and five inch shells were proving to be less cooperative. There were fewer of them and they rattled around on the pitching and rolling deck like bowling pins. It would only take one to somehow get set off, and who knows what would happen. If one blew, the entire fantail could go up, along with the ammo-filled barge. Nerves were frayed and tempers began to flare.

"Goddamit!" someone yelled, "we're gonna get our asses blown the fuck up!"

"Shut up!" Pea yelled back. "Just do your friggin' job!"

Because of the volatile situation with the ammo, around 0500 hours Lieutenant McCarthy ordered all but three sailors to leave the fantail. The three who stayed on the fantail, Pea, Jimmy Dole and Chief Boatswain's Mate Fred Billings were charged with controlling the rolling ordinance as best they could. The rest of the crew mustered on the forecastle, certain there would be a huge explosion. The three sailors on the fantail accepted the fact that they had become expendable, and it wasn't a pleasant feeling. The presence of Chief Billings calmed Pea and Jimmy. The chief boatswain's mate was a big man, over six foot, and weighed over two hundred pounds. There was no fat on the chief. He exercised regularly and kept himself fit. He didn't smoke, didn't drink to excess and didn't carouse with whores. He was happily married, and had been so for over ten years, dedicated to his wife, and although they could not have children of their own, he considered himself a stable, family man. He had welcomed his wife's much younger brother into his home after his mother-in-law had passed away, and for seven years had raised the boy as his own. Chief Billings wore four gold hash marks on his sleeve, one for every four years in the Navy. The gold color of the hash marks denoted exemplary service. Fred Billings had never had a negative report written about him, his performance had always been 4.0 on a 4.0 scale, and the Navy was his chosen career. He would not abide sloppiness or carelessness, and treated his subordinates with kindness and caring. He was one of the most respected men aboard the Knox.

On the 03 level, Lieutenants Lamb, Holliday and Darby donned battle helmets and cautiously watched the fantail operation. Mr. Holliday pointed at Chief Billings.

"The chief of the boat should not be endangering himself like that."

"Who's gonna stop him?" Geoff Darby grinned.

Mr. Holliday looked over at Roger Lamb, who was staring down at the fantail, his brow furrowed. "Roger?" Mr. Holliday patted his friend on the shoulder. "You still with us?"

"I was thinking, maybe I'll ask the captain if I can put Chief Billings in charge of first division."

"Might as well," Mr. Holliday agreed. "Hell, he's running the deck force now."

"He's only got about a dozen men," Mr. Darby said. "The rest of them have been evacuated."

"I wish you wouldn't use that term, Geoff," Mr. Lamb admonished the engineer good-naturedly. "Let's say they've been temporarily transferred, okay?"

"Yes, sir," Mr. Darby said, chuckling along with the exec.

"He deserves the recognition, Roger," Mr. Holliday agreed. "He's a good man."

Mr. Lamb and Mr. Darby watched the chief working with the hedgehogs and slowly nodded their heads in agreement.

Pea, Dole and Chief Billings formulated a plan, the only one they had. They lay across the shells, throwing their bodies over as many as possible to keep them from rolling around. About the only thing they could think to do was get the shells to the side of the ship where they could roll them off into the drink. It was too dangerous to try to load them on the barge. Half-crawling, they slid or carried the hedgehogs slowly toward the side and let them slip into the water. A few hedgehogs slipped off the deck and got stuck, fins up, between the ship and the barge. Chief Billings watched the barge slam into the ship, and prayed that the hedgehogs wouldn't explode from the concussion. He decided not to say anything to Pea and Jimmy Dole about the hanging hedgehogs. Finally, they slipped through and dropped into the drink. Chief Billings looked up into the rainy sky and offered silent thanks. *Only a couple dozen or so to go,* the chief thought hopefully. *We sure could use some help.*

Up on the forecastle, Gunny Terry Davis pulled off his campaign hat and ran his hand through his thick, black hair. *This is no place for the Marines,* he decided. "Muster up!" he yelled at his charges. The Marines jumped to their feet. "We're going aft to help those people," he said firmly. He looked into the eyes of his men. "Anybody wanna stay here?" No one wanted to stay.

"Belay that order, Gunny," Mr. McCarthy said. "No one else is going into harm's way."

"Sorry, Lieutenant," T.D. replied, pulling on his hat and squaring it on his head. "In case you forgot, sir, that's what Marines do." He stared unblinking at the lieutenant.

Mr. McCarthy looked into the steely eyes of the gunnery sergeant and realized he was not going to change his mind. *Stubborn jarhead!* "Very well, Gunny," he relented. "Thank you."

"Let's go, men!" Gunny Davis led his Marines aft.

Slowly, almost painfully, the Marines and three sailors eased the remaining ordinance over the side and into the sea where it seemed to be deepest. The Munsee towed the barge back to the Iwo Jima slowly, the flat barge bouncing and rolling dangerously on the choppy sea.

On the fantail of the Knox, BM-3 Peacock, dripping with perspiration, his face and clothes covered with grime, looked over at Jimmy Dole. "Man, I thought we was dead!"

"Yeah," Jimmy said absently. He stared at the bobbing barge making its way cautiously toward the Iwo Jima. "Me too." He cupped his hands against the light rain and started to light a cigarette, but his hands were shaking so hard he couldn't work the lighter. Pea tried to give him a light, but his hands were shaking, too. Gunny Davis stepped up, calmly lit his Zippo, and Pea and Jimmy leaned forward to accept the light. They could not help but notice the gunny's hands were not shaking at all.

"Thank God for the Marines, huh buddy?" Pea asked, watching the gunny muster his men.

Jimmy looked down at his still-shaking hands. "Yeah," he mumbled, puffing hard on his cigarette, "thank God for the Marines."

Captain Pizzonovich read the status reports with half-hearted interest. The initial shock of the past two days had worn off, leaving him depressed and weary. He thought he could sleep for a month, and his body ached for his bunk, but his mind was racing at high speed. So much had happened so quickly. Thank God they got all the ammo off before Gilda arrived, though recent reports on her indicated she had turned southeast and her impact on the salvage operations would not be as dramatic as first thought. It was early, almost time for breakfast, but he wasn't hungry. He'd been up all night, unable to sleep, but now he felt so tired he knew he couldn't last much longer. But Gilda's winds were already lessening, and that was a good thing. The captain initialed each report and stacked them neatly in a folder to return to Mr. Lamb. He stood and stretched, deciding to take a shower and get some sleep. The shower would have to be a short one, fresh water was at a premium, so Captain Pizzonovich took a quick, Navy shower and climbed into bed. Within moments he was sound asleep.

CHAPTER ELEVEN

Tuesday, July 20, 1965

Day 3

The Prairie arrived in the morning when the storm was breaking up. Still, rain pelted the signal bridge as R.J. ran to his light. The first flashing light came from the Grapple, and requested Prairie manufacture fresh water containers for the Knox. The containers would be lifted over by Marine helicopters. The Knox was in dire need of fresh water.

"Man, would you lookit all those ships!" Charlie pointed toward the task force, gathered to rescue the Knox. "Shit, you'd think the Navy's got enough on its mind with all this Viet Nam crap. Now we all gotta come out here and wipe the butt of some dumb-ass destroyer?"

R.J. was on the light, receipting for the latest message. He had on his foul weather gear, and the plastic hood covered his face. He laughed at the sight of Charlie, standing in the rain, no foul weather gear, wearing just his steaming cap, and holding the ever-present cup of coffee. Water dripped off his cap and rain sprinkled into his coffee, but Charlie seemed oblivious to it all.

The Iwo Jima flashed and advised the commanding officer, USS Prairie that Admiral Wilson would transfer his flag to the destroyer tender.

"Oh, great," Charlie Mayweather complained. "We're gonna have an friggin' admiral on board."

"What's so bad about having stars aboard?" R.J. asked. He spun the light around to answer the flashing message from the Frank Knox.

"Everybody gets all paranoid with an admiral on board," Charlie explained. "Especially the officers. They want everybody to be squared away, regular Navy, you know." He looked down mournfully at his coffee cup, then up at the sky, as if he'd just discovered it was raining. "And boy, are we gonna be handling a shit load of traffic." Charlie looked up at the rain disgustedly and turned to go back inside the signal shack. "You hear me, R.J.?" he called above the rain.

R.J. had not heard Charlie. His concentration was on the flashing light from the Knox signal bridge. *This guy is good,* R.J. thought. He smiled as he read the smooth, even code, the characters perfectly constructed. *And rhythm. Man, does this guy have some rhythm!*

The Knox needed Prairie to accommodate the members of the

Knox crew the Iwo Jima and Mars couldn't handle. R.J. receipted for the message and stared through the rain at the grounded destroyer. *Too bad we're not in port,* R.J. thought. *I'd love to shoot the breeze with this guy*. R.J. tried to think of a way to show the guy on the Knox how he could send code, but he would have to wait for something official.

"Hey Charlie," R.J. poked his head into the shack. Charlie had assumed his usual position, leaning back in the chair, feet up on the desk, coffee cup in one hand, cigarette dangling from his lips, concentrating studiously on his crossword puzzle.

"Wha?"

"I'm gonna run this message down to the captain and I'll be right back." R.J. headed down the ladder to the bridge wing.

Charlie looked up at the door. "What?" he asked, but R.J. was gone. Charlie shrugged and sipped his coffee.

R.J. knocked softly on the captain's cabin door and waited for the order to enter. A voice behind him startled him.

"He's not in there."

R.J. turned around and came face to face with his commanding officer, Captain Frederick Marshall. The captain grinned as R.J. came to attention and saluted.

"As you were," the captain said in his easy-going way. Captain Marshall was a four-striper who was loved and admired by his crew. He was an excellent commanding officer, never ruffled, never surprised, and always calm. He was a veteran of World War Two, and on inspection day, when everyone was in dress uniform, the rows of decorations on Captain Marshall's chest humbled those of the other officers. Among those decorations, pinned above the others, was the distinctive single vertical white line on a deep blue ribbon, holding the bronze-finished Navy Cross.

"Some messages just came in, sir." R.J. handed the clipboard to the captain.

Captain Marshall read the message. "Hmmm." He handed the clipboard back to R.J. "Tell the Grapple we will start on the problem immediately. Tell the Iwo Jima we are delighted to have Admiral Wilson aboard, and tell the Knox we will provide billets for as many men as they need. And ask them if they need anything else at this time."

R.J. was scribbling frantically.

"You got that, Davis?" the captain asked, smiling good-naturedly.

"Yes sir," R.J. replied. "I'll send this right away." He saluted again and hurried back to the signal bridge. He stepped into the shack and closed the door behind him.

"What's going on?" Charlie asked. He sat at the desk, a crossword puzzle in hand.

"I have some messages to send," R.J. answered. He was going over his notes and formatting the messages. He wanted these to be sent perfectly. *Show that hot shot on the Knox some pure code!*

"Want me to send one?" Charlie asked half-heartedly, without looking up.

"Naw," R.J. replied. He took his clipboard to the port signal light and called up the Grapple. He would send the replies in the order the messages had been received. He had no doubt he would be observed by the Frank Knox signal bridge.

Lincoln Jones was indeed observing the messages being sent by the Prairie. He studied the code carefully. First the message to the Grapple, then the message to the Iwo Jima, and then the light turned in his direction and addressed the Frank Knox. He nodded to himself and set his mouth in a tight grin. Linc had never met R.J. He had never seen him and he had never exchanged flashing light with him, but he instinctively knew the code being flashed from the destroyer tender was the hand of R.J. Davis. "Damn, this guy can jam!" he said to himself as he opened the light and sent the letter 'K' for 'go ahead.'

R.J. was completely at ease on the signal light. He operated the handle smoothly, quietly, almost without any real effort, sending perfectly formed dits and dahs that would be translated into English at the receiving end. The message translated automatically into code in his mind, then down his arm to the signal light's handle, where it was transmitted effortlessly to its intended recipient. R.J. felt the light was an extension of his hand, that the Morse Code existed for the sole purpose of displaying his talent, and he never hesitated to take advantage of circumstances which would put him on center stage.

He sent a little more slowly than he had to, knowing the hot shot on the other end would hold his light open instead of flashing once for every word he received, as was the routine. Fast code senders often keep the light open for another fast sender as if to say, "I read you easy."

Linc knew the strategy. He knew R.J. wanted him to ask him to send faster, but the message was pretty short, and was over before Linc could react. In port, making conversation with the code, Linc could really show R.J. what he could do. He receipted for the message, and then took a chance. It was only a little chance, and Linc doubted he would get in trouble for it, so after he had sent the letter 'R' for 'received' he added two short words: *Good Code*.

R.J. grinned and sent two single characters: *U 2*. Both signalmen stared into the rain toward each other, not able to actually see each other, but knowing the other was out there. Through the dim morning mist they stood watch and waited, brothers of the code, keepers of the secret language. *Keepers of the faith,* Linc mused. *Like the Templar Knights.* He decided he liked the analogy. Linc grinned. He had to admit that R.J. Davis sent some of the prettiest code he had ever seen. This was going to be fun. He was happily aware that every signal bridge in the rescue fleet would be watching for signals from the two ships: the Knox because she was the subject of the salvage effort, and the Prairie because the admiral was on board. He and R.J. Davis could show the other signal bridges how it was done!

On the Frank Knox

The captain came out of his cabin early that afternoon, shaved, showered and apparently refreshed. The storm was moving southeast and small patches of sunlight broke through the dispersing clouds and shone down on the mournful destroyer. She looked old and tired in the bright sunlight. She listed to starboard, leaning on the reef as if trying to take a moment to gather herself. The captain looked over the side from the starboard wing and smiled self-satisfactorily when he saw several large sharks circling the reef and the tired old destroyer. They circled patiently, seeming to expect death, and they were there to clean it up.

The captain stepped into the pilot house and grabbed the microphone from the 1-MC. "MR. LAMB, MR. HOLLIDAY PLEASE REPORT TO THE BRIDGE!"

Within a few minutes the exec and the operations officer arrived on the bridge. The captain nodded at them and leafed through a clipboard containing damage reports. He didn't say anything, preferring to leave them standing there, fidgeting, wondering what the captain wanted. Finally he looked up. "I told you there would be sharks," he grinned broadly, then his face closed, like when the lights go out on a neon sign but the outline of the design remains. "I want you to issue side arms to any petty officer who wants one." He watched their faces to be sure they understood him. "And bring me an M-14. I'm going to take out some of those lousy sharks." He walked out to the wing bridge without waiting for a reply. The exec and Mr. Holliday stared at each other, each thinking the same thing: *Should the captain be armed while in his present state of mind?*

CHAPTER TWELVE

'Knox on the Rocks'

The activity was picking up at a fast pace as Gilda headed southeast. Joining the ships already on station, two more fleet ocean tugs, the USS Cocopa ATF-101, the USS Sioux ATF-75, and an auxiliary ocean tug, the USS Mahopac ATA-96, arrived to assist. With the admiral due to transfer his flag to the Prairie, helicopter activity increased dramatically. Salvage experts from BuShips, ComServe and ServPac arrived aboard the Prairie to confer with the salvage officers from the various ships. Things were starting to get hectic.

R.J. manned the starboard light while Charlie manned the port. So far, the traffic was active but manageable, and R.J. was enjoying himself. He watched the Frank Knox sway slightly on the reef and was privately glad he wasn't aboard her. He wanted to get in touch with Pea, but didn't want to risk a personal message. As if his mind had been read, a light flashed from the Knox. R.J. pointed the light and sent 'K.' Linc Jones sent the message smoothly, easy to read, and R.J. kept his light open. The Knox needed several types of tools and submitted a requisition list. They were sending the motor whaleboat to pick up the tools. For no apparent reason, Jones identified the coxswain of the motor whale boat: BM-3 Peacock.

R.J. grinned. Linc had managed to let him know his old friend would be coming aboard the Prairie.

On the Knox signal bridge Pea shook hands with Linc and thanked him for the favor. He hurried down to the fantail and stepped into the pitching boat. He started the engine and nodded to Jimmy Dole who threw off his tether, and Pea eased the boat away from the ship. Gilda had left some choppy water behind, so Pea carefully and skillfully piloted the small craft toward the big destroyer tender.

R.J. watched the motor whaleboat cover the distance between the Knox and the Prairie and was eagerly looking forward to seeing Peacock again. He told Charlie he was going down to deliver the tools requisition and then to the boat deck to greet Pea. Charlie just nodded, waved, and went back to his crossword puzzle.

Pea maneuvered the motor whaleboat expertly into position and tossed his line to a sailor on the Prairie's boat deck. Once tied up, Pea climbed the bosun's ladder and bounced up on deck. He was immediately greeted with a big hug from R.J.

"How the hell you doin', little dude?"

"I'm cool, I'm bad, I'm a BM-3!" Pea proudly showed off his third class crow.

"Good for you, partner." R.J. beamed at his friend. "Let's get the hell out of the way," he advised, as several sailors milled around them, doing various tasks. He led Pea to a vantage point above the helipad where copters were landing, dropping off their passengers and taking off again.

"Boy," Pea explained, "I thought the Knox was a lot bigger than the Haverfield, but this baby..." He looked around appreciatively at the destroyer tender. "You guys still eating those Prairie burgers?"

"Damn right. Can you stay for chow?"

"Depends on how long they take gettin' my stuff together." He motioned toward the boat deck.

"C'mon with me," R.J. motioned for Pea to follow him to the mess decks. Once seated inside, trays of food in front of them, R.J. leaned over and asked his friend, "Who's that hot shot you got on your signal bridge?"

"You mean Linc?" Pea asked, his mouth full of food. "He asked me the same thing about you."

"The guy sends pretty code," R.J. mused. "Very pretty."

"He said the same thing about you," Pea grinned. "Maybe you guys should go out on a date."

After talking about old times, and getting caught up with each others' lives while gulping down lunch, R.J. and Pea left the mess decks and returned to the 04 level where they could watch the helicopters land and take off. A steady stream of copters shuttled between the Prairie, the Knox, the Iwo Jima, and the Mars. More ships were arriving on the scene.

"Man, this is a big operation!" Pea observed. "Lookit all them ships. Looks like a task force, huh?"

"It is a task force, little buddy. It's Task Force 73."

"Hey! You from the Knox?" one of the Prairie's deck gang called up from the boat deck, a sly grin on his face.

"Yeah, I am," Pea answered cautiously. "Why?" Thus, Pea became the first to hear the popular joke circulating around the Prairie, a joke which quickly would grow very old to the Knox sailors, very old, indeed.

"What's a Knox sailor's favorite drink?"

Pea shrugged. "I dunno."

"Knox on the Rocks!" The jokester and several other sailors laughed loudly. Pea squinted down at them, trying to think of some clever retort. "Hey," he called. "Fuck you!"

The Prairie sailors laughed again.

A large helicopter roared above and began descending toward the pad. "Wow!" Pea shouted, looking up at the big bird. "That's a big copter. Can she land on that tiny pad?"

"Been doin' it all day, little man," R.J. assured him. "These guys can do anything."

The copter landed and several officers began filing off. "Whew!" R.J. exclaimed, chuckling at the sight. He was watching the scene through a pair of binoculars. They piped aboard the admiral while several other high ranking naval officers followed him down the ramp. "An admiral, two four-stripers, two commanders, and...a lieutenant jaygee! How did he get on that copter?"

"Lemme see," Pea grabbed the binoculars and adjusted them to his face. "Yep, he ain't nothin' but a JG! Hey, I bet he's the criminal investigator." Pea stared through the glasses and tried to adjust the lenses. "Oh, no. It can't be!"

"What?" R.J. asked, alarmed.

"It can't fuckin' be!" Pea handed the glasses to his friend.

R.J. adjusted the binoculars and stared into them, focusing on the lieutenant (jg) who had taken off his hat, wiped his brow and was looking around. His salt and pepper hair danced about in the breeze and his face came clearly into view.

"Oh, crap!" R.J. gasped. "It's Deavers!"

PART TWO:

THE SHIP

CHAPTER THIRTEEN

Day 3

A storied history

Gerald Pizzonovich sat on his bunk, his head resting in his hands. *It was all an ugly dream,* he thought, *and it would be over soon.* But even though Captain Pizzonovich was quickly losing his grip on reality, he knew in his heart that this was no dream. All he had to do to verify that was to look out his porthole, which provided a stark and disturbing view of the reef, and of the waves slapping against the starboard side of his ship.

He tried to occupy himself with the progress reports submitted by the department heads. The ammo and fuel oil had been safely off-loaded, thanks to some brave crew members and a squad of single-minded Marines. Salvage experts were due to come aboard the Knox early the next morning for a visual inspection of the damage and to try to formulate a plan to get her off the damn reef. How did this happen to him after twenty years of impeccable service? *All it took was one idiot in the wrong place at the wrong time and...* "Jesus," the captain moaned. "Jesus fucking Christ!"

The USS Frank Knox was a proud and beautiful ship, with a proud and distinguished record, a bright jewel in the Naval crown known as the U.S. Seventh Fleet. A 'Gearing Class' destroyer, her keel was laid in May of 1944. She was commissioned in December of that year, and was named for the Secretary of the Navy, Frank Knox. The ship was deployed to WestPac in the summer of 1945 and participated in the attacks on Japan launched from American carrier-based aircraft. Frank Knox was one of the ships participating in the Japanese surrender in Tokyo Bay in September, 1945.

In 1949 she was re-designated a DDR (destroyer, radar picket ship) and participated in several operations during the Korean War, including support for the Inchon invasion in September, 1950. She remained in the Far East following the Korean War as part of the U.S. Seventh Fleet.

In 1960, Frank Knox was one of the many destroyers that underwent a modernization refit known as Fleet Rehabilitation and Modernization, or FRAM, instituted by the Chief of Naval Operations, Arleigh '31-Knot' Burke. Modernization was necessary because the Soviet Union had launched a global submarine service, and American World War II-era destroyers were not much of a match for the new Soviet fast-attack submarines. Because of tight budget constraints, refitting the warships was more practical than building new ones. The FRAM rehabilitation fitted new weapons systems on to older warships. The two most important systems were ASROC (Anti-Submarine Rocket) and DASH (Drone Anti-Submarine Helicopter.)

In 1964 the Frank Knox was a participant in the goodwill tour of the First Concord Squadron, and sailed to Madagascar, Mombasa, Kenya, and Aden where the crew helped rehabilitate a school and playground. Returning to the west Pacific, Knox took up patrolling Yankee Station off the coast of Viet Nam. 'Our Navy Magazine' named Frank Knox the 'Ship of the Year' in 1964. She was fast, she was beautiful and her officers and crew operated at high efficiency. Then the proud ship hit Pratas Reef.

CHAPTER FOURTEEN

Pearl Harbor
Two days earlier

Deavers

Deavers had fully intended to retire after his successful investigation of the Haverfield incident. It had been an unusual case; one which he believed would be an appropriate swan song to his Naval career. He had spent a full day preparing his papers for submission to his C.O., Captain Peterson, but when he walked into the office and placed them on the center of the captain's desk, his C.O. merely glanced at them and grunted.

"What is this all about, Deavers?" Everyone just called him Deavers, though his name was William C.

"It's self-explanatory, Captain," Deavers retorted, a little impatiently. *Screw him if he doesn't like it.*

"I can't accept your retirement, Deavers."

"And why not, sir?"

Captain Peterson took off his glasses wearily and looked up at Chief Warrant Officer William C. Deavers, his best criminal investigator. "I'm losing a lot of people to this Viet Nam crap," the captain scowled. "I'm down to three investigators, including you, and one of them is a goddamn rookie." He sighed and glanced through Deavers' paperwork. "You have almost twenty-three in," he observed, studying the file. "Why not wait until you've got twenty-five?" He looked up questioningly at his investigator.

"Sorry, captain, but I'm out of here."

"Well, I'll make you a deal," Captain Peterson picked up Deavers' paperwork and held it out to him. "Wait until you have twenty-five, you'll get a better pension." He paused. "I'll make it worth your while."

Deavers stood motionless, staring at the papers in the captain's hand, but making no move to take them from him. "Make it worth my while how?" *There was only one way he'd stay in the Navy.*

"How about getting a bump to lieutenant (jg)?"

Bingo! "You can do that, sir?" Deavers stared at the captain. *No longer a warrant officer, a half-assed cross between an officer and an enlisted man. A lieutenant (jg)? Hell yes!*

"I can," the captain assured him. "It would be a temporary promotion, but by the time it came to making it permanent, you'd have your twenty-five in and be able to retire as a lieutenant junior grade."

The captain wasn't sure he could deliver on the promise, but he needed Deavers, so he made the promise anyway.

Deavers decided to push his luck. "I might consider staying if I was a full lieutenant," he mused.

The captain frowned up at him. "Lieutenant (jg), take it or leave it," he growled.

It took Deavers about two seconds to decide. "Okay, I'll take it." He reached across the captain's desk and shook his hand. The captain didn't know it, but Deavers would have stayed on as a lowly, fuzz-butt ensign. He chuckled to himself as he left Captain Peterson's office. That had been almost a year ago.

Now Deavers stood again in front of Captain Peterson, this time as a lieutenant (jg). The captain had summoned him with instructions to turn over anything he was working on to the other investigators and to report to the captain's office at once. Something was up.

"I've got a murder for you," the captain said.

Deavers perked up. "Murder?" he asked. He decided he liked the sound of that.

"Don't get too happy," the captain cautioned. "This one's a bitch." He handed the case file over to Deavers who leafed through it.

"First class boatswain's mate?" Deavers continued glancing through the file. "No suspects, no sign of a murder weapon, no witnesses..."

"That's why you've got it and no one else," the captain stated. "We've got to wrap this up quickly, Deavers. The Navy already has a black eye because of this grounding, and this is only going to make it worse."

Don't get any easier, do they? Deavers thought to himself.

"I'm depending on you to bring this case to a quick conclusion," the captain went on. "The eyes of the Seventh Fleet are on you."

Well, I certainly didn't need that pressure, Deavers thought wryly.

Captain Peterson stood and offered his hand, which Deavers shook. "You need anything you contact me, got that?" the captain asked. "Good luck, Deavers."

Deavers left the captain's office with the Knox file in his hand. *A murder case!* Deavers decided he was a very happy man. *No more low-end crime like forgery or robbery or embezzlement. He had a murder!* All his antennae were up and he felt ten years younger. He hurriedly made arrangements to fly to Subic Bay, then to the USS Iwo Jima, and finally by helicopter to the Prairie where he would meet with the powers that be and take over the investigation of the murder of BM-1 C.C. Green.

Two days later, debarking from the helicopter on the tender, he took off his hat, wiped the perspiration from his face and scanned the scene. It was a hot and humid day. Puffy clouds dotted the sky as Typhoon Gilda departed, and Deavers got his first look at the Frank Knox, perched unhappily on the reef. *Good Lord,* he thought, *this is gonna be a bitch*, but he couldn't wait to get aboard the destroyer and begin his investigation.

CHAPTER FIFTEEN

The Body

Regular trips to the Knox were handled by the deck crew on the Prairie boat deck, some of the best sailors aboard. Almost every one of the various small craft in the Prairie's inventory took part in ferrying personnel and supplies back and forth between the tender and the stranded destroyer. Naval criminal investigator Deavers caught a ride on an LCM dispatched to off-load unnecessary equipment from the Knox.

After a brief meeting with the admiral's staff and the reading and re-reading of the report about the discovery of the body filed by Captain Pizzonovich, but written by Mr. Lamb, Deavers knew he faced a difficult challenge. Almost three hundred men called the Knox home. C.C. Green was relatively new on board, having been assigned to the destroyer after a tour of duty at the Navy boot camp located within the sprawling San Diego Naval Training Center. Deavers made a note to check into Green's service at the Navy boot camp. If there were a hint of a problem, he'd find out about it, though the file provided by Mr. Holliday indicated nothing amiss.

According to Mr. Holliday, no one aboard the Knox seemed to know C.C. Green. He was a stranger among the crew, and had not made a single friend in the three months he had been aboard. There appeared to be no clear motive for the killing, and there were no initial suspects. Deavers sighed. He knew what that meant: he had three hundred initial suspects. His first task was, therefore, to eliminate as many as he could, and as quickly as possible. Most of the Knox sailors had already been taken off the ship and billeted aboard the Iwo Jima, Mars and Prairie. Without understanding why, Deavers firmly believed the killer was still on board the Knox, part of the volunteer salvage crew. *That's how I would do it,* he reasoned. *Stay close to the scene so I could monitor the progress of the investigation.* Of course, he could be totally wrong about that, but he didn't think so. Many years of culling the truth out of a situation had provided Deavers with a sixth sense about these things. He followed his nose because his nose had rarely let him down.

Deavers understood that, while he was probably right, he couldn't be a hundred percent certain his theory was correct. He would have to eliminate the crew members as suspects, one by one. *Where to start? First things first.* He had to examine the body and come up with a cause and approximate time of death. The cause of death shouldn't be difficult to determine, but pinpointing the time of death could be problematic.

The LCM pulled alongside the Knox and was secured. Deavers climbed out of the craft and stood, a little unsteadily, on the fantail. The ship listed to starboard and waves off the reef buffeted the stern about, making footing difficult.

"Mr. Deavers?" The exec approached the investigator and held out his hand. "Glad to have you aboard," he said wearily. "I'm Lieutenant Lamb, executive officer."

Deavers shook the lieutenant's hand and looked him over. The exec seemed very tired, and Deavers imagined the last two days had not been pleasant. "Just Deavers," he said, smiling affably. "Like beavers."

The exec motioned for a seaman to take Deavers' bag. "Put that in Mr. Prentiss' quarters." Medford Prentiss II had been airlifted to the Iwo Jima on the first helicopter. The Marine copter crew had assumed he'd received his black eye during the grounding. The exec turned to Deavers. "Come with me, Lieutenant, I'll show you the body."

Mr. Lamb led the investigator down the ladder to the after crew's head. The odor reached them long before they stepped through the hatch to the shower area. Deavers and the exec held handkerchiefs to their noses. The watch on duty wore a gas mask and displayed a 1911 style .45-caliber automatic in a holster on his hip. The exec motioned him out of the shower area and the watch stepped through the hatch and stood at parade rest. He looked relieved, even through his gas mask.

It had been 48 hours since the grounding, which, in the absence of evidence to the contrary, was accepted as the approximate time of death. Deavers leaned down and took a quick look at the entire scene. The body remained in the position it had been found, bent over at the waist, but it had fallen back on its side, face toward the investigator. Rigor had set in, but had subsided after 48 hours, making the body appear relaxed. The odor was unbearable, the corpse was beginning to swell, and Deavers knew that in a few hours the body would become grotesquely bloated and fluids would begin to seep out of every orifice. He did a quick survey of the body and made mental notes of what he observed.

Deavers had been informed that C.C. Green was a black man, but his skin had a pale gray-green pallor to it, as if his skin color had drained out of him along with his life. The black, woolen watch cap still covered the victim's face and his hands were bound behind his back. Deavers leaned over the body and examined the wound on the back of the head. It was a deep gash, caused by a hard object swung with great force. The investigator got down to the level of the shower floor and peered under the body. He got back up on his knees and examined the wound again. "This man was killed with a chipping hammer," he stated confidently.

The exec was impressed. "You can tell that by examining the wound?" he asked through his handkerchief.

Deavers smiled. "Not exactly." He took hold of the body and pulled it forward, so it was once again face down. He motioned for the exec to step in and take a look. Lying on the shower floor next to the body was a chipping hammer, used by the deck force to chip away rust and paint. It had apparently been dropped there by the killer. Dark blood encrusted the steel head. The murder weapon lay there almost defiantly, its bloody head a stark contrast to C.C. Green's lifeless, colorless body. It stood out like a brightly colored object injected into a black and white picture.

Deavers produced a small 35mm camera with a fast lens. He opened the aperture all the way and very slowly, very deliberately took a series of pictures. He took several of the body, a few of the shower stall and a few of the passageway leading to the shower. "I'll have these developed on the Prairie," he said, absently rewinding the film. "They've got a cracker-jack photographer and a good darkroom on board."

"Can we get rid of the body?" the exec asked hopefully.

"I just need to check a few things," Deavers mumbled. He folded his handkerchief and put it into his pocket. He suddenly seemed oblivious to the smell as he examined the nylon line used to bind the hands. "Be just a couple of minutes." He turned his attention to the watch cap. Something clicked in the back of his mind and he reached for it, but it disappeared. *Something about the way the watch cap was pulled over the victim's face...*

"Let me know when we can get it...him...out of here," Lieutenant Lamb said through his handkerchief. "I'll be on the fantail. And, Deavers," the exec stopped and looked back at the investigator. "You WILL keep me advised of any developments." It was not a request.

"Of course, Mr. Lamb," Deavers mumbled absently, concentrating on the body.

The exec nodded and murmured something to the watch, who replied through his gas mask with a muffled, "Yes, sir." Lieutenant Lamb took one last scowling look at the body, and headed topside.

CHAPTER SIXTEEN

Captain Pizzonovich

The exec had just arrived on the fantail when the first shots rang out. Some of the men on deck ducked and scrambled behind any cover they could find. Others froze where they stood, as if they doubted what they had heard. More shots rang out, followed by excited shouting, and seemed to be coming from the starboard side of the bridge.

POW!

"TAKE THAT YOU SON OF A BITCH!"

POW-POW!

The exec hurried forward and ran into Mr. Holliday who was shielding himself behind the motor whale boat davit. "What the hell's going on?" Mr. Lamb demanded.

"The captain's on the wing bridge shooting sharks."

"Shooting sharks?" the exec gasped.

"Yeah, shooting sharks." Mr. Holliday peeked around the corner of the davit and up at the bridge. He turned back to the exec, a big grin on his face. "I gotta tell you, Roger, he's good! Killed three sharks already."

The exec stared at the operations officer as if Mr. Holliday had just lost his senses. *Was everybody on this ship going nuts?* He peered around the davit and spotted the captain on the wing. He was reloading the M-14 and laughing loudly. "I thought I gave instructions that the captain was not to get a rifle!"

"He showed up at the armory and scared the hell out of poor Leo Banks, the gunner's mate. He just intimidated him into giving him the gun. He only got two clips of shells, though." Mr. Holliday peered around the davit again and chuckled. "Should be out of ammo pretty soon."

"I don't think this is funny, Bill," the exec said seriously.

"Oh, sure it is, Roger. Hell, how many times does something like this happen? He'll be out of ammo soon, we'll have Doc give him something to make him sleep, and then we'll get on with the task of salvaging our ship."

The exec studied Mr. Holliday skeptically.

"Think of the story we'll have to tell at the O-club," Mr. Holliday urged.

The exec broke into a wide grin. "Let's make sure he gets some sleep," he said, simulating a hypodermic needle shooting into his vein. "And, please don't let him have any more guns."

POW-POW-POW-POW!

"HA HA! GOT THAT SLIMY BASTARD!"

Both officers ducked behind the davit and grinned nervously at each other.

"The investigator beginning to investigate?" Mr. Holliday changed the subject.

"Yeah," the exec looked thoughtful. "He's kind of a strange duck," he decided.

"Strange? Not like the captain!"

"No, no," the exec laughed. "You'll meet him. You'll see what I mean."

The shooting stopped and the officers peeked around the davit. The captain was leaning forward on the side of the wing, smoking a cigar, the rifle propped against the bulkhead beside him.

"Okay, he's out of ammo," Lieutenant Holliday announced. "Let's go talk him down."

"Are you sure he's out?" the exec worried, but Mr. Holliday had headed forward, so Mr. Lamb hurried after him, concerned that the operations officer was enjoying himself a lot more than he should be.

They reached the wing bridge and approached the captain slowly. He turned when he heard them coming and smiled. "Gentlemen," he greeted, "how goes the battle?" He took a long, slow pull on the cigar and let the smoke drift out through his nose. He seemed relaxed, calm, a man with absolutely no cares.

"Are you alright, Captain?" the exec asked.

"Yes, yes. Just getting in a little target practice." He stared blankly at the reef. "Can't sleep," he stated flatly.

"Let me get Doc up here," Roger Lamb said. "He'll give you something to sleep."

The captain continued staring down at the reef. Mr. Holliday gently moved the M-14 away from the captain and held it behind his back.

"That's okay, Bill," the captain smiled wanly at his operations officer. "Have that returned to the armory and tell Banks I didn't mean to scare him."

"Captain?" The exec was concerned and looked into the captain's face.

"Yes, yes, Roger," the captain agreed wearily, "Ask Doc to bring me something. I'll be in my cabin." He stepped into the pilot house and started toward his cabin. He stopped and looked back at his worried officers with a bemused look on his face. "You feel better now?" he asked, and disappeared into the pilot house.

Mr. Holliday and Mr. Lamb stared at each other. "You feel better?" Mr. Holliday asked.

"Nope. You?"

"Nope."

The killer lay in his bunk, staring into the dark. He had only been able to snatch a few hours sleep since the ship ran aground, and he, like every other man aboard, was tired to the bone. The salvage crew was so small, numbering only seventy, and there was so much work to be done, it didn't seem possible to accomplish everything. He had to stay on board though. Forget his dedication to the Navy and to the ship. Everyone who stayed felt that way, but he wanted to stay close to that nosy investigator, Deavers.

He closed his eyes and thought again about his plan and how it had been derailed by that idiot Prentiss' running the ship aground. The plan had been perfect. He had waited in the after crew's head, knowing C.C. Green would get up at 0200, which was his habit, to take a leak. Bury the hammer in his head and tie him up. Then the coup de grace: pull the watch cap over his face, just as Green had done to...

Then drag him up the aft ladder to the 01 level and ease him over the side while the ship was dark. If the body was ever found, and he doubted it would be, he hoped the watch cap stayed in place. If the body was never discovered, the watch cap would remain a private message between him and Green. He knew Green would grasp its significance.

But the Frank Knox had hit the reef just as he was tying Green's hands behind him, and he had to leave the body where it was, so he posed him and rushed back to his compartment to join others who were fumbling around in the dark. No one had noticed.

CHAPTER SEVENTEEN

The Dental Tech

The first thing the salvage experts wanted to do was try to pull the Knox off the reef using the fleet tugs Cocopa, Munsee and Sioux. The Mahopac would stand by to assist. The crews had worked hard to off-load as much unnecessary weight as possible, hoping to lighten the ship enough so it could be tugged off at high tide.

It was a futile attempt. The tugs took a strain on the cables attached to the fantail of the Knox and began to pull very slowly, very deliberately, almost afraid of pulling too hard. The ship moaned and groaned and moved about two feet, causing a horrible grinding and popping sound. The tugs were ordered to back off. The attempt had the effect of snaring the ship on the reef worse than before. The salvage team decided the ship had to be lightened further or the reef had to be minimized. It was agreed that an underwater demolition team could plant explosives on the reef and blow a part of it away. Confidence was high that it would work.

Meanwhile, the talented craftsmen of the Prairie manufactured several large aluminum containers for fresh water. Helicopters from the Iwo Jima shuttled the welcome fresh water to the Knox several times a day, and the Knox sailors took precautions to make the water last as long as possible. 'Bird bath' showers were taken to conserve water. A sailor got into the shower, turned the water on only long enough to get wet, turned the water off and soaped down, then back on briefly to rinse off. It was better than no shower at all.

The off-loading of unnecessary gear continued. The LCM's, motor whaleboats and helicopters ferried men and equipment back and forth daily, as long as they had sunlight. Chief Billings stood on the 02 level, watching the activity on the fantail. He was proud of his crew. They slaved in the hot sun with few complaints. He welcomed the occasional bitching because he knew he only had to worry when the bitching stopped. He watched with curiosity as four of his men helped to load an LCM. *Curious,* he thought. *There's a man down there I don't know.* The man was vaguely familiar, but Chief Billings prided himself in knowing everyone under his command. With most of the crew gone, individuals were more noticeable.

"Peacock," Chief Billings called down to the fantail. Pea looked up, shielding his eyes with his hand. The chief motioned for Pea to join him on the 02 level.

"Yes, Chief?" Pea bounded up the ladder and stood in front of Billings. "You want me?"

"Who the hell is that guy?" Chief Billings pointed toward the men loading the LCM. A dark-haired sailor, wearing sunglasses, his hat tucked into his back pocket, worked furiously, passing equipment to the LCM. He looked to be in his twenties, wore a third class crow, and, therefore, must have been in the Navy for a few years. Yet his dungaree uniform was almost new, as were his boondockers. He didn't fit in somehow and Chief Billings frowned. A nagging voice in the back of his head began to whisper to him.

Pea looked down to where the chief pointed. "Him? That's Parker. He's been aboard a coupla months."

"How come I don't know him?" the chief mused.

"He's a dental tech. Don't spend a lot of time on deck."

"A dental tech?" The chief narrowed his eyes as he watched Parker work. He thought, *why the hell do we need a dental tech on a destroyer? We got no dental lab.*

"Yeah," Pea replied. "But some of the guys think he's a spy." Pea grinned broadly, but the grin faded when he saw that Chief Billings was not amused.

"Spy?"

"We were givin' him a hard time, 'cause he don't have much to do. Hangs around sick bay with Doc most of the time." Pea chewed his lip and added, "Seems like a good guy, I mean, he don't start no shit."

Chief Billings sipped his coffee and watched Parker over the rim of his cup. The man certainly worked hard, but his eyes were constantly darting about, as if he were afraid he'd be noticed...or discovered. *Now why was that?*

"That all, Chief?"

"Yes, yes," Billings said absently, watching Parker on the fantail. "Thanks, Pea."

"No prob, Chief," Pea grinned and slid down the ladder to the fantail.

Fred Billings stared down at the working party, and made a mental note to look into the personnel file on Parker, the dental technician. Something didn't add up.

CHAPTER EIGHTEEN

Deavers waited in the darkroom for Jeff Samuels, the Prairie's photographer's mate, who was in the black room, threading the 35mm film from Deavers' camera into the film tub. Samuels opened the door and stepped into the darkroom, illuminated only by a red safe light. He held up the film canister and smiled.

"Just have to develop the film," he said. He carefully poured developing fluid into the small film tub and turned the film around and around, making sure it was all soaked with developer. "Only be a couple of minutes." Samuels busied himself with mixing liquids in three trays for developing the prints; developer in the first tray, stop bath in the second and fixer in the third. Once the print was 'fixed' it would be rinsed with plain water and put through the dryer.

Jeff poured the developer out of the film tub and opened it up, unrolling the developed film. He hung the film on a line with a clothespin to let it dry. Deavers could make out negative images on the film, and he felt himself getting excited about seeing the prints.

While they waited in the darkroom, Deavers looked around. Samuels certainly was a squared away sailor. Everything in its place. Samuels himself was squared away, too. His dungaree uniform was starched and pressed, he was clean shaven, his hair neatly combed, and his boondockers were carefully polished. Deavers appreciated that sort of organization and professionalism.

"Okay," Samuels announced as he pulled the film down and inspected it. "We're dry. Let's set up the enlarger." He fed the film into the enlarger and turned on the light, projecting the negative image down on the easel. Samuels focused the image until it became clear, and then turned off the enlarger. He pulled a sheet of eight by ten photographic paper out of a black envelope and situated it on the easel. He turned the timer on the projector to fifteen seconds and pressed the ON button. The enlarger projected the image onto the paper, and when the timer went off, the enlarger light went off. Jeff Samuels picked up the paper with a pair of plastic tongs and slipped it into the developer tray. Almost immediately, the positive image began to appear, and Deavers smiled at his photography. The picture was clean and clear, very well defined.

Samuels smiled at Deavers. "Good shot," he said, and transferred the print to the stop bath. After about thirty seconds, he lifted it out of the stop bath and put it into the fixer.

The rest of the prints were as good as the first, and soon twenty four eight by ten pictures came out of the print dryer. Samuels slipped them into an envelope and handed them to Deavers.

"Thank you, Samuels."

"My pleasure, sir, let me know if I can be of any more help."

Deavers stepped out the hatch, leafing through the prints, smiling at the clear quality of the shots. He stood on the 04 level admiring his pictures, when the hatch to the bunting locker opened and he found himself face to face with R.J. Davis.

They stood there staring at each other for what seemed like minutes. Deavers smiled widely and put out his hand. "R.J. Davis! Long time no see."

Memories of the Haverfield incident flooded R.J.'s mind. He took Deavers' hand and shook it. The first time he had met Deavers, almost a year ago en route from Subic Bay to Pearl Harbor, he didn't like the man. More accurately, he didn't trust him, but Deavers' handling of the Haverfield incident and its aftermath had greatly impressed R.J. What could have been a very difficult situation for him and two of his friends had been defused deftly by Warrant Officer Deavers, who was now a lieutenant (jg). R.J. was genuinely glad to see him.

"Congratulations on your commission, sir," he offered.

"Thanks, R.J.," Deavers replied, still smiling. "How do you like this duty station?"

"I love it, sir," R.J. replied enthusiastically. "This is a great ship."

"You hear about the murder?" Deavers asked conspiratorially.

"Rumors about it," R.J. admitted. "My friend Peacock is on the Knox and he mentioned it."

"It's a tough case, R.J." Deavers spoke to him as if he were an old friend. "Not much to go on."

"Lots of pieces, huh, sir?" R.J. grinned at a shared memory.

Deavers nodded, chuckling. "It's always a puzzle, to be put together piece by piece."

"Knowing you, sir," R.J. assured him, "you'll have it solved in no time."

"From your lips to God's ear," Deavers said, smiling. "I'll come up to the signal bridge and visit sometime, if that's okay with you."

"Yes sir," R.J. replied. "Please do."

"Take care, sailor."

"You too, sir." R.J. watched Deavers walk aft, looking into his envelope. R.J. wondered what was in there. He looked at the hatch to the photography shop and nodded to himself. He opened the hatch and stepped in. "Samuels?" he called. "You in here?"

The Puzzle

Deavers sat on his bunk and stared down at the array of photographs he had spread out on the deck. This was not a complicated murder. It was probably over quickly, and the victim, BM-1 C.C. Green, probably didn't suffer too much, if he even knew what hit him. The killing was carried out with apparent precision and premeditation, and therefore must have been thought out carefully. *Running into the reef gave him his chance, but how could the killer have anticipated the grounding? Unless the murder was planned for that very night and the killer was as surprised as everyone else when they hit Pratas Reef. Was it his plan all along to leave Green where he could be found easily? Or was there another plan, a plan that was interrupted by the accident? Perhaps the killer didn't mean for his victim to be found. Then why the black watch cap? It was clearly posed. And what the hell was it about that picture...*he rummaged through his prints until he found the one that clearly depicted the position of the watch cap. A fleeting feeling of recognition, there for a moment, then gone, whispered through his memory. He tried to recover it, turning his head sideways as if he were having trouble hearing someone speak. It was gone. *Damn, this is infuriating,* he thought.

He stared at the pictures, letting his mind roam free. Sweet memories of Maggie swept in and danced before his eyes. He didn't think Captain Peterson knew about him and Maggie. They had kept their liaison private, knowing the Navy frowns on co-workers becoming romantic. He smiled to himself, and then shook his head. *Not that free,* he thought, shaking Maggie out and urging C.C. Green in. He stared again at the picture of Green's face covered by the watch cap. For some reason, he felt short of breath, but only for a single heartbeat, then that, too was gone. *The watch cap. That's the key, I'd bet money on it.*

He sat back and smiled. It was good seeing R.J. Davis again. It brought back good memories, memories of how the huge bureaucracy known as the United States Navy could bend, flex and adjust to the changing times. They were good memories. *Okay, enough of that. Back to the watch cap. What was its significance?*

Chief Billings had two personnel files on his desk: Green, Charles C. and Parker, Jude I. What was the common denominator for these two files? The only common denominator Chief Billings could determine was that they had reported on board within a few days of each other; C.C. Green first, then J.I. Parker three days later, just before the ship got underway for Yankee Station. The chief kept struggling with one important fact: Parker, J.I. was a dental technician. *What was a dental tech doing on a destroyer? Did his arrival coincide deliberately with Green's? Could it be he was sent here purposefully at the same time as Green? If so, why? Was it all a coincidence?* Chief Billings was a cautious man, and did not believe in coincidence. So much didn't add up. The chief firmly believed that something was not exactly kosher with J.I. Parker, and he would scratch around and find out what. He closed the files, put them out of his mind, and took out his personal stationery. He needed to write to Janice again and try to cheer her up. It wasn't easy this far away, he knew she hurt, and was frustrated he couldn't be there with her when she needed him. Her letters were brave and optimistic, but he could read between the lines. He put pen to paper and started his letter: *Darling Janice...*

CHAPTER NINETEEN

Day 5

Styrofoam

"Damn!" Lieutenant Holliday swore and threw the latest damage report on the wardroom table. Roger Lamb picked it up and glanced through it.

"Looks worse," the exec said.

"Much worse," Bill Holliday agreed, shaking his head sadly.

With the combination of the aggressive waves caused by Gilda and the aborted attempt at pulling the Knox free, the ship had become further impaled on the reef, causing more damage to her hull and more flooding. Every available water pump was put to work and all lower compartments were dogged off and secured by watertight doors. The pumps eventually began winning the contest. Most of the excess water was pumped out of the ship's lower decks and more compartments were sealed off. At high tide the ship moved ever so slightly, and seemed to sigh as she tried to find a comfortable position.

At the daily salvage operations meeting aboard the Prairie, it was determined that Knox needed to be even lighter in order to get her off the reef. Her main girder had been weakened and needed to be strengthened. Many holes along her hull had to be patched. Finishing these repairs and making the ship even lighter would be their only chance of getting her off the reef. It was decided they would redouble their efforts and pull everything non-essential off the ship. "Strip her down to her skivvies!" Admiral Wilson ordered. The salvage crew accepted the order and stormed through the ship, grabbing everything that wasn't actually in operation at that time. They took off all top deck hatches, all furniture except in officer's country, and all unnecessary tools from engineering. They even took the ship's bell.

Next, some of the salvage experts wanted to try a new, untested method for lightening the ship. They proposed to pump liquid Styrofoam into her keel and wait for it to dry. The theory was that the foam would displace all remaining water, and would dry, adding greatly to the buoyancy of the ship, which should make it easier to pull her free.

"We introduce the chemicals through a narrow-holed nozzle, so it shoots in under pressure and expands as it sets up, displacing the water, forcing it out," a lieutenant commander from BUSHIPS explained. "It is supposed to put the buoyancy ratio at about twenty to one." He paused and looked around at his audience. "That oughta lighten her up quite a bit."

Another group insisted that their best chance was in removing some of the coral, and they wanted to bring in an underwater demolition team to set charges and blow away a portion of Pratas Reef. Hopefully, enough of the reef could be cleared so that they could pull her off with the tugs.

A spirited debate raged between these two factions until Admiral Wilson, weary of the argument, held up his hand for silence. The group became silent.

"We'll do both," he decreed. "But first we have to get the water pumped out of the lower compartments. See to it."

By the end of the day, liquid foam had been ordered to be flown in from Japan, which would take a minimum of fifteen days, and a team of Navy Seals was put on stand-by at Subic Bay. The salvage teams smoked cigarettes, pored over schematics and blueprints, and fretted. In the meantime, they would strengthen up that main girder and patch the holes in the hull, so they could pump as much excess water as possible out of the compartments.

The Prairie continued to supply fresh water and food to the Knox, as did the Iwo Jima, and the Knox crew, ably assisted by Gunny Davis and his Marines, continued to offload tools and equipment. Everybody agreed there was good news for the Knox. The weather would be hot and calm for the foreseeable future, with no more storms, no more battering by angry waves, no more slashing rain in the face. The salvage task force would carry on their mission under a bright sky and a brighter sun. After a few days working in the Western Pacific's hottest summer days, those same sailors would look to the sky and yearn for rain.

The wait for the underwater demolition team provided a brief respite from the hard work and boring routine of the salvage operation. The remaining Knox crew continued to offload anything and everything possible, but the pace was slowing as fewer and fewer items were located and taken off the ship. The holes had been patched and pumps had sucked out most of the water. Captain Pizzonovich authorized the crew to do some fishing, and, after posting men on the upper decks with M-14 rifles to watch for sharks, he okayed swim call.

The Knox salvage crew responded with youthful exuberance, and within minutes fishing lines were in the water off the forecastle, and swimmers splashed around off the fantail, ever mindful of sharks. They swam across the reef, some with snorkels examining the marine life, but most simply enjoying themselves. The sun was high and bright in the blue sky, and a few white clouds clustered on the horizon. A gentle breeze whispered across the water. After five days on the reef, the time off was like being on liberty...almost.

Pea stood in the cool, aqua water of the reef, his head just above the surface, looking around at the vast scene. It certainly looked like a major operation was underway. Navy ships dotted the seascape and helicopters constantly shuttled between the Mars, the Iwo Jima and the Prairie. Pea grinned. The Navy had closed ranks, circled the wagons and come to the aid of one of her family, and now the Frank Knox was securely nestled in the protective bosom of the U.S. Seventh Fleet. For the first time since they had run aground, Pea felt everything was going to be okay, and that feeling permeated the crew, instilling them with confidence and renewed energy. Pea floated on his back, listening contentedly to the happy laughter of the crew. It had been a while since he had heard laughter on the Frank Knox. It sounded like music to him.

On the Prairie, R.J. sat in the signal shack with Ricky and Charlie. R.J. and Ricky had the watch, and Charlie was killing time until his duty section took over. He sat at the desk while R.J. leafed through a clipboard of message slips. Ricky leaned in the doorway, keeping an eye out for signal traffic. Tommy Blanchard came up the ladder with an armful of envelopes and packages.

"Mail Call, you lucky dogs!" he announced. The signalmen jumped to their feet and gathered around Tommy. They hadn't received any mail since they were in Hong Kong, and were eager for letters from home.

R.J. collected five letters, all from Longmont. One from Renee, one from Chuck, and three from Millie. He sighed as he inspected the letters.

"That crazy chick write you again?" Charlie asked, grinning.

"Yep," R.J. replied, examining the letter from Millie.

"You ain't gonna go and marry that screwy broad, are ya, partner?" Ricky asked seriously.

"No, I am not," R.J. replied, a little irritated. He wasn't irritated with Ricky, but with the unhappy anticipation of what kind of crap was in Millie's letters...this time.

"You might as well marry her, R.J.," Charlie mused. "She's already starting to nag you, hating you is just around the corner. It's the natural progression of these things, you know."

Tommy Blanchard grinned broadly and nudged Charlie. "How many ex-wives you got now, Charlie?"

Charlie brought a hand up to his chin and stroked it thoughtfully. The mischievous smile appeared on his face. "Goin' on three," he said to the accompaniment of laughter.

Ricky snorted. "You mean the present Miz Mayweather is the future ex-Miz Mayweather?"

Charlie nodded solemnly. "Let's just say she's exhibiting all the symptoms."

"All Charlie's exes hate him with a passion, right, bud?" Tommy asked.

Charlie sighed. "I blame myself," he said. "I always had magic when it came to women. I used to sprinkle it on them, you know, like Tinker Bell's magic dust, and they would fall into my arms." His mischievous grin was back. "And subsequently into my bed." More laughter. "But sometimes, when I was younger and more impetuous, I would end up using too much of it, and they would fall madly in love with me."

"Well, hell," Ricky exclaimed. "What's so bad about that?"

Charlie lit a cigarette and blew a perfect smoke ring. "Listen up boys, I'm gonna give you pearls." The others gathered around for some Mayweather philosophy.

"Lots of people think love and hate are opposite emotions, but they ain't. Actually, they're very close, because they're both extremely strong emotions." He looked around to make certain his audience was listening. R.J. sat back in the chair with his hands behind his head, Tommy leaned against the rear bulkhead, and Ricky slouched against the doorjam to hear Charlie's 'pearls.'

"The degree to which a woman ends up hating you is in direct proportion to how much you make her love you, dig?" Charlie pulled himself into a sitting position on the desk and continued. "I used to make 'em love me too much, that's why they ended up hating me so much. See, the opposite of love is not hate, the opposite of love is *indifference.* I feel indifferent toward my exes, and I only wish they would feel the same for me."

"How do you get chicks NOT to hate you?" R.J. asked sincerely. "You said that's the natural progression, so how do you get them to just be indifferent?"

Charlie stroked his chin. "Well, it's a delicate balancing act," he acknowledged. "It takes years of practice." He nodded toward R.J. "You got some of that magic dust, too, my boy. Use it judiciously or they will end up hating you, too."

R.J. nodded and looked down at Millie's letter. *Too late for that, I think.*

"Thus spaketh the Master!" Chief Benson stuck his head in the door and winked at Charlie and glowered at Ricky. "Ricky, goddamit!" he yelled, "you got the watch up here or what?"

"Yeah, Chief," Ricky replied with what he hoped was a totally innocent expression. "I got it handled."

"Then maybe you can tell me why we gotta friggin' light flashing at us from the friggin' Mars!" He pointed aft to the combat supply ship. A flashing light blinked incessantly.

"Oh, shit!" Ricky exclaimed, and ran out to the aft deck toward the rolling signal light.

"Careful with my light, Ricky!" R.J. yelled after him. He opened the envelope and extracted Millie's letter carefully, as if he were holding a baby's soiled diaper by one corner.

Chief Benson watched R.J. with the letter. "That crazy chick write you again?" The signal shack erupted in laughter and the chief looked from one man to the other, a confused expression on his face. "What?"

R.J. grinned and unfolded Millie's first letter. *Might as well get it over with*, he thought. As he opened the envelope and caught a whiff of her perfume, he drifted back to Longmont, Colorado and the hilarious wedding of his friends, Renee and Chuck.

CHAPTER TWENTY

Longmont, Colorado
August, 1964

The Little Voice

The rehearsal dinner had been an interesting affair. The VFW hall was packed with family and friends of Renee and Chuck, who beamed with happiness, though they worried that their best man, Benny Ortega, hadn't shown up yet. His girlfriend Karen kept peeking out the front window, hoping to see Benny's customized Olds pull up.

After a few glasses of champagne, Millie became amorous. She cuddled up to R.J. in a booth, giggling and nuzzling his neck with little kisses. Her glasses were steamed up and her eyes gaped large at him through the mist. "Do you love me, R.J.?" she pleaded, squinting to focus on his face. "Mmmm? Do you?"

"Hey Millie!" Dean Phillips yelled from across the room. "You gonna climb in that guy's shirt or what?" The hall filled with laughter and Millie, mistaking the laughter for encouragement, ran her hands up inside R.J.'s uniform jumper and tweaked both his nipples.

"Ow!" R.J. pushed her hands away irritably and jumped to his feet, smoothing down his jumper. Millie fell sideways in the booth, laying her head on the vinyl and laughing uncontrollably. She laughed long after everyone else had stopped, and R.J., embarrassed, walked out the side door and leaned against the brick building. He lit a cigarette and looked up into the Colorado sky, sparkling with stars. The constellations were clearly defined against an inky background and R.J. smiled happily. It was almost like being at sea; staring up at the sky above the blue Pacific, tracing constellations and the other planets in the solar system...*where everything is peaceful and worries evaporate in the salt spray.* He had a sudden urge to go home, pack his sea bag and catch the train to San Diego.

Run!

R.J. sighed, ignoring the voice, took a deep drag off his cigarette and thought of Renee and Chuck. He had to admit he envied them. His own romantic dalliances always turned sour somehow, as though they were meant to be that way. That included his relationship with Renee, who was now marrying one of his best friends. His recent failures were fresh in his mind. His thoughts drifted back to Guam and to Annie. He chuckled to himself about Annie. *How do I always get the weird ones?* he pleaded up at the stars. *Why does this shit have to be so complicated?* He took a last drag on his cigarette and flipped the butt in a high arc toward the parking lot, where it landed in a short burst of sparks. *Fuckin' women!*

"You out here, R.J.?" Chuck came out the side door and squinted in the dim light.

"Over here," R.J. called and lit another cigarette. Chuck followed the glow to where R.J. was standing. "Millie's afraid you might be pissed off." He accepted a smoke and a light from R.J. and leaned up against the wall next to him.

"Yeah?" R.J. said sarcastically. "Millie's got a right to be afraid. I am pissed." R.J. changed the subject. "Any sign of Benny?"

"Not yet, but you know Benny."

"Yeah," R.J. chuckled, "I sure do. He got us into a lot of fights at the swimming hole."

"We won most of them," Chuck grinned.

"Yeah," R.J. replied, remembering the summers at the swimming hole. "But not all of them." He looked seriously at his friend. "Renee's folks aren't getting along, I take it."

Chuck laughed out loud. "Now, what gives you that idea?" They both laughed, remembering the angry scene between Renee's mother and father. "But now that you mention it, R.J., no, I don't believe they are getting along." They both laughed again until tears were rolling down their cheeks.

"I'm happy for you, Chuck," R.J. said suddenly. "I don't think I'll ever find the right girl."

"What about Millie?"

"She gets on my nerves, you know? She's cute as hell, and that body..."

"She had a little too much champagne," Chuck explained half-heartedly. "Anyway, she's Renee's best friend and..."

R.J. got a big grin on his face. "...and you wouldn't be out here if it weren't for Renee?" R.J. put his arm around his friend's shoulders and gave him an affectionate hug. Chuck smiled sheepishly. "Damn, Chuck, you ain't even said the 'I do' yet and already you're pussy-whipped."

"I do...believe you are right," Chuck replied, grinning.

"You do?"

"I do!" They were laughing so hard they didn't notice Millie come up behind them.

"R.J.?" she whined.

R.J. and Chuck turned to face Millie. She stood with her feet apart, arms folded across her chest, a childish pout on her face. "R.J.?" she whined again. R.J. and Chuck looked at Millie, then at each other. The laughter was gone.

Chuck smiled knowingly. R.J. winked at him and put his arm around Millie's shoulder. "C'mon, baby, let's go for a drive." He led Millie to her car and put her in the passenger seat. As he came around the back of the car toward the driver's side, he looked back at Chuck who was standing in the doorway of the VFW, waving. He looked relieved. R.J. smiled and waved back. *Run!* the little voice said again. R.J. climbed behind the wheel and started the car. He looked over at Millie who was asleep in the passenger seat, her head resting on the side of the door. She looked beautiful, her face so peaceful, and he reached over to brush some hair from her eyes. She murmured, eyes closed, shifted in her seat and smiled so sweetly it melted his heart. It was easy to ignore the little voice, even as persistent as it was becoming.

He drove north on Main Street toward the Silver Spur. Traffic was sparse, as usual late at night in a town of twelve thousand people. R.J. cruised at thirty miles per hour, only five miles over the speed limit. When he pulled into the Silver Spur parking lot, Millie woke up, ran her hands through her hair and checked her lipstick in the rear view mirror. R.J. killed the engine and pulled the emergency brake. He came around the car and opened the door for Millie. She accepted his hand and hopped out of the car, her step full of bounce. She appeared to be completely sober.

"Let's get a Pepsi and go visit Penelope!" she said enthusiastically, looking across the street at the cemetery.

"Let's get a Pepsi and talk a while, okay, Millie?" She frowned at him and R.J. knew he sounded terse, impatient, but he didn't give a shit. *I've been in town for two weeks and she dragged me to that damn grave seven times already! I don't feel like visiting Penelope. I don't want to see Penelope. I don't like Penelope. In fact, Penelope can kiss my ass!*

Inside the restaurant, Millie took R.J.'s hand and looked up into his eyes. "Are you okay, R.J.?" she asked softly. "You're not mad anymore are you?"

He looked down into her soft brown eyes and smiled. "Naw, I ain't mad, but let's not disturb Penelope tonight, okay?" He tried to make it sound like a statement and not a request while he was looking around for Mr. Cozner. If the old man was there, he would certainly toss Millie out of the restaurant for throwing that ketchup bottle through his front window.

"What are you doing?"

"Looking for old man Cozner."

"He's not here this late."

"Good, then we can stay."

"Don't be sarcastic. You sound so sarcastic," she pouted at him. "Besides, I was a little drunk and Benny dared me to do it."

"Well, that explains it," R.J. said sarcastically.

"Don't be cross. You sound so cross."

They were interrupted when a couple of diners, friends of his parents, came over and welcomed R.J. home. He answered their questions politely and respectfully, thanked them for coming over and wished them well. All the time he was painfully aware of the bored, impatient look on Millie's face. When he looked directly at her, she brightened quickly, cocked her perky head and flashed a big, phony smile.

"What is it with you, Millie?" R.J. challenged.

"What do you mean?" The wide-eyed, innocent look.

"You're up, you're down, you're happy, you're pissed off..." He stopped and ordered two Pepsis from the waitress.

"Am I really that bad?" Millie asked after the waitress left.

"Yes." *And I'm getting damned sick of it*, he thought.

"Well, to tell you the truth, you've changed, R.J."

"Yeah, how?"

"You're not as much fun as you used to be."

"Why, because I don't think throwing a bottle through the window is a fun thing to do?"

"Don't be sarcastic!"

"Don't act like a child!"

Her expression softened, and she leaned across the table, taking his hands in hers. Her whole demeanor changed, as if he had switched television channels and was watching an entirely different program. "Can I make it up to you, R.J.?" She smiled very sweetly and gazed into his eyes.

Run!

He looked at her skeptically. "You gonna behave like an adult and not some spoiled-assed brat?"

She squeezed his hands and looked dreamily into his eyes. "Tomorrow is the wedding, you know."

"Yeah, I know." He straightened up as the waitress set down the two Pepsis, smiled at R.J. and walked off. "So what?"

"Renee and Chuck have a room at the Howard Johnson's for their honeymoon."

R.J. stuck straws into both glasses and shrugged. "So?"

"So, it just so happens that I have a room at the Howard Johnson's, too." She got a wicked look on her face and her voice dropped an octave. "How 'bout it, Big Shot?" she teased. "You want to have a honeymoon, too?"

Run!

R.J. stared at her, trying to decide if she were serious or just playing some childish game. "If you're serious..." he started.

"Of course I am," she insisted. She sat up in the booth and coyly sipped her Pepsi. "I've been waiting for it for a long time, R.J." She could see he was weakening. "I'm twenty years old and I'm tired of being a virgin." She said it a little louder and more forcefully than she meant to, and several other patrons looked around at them. Millie lowered her voice. "I'm nuts about you, R.J. I've been planning this for a long time." She sipped her Pepsi and looked up at him. "Well, what's it gonna be?"

R.J. sipped his Pepsi and studied Millie. "Okay," he grinned. "You've got a date. Let's see who chickens out."

"It won't be me," Millie assured him. "Just one thing, though." She nibbled at her thumbnail and studied him intently.

"What?"

"You gotta do something for me."

"What?"

"Tomorrow, after the wedding, you gotta go talk to Penelope with me."

Again? he thought, and then said aloud, "Again?"

She pouted. "I want you to make friends with Penelope, R.J."

"I am friends with her," he insisted. "I go there with you to see her, don't I?"

"I want you to talk to her. Tell her you love me and ask her if you can go to bed with me."

Run!

Had R.J. thought about it long enough, he probably would have listened to the little voice and got as far away from her as he could. Unfortunately, in the presence of Millie's tight little body, R.J.'s thinking processes were taking place a good distance south of his brain.

"I know she'll say yes," Millie said softly.

Man, he thought, *and I was giving Chuck a hard time about being pussy-whipped.* "Okay," he said aloud.

Millie smiled widely and squeezed his hands. "Well," she exclaimed, and the channel switched again, "we better get home and get some rest. Big day tomorrow." She slid out of the booth and picked up her purse and car keys. "I'll drop you, okay?" She was out the door.

R.J. shrugged, paid the check and followed Millie to the parking lot, fighting hard against the persistent whispering of the little voice.

Front Porch

The moon, full and golden in the high sky, shone down on R.J. as he stood on his parents' front porch and watched Millie's car speed away down Sunset. He lit a cigarette and leaned forward on the railing, remembering the many times he had spent out on the porch, sneaking cigarettes when his parents were away, or waiting for Chuck to pick him up on his Vespa so they could cruise town, throwing firecrackers at dogs that chased the scooter. In the summer, he would wait on the porch for the gang to pick him up so they could walk up to Sunset Park and the swimming hole. That's where he had met Renee when he was twelve years old. He had also met Millie, but didn't remember her well. They all got together each day at the pool, and soon they became inseparable. Benny Ortega, the mischievous troublemaker who could make you laugh until your stomach hurt. Jim Wallace, expert on car engines and cheating on tests, who could steal more candy bars in one trip to the drug store than the rest of them combined. Chuck Phipps, all around nice guy, who had always been in love with Renee. Millicent Brewer, who hung around in the background, braces on her teeth and cats-eye eyeglasses; the ugly duckling who became the beautiful swan. Dean Phillips, the organizer, who did nothing without a plan except woo girls, which was why he did so poorly at it. He once organized a massive walkout of third period at Longmont High School. Fifty students at a time, in several different classrooms, suddenly got up from their seats, in five minute intervals, and walked out of class, assembling on the front lawn of the school. Within fifteen minutes he had emptied the school of the entire senior class, about two hundred students, and had done so in a calm and organized manner. He told the principal, during his subsequent disciplinary visit, that he was demonstrating the proper way to evacuate a school in case of an emergency, and he had organized the exercise as a project for his Social Sciences class. The principal suspended him for three days, and met with his parents. Mrs. Proctor, the Social Sciences teacher, gave Dean an A+, with the promise that he would never do anything like that again.

And there was Renee, the beauty who turned every boy's head, but had eyes only for R.J. She was perfect. A perfect student, a perfect daughter, a perfect friend. She did everything perfectly, including swimming, and all the boys were crazy about her. The girls all wanted to hang out with her and R.J. and the rest of the boys benefited from her magnetic attraction. They were assured of having plenty of girls around.

R.J. chuckled to himself. He thought he had been so very clever, sneaking smokes outside so his folks wouldn't smell it in the house. One evening his father had lighted a cigarette and turned to him, offering him the cigarette pack.

"You smoke cigarettes, don't you, R.J.?" he asked wryly. R.J. knew at once that he had not been as clever as he had thought. He remembered blushing, embarrassed he had been busted. He also remembered fondly the soft, kindly smile on Granny's face.

Only a week to go before he had to leave. He felt obliged to spend a little time with his mother in Denver, though he wasn't really looking forward to it. Growing up with a drunk for a mother had left a deep hollowness in his soul, and thinking of seeing her always brought on a headache. His mother and father had divorced when he was eight. R.J. was the oldest of four, and took over the responsibility of watching out for his sisters. His relationship with his mother gradually deteriorated to the point that their places in the family hierarchy reversed. He became the responsible adult at age nine, and she became the incorrigible child. On more occasions than he could remember, he awakened in the middle of the night to his mother's noisy return from a night of drinking. She would rail in a drunken rage until R.J. got her calmed down and put to bed. In the morning, he would rise early and help his younger siblings get ready and off to school. If they needed a parental note for any reason, R.J. would write it for them and sign his mother's name. He was quite good at forging her signature, a talent he employed extensively on behalf of himself and his younger siblings.

After his mother had remarried (to one of her drinking buddies), he soon found himself the oldest of seven, his responsibilities grown exponentially. When all of the money they earned ended up in the cash register at Danny's 39 Club, his mother and stepfather moved them out of their house in the Chafee Park area and into the Lipan Street projects. He soon discovered that many of the poor black people in the projects had better home lives than he did, and that was enough for him. He fled into the warmth of his grandparents' home, and they nurtured him, bolstered him, encouraged him. He rarely went back home, and when he did, it always ended in a loud argument with his mother. When his father finally resurfaced four years later, R.J. went with him to Longmont. There, living in a clean, uncrowded environment, his parents coming home every night after work instead of heading for the nearest bar, and no younger kids to be responsible for, he found he had no further reason to stay in Denver. Longmont was his home. Denver was just a place to visit.

The screen door creaked open and Granny stepped out on the porch in her robe and slippers.

"R.J., are you smoking out here?" she teased.

R.J. laughed out loud and put his arm around his stepmother. "I really thought I had you guys fooled."

She put her arm around his waist. "Oh, you'd be surprised all the things your father and I knew about."

"Yeah?" he said, turning to face her. "Like what?"

"Let's see. How about the time you let the neighbor's dog out of the yard, after being told not to, and you and your buddies chased that dog all over town until you caught it." She held her hand up to stop him from interrupting. "And, then, because the dog had been through yards, alleys, mud and water, you guys decided to give her a bath."

R.J. chuckled at the memory.

"But the poor dog, Cookie was her name I think, hated being bathed." Granny was clearly enjoying the telling. "So she bit poor Chuck pretty badly, I think he ended up with six stitches, and you and your buddies made up a story to tell his mother."

R.J. was laughing out loud at the story, even though it was personally humiliating. For a twelve-year old, it had been an incident of disastrous proportions.

"Yeah, I remember that." His father's voice came through the screen door and R.J. looked over at him. All he could see through the screen was a dim outline and a bright orange glow every time his dad took a drag on his cigarette. The image prompted a quick childhood memory that flooded his mind. His image of his father had always been dim, tentative, unfocused. R.J. had only a misty memory of his father from age eight, when he was still blaming himself for his parents' breakup, and the soft, diffused specter behind the screen door reminded him of that time and that memory. He shook his head hard to clear it, and half-expected a headache to tap him on the back of his eye.

"And what a clever story you dumb shits came up with." His father stepped out on the porch and patted R.J. on the shoulder. "How did you Einsteins think that up, anyway?"

"It seemed like a good idea at the time," R.J. replied, laughing.

His dad turned to his stepmother. "I can just hear it now: Mrs. Phipps," he crooned in his best twelve year-old voice, "we were out in the woods and a big bear attacked us and bit Chuck while we were fighting it off."

They had a good laugh about that, and Granny continued. "Then there was the time Benny stole the putter off the golf course, you and Chuck got in trouble for breaking that girl's screen door, you stole your dad's car and took the guys for a joy ride..."

"Yeah, and by the time I got home, you had already heard about it," R.J. recalled.

"Small town, my boy," his dad explained. "Small town."

"And then," Granny began ticking off more incidents on her fingers. "You threw the firecrackers in the girl's restroom, you tipped over the mailbox on 4th and Main, you threw the dead trout in the girl's restroom, you reversed all the street signs on Mountain Avenue, you threw a stink bomb in the girl's restroom..."

"Anyone else beginning to perceive a theme here?" his dad cracked.

"You had a storied career," Granny forged on. "And then you got to high school."

That was enough for R.J. "No, please," he begged, holding his arms in front of his face. "I confess, I did it, I chopped down the cherry tree."

"Actually," Granny corrected him, "that was an apple tree. Mr. Ahern's apple tree." She frowned at him disapprovingly and shook her head slowly. "R.J," she clucked.

"Old Ahern was quite proud of that apple tree," R.J.'s father reminisced. "The bald-headed old bastard."

"Now dear," Granny scolded.

"He was a mean old crab," R.J. said. "Besides, we picked all his apples off the lower branches and climbed as high as we could for others, but the best apples were way up at the top, and we couldn't climb that high, so Benny suggested the obvious."

"How long did it take you to do the job?" his dad asked, grinning.

"There were eight of us, working two-man shifts...all night actually."

"I don't want to hear the details," Granny protested. "I'm going to bed." She kissed them both on the cheek and slipped through the door.

R.J. and his father stood on the porch, watching the screen door close. It became very quiet and still, and they stood there, smoking cigarettes and enjoying the evening. R.J. had no idea why he was always a little uncomfortable in his father's presence, but he always had been.

"Those were some good apples," R.J. said.

"I remember," his father said, nodding agreement.

"Were we really that bad?"

"You guys were pains in the ass. But, I gotta tell you, you were entertaining as hell."

"So, you musta told a lot of stories about us at the American Legion, huh?"

"Oh, hell yeah." His father winked at him conspiratorially. "Especially the one about you mutts thinking we old folks didn't know shit."

R.J. chuckled. It was good to be home.

"I must now retire," his dad announced, "for I am weary. Goodnight, R.J."

"Good night, Pop."

R.J. lit another cigarette and looked up at the dark sky. It felt great to be home. Watching the twinkling stars, he realized he wasn't the irresponsible kid he used to be. He was becoming a man, and his father seemed to recognize that. He'd treated R.J. a little differently since he had come home on leave, as if he were signaling subliminally his realization that his son was no longer a kid. R.J. smiled, and a curious pride enveloped him. He looked around at the porch fondly. Boy, he thought, *this old porch has seen a lot of history, a lot of changes, a lot of life and a lot of...*

He loved the mountain sky, especially late at night. The moon always seemed to beam so much brighter late at night. The thin air and semi-rural location allowed a wide blanket of stars to sparkle bright and brilliant in the indigo sky. *Wow,* he thought, breathing in the crisp Colorado air. *What a beautiful night!*

He had spent a great deal of time on the porch when he was growing up. He would lean against the railing and daydream about joining the Navy and going to sea. He'd imagine himself at sea, on the deck of an aircraft carrier, at the center of a task force. He chuckled at the memory. At sea, he often leaned on the lifeline and daydreamed about standing on the old porch back home. Now each memory would remind him of the other, like an unexpected bonus. He took in one more deep breath of air and went inside.

CHAPTER TWENTY ONE

Penelope

Twenty four hours later, a slightly drunk R.J., pieces of wedding cake stuck to his dress blues, stood unsteadily in the cemetery and glared down at the grave of Penelope Laine, Beloved Wife of Jonathan, *blah, blah, blah*. Millie was on her knees, brushing off the grave. She had little pieces of frosting and wedding cake stuck in her hair. She gathered up her bridesmaid's dress and held it off the ground. She was still tipsy from too much wedding reception champagne, and rocked slowly from side to side. She was humming a song R.J. could not place, and he was unhappy about being dragged in front of Penelope again. But he had to admit, *it had been one hell of a funny wedding!*

"Penelope, Penelope," she hummed dreamily. "We've come to ask your blessing."

R.J. lifted a half-empty bottle of champagne to his lips and took a long pull. "Yeah, Penelope, old girl," he shouted down at the grave. "We want permission to DO THE DEED!" He staggered a bit, giggling at Millie who scowled back at him, her finger held to her lips.

"You have to talk to her, R.J.," she scolded in a quiet voice. "And be nice, she's been through a lot."

R.J. sat on the grave and draped his arm over the headstone, dangling the bottle of champagne. He looked at the headstone solemnly and cleared his throat. "My dear Penelope," he began. "We are here this evening to ask your permission to, uh, consummate our relationship." He motioned toward Millie, who stood to the side, frowning disapprovingly. "Me and the lady over there." R.J. gestured limply and took another drink of wine. He grimaced as he swallowed it down and turned to look, once again, at the headstone of Penelope Laine. "Whadda ya say?" he asked the stone seriously, eye to eye.

"You have to listen, really listen or you won't hear her," Millie warned in a small voice.

R.J. put his head down on the grave, listening intently. He held a finger in the air. "What's that, Penelope?" he listened again. "Okay, thank you and we'll be back to see you real soon." R.J. patted the grave gently, set the half-empty bottle of champagne in front of the headstone, got up and brushed the dirt and leaves off his blues. "Okay," he said to Millie confidently. "We can go now."

"Did she speak to you, R.J.?" Millie looked skeptical.

"She blessed our union," R.J. insisted. "And asked for some champagne, c'mon, let's go."

"R.J.!" She stood with her feet apart, arms crossed, a scowl on her face. R.J. was becoming familiar with that posture. "Tell me what she said to you."

"Okay." R.J. stopped and turned to face her, then took his best shot. "She said that you wanted to go to bed with me, and if it happened it would be up to me. She said she advised you to go slowly." R.J. looked into Millie's eyes and tapped his finger gently on her chin. "That right?"

"Yes," she admitted grudgingly.

R.J. silently congratulated himself. *Nailed it!*

"Not in so many words, but I knew what she meant." Millie pouted and chewed on her lip. "But get the champagne, R.J. Penelope doesn't drink."

"Then why the hell did she ask me for it?" he demanded, his eyes wide, his hands on his hips, mocking her.

"You're mocking me." She turned and started to leave.

"Okay, okay, okay." He relented, retrieved the champagne and hurried to catch up with her. "I'll bring you champagne later, Penelope-old-girl," he promised the headstone. "A full bottle, just for us to share." He sipped the champagne and belched. Then he chuckled and looked back at the grave. "See ya later, baby!"

"R.J.!"

"Coming, dear," he mumbled and caught up to her. They walked out of the cemetery and climbed into her car. R.J. was sobering up and slid behind the wheel. Like most twenty-one year old guys, R.J. believed all roads led to pussy, and he was willing to put up with a lot of grief in the pursuit of that most desirable destination. "Next stop, Howard Johnson's," he announced. Millie smiled demurely and put her head back, eyes closed. They made it to the motel in less than five minutes.

The reception had long been over, he observed, when they passed the closed up VFW, neon lights flickering off, parking lot empty, except for various paper plates, cups, napkins and various other wedding reception debris. One of the small windows on the door had been broken out. *Can't blame that one on Millie*, he thought, grinning. R.J. pulled into the motel lot and found a spot up front, directly across from the office.

"Not here, R.J.!" Millie snapped. "Not in front of the office, my God, everyone will see us going in and going out."

Going in and going out, he mused. *Oh, yeah!*

"Okay," he said. "We'll sneak in. In fact, what the hell, we'll make a military operation of it!"

He made a big production of driving to the farthest point in the parking lot. He looked around dramatically to make sure they weren't being tailed, backed the car up to the perimeter fence and turned off the engine. "Just in case we have to execute an emergency escape," he grinned conspiratorially. "Now, grab your gear, 'cause we're gonna make an assault on room...," he looked at her room key, "...three-one-niner."

"You're being silly," she scolded, but she had a sly smile on her lips.

"Go! Go! Go!" He jumped out of the car, ducked and ran an exaggerated zigzag pattern to the side of the motel where he pulled up and threw his back up against the brick wall, his head on a swivel, looking left and right. Millie followed after him clumsily. Having lost the heel to one shoe, she carried the other, along with a gathering of the front of her dress. She giggled uncontrollably as she tried to duplicate his zigzag route, but, due to the late hour or to the anticipation of the night ahead, added to the champagne she'd consumed at the reception, Millie's evening ended when she stumbled up next to R.J. and crashed, head first, into the east wall of the Longmont Howard Johnson's Motor Hotel. She slumped to the ground like the lead ballerina in Swan Lake, and landed in a lumpy pile at R.J.'s feet.

R.J. watched her wilt and slowly shook his head. "There goes my honeymoon," he muttered sadly. *And the military operation had been such a huge success...* He looked down sadly at the pile of Millie *...until now.* It occurred to him briefly that a monument of some sort should be erected on the site to commemorate the end of a long and crazy day. He shook the bottle of champagne and discovered a little bit left. He drank it down, tossed the bottle aside, and reached down, grabbing Millie by the waist and hefting up her limp body so he could lean her against the wall. Holding her up with one hand, he reached down and picked up her shoes, purse and keys. Then he leaned down, let her fall across his shoulder and lifted her, shrugging her up and down until he found a comfortable position...for him. He carried her up the outside stairs to the third floor and to room 319. He unlocked the door, carried her over to the bed and gently laid her down. She had a bump on the top of her head, but it was a small one. He covered her with a blanket and dropped her shoes and purse on the floor. He put her keys on the small table by the window. He pressed the room key into her limp hand, and she grasped it firmly, the way a sleeping baby grasps her mother's finger. He turned off all but the bathroom light and slipped out the door, pulling it shut behind him. Millie was snoring softly and R.J. listened at the door for a moment, shaking his head sadly, then chuckled and hung the 'Do Not Disturb' sign on the knob. He made his way back down the stairs and through the front doors to Main Street. *Perhaps this is a good thing,* the little voice whispered to him. *Perhaps now you can take a moment to reflect on...*

"Shut up!" R.J. barked at the little voice. "I don't wanna hear it."

He paused, smiled to himself, and took a deep breath of the thin air. He felt incredibly good. The champagne was wearing off, Millie was sleeping it off, and his mind was clear and sharp.

It was a pleasant late summer night, with just a hint of a breeze, and R.J. didn't mind walking the eight blocks to the American Legion Club. It was just before midnight. He knew the bar would be open, and there was a good chance his father would be there, perched on the usual stool, holding forth on what's wrong with the country and what's wrong with the world. R.J. smiled to himself. It would be good to hang out with his dad after eighteen months overseas, and tell him the hilarious story of Chuck and Renee's wedding. He looked forward to seeing his father at his favorite haunt, and was delighted when he spotted the old man's Chevy El Camino parked out front. He rang the buzzer and waited to be buzzed in. The answering buzz released the door and R.J. went in and closed it behind him. He looked up the steep stairs at the bright warmth of the American Legion bar on the second floor and smiled to himself. This building brought back a lot of memories for him. As he climbed the stairs, the soft sounds of muted conversations and Patsy Cline crooning from the jukebox became mixed with the familiar smell of peanuts, beer, pretzels and hamburgers. The closer he got to the bar the louder the sounds became, the smells grew stronger and he shivered in anticipation. For the first time in his life he would sit and have a beer with his father in the Longmont American Legion Club. He thought of Renee and Chuck's wedding and began chuckling. His dad was not going to believe this story!

CHAPTER TWENTY TWO

Aboard the Prairie
Pratas Reef

R.J. sat back in a corner of the bunting locker and tore open the first letter from Millie. Her letters always came in threes. She wrote every Monday, Wednesday and Friday, and always mailed them together on Saturday. He unfolded the pages of the Monday letter and concentrated on Millie's tiny, cursive penmanship. Even her handwriting seemed to whine.

Dear R.J.,
It's hot and humid today, and so I didn't get to spend a lot of time with Penelope, but we had a nice talk. I asked her if she thought I should let my hair grow out like hers, and she thought that would look lovely, so now I'm just letting it grow. My boss at the paper is giving me a hard time about being late too much, but I don't care. She's an uptight old hag who thinks she knows everything just because she has some uptight job in this rotting establishment. Her generation sure didn't help the planet much, so she takes it out on us with her pathetic little power trips. My mom is getting just as bad. I'm almost 21 and she still thinks she can boss me around all the time. I'm going to move out when I can get a place of my own. She's constantly bum-tripping me.
I can't wait for you to get out of that stupid Navy. Do you know what's going on? I mean, all this stuff with the war? A lot of us think this country should stay out of Viet Nam. What do you think? You're probably for the war, since you're in the military, like that's supposed to mean something.
I gotta go. A bunch of us are getting together at the park to sing songs and discuss the illegal war America is perpetrating on a sovereign nation of people who never did nothing to us.
Love,
Millicent

Well, that was pretty typical for a Monday letter, he thought as he folded it and put it back into its envelope. He chuckled to himself. Wednesday's letter would be different, he knew.

He opened the next envelope and took out Wednesday's letter. It was different, that was for sure. Monday's letter was a one-pager. Wednesday's letter was fifteen pages. R.J. knew what it would say before he read it, but he read it anyway. She professed undying love for him, couldn't wait for him to get home, was so confused about everything that was happening, was so sorry for taking it out on him, etc, etc, etc. He waded through all fifteen pages, mostly saying the same thing on each page, then slowly folded the letter and stuffed it back into its envelope. He also knew what Friday's letter would be about. Millie always ended her week with Penelope. Friday's letter would be all about that, and how close Millie feels to Penelope, *blah, blah, blah*. He was right about Friday's letter:

...I feel her, R.J. I feel her life inside me. It's almost as if we were merging our souls together, becoming one person. I sit and listen to her voice in my mind. She understands everything, R.J. She says her time was a much more peaceful, simple time. She wishes I could live as simply as she did. I've been thinking that maybe I could live like Penelope, simply, peacefully, without all this chaos.

My friend Alice came home from school for the summer. She goes to the university of California, in Berkeley. That's close to San Francisco. You should hear some of the things she says about the world. She's learning so much out there. I wish I could go to school there. You can't learn anything in this town. It's so far behind times. Alice says, "Welcome to Longmont, Colorado. Please turn your clocks back one hundred years." Isn't that a scream? I took Alice to meet Penelope and they got along great. We sat there in the cemetery until two in the morning, just talking. It was so cool...

The letter went on like that and R.J. rubbed his temples. The headache was trying to break through, and he closed his eyes, trying to will it away. *So, now she's got a real, live Penelope to play with,* he thought. Her letters were getting more and more curious. She was a little squirrelly before he left, but lately she had been getting downright weird. *At least she quit telling me how much I owe her for taking her virginity.*

He saved Chuck's letter for last, because he knew it would be short and full of funny comments about Longmont and everyone in it. He opened Renee's letter and read it slowly. Then he read it again.

Dear R.J.,

I hope you're doing well. We keep hearing all this stuff about war in Viet Nam.

You aren't close to all that, are you?

I don't know if you've heard from Millie, but we haven't seen her in weeks. She doesn't hang out with us anymore. She has a new set of friends, and I don't think they are very good for her. They all hang out in the park and smoke pot and sing stupid protest songs. We can't

even go up there anymore. They lay all over the place and throw trash everywhere. Chuck thinks some of them are living in the park. Millie quit shaving her legs or underarms, let her hair grow out long, goes around barefoot everywhere, and I don't think she bathes much.
She got fired at the newspaper for fighting with her boss. She's still living at home, but all she does is hang around the park or the cemetery with her weird friends and smoke pot. If you write to her, let her know I'm worried about her. She won't talk to me when I call. She told her mom she was just dropping out. Whatever that means!
Take care of yourself,
Love,
Renee

R.J. put the letter back into the envelope and gathered up his mail. He was very glad he wasn't back in Longmont. Millie had been the worst mistake of his life, and he'd made some big ones. He had remained noncommittal when she had babbled on about getting married after he got out of the Navy, but he knew he wouldn't go through with that. He wasn't planning on going back to Longmont. His plan was to settle in California. Sooner or later Millie was going to have to be made to understand that. *But not today*, he thought, making his way up to the signal bridge.

Day 6

Linc sat relaxing in the bow of the motor whaleboat and grinned as Pea piloted the boat toward the Prairie. Linc was finally going to meet R.J. Davis for the first time, having hitched a ride with Pea on his regular run to the tender for supplies and tools.

He chuckled, remembering the exchange of flashing light messages with R.J. earlier that morning. Linc had flashed the Prairie signal bridge and asked for a favor. "We been flying Bravo so long, we are out of red bunting. Can you spare some?" Linc included the question mark.

R.J. read the message and chuckled. The guy even sends punctuation. He receipted for Linc's message and sent only two characters in reply: The letter 'C' which means correct, and an exclamation point, just for drill. He actually thought he could hear Linc laughing appreciatively over on the signal bridge of the Knox.

Pea piloted the motor whaleboat into position next to the side of the Prairie and Linc tossed the bow line toward the boat deck sailors. They quickly tied up the boat and Linc and Pea climbed up the ladder.

"Knox on the rocks, arriving!" some wise ass called out.

Pea ignored him but lifted his middle finger into the air. The Prairie deck crew laughed.

"It's a little game we play," Pea explained to Linc while leading him forward toward the signal bridge. "They yell out 'Knox on the rocks" and I flip 'em off."

"Sounds like fun," Linc said absently, but he really didn't think it sounded much like fun. He stopped on the 03 level and stared out at the Frank Knox, tossing restlessly on Pratas Reef, like an insomniac who can't get to sleep. "She looks worse from here," he said quietly.

Pea stood next to Linc and leaned forward on the railing. "She looks so sad."

"Yes, sad and old," Linc agreed, watching his ship being pummeled by white-capped waves at high tide. She looked beaten up and deflated, as if she had given up and was just waiting to die. He nodded slowly. "Sad and old."

They climbed the ladder to the signal bridge and spotted R.J. across the deck on his rolling signal light. He and the Iwo Jima were exchanging daily reports. Ricky Buford stood next to him, a clipboard in hand, writing down the message as R.J. read the light.

Linc stood next to the signal shack, unseen, and watched R.J. manipulate the handle on the light. Linc read the light from the Iwo Jima easily, although the sending signalman was very fast. R.J. held the light open and read the message aloud as if he were reading from a novel. Linc grinned broadly. When the Iwo explained the cannibalization of one helicopter for parts for the others, R.J. read it without missing a beat, light held open, adding inflection and drama to his voice, so that the saga of the helicopter parts became a dramatic and engaging story. Linc, and the other signalmen admiring R.J.'s expertise, found themselves eager to learn the story's outcome.

R.J. signed off and took the clipboard from Ricky, examining it for errors. There were none.

"Ricky, you are one hell of a message writer," R.J. exclaimed.

"Bet yer ass, Yankee," Ricky replied, pleased at the compliment.

R.J. started toward the signal shack and spotted Pea. "Hey, little buddy," he called. "How long you gonna stay this time?"

"Till you throw me out," Pea replied, smiled broadly and hugged his friend.

R.J. returned Pea's hug and noticed a tall, black sailor standing off to one side, a sardonic smile on his face. He leaned against the signal shack, his arms crossed, and studied R.J. carefully. R.J. knew immediately who he was. The SM-2 crow on his left arm gave away his identity.

"This must be Lincoln Jones," R.J. said, walking up and offering his hand.

"Guilty as charged, your honor," Linc replied with big, toothy grin, taking R.J.'s hand. "And that's the last time you ever gonna hear that from a black man. At least a black man from Detroit."

R.J. liked him immediately. "I been looking forward to meeting you," he said. "Where'd you learn to send code like that?"

Linc grinned his big, toothy grin. "I instructed at the SM school in Pensacola for two years. Got a whole hell of a lot of practice, trying to teach them young'uns how it's done. So how'd you learn to send that pretty code you send?"

"It's a long story," R.J. replied automatically. "But I went through radio school."

"You was an RM before you became a SM?"

R.J. nodded, and then grinned. "I don't wish to appear less than humble, but the code comes easy to me."

"Me, too," Linc agreed, grinning back. *This white boy and me gonna get along jus' fine.*

Pea stood off to the side, a big smile on his face, watching two of his best buddies becoming friends.

R.J. snapped his fingers, as if he had just remembered something, and pointed at Linc. "Let's head to the bunting locker and I'll help you sew up those Bravo flags." He glanced over at Pea. "You comin' buddy?"

"Naw, I think I'm gonna go get me some of that good chow." He headed down the ladder. "I'll catch up with you guys later!" he called as he hurried toward the mess decks.

Inside the bunting locker, Linc let out a low whistle. "Man, look at this joint." He let his eyes wander over the treasure trove in the bunting locker. It was a large compartment, about fifteen feet by twenty feet, and it had a lot of counter and shelf space. There were two heavy-duty sewing machines, bolts of bunting in all colors, too many spools of thread to count, and a long, wide counter in the middle of the compartment for cutting and sizing the signal flags. Linc ran his hand over the table. "Man I wish we had room for this."

R.J. nodded and selected a bolt of red bunting from the shelves. "That table is perfect for pinochle."

Linc laughed. "Mind if I explore a little?"

"Make yourself at home," R.J. replied. He was already cutting the measured bunting in the dimensions of the Bravo flag. It was one of the two flags which weren't in a perfect square. The Bravo and Alpha flags had narrow triangles of cloth cut out of the front of the flags, indenting inward, leaving twin points to the front. Still, they were easy to make...if you were good on a sewing machine, and R.J.

was very good on a sewing machine. In fact, he was the second best seamstress in the signal gang.

Linc walked around the roomy locker, admiring the vast space. Space was at a premium on a destroyer. It just didn't exist. *This place is as big as the Knox's pilot house*, he thought. Linc spotted a stack of several books in a corner of the counter. He glanced through the titles and recognized several he had read himself. They were all older novels. No current, popular fiction was represented, with the glaring exception of a tattered, dog-eared paperback edition of Ian Fleming's "Dr. No." Linc picked up a large, worn, well-read volume and a small smile crossed his lips. "THE COMPLETE WORKS OF EDGAR ALLAN POE." He turned when he sensed R.J. come up beside him.

"You like Poe?" R.J. asked.

"I read a lot of his stories," Linc nodded. "But he always spooked me with all that weird death shit." He looked at the book in his hand. "This yours?"

R.J. nodded. "I've never read any of his stories," he explained. "But I consider myself a student of his poetry."

"So you studyin' his stuff?"

"Yeah."

"What's your favorite Poe poem?"

"I like 'em all, but right now, the one I'm studying is 'The Raven'."

"You understand that poem?" Linc asked skeptically.

"Understand?" R.J. replied. "Let's say I'm trying to get a handle on it."

Linc handed back the book and re-appraised R.J. He wasn't just a very fast signalman; he was a student of poetry. *This R.J. Davis got some soul*, Linc thought, and decided he liked him. An object in the far corner caught his eye. "Damn!" he swore, staring incredulously. "You dudes got a RECORD PLAYER up in here?"

"Yeah, it belongs to Charlie Mayweather, but he never plays anything but Hank Williams on it." R.J. looked at the small record player. It held only one record at a time, the records had to be replaced by hand, but it was set up for 45, 78 and 33 rpm.

"I got some albums on the Knox," Linc said, turning the turntable with his finger and inspecting the needle. It would do. "Good music. Jazz, you know? Good ol' southern jazz."

Ricky had just come into the compartment, Peggy Sue under his arm, and heard the last comment.

"Looseyanna jazz?" he exclaimed. "Now, that's music." He offered Linc his hand. "Ricky Buford," he introduced himself. "From Nawrlans."

"Lincoln Jones," Linc replied, shaking Ricky's hand. "From Deetroit, Michigan."

"We been dyin' to get some good music around here," Ricky explained. "Not that I got anythin' agin Hank, but enough is e-fuckin'-nough."

"I got Oscar Peterson," Linc said, ticking off names on his fingers. "I got the great Jimmy Smith on organ, I got some Brubeck, some Dizzy Gillespie, some Charlie Parker, and I even got some old King Pleasure stuff that I bet none of you boys ever heard."

R.J. began snapping his fingers and singing:

"There I go, there I go, there I go...there I go,
Pretty baby, you are the soul who snaps my control..."

Linc stared at R.J., surprised, and then joined in, snapping his fingers:

"Funny thing but every time you're near me,
I never can explain, you give me a smile
And then I'm wrapped up in your magic..."

"Man that sounds good!" Ricky exclaimed.

R.J. and Linc grinned. Linc took another, more appraising look at R.J. Davis. The fleet's fastest signalman was full of surprises. "Where'd a white boy like you pick up on King Pleasure?"

"North Denver," R.J. replied with a grin. "All the potheads I knew loved King Pleasure."

"All the potheads I knew in Detroit did, too." Linc winked conspiratorially at R.J.

Ricky stopped strumming Peggy Sue and looked up, feigning shock and disapproval. "You mean to tell me I'm consortin' with a couple o' coon-ass DOPERS?"

R.J. and Linc had a good laugh over that one.

"You gotta bring over your records, Linc," R.J. said.

"Yeah, man," Ricky readily agreed. "Get permission to stay over here to get all your flags done, we'll have a jam session." Ricky held up Peggy Sue enthusiastically.

"You play?" Linc asked.

R.J. and Ricky grinned at each other. Ricky sat on a stool and balanced Peggy Sue on his knee. He strummed her strings a little, then launched into the guitar riff from Chuck Berry's "Roll Over Beethoven."

Linc watched admiringly as Ricky's left-hand fingers danced along the neck of the guitar, as his right hand picked the melody. "Damn, you are good!" Linc began tapping a beat on the table with his hands, and he and Ricky rocked through "Roll Over Beethoven."

"I think we got the beginnings of a real cool combo here," R.J.

said appreciatively. "You think you can get an okay to stay here for a few days? It's not like we're doing much, just waiting for the frogmen."

"Depends on who I ask," Linc replied. "If I ask Mr. Holliday, he probably say okay...ain't had any signal traffic all day. Everybody's just taken a break for a few days."

"Yeah, the boys on the Knox probably need the time off," R.J. said.

Linc looked at his watch. "I wonder where Pea ran off to."

R.J. smiled warmly. "Any time now my little bud is gonna come crashing through that hatch there, bragging about the chow."

"He do like the Prairie mess decks," Linc agreed.

Pea came bounding noisily into the bunting locker, a toothpick hanging from his teeth. "Man, that be some damn good chow!" he declared. He looked at the three signalmen who were laughing at him. "Wha?" he asked.

"We're starting a band," R.J. said kiddingly. Linc and Ricky started laughing again.

Pea looked around at them, frowned and picked at his teeth. "You flag-fags are all nuts, you realize that?"

Aboard the Frank Knox
Day 7

Frank Knox Departing

"You asked to see me, sir?" Roger Lamb stuck his head in the door of the captain's quarters and was directed to take a seat. Bill Holliday was seated on the captain's bunk, and the captain was sitting at his desk, in his robe, holding a message slip in his hand. Roger took one look at Bill Holliday and knew this wasn't going to be a pleasant meeting, whatever its purpose.

Captain Pizzonovich handed the message slip to the exec. "I'm relieved of command," he said before Roger could read the message. "And you are to assume command of the ship." He said it matter-of-factly, as though the decision didn't surprise him at all.

"Sir?" Lieutenant Lamb asked. He read the message quickly and looked up at the captain. "I don't understand."

"It's simple, Roger," the captain replied wearily. "I'm on my way to Pearl to face a board of inquiry and you are the interim captain of the Frank Knox."

Roger Lamb looked stunned. He looked over at Lieutenant Holliday, who avoided his eyes. "When..." he began, but the captain interrupted him.

"Right now, Roger," he said softly. "Right now. I'm going to pack up and leave. After I'm gone, you can inform the crew. I don't want to be aboard when you do that." He got up, pulled open his valise and began filling it with his personal items. He looked up again, surprised to find the two officers still there. "See to your ship, Captain!" he ordered, and went back to his packing.

Lieutenants Lamb and Holliday stepped into the passageway and pulled the hatch shut on the captain's cabin. They looked at each other for a few moments, and Bill Holliday said, "A man like that, career deep sixed by an act not of his doing."

"It certainly isn't right," new Captain Lamb agreed. "But he's the CO, he's responsible and that's the way the Navy sees it."

"Well," Lieutenant Holliday said, "It may be the Navy way, but it stinks, if you ask me."

Roger Lamb nodded and looked around dejectedly. "My first command is a mortally wounded ship that is probably beyond salvaging."

"Cheer up, Captain," Mr. Holliday said cheerfully, slapping his friend on the back. "Things could always be worse."

"Oh, really, Bill?" Lieutenant Lamb replied irritably. "Just how do you think it could be worse?"

"Well," Lieutenant Holliday said, smiling, "Medford Prentiss could still be aboard."

Roger Lamb stared at his friend, and a slow grin crept onto his face. "Well, when you put it that way," he said, grinning widely, "I guess things could be worse." He looked seriously at his friend. "You're my exec," he said flatly.

"Aye, sir," Holliday nodded. "Any orders, Captain?"

"What?"

"Do you have any orders, sir?"

"Yes." The new captain turned to Mr. Holliday with a grave look on his face. It was as though he had suddenly accepted the burden of command and found its weight to be a lot heavier than he had imagined. "With the exception of the two gunners mates, I want all firearms collected and stored, and Bill," Roger Lamb put a hand on his friend's shoulder, "when Captain Pizzonovich leaves the ship I want him to be announced. Understand?"

"Aye, sir." Lieutenant Holliday saluted his new C.O. and headed aft to find Chief Billings. After a few words with the chief boatswain's mate, Mr. Holliday returned to the bridge.

A Marine helicopter hovered over the Knox as Gerald Pizzonovich, leather valise in hand, made his way to the small flight deck. The copter landed and cut down the engines, allowing the former captain to climb aboard. The 1-MC crackled and Chief Billings' voice boomed out, "FRANK KNOX, DEPARTING!"

All the sailors on the fantail stood at attention and saluted the Marine helicopter as it pulled up and away from the ship. Gerald Pizzonovich looked down and smiled wanly at the showing of respect. It was a reminder of the caliber of men he had commanded. As he settled into his seat, he looked around and realized he was on the same helicopter which had taken Medford Prentiss away. As the helicopter lifted off and pointed its nose toward the Iwo Jima, he sighed, sat back, closed his eyes, and pondered his uncertain future.

PART THREE:

THE INVESTIGATION

CHAPTER TWENTY THREE

Aboard the USS Iwo Jima
July 26, 1965

Day 9

Lieutenant Commander David Van Ryn, M.D., pulled the gloves off his hands and threw them into the trash bin. "Can't be any more specific under these circumstances," he said wearily.

"That's a pretty large window, Doc," Deavers observed quietly.

"In this climate, considering how long he lay there until we got him, I can't be more accurate." The doctor slumped down wearily in the chair behind his desk. They sat cramped in his small office adjacent to the sick bay. "I'm going by the condition of the body when you found it. He died between midnight and zero-four-hundred. A full autopsy might pin it down, but we aren't equipped for that."

Deavers nodded his understanding, busy studying the results of Dr. Van Ryn's report. "It had to happen during or just before the grounding. Otherwise, I have to believe he would have had time to dispose of the body."

"How do you figure?" Dr. Van Ryn was becoming intrigued with the case, and especially with the theories of Lieutenant (jg) Deavers.

"Because he planned it for late at night, thinking perhaps that Green would get up to go to the head, and he waited. Maybe he waited on previous nights, I don't know. He obviously had a plan, and I think it was interrupted when the ship hit the reef."

"Then what about the watch cap and the manner in which the corpse was staged?"

Deavers rubbed his face. He needed a shave. "Staging the body was improvised," Deavers mused, leafing through the report. "It was for whoever found him."

"And the watch cap?"

"The watch cap was for Green. It was part of the reason for killing him; I just can't put it together yet." Deavers tossed the report on Dr. Van Ryn's desk and stood, stretching his arms out. "It'll come to me, though," he said with more confidence than he felt. "It's rattling 'round up here." He pointed to his temple. "I'm gonna have dinner and get some sleep. 'Night, Doc."

"'Night." Dr. Van Ryn picked up the report and put his feet up on the desk. He read through the report again, trying to find something that would narrow down the approximate time of death. There was nothing there.

Deavers was assigned a billet on the Prairie, but most nights he spent aboard the Knox. That evening he remained on the destroyer tender, showered, spent a long time shaving, dressed in fresh khakis, and prepared to join the other officers for dinner. He was running a comb through his hair when someone knocked on his door.

"Enter!" He looked up, slightly irritated by the interruption.

The door opened and a messenger from the radio shack handed him a clipboard with a message slip clipped to it. Deavers smiled, took the message, signed the log and handed the clipboard back to the messenger, who nodded and left the compartment. Not one word had been spoken.

Deavers looked at the message:

CONFIDENTIAL!

DATE:26 JULY 1965

TO:LT. (jg) W.C. DEAVERS
c/o USS PRAIRIE AD-15

FROM:CAPT. D. PETERSON
SUBJ:GREEN, C.C. vis a vis CAMP NIMITZ

1.RECORD INDICATES SUBJECT GREEN, C.C. SUSPECTED OF BEING RESPONSIBLE FOR DEATH OF RECRUIT ON OR ABOUT 12 FEB 1965. NO CHARGES HAVE BEEN FILED.

2.DUE TO SENSITIVE NATURE OF MATERIALS, COPY OF COMPLETE FILE BEING FORWARDED TO YOU via PRAIRIE THIS DATE.

CONFIDENTIAL!

Deavers studied the message closely. It didn't say much, but what it did say certainly piqued his interest. This was the first hint of a motive, a small piece of the puzzle falling into place, like the tumblers of a combination lock on a secret safe. He was no longer tired, thanks to the shot of adrenaline provided by Captain Peterson's message, and the prospect of pinning down a motive. *I'll find out the name of the recruit Green was suspected of getting killed in Camp Nimitz,* he figured, *and match the name with the crew roster of the Knox. Match the name and we probably have the killer.* Can it really be that simple? He shook his head angrily. *Of course it can't! Just because someone might have the same last name didn't mean he was a killer. Besides, C.C. Green could have been killed for another reason, another motive entirely. Maybe someone aboard served under C.C. Green in boot camp and carried a grudge. Wait for the file, and we'll go from there.* Deavers knew if he couldn't find a link in the files, he would have to interview each member of the Knox crew, and he did not look forward to that. But at least none of them was going anywhere. The crew members who were not on the Knox were tucked away safely on the Prairie and Iwo Jima where he could find them easily.

Deavers couldn't have been more disappointed when he received the file the next day. A quick scan of the Knox personnel list revealed no match to the name of the dead recruit, Andrew Tompkins. The file seemed incomplete, almost as if someone had sanitized it by removing pages. It did not indicate how the recruit died, other than as a result of a training accident. Maybe Captain Peterson didn't think the cause of death was important, but Deavers doubted that. His boss would have sent him everything he had, so that particular fact must have been deleted from the official file. *Why?* Another thing not explained in the file was the fact that the investigation was never officially closed, meaning the file represented an open case, but the last entry in the file noted the transfer of C.C. Green, BM-1 to the Frank Knox on 15 March, 1965. After that, nothing.

Deavers tossed the much anticipated file on his bunk. It had presented more questions than answers. This was going to take some thought. *If the investigation is still open, then someone must have been watching Green. Hmmm.* He wrote a confidential note to Captain Peterson asking why the cause of death wasn't identified. He would hear back soon. In the meantime, he would pursue the one thin lead he had: Andrew Tompkins. He decided to go through the personnel file of everyone aboard, looking for a reference to a relative named Tompkins, or for any sailors who were in boot camp under C.C. Green. He also realized he would need some help, a few people he could trust to keep all information confidential. He wanted Chief Billings to help because he liked the boatswain's professional work ethic, and he wanted R.J. Davis to help because he liked and trusted the young man. He was loyal and honest, traits Deavers had discovered in the young signalman during his last mysterious investigation. Deavers felt energized. He was organizing things, setting things in motion, and something was going to break. He just knew it. He made his way to the officers mess happily humming "Anchors Aweigh."

CHAPTER TWENTY FOUR

"Sure, I'll help any way I can, sir," R.J. nodded eagerly. He eyed the box of files Deavers had sitting on his desk. The investigator had asked R.J. to join him in his cabin for some volunteer work, after getting permission to use him. As an officer, Deavers might have gone to the operations officer with the request, but the investigator had come up through the ranks, and he knew who actually ran the departments aboard a Navy vessel. So, he went to Chief Benson, who, recognizing and appreciating Deavers' wisdom, readily approved R.J.'s part time job.

"These files are confidential, R.J.," Deavers explained. "We are looking for any connection to a man named Tompkins, Andrew Tompkins."

"Who's he, sir?"

"Again, this is confidential. Andrew Tompkins died in a boot camp accident and C.C. Green was suspected of negligence in that death. He has not been charged with anything, but I think Tompkins' death may present a motive."

"Some friend or family of Tompkins killed Green for revenge?"

"As I said, it's a possibility." He studied the young signalman for a moment, and decided to confide in him a little more. He pulled out a picture of C.C. Green's body, as it was discovered in the head, and gave it to R.J. "Does that picture tell you anything, R.J.?"

R.J.'s eyes grew large when he looked at the picture. Jeff Samuels hadn't shown him the prints. "You mean the way he was posed, sir?" He had heard rumors about the killing and the body, but this picture...

"Yes. There is something about that watch cap..." A small piece of a memory wafted through Deavers' mind, then evaporated again before he could grasp it.

"It seems familiar to me, Mr. Deavers," R.J. agreed, studying the photo and searching his memory. "I don't know what it means, but every sailor has at least one of those watch caps." He looked up from the picture. "Maybe whoever killed him used it as a blindfold."

Deavers nodded thoughtfully. "Take those files with you and see what you can find. I'm going to ask Chief Billings on the Knox to help me with this, too."

R.J. gathered up the box. "Thanks for trusting me, sir."

"No problem, just let me know if you find a connection."

"Aye, sir." R.J. left the cabin with a smile on his face. This was going to be fun. At least it would break up the monotony.

He carried the box of files into the bunting locker and plopped it down on the counter. Ricky was on the sewing machine, creating a blue and white checkered November flag. Ricky was as adroit a seamstress as he was a guitar player. "Whatcha got there?" he asked, skillfully moving the flag around the bobbing needle.

"Nunya," R.J. replied over his shoulder.

Ricky grinned. He knew what 'nunya' meant: *Nunya fuckin' bidness!* He returned to his flag sewing.

R.J. looked into the box, and carefully counted the personnel files. There were about seventy five of them. Most of them were pretty thin, only a few bulged with paperwork. R.J. ignored Ricky and began going through the files. Ricky politely minded his own business. R.J. found the longer a man had been in the Navy, and the more trouble he had gotten into, the fatter the file. Some of the entries for Captain's masts and other disciplinary measures were hilarious. R.J. shook his head in wonder at some of the hijinks sailors would pull, especially overseas, where most of the infractions occurred. Hijacked taxi cabs, fighting in public, drunk and disorderly, inciting a riot in a whorehouse. The list went on. One sailor had insisted he could milk a goat and climbed into the admiral's compound to demonstrate on his goat, which turned out, unfortunately for the sailor, to be a ram. Another sailor, obviously in love, didn't want to leave his honey behind in Hong Kong, so he tried to smuggle her aboard in his sea bag. Unfortunately, he had not provided for a breathing hole, and was busted by the officer of the deck when the girl started squirming and yelling inside the bag just as the sailor arrived on the ship's quarterdeck. But R.J. was not finding any reference to anyone named Tompkins, and as he struck out on each file, he became less and less optimistic about finding one. He was more than half-way through the box when the participants for the evening pinochle game began arriving. He put the files in an overhead cabinet and secured it with a padlock.

Chief Billings

Deavers didn't think he needed permission to use Chief Billings in the investigation. He went directly to the source.

Chief Billings was taken aback for a moment. The death of C.C. Green was of particular interest to the 'Chief of the Boat,' and he had intended to keep a close eye on the investigation as was expected of him. Being the ship's bosun, he was responsible for everything that happened on board, especially when it concerned his deck force. The chief sat staring at the files, lost in thought.

"Chief?"

"Oh, sorry, sir," the chief snapped out of his reverie. "Yes, sir. It would be my pleasure, Mr. Deavers." Chief Billings began sorting through the files. "What are we looking for?"

"We are looking for anyone related to Andrew Tompkins or anyone who has a family member named Tompkins, maybe next of kin."

"Who's Andrew Tompkins, sir?"

"This is just between us, chief. I want to be able to trust you to keep quiet about all this." Deavers stared at the chief intently.

"Yes, sir," the chief said firmly.

Deavers handed the chief the incomplete file from Captain Peterson. Chief Billings looked through the file, then up at Deavers. "This boy is dead?" He sounded very sad, his expression strained.

"That's right, Chief," Deavers replied. "C.C. Green was suspected of being responsible for the death of Andrew Tompkins. Nothing has been proven yet, but the case is still open, and I believe Green was transferred to this ship to get him away from the investigation, and so someone would know where to find him."

Chief Billings stared blankly at Deavers, but his mind was racing. *Deavers thinks Green was sent to the Knox in order to leave him in cold storage?* Aloud he asked, "And that someone killed him?"

"I don't know for sure," Deavers replied, rubbing his temples. "Maybe it was someone else. All I know is, we have a lead, so let's look for a connection."

"Aye, sir. I'll look through all these files and I'll keep it quiet."

Deavers nodded, still looking at the chief. "I hear Captain Lamb asked you take over as First Division department head until after this is all over."

The chief smiled proudly. "Yes, sir. I'm only going to supervise a handful of men, but these men, you know, can be a handful."

Deavers chuckled. "Yes, I'm sure they can. Well, congratulations, Chief, let me know what you find, and I do hope you find something."

Deavers carried the remaining files back to his cabin and began combing through them. He was relieved to have someone as professional as Chief Billings on his team. The chief had displayed his competence over a long period of time. Roger Lamb had recognized that and put him in a position of authority. *The cream always rises*, he thought. *Same with R.J. Davis. He is a leader, no doubt*. Davis might be young, Deavers realized, but he knew Davis possessed a maturity beyond his years. Deavers silently wished all U.S. Navy sailors could be as dependable as Fred Billings and R.J. Davis.

Chief Billings set the files aside as soon as Deavers left. He pulled out the file on Parker, J.I., and opened it. He had been through it many times, but he wanted to go through it again. He wanted more than anything to find a connection to Andrew Tompkins in Parker's file, expose him and put an end to the entire mess. The chief thought he had the whole thing figured out, and for the first time in a long time, he felt a brief moment of peace. Circumstance and his sharp eyesight provided the perfect solution: Jude Parker had reported aboard only days after C.C. Green, which was a fact. Green was under suspicion for killing a boot camp recruit, which was a fact. These facts had to be related, it couldn't be a coincidence. It was too perfect. The chief let out a sigh. *A dental tech on a destroyer? I don't think so.* Then he thought about the reef and about his wife, and a heavy feeling of melancholy engulfed him.

Being aground on the reef was particularly painful and humiliating for a fleet sailor like Chief Billings. He was Chief of the Boat. It was his responsibility to see that the ship and the deck crew operated smoothly with a minimum of fuss and bother. The Ship of the Year award bestowed upon the Frank Knox was a source of personal pride and pleasure for Chief Billings. He and his deck force had worked hard to win that award, and boasted of it proudly wherever they went on liberty. Now his proud ship was impaled mercilessly on this reef. Fred Billings considered it the most painful event in his life...then he thought of his wife. *Poor Janice, she's so lost and there is absolutely nothing I can do from here,* he thought, frowning sadly. *Maybe I can wrangle another short leave when we get off this damn piece of coral rock...*He shook his head bitterly, thinking of his crumbling marriage, of Janice and what she was going through. *I've done everything I know how to do,* he told himself, but he didn't really believe it.

Working through the files when he wasn't on watch, it took R.J. only one day to get through them. He had come up with nothing, except the funny stories he would be telling and re-telling, without mentioning names of course. He was disappointed he didn't find any connection to Tompkins; he felt he was letting Mr. Deavers down. He stood and stretched. The bunting locker was deserted, and R.J. put the box of files in his cabinet and locked it up. He decided to get a good night's sleep, and in the morning he would go through the files again, with fresh eyes. Perhaps he would find a link tomorrow.

After a hot shower, albeit a short one, R.J. lay back on his bunk and pulled Chuck's letter out of his pocket. He had almost forgotten Chuck's letter when Deavers showed up with the files. He lay back on his pillow, turned on his reading light and opened the letter.

When R.J. finished Chuck's letter he was sitting up in his bunk, laughing and wiping tears from his eyes. He had saved Chuck's letter for later, and he was happy he had. His friend had referred to last year's almost-disastrous wedding, and revealed some previously-unknown details about the ensuing honeymoon that had R.J. in stitches. Chuck swore him to secrecy, and R.J. vowed never to repeat anything. However, he was a little disturbed by Chuck's last lines:

> *I hate to tell you this, buddy, but Millie is not sitting around waiting for you. She hangs out in Sunset Park with some strange people, who seem to believe in only two things: "America sucks, and all sex and love ought to be free."(I'm reading this off one of their mimeographed hand-bills.)*
> *Remember what my Mom used to tell us when we were kids?*
> *Fore-warned is fore-armed!*
> *Don't take any of her crap, R.J. She's a nut case.*
>
> *Chuck*
>
> *P.S. Remember: don't ever let Renee know*
> *I told you about 'Mr. Buzzy.'*

R.J. chuckled a little more, folded up the letter and stuffed it back into its envelope. He would save it and re-read it later, when he needed a good laugh. He lay back on his bunk and closed his eyes. The wedding and the following few hectic days, his last in Longmont prior to reporting to the Prairie, were vivid in his memory, despite the full year that had elapsed since then. He thought of Chuck's letter and grinned to himself. *That sure was one crazy wedding.* He dozed off thinking about it.

CHAPTER TWENTY FIVE

Longmont, Colorado
August, 1964

Something awakened Millie just after midnight. It was a low, droning sound, and as Millie emerged from her near-coma, she imagined she was in the dentist's chair. Her eyes popped open and she stared blankly at the ceiling. *What is that sound? Where am I?*

Slowly, the evening's events came back into focus and she groaned, tried to lift her head, groaned again and let it fall back on the pillow. The droning sound was beginning to get on her nerves and she forced herself into a sitting position, peering around the dark room through squinted eyes. The top of her head hurt, and when she touched it gingerly, she winced and groaned again. *This is all R.J.'s fault,* she thought testily.

The droning sound seemed to be coming from behind the headboard. Millie got up on her hands and knees, crawled up to the headboard and put her ear against it. All that did was muffle the droning sound. Then she realized it was coming from the room next door, so she stood and put her ear to the wall. The droning sound was louder, more distinct, and it was accompanied by giggling sounds.

"Hey!" Millie yelled and pounded on the wall. "Run that friggin' vacuum cleaner some other time!" *Dumb ass maids,* she thought, standing and gingerly touching the bump on her head. *Vacuuming at this time of night? Dumb ass maids!*

The droning stopped but the giggling didn't. Millie decided to go into the bathroom and survey the damage the evening had done to her face. She examined her image in the mirror, and a look of despair stared back at her. Mascara had run down both cheeks and caked on her eyelashes. Her cheeks were bright red, her lipstick was smudged across her face, and her hair poked out at all angles from her head like the quills of an angry porcupine. "Great," she said disgustedly, picking pieces of frosting from her hair, "I look like Raggedy Ann."

She quickly brushed her hair, pulling out pieces of wedding cake, and worked frantically to repair her face. Squinting into the mirror at the results she figured she had done all that could be done, so she set out determinedly to have it out with R.J. She had a pretty good idea where he could be found. *Dump me on the bed and walk away?* She found only one shoe and decided it had to do. *I don't think so, mister!*

The Legionnaires

R.J. had just finished telling the story. His father and fellow Legionnaires were laughing uproariously, tears streaming down their cheeks, when the outside buzzer began buzzing and didn't stop. The bar patrons quit laughing and looked around at each other, eyebrows raised questioningly. Normally, people ring the buzzer once and wait to get buzzed in. Maybe it got stuck?

The bartender, Truley Johansen, a big, gregarious Swede, reached under the bar and hit the release buzzer. The outside buzzing stopped and the bar patrons grew quiet. They turned toward the stairs in anticipation, watching the door and listening to the footsteps ascending the stairs hesitantly, unevenly.

Reaching the top, Millie thought she had one more step to go. She stepped up to it, came down on nothing but air, and suddenly, surprising everyone, especially herself, she came bursting into the bar, her nylon-stockinged feet slipping and sliding on the polished wooden floor, her arms flailing around in a pitiful attempt at gaining her balance. She held her single surviving shoe in one hand and a handful of her bridesmaid's dress in the other. Her dress was soiled and torn in a few places, but she didn't seem to notice or care. She glared around the room, trying to locate the cause of her misery.

The bar patrons stared silently, wide-eyed at the frightening apparition that had materialized so dramatically in their midst. Despite her best efforts at repairs, Millie was a mess. Her hair stuck straight out in the back, and in the front, fell undisciplined down the front of her face. She tried to blow up at it, but it just shot up into the air and fell back down on her face. She tried it three times in quick succession, the result of which was quite comical, and the bar erupted into laughter again. R.J. ducked down and hid behind his father.

"Chicken shit!" his father whispered. R.J. giggled and hunched down farther.

Millie swayed uncertainly and squinted at the room. "R.J.!" she yelled at the group of startled onlookers. "YOU LEFT ME ALONE ON THAT BED, YOU SON OF A BITCH!"

Once again, the laughter roared, which seemed to confuse Millie or at the very least give her pause. "R.J.!" she whined again.

R.J.'s father shielded his eyes with his hand and slowly shook his head. He whispered to his son, cowering behind him, "Go take her home, R.J."

Millie looked around angrily and started to say something, then shook her head and turned, retreating clumsily down the stairs.

When she got outside and slammed the door, the bar erupted in laughter again, and everyone started chanting, "R.J.! R.J.! R.J.!"

Crawling out of his cowardly hole, R.J. looked around sheepishly as the American Legionnaires chanted his name. His father was frowning and shaking his head, as if he were ashamed, but he had that twinkle in his eye, and R.J. knew he would be telling this story for a long time to come.

"I guess I better take her home," R.J. said.

"Yep, that'll do," his dad agreed. "Take the El Camino, I'll catch a ride with Truley." He tossed his keys to R.J. "Be a gentleman," he said quietly.

"Yes, sir." R.J. took the keys and slinked down the stairs, serenaded loudly by the Legionnaires.

"R.J.! R.J.! R.J.!"

The Brewsters

The next evening R.J. sat impatiently in the Brewster living room, waiting for Millie to get ready for their big night. Millie had the key to the newlyweds' apartment, and she and R.J. were going there to be alone. Mr. and Mrs. Brewster were in their sixties. They'd had Millie when they were in their forties; she was their only child, and a surprise one at that. R.J. sat on the flowered couch, sipping a cup of coffee provided reluctantly by Mrs. Brewster. Mr. Brewster, almost completely deaf, sat quietly in his easy chair, reading the Sunday paper and ignoring the rest of the world, as if he were unaware of it.

Millie's mother did not like R.J., but he didn't take it personally, because Mrs. Brewster disliked and distrusted all males, including Mr. Brewster. She sat stiffly, perched on a high-back chair, sipping her tea and watching R.J. suspiciously over the rim of her cup. Her rag mop of a dog, Winky, sat at her feet staring dewy-eyed at R.J. and passing gas. Mr. Brewster occasionally sat forward, mumbled some expletive, and waved his paper at the dog, trying to dispel some of the odor.

"Oh, George, Winky can't help it, she's old."

"Then maybe we ought to put her out of her G.D. misery," George mumbled behind his paper.

"Don't swear, George," Mrs. Brewster scolded. "It's the Sabbath."

R.J. was becoming bored, and decided to entertain himself. "You know, Mrs. Brewster." He leaned forward conspiratorially, glancing at Mr. Brewster, who seemed not to hear him. "The ancient Egyptians used to have their dogs buried with them when they passed on." He motioned toward Winky. "If you like, I'll be happy to toss Winky into your grave when you go." R.J. sat back and smiled his most supercilious smile. "That way you and she can be together through eternity."

Mrs. Brewster did not seem to be amused. Winky looked alarmed and passed more gas. Mr. Brewster rattled his newspaper and grunted.

"Millie!" Mrs. Brewster yelled at the hall.

"Coming!" Millie yelled back.

"Also," R.J. continued, "if that dog keeps farting up this house, you may wish her to precede you in death." He grinned evilly. "I can arrange that, too."

"Millie!"

"I'm coming, mother!"

R.J. stood as he heard Millie coming down the hall. "Hey, Mrs. Brewster." He winked at Millie's mother and again showed her his evil grin. "You ever been French-kissed?" He wriggled his eyebrows up and down ala Groucho Marx.

"MILLICENT!"

"For God's sake, mother, I'm here!" Millie burst into the living room, scowling at her mother. She looked over at R.J. as if she were surprised to see him there. "Hi, honey," she said sweetly.

R.J. and Millie said goodnight to her parents and stepped out into the night air. Mrs. Brewster seemed relieved they were leaving. Mr. Brewster didn't notice.

"You've been messing with my mother again, haven't you, R.J.?"

"What are you accusing me of?" he replied, as innocently as he could manage.

"Of messing with my mother! You know damn good and well what I'm accusing you of." She stood on the front walk, halfway between the house and the car, hip cocked, arms crossed, glaring angrily at him. R.J. thought she looked lovely.

"Whatever your mom told you, baby, she's lying. She's crazy, you know that. She's always accusing me of saying shit I don't say. Does your dad complain about me?"

"My dad's deaf."

R.J. grinned down at her. "Well, there you go, then," he whispered, and kissed her on the tip of her nose.

"Just don't mess with her so much," Millie pouted.

"Okay, okay." He kissed her again, this time on the mouth, and ushered her quickly to the car. He was anxious to get her alone.

They were quiet on the drive to Chuck's apartment. Renee and Chuck were in a hotel suite in Denver, spending their honeymoon exploring the mile high city. As far as R.J. was concerned, they could have it. Millie was feeling much better, having managed to sleep fourteen hours. Her eyes were bright, that sly smile was back and she looked lovely. They sat on the living room floor, eating pizza and watching The Three Stooges on television.

Millie had forgiven him for abandoning her at the Howard Johnson's the previous night when he explained he was just trying to make sure she was safe. She cuddled up to him and whispered that she was sorry they'd wasted the motel room. He picked her up and carried her to the bedroom. That night they consummated their relationship and murmured promises of never-ending fidelity and commitment. When R.J. awakened early the next morning, he was already looking forward to leaving.

R.J. lay awake, staring at the ceiling. It was 6:00 A.M., and early morning sunlight streamed sharply through the bedroom window, splashing yellow and gold across the far wall. Millie lay snoozing softly beside him, her head resting in the crook of his arm, which had fallen asleep. He pulled his arm free, slowly, gently, trying not to awaken her. She murmured, rolled over on her side, and resumed snoozing. R.J. sat up, took several deep breaths, and tried rubbing some feeling back into his numb arm. He glanced over at Millie and stood, stretching, attempting to get out some of the kinks she had put in his body. Millie had, indeed been a virgin, but apparently had been storing away her sexual energy to be released on him all in one night. It had been quite a night. *Good thing I'm leaving,* he thought, looking down at the sleeping Millie. *I could get used to that and then I'd be stuck here like Chuck, and Dean...*he shuddered...*and the others.* He stumbled toward the bathroom and turned on the shower to warm up the water.

Standing under the shower spray, R.J. turned the water as hot as he could stand it, letting it run down his body, soothing his aches and pains. *Long, hot showers*, he thought. *Another pleasure I could get used to.* He lathered and rinsed several times, washed his hair and brushed his teeth. He climbed out and toweled off quickly. He wrapped the towel around his waist and peeked out the door. Millie was still on her side, just as he had left her, sleeping contentedly. R.J. left the door open to let out the steam and leaned forward on the sink, watching the fogged-up mirror slowly defrost, bringing his reflection into focus. He rubbed at the light stubble of beard forming along his jaw, and decided he wasn't going to shave today. *Screw it,* he thought, *I'm only gonna shoot pool with the guys.*

"R.J.?" Millie's tentative voice called out to him.

R.J. leered at his reflection, and it leered back at him lasciviously. "In here, baby," he called back. He combed his hair quickly, grinning at his image in the mirror.

"R.J.?" She sounded whiney. *Big surprise.*

"I'm in the bathroom," R.J. called. He slowly shook his head while he finished primping. Millie had been all he could think about for the past several days, and now, the morning after, he discovered her appeal had dimmed. As with all his other girlfriends, he lost interest in them immediately after having sex with them. *Except Renee,* he reminded himself. She had never let him get past first base!

Millie stumbled into the bathroom, squeezed past R.J., and sat down on the toilet. She peed, yawned and grinned up at him. "How you feeling this morning, Big Shot?"

Uh-oh, he thought, *the attitude's back.* "Good, I'm good, just in a hurry."

"Hurry for what? It's not even 7:00 A.M."

"I promised my folks I would have breakfast with them," he lied.

"Why can't you stay and have breakfast with me?" she purred, running her hand under his towel.

"Knock that off," he protested, pushing her hand away.

"You couldn't wait to get me here last night," she pouted. "Now you can't wait to get out of here."

R.J. walked out of the bathroom and began getting dressed. "I haven't spent a lot of time with my folks," he explained. "I'm leaving day after tomorrow and I want to see some of them before I go."

She followed him and perched cross-legged on the bed, holding the sheet up to her chin, and whined with a pouted lower lip, "Can I go with you?"

"I'll call you later," he said, buttoning up his shirt. He pecked her on the cheek and hurried toward the door.

"I'll be right here!" she called after him. The door slammed. "In case you're interested," she whispered to the closed door.

Two days later, R.J. packed his sea bag in his parents' living room and plopped it down on the front porch. The Greyhound bus left for Denver in less than an hour. He would spend a week in Denver, visiting his friends, his grandparents, and even his mother. Then he would catch the train to San Diego. He was looking forward to reporting to the Prairie and taking his place on her signal bridge. Granny came into the room and put her arms around him. "Your visit went by so fast," she said. "It was so good to have you home." R.J. hugged her back and blinked away tears. The El Camino's horn blared in the driveway and R.J. put on his white hat and saluted his stepmother.

"See you in a little more than a year," he promised, kissed her cheek and stepped out the front door. He tossed the sea bag into the bed of the El Camino and slid into the front seat with his dad.

They drove silently, R.J. staring out the side window and his father staring straight ahead. Finally his father broke the silence. "Good visit."

R.J. grinned. His father was a man of few words. "I had a lot of fun," he replied. "Especially at the wedding." He grinned at his father. "Boy, that was a funny wedding!"

His father responded with a big grin of his own. "Yep, sounds like it was. Sorry I missed it."

Outside the Greyhound Bus station, several of R.J.'s friends had gathered. Benny Ortega was there, as were Dino and Jim and their girls, including Millie, who stood off by herself, pouting. Chuck and Renee were still in Denver. R.J.'s dad pulled the El Camino into a parking spot and turned off the engine. He turned and looked at his son.

"I wish I were goin' with you, R.J. It's been a long time since I wore that white hat."

"I think you'd like today's Navy, Dad. Lots of things have changed, though."

"Yeah, like I hear you get to sleep in a bed. Hell, in my time we had to sleep in hammocks, for cryin' out loud!"

R.J. laughed and embraced his dad. His father hugged him back, hard.

"'Nuff said?" his father asked self-consciously.

"See you next year, Pop," R.J. said. He gave him one last hug and got out of the car, retrieved his sea bag and carried it to the baggage area. When he was checked in, he joined his friends. Millie was still pouting.

They talked and laughed, especially about the wedding, until the first call for the bus was announced. R.J.'s friends bid him farewell, with promises to write, and piled into their cars. Millie stepped up next to R.J. and waved with him at their departing friends.

"R.J., I have to talk to you about something."

R.J. turned to face her. "What?" For reasons he didn't fully understand, R.J. had held Millie at arm's length since the day they did the deed. He looked into her brown eyes and realized he was no longer smitten with her. It was always like that with him. He lost interest quickly, once his original goal had been accomplished.

"Don't be cross!"

"I'm not, I just have to catch that bus." He looked around furtively, as though he were trying to locate an escape route.

"You have a couple of minutes."

He sighed resignedly. "Okay, what's on your mind?" He put his arms around her to comfort her.

"I don't want you to go," she whined. "Especially now."

"What's wrong, Millie?" He was becoming impatient with her, and he didn't care if he showed it.

"I...Penelope thinks I might be pregnant."

He stared at her and almost burst out laughing. "Millie, I don't think that's something you know about after only two and a half days."

"I talked with Penelope..."

The second call for the bus was announced and R.J. decided to take advantage of it. "I gotta go, kiss me goodbye." *He did not want to hear about that fucking Penelope.*

"R.J.!" She was crying.

He leaned over and pecked her on the cheek. "I'll write as soon as I'm on board ship. Bye, baby." He jumped on the bus, ignoring her whining pleas to stay a little longer, and found a seat in the rear next to a window. Millie stood in the parking lot, amidst the swirling dust kicked up by the bus, shielding her weeping eyes against the sun and waving at the Greyhound's rear window. R.J. sat staring straight ahead and ignored her. His focus was ahead, not back. The farther down the road the Greyhound traveled, the farther Millie faded from his mind. *Forward steps*, he thought, smiling fondly at a private memory. *Forward steps!*

CHAPTER TWENTY SIX

Aboard the Prairie
July 27, 1965

Day 10

Lincoln Jones was having a great time on the Prairie. He was developing close friendships with R.J. and Ricky, and the three of them were almost always together. Charlie Mayweather called them Manny, Moe and Jack, the Pep Boys, but they were never sure who was supposed to be whom.

Linc brought over his record albums, along with Pea, who could only stay a couple of hours and had to be back aboard the Knox for the evening watch at 2200 hours. R.J. and Ricky were also scheduled for the evening watch, but they had a little time to kill. The four of them sat around the bunting locker, listening to jazz and talking about music.

R.J. really liked Jimmy Smith and his album, "Who's Afraid of Virginia Woolf." Ricky listened carefully as the music flowed from Jimmy Smith's magic organ, and he began picking at Peggy Sue. Soon, he was playing along with the organ as Linc and R.J. urged him on. Pea sat in a corner and smoked a cigarette, smiling dreamily, imagining that the four of them might be hanging out in one of their living rooms back home instead of part of a massive Navy salvage operation.

Linc put Oscar Peterson on the record player and sat back with his eyes closed, slowly nodding his head to the beat of "Night Train." Along with Oscar Peterson, Linc had brought some Cannonball Adderley and an album by Cal Tjader that R.J. had never heard of called "Soul Sauce." Linc knew all about music, particularly jazz, and introduced the others to different cuts on different albums. The atmosphere inside the bunting locker was mellow and comfortable with the soft jazz playing in the background.

"Uh-oh!" Pea said, looking down at his watch. "I gotta get back or Billings is gonna tear me a new one. See you dudes tomorrow." He slipped out the hatch to a chorus of goodbyes and made his way to the boat deck.

When time for the evening watch arrived, Linc helped R.J. and Ricky tidy up the bunting locker and stow away the record player. Linc gathered his albums up in his arms and looked around. "You got somewhere I can store these?" he asked R.J.

"Over here." R.J. opened a cabinet. "We each have one of these cabinets, and nobody ever opens somebody else's cabinet." Linc stacked the albums inside, next to R.J.'s box of Knox personnel files. "Is my file in that box?" he asked mischievously.

"How did you know what's in that box?"

"The skeleton crew on the Knox is very small," Linc winked at him. "Personnel files get gathered up and the word get around. I seen 'em puttin' the files in boxes just like that one." Linc smiled his big, gregarious smile. "I'm pretty smart, huh white boy?"

R.J. laughed and closed the closet, snapping the padlock shut. "I'm doing some research for Deavers..."

Linc interrupted him, holding his hand up, palm out. "Ain't none o' my never mind."

R.J. chuckled. "Anyway, your albums are safe here. Nobody pokes around in here."

Linc looked doubtful, but followed R.J. and Ricky to the signal bridge, figuring he might as well hang out there. *Nothing better to do.*

After relieving Charlie on the signal bridge, R.J. took a quick look at the paperwork and smiled. *Good ol' Charlie, always loved to write up reports.* "Well, we got nothin' to do up here. Charlie already did the dailies, so unless we get some traffic..." he let the thought hang in the air.

The three of them leaned together on the railing and looked out at the ships of Task Force 73. There was no moon, and the various ships' outlines were hard to make out, but their running lights indicated which way they faced. Red for port and green for starboard, just like the filters on the signal lights. The lights were filtered to cut down their brilliance at night.

Occasionally, a signal light flashed from one ship to another, mostly routine reports, and the three signalmen stood quietly, leaning on the railing and silently reading the mundane messages. During the day, the signal traffic would be significantly higher, and everyone would be very busy, but at night the traffic was minimal, and gave the signalmen some quiet time to talk and get to know one another. Mostly they talked about home and family, and Linc began to think he belonged with the Prairie signal gang. He decided he would ask to be transferred there if the Knox became decommissioned.

"How would you guys feel if I asked to be transferred here?" he asked without looking at R.J. and Ricky.

"Okay by me," Ricky readily agreed. "But you gotta bring over the rest of your albums."

"So," Linc got a twinkle in his eye. "You wouldn't mind havin' an integrated signal crew?"

"Hell, we already integrated," Ricky replied. "We got crazy-ass Charlie Mayweather, big brother Chief Benson, two or three good-for-nothin' strikers, not to mention the great R.J. Davis, and if I may be less than humble, a risin' star in yours truly." Ricky grinned. "We got every kinda coon-ass they is!"

R.J. and Linc laughed. "Well, you gonna have a real-life coon-ass," Linc stated. He grabbed his buttocks with both hands. "An extremely nice ass...if *I* may be less than humble."

"Signal bridge!" The OOD was calling from the wing.

R.J. leaned over the rail, "Signal bridge aye, sir!"

"We have a message to send to the Mars!"

"I'll get it," Ricky declared and scooted down the ladder.

Linc watched him go. "Ricky's a funny dude," he said, smiling broadly. "Full speed ahead, huh?"

"Yeah, he's one o' the best," R.J. replied. "He is the best message writer I ever seen. That boy has got some fingers on him. He can sew flags together faster than anyone, he plays the guitar like a maniac, and he can write down my messages as fast as I read the code." R.J. watched the OOD give the message slip to Ricky, who turned and headed toward the ladder. "I'm sure gonna miss Ricky," he murmured.

Linc nodded. "That's right, I hear you due to get out in September. That's only a few weeks away, m'man."

"Eight weeks, two days, six hours and," R.J. looked at his watch, "thirty seven minutes."

Linc chuckled loudly. "Course that's just a rough estimate, right?"

Ricky came bounding up the ladder. "It's a quick message to the Mars about supply levels," he called out. "You want me to send it?"

Linc held his hand out for the message. "Mind if I send it?"

Ricky and R.J. shrugged at each other. "G'head," Ricky agreed, and handed him the message slip.

R.J. got a glint in his eye. "Use my light," he said, pointing at the rolling signal light. It was tied up to a stanchion to keep it from traveling around the deck un-piloted.

Ricky looked at R.J. and raised his eyebrows. They nodded slightly to each other, and Ricky got a big grin on his face. "Here y'go, Linc, I'll untie it for you."

Linc looked at the rolling light suspiciously. The signal light was mounted on a round piece of plywood, about three feet across, with three multi-directional wheels on the bottom. Its purpose was to provide a hundred percent access to the entire signal deck, which made it much easier to take and send messages to different ships in different positions. R.J. had two friends in the wood shop make it up for him in trade for five minutes each on the big eye binoculars when they got to Hong Kong.

R.J. had taken it one step further. He liked to step up on the platform and move the light around like a scooter while he was sending or receiving messages, and it took skill to keep the light pointed in the right direction. It created a high level of difficulty, but R.J. mastered the moving light in less than an hour. Now Linc, unbeknownst to himself, was going to get his chance.

Linc turned on the light and pointed it at the Mars. They were on the port side, so his filter was red. He took hold of the handle and looked down at the message slip.

"Whoa, whoa," R.J. called. "What're you doin', Linc?"

"Gettin' ready to send this here message," Linc said, as if it were obvious to everyone.

"Not like that," Ricky stepped in, pointing to Linc's feet.

Linc looked down. "What?" he asked, a little impatiently.

R.J. was enjoying this. "Up on the platform," he explained. "You stand on the light and move it around by shifting your feet and weight. Like on a surfboard."

"I ain't never been on no surfboard!" Linc exclaimed, beginning to laugh. "We'da cut any surfer showed up in Detroit." He climbed cautiously onto the round plywood platform and moved around a bit, getting comfortable. "Piece of cake," he insisted. He pointed the light at the Mars and began his message.

R.J. nodded at Ricky and he stepped up behind Linc, put his foot on the edge of the round platform, and gave it a strong push. The rolling light took off across the deck, turning and spinning, almost throwing Linc off.

"Whoa, Mamma!" Linc hollered, holding on desperately to the light and trying to stay on the platform which was spinning around rapidly.

"The message!" R.J. yelled at him. He pointed toward the Mars. "Send the message!" R.J. bent over laughing, holding his stomach.

Ricky was much in the same condition, but every time Linc would get the light pointed toward the Mars, he or R.J. would give the platform a little spin. The flashing red signal light was bouncing off the bulkheads of the signal shack, off the mast, and off Ricky and R.J. as it got sprayed around in every direction.

Finally, Linc got control of the light and R.J. and Ricky stood back, laughing. Linc sent the message, got the receipt, and hopped off the light.

"A little Prairie-signal-bridge-initiation?" he asked, grinning.

"Jus' a little test you gotta pass," Ricky replied.

"Well, tell you the truth," Linc grinned, looked back at the rolling light, "that was kinda fun."

"WHAT'S GOING ON UP THERE?" The OOD again.

Linc held up an index finger at the others and leaned over the railing. "Message sent to the Mars and receipted for, sir!" he called down.

The OOD looked up at Linc and frowned. "Who the hell are you?" he demanded.

Linc turned his left sleeve so the OOD could see his crow. "Lincoln Jones, SM-two," he replied, as if that explained everything.

The OOD looked thoughtful. "Very well," he said finally. "Carry on."

"Aye, sir." Linc turned and grinned at R.J. and Ricky.

"Oh, yeah," Ricky decided, nodding thoughtfully. "You gonna fit in jus' fine up here."

Day 11

The salvage team met to assess their progress. Most of the heavy preliminary work had been done in the first ten days of the operation. A majority of the excess gear had been off-loaded from the Frank Knox. Some of her crew was transferred to the Mars, some to the Iwo Jima and the rest to the Prairie. Regular water deliveries continued through the use of the heavy tanks manufactured by the Prairie, so the Knox wouldn't run short. Since the next big effort would involve the blowing of the reef, most of the task force settled into a slow, numbing routine, waiting for the arrival of the Navy underwater demolition team. The wait was made more difficult by the oppressive heat and humidity. Occasionally during the day, a strong breeze would kick up and temporarily cool the sailors of Task Force 73, but mostly the breeze blew at night, and at times very strongly.

On the Knox, three more sets of beach gear were employed. The thick cables led like umbilical cords from the heavy anchors to the ship, and kept the Knox from settling farther on the reef.

The off-loading continued on the stranded destroyer, although the pace had slackened. The men of the volunteer salvage crew were miserable; their meals usually consisted of sandwiches and water, they were limited to one two-minute shower per day, and there was no air conditioning, so most of them slept up on deck at night. Working under the tropical sun all day left very little energy for card games or any other usual shipboard activity. As a result, the families of the salvage crew were not hearing from them, and some were writing their concerns to the Navy.

Bob Harp was an exception. After his brief shower each night, he would sit on the edge of his bunk, relaxing after another taxing day, and write a short letter to his parents:

Dear Mom & Dad,
Guess where I am? Yep, same place...

Captain Marshall of the Prairie suggested a crew exchange. Several members of the Prairie deck crew would change places with some of the Knox sailors for a week, on a rotating basis, giving the Knox's salvage crew a much needed rest. Admiral Wilson endorsed the plan enthusiastically, and it was put into motion. The Knox sailors loved the plan and were delighted. The Prairie sailors...were not.

Chief Billings was instructed to pick the first dozen men. He chose Pea and several others. He did not select Parker, the dental tech. The chief wanted Parker where he could keep an eye on him.

Pea maneuvered the motor whaleboat full of happy Knox sailors toward the Prairie, a big smile covering half his face. He was going to get to spend a week on the Prairie, which meant better food, longer showers, easier labor, and air conditioned compartments. It also meant he would get to spend more time with R.J., Linc and Ricky.

As he tied up his boat to the Prairie and allowed the rest of the men to file up the ladder ahead of him, the unhappy Prairie sailors began climbing down into their boat for the trip to the Knox. Pea recognized a few of the Prairie deck crew. As they pushed away from the tender, and pointed the bow toward the reef, Pea waved and yelled to them.

"Hey! Knox on the rocks, muddafucka! KNOX ON THE ROCKS!" He grinned at the middle fingers lifted in reply from the Prairie boat, and climbed up the ladder to the boat deck. *Wonder what's for chow?* he thought, grinning happily.

Linc stuck around on the Prairie for a few days, after getting Jimmy Dole to agree to handle the flag raising in the morning and lowering in the evening. Beyond that, there wasn't anything for a signalman to do on the Knox. There was very little signal traffic during the lull in activity, and when another ship did flash the Knox, Linc could answer from the Prairie, and relay the infrequent messages by radio to the stranded destroyer. Soon, he became a recognized fixture around the signal bridge, lent a helpful hand with signal traffic and flag hoists, most of which were conducted as training drills, and he was quickly accepted as one of the Prairie's signal gang.

Almost immediately, Chief Benson and Charlie Mayweather began scheming on how to get Linc assigned to the Prairie permanently. The chief knew he had an open billet coming up. R.J. Davis' enlistment was up on the twenty-third of September, less than two months away, and R.J. had made it clear he would not consider reenlisting. "Four and no more," was his mantra and there was no changing his mind.

Day 12

Pea came bouncing up the ladder to the signal bridge, rubbing his hands together. "Hey, flag-fags, what's goin' on up here?"

R.J. grinned at Linc and Ricky and glanced at his watch. "Must be time for lunch," he mused. Linc and Ricky laughed. Charlie poked his head out of the signal shack, saw it was Pea arriving on the signal bridge, and sat back down at the desk, refocusing on his crossword puzzle.

"C'mon," Pea urged. "Let's go get chow! Mess decks gonna close in thirty minutes!"

"Yeah," Ricky agreed. "Let's go get some chow."

R.J. stuck his head into the signal shack and let Charlie know he would be alone on the signal bridge. He waved them away, scowling, and went back to his puzzle.

On the way to the mess decks, Linc remarked, "Charlie's always workin' on them crossword puzzles, huh?"

"He always workin' on 'em, but he don't never finish any," Ricky observed.

R.J. chuckled. "The guy's got about three dozen crossword magazines, all the puzzles unfinished. Sometimes he goes into them and works on the puzzles, but he never finishes one."

"How come?" Pea asked, hurrying to keep up with the three taller signalmen.

"'Cause he a crazy Yankee, that's why," Ricky explained. "Says if he ever completely finishes a puzzle, the world as we know it would end, and he don't wanna be responsible for that." Ricky shook his head sadly. "Crazy-ass Yankee!"

The mess decks were emptying out when the foursome got there. Most of the crew had finished lunch, and only a few stragglers remained. Linc made his way through the chow line, filling his tray and looking around with a puzzled expression. "Hey, R.J.," he said quietly. "What's this all about?"

A group of about a dozen black sailors sat around two tables in the corner of the mess decks, huddled together and talking quietly. When Linc and the others walked past them with their trays, the blacks became silent, their conversation stopped. Most of them glared at Linc as he sat at another table with the three white sailors.

"Dunno," R.J. said, spooning beef stew into his mouth. "They meet here during noon chow almost every day. I got no idea what they're up to."

"Maybe they plannin' to overthrow the gov'mit!" Ricky offered, grinning. "They call themselves the 'Black Summit,' and it started with just four or five, but they been growin'."

"So why they givin' me dirty looks?" Linc asked.

"I guess 'cause you're with us," R.J. offered. He frowned and looked over at the Black Summit members. "They're isolating themselves from the rest of us, guess they wanna form their own Navy or sumthin'."

Linc glared back at the Black Summit. "De facto segregation," he murmured.

"What?" Pea asked.

"They goin' about it all wrong," Linc observed. "They're segregating themselves. That's not what the movement is all about." He looked around at his table mates, shaking his head slowly, sadly. "Back home Doctor King preaches a non-violent approach to civil rights. He just wants black Americans to be able to live and work with white Americans on an equal footing." He glanced back at the Black Summit. "We're Americans, too," he went on. "We don't want nothin' but an equal chance...at everything America offers."

Pea looked at R.J. and a silent understanding passed between them. "Sounds familiar, huh R.J.?"

R.J. nodded thoughtfully. "Yeah," he said quietly, thinking about his last ship, the USS Haverfield, and his friends, Andy and Rafer Sample.

"Who's that little guy?" Linc asked, nodded toward the Summit. A short, light-skinned black sailor was standing and talking urgently to his group, punctuating his comments with exaggerated hand gestures. He wore a third-class electrician mate's crow on his left arm.

"That's the Hawk," R. J. explained. "His name is Hawkins Wilson, but everybody just calls him Hawk." R.J. finished the last of his milk and set the cup down hard on the table. "Hawk's the leader of that group," he went on to explain impatiently. "He's a militant guy, and he don't agree with that non-violent stuff."

Linc looked over at Hawkins Wilson, then back at R.J., who seemed irritated. "You and him got problems?" Linc asked.

"Naw," R.J. answered. "I just think he's goin' about it all wrong, like you said."

"We had some friends on our last ship," Pea said quietly, then let the thought drift.

Linc looked at Pea curiously. "And?" he asked.

"Nothin'," Pea said absently. "We been through this before and that ain't the way to go about it." He nodded toward the Black Summit which seemed to be winding down.

The meeting had apparently broken up, and Hawk Wilson stared at Linc as he gathered up a few books and papers. It wasn't a challenging glare, but more a curious look, studying Linc's face. Linc stared back in the same manner. Hawk put his books under his arm, nodded politely to Linc, who nodded politely back, and slowly strolled out the hatch and down the passageway. Linc smiled to himself. *Brother Hawk got his act down pat*. Somehow, Linc knew he and Hawkins Wilson would meet again, and soon.

The UDT's arrival was only a few days away. Everyone in the task force realized that. The weekend arrived, the last easy-going weekend they would have until the Knox was pulled off the reef, and no one knew how long that would take. The optimists among them believed the ship would come off after the reef was blown. Others worried they would never recover the Knox.

Throughout it all, Admiral Wilson led Task Force 73 with a deft mixture of charm, praise and selective ass-chewing. He kept everyone on their toes, even during the lull period, and read the daily reports from start to finish, even when he knew nothing had changed from the prior day.

He discovered the Prairie's twenty-fifth birthday was coming up on August 5. She had been commissioned in August 1940. Since the UDT boys were arriving on the fourth and the ensuing few days would be hectic, Admiral Wilson quietly planned a silver anniversary celebration for the following week, on August 12, hoping that when the 12th arrived, they would all be gone from Pratas Reef. He had steaks and soft drinks flown in for the enlisted men, and steaks and champagne for the senior officers. The bakers were instructed to create a special cake for the occasion. Admiral Wilson shared his plans with only a few officers and enlisted men who would be directly involved, and he swore them to secrecy, which was probably why it took a full two hours for the word to spread throughout the ship. The crew was delighted at the thought of having a party, anything to break up the boring routine, although they hoped that they would celebrate Prairie's silver anniversary somewhere other than Pratas Reef.

Day 14
The Burning of Atlanta

Late in the evening, up on the signal bridge, Pea, Linc, R.J. and Ricky sat around the signal shack, trading sea stories. Ricky and R.J. had the watch, so Ricky had left Peggy Sue below in the compartment, tucked under a blanket so she wouldn't catch cold. When the UDT arrived, Pea and Linc would have to return to the Frank Knox for as many more 'maximum efforts' as it took to free her, so they wanted to enjoy their last few days in relative comfort aboard the big destroyer tender.

Pea spoke about patrolling off Yankee Station, wondering if they were going to be fired on. "We was pretty close to the beach," he said. "Maybe a couple of miles off, that's all. I wasn't afraid of runnin' into those PT boats, I was afraid some little slant on shore would shoot us with a SAM."

"SAM's are surface to air missiles, Pea," R.J. corrected him. "They shoot down planes with 'em."

"Well, they could shoot it at us, too," Pea insisted. "They sneaky little fuckers."

"Y'all see any action down there?" Ricky asked.

"Naw, we just patrolled," Pea replied. "Up and back, up and back, up and back, up..."

"We get it, Pea," R.J. laughed.

Pea scowled. "...and back," he finished with a tone of finality.

"We did see a town burning," Linc said.

Everyone turned to look at him. "What town?" Ricky asked, becoming interested.

"'Member that, Pea?" Linc turned to Pea who nodded. "We were patrolling off the coast near Nha Trang," Linc explained. "We were in close because we were picking up some officer who was ashore doin' some damn fool thing..."

"What officer?" Pea interrupted. "I didn't hear about no officer."

"That's 'cause you deck apes are too busy scraping rust and clankin' anchors to pay attention to what's goin' on," Linc said with a wide grin. "You don't remember that fire?"

"I remember the fire," Pea said, petulantly. "But I didn't know about the officer. What was he doin'?"

"Hell, I don't know," Linc said, irritated his story was being interrupted. "You wanna tell the story?"

"No, I just wanna know what the friggin' officer was doin' ashore, WHOEVER he was."

Linc sighed and looked exasperated at Pea. "Anyway," he

returned to the story. "We're sittin' out there when all of a sudden, BLAM!" Linc stood up and held his arms out wide. "The whole mammy-slammin' town of Nha Trang went up, man. BLAM! The fire was red, and orange and *black*. I jive you not, black fire. Later we learned it was napalm. Navy jets blew the place away." Linc smiled at the memory. "It was a cool sight, though, watching that fire. The burning of Atlanta musta looked like that."

"Yeah," Pea agreed. "Real 'Gone With The Wind' shit!"

"We ain't seen no action," Ricky said, absently strumming the air where Peggy Sue would be. "We go from one port to another, takin' care of destroyers. Some o' them seen action."

"Yeah?" Linc asked. "Like who?"

"Like the Turner Joy," R.J. interjected. "We were in dry-dock with the Turner Joy in Long Beach last Christmas. We met a couple of the signalmen at the EM club, and they told us about getting shot at by PT boats in the Tonkin Gulf."

Pea looked at R.J. intently, a curious, smug smile on his face. "That musta scared the crap outta you," he said softly, that curious smile becoming wider.

R.J. nodded. "It did," he agreed, "it truly did." He and Pea stared at each other, smiling and nodding. They had shared a combat experience on the Haverfield, and they had promised each other they would never speak of it again. There were three others who had taken the oath along with them.

Linc and Ricky looked at Pea and R.J. curiously. Ricky got up and put on his white hat. "I'm gonna walk the deck a little," he announced. "Make them coon-ass officers think we workin' up here."

"Lemme put on some music," Linc offered, not quite understanding what just passed between R.J. and Pea. Linc was not one to meddle, considering others' business to be 'none o' his never-mind.' "I think we need a little pick-me-up." He put Cal Tjader's album 'Soul Sauce' on the turntable. Soon the snappy sounds of Cal Tjader, pounding away at his vibes, echoed through the shack, the volume low enough so that the OOD couldn't hear it. Everyone's spirits were lifted, and outside the shack Ricky danced a little cha-cha-cha across the deck.

"WHAT'S GOING ON UP THERE?"

"Nothin', sir." Ricky stopped dancing.

"SOUNDS LIKE A STAMPEDE UP THERE!"

My dancing? Ricky thought. *Coon-ass OOD!*

"Just movin' the light, sir."

"WELL, MOVE IT A LITTLE QUIETER!"

"Aye, sir!" *Dumb-ass Yankee!*

Sunday, August 1, 1965
Day 15

The Hawk

It didn't take long for Hawkins Wilson to introduce himself to Linc. It happened on Sunday at the Baptist church services held at 1000 hours in the ship's library. About 20 sailors showed up, mostly black, each and every Sunday to listen to the sermon from the Prairie's chaplain, Lieutenant Commander C. R. Charles, arguably the most popular officer aboard ship. Hawk liked to use the services as a recruitment event. He also liked to engage the chaplain in social debate. Chaplain Charles was a peaceful, non-violent man, a true believer in the philosophy of Martin Luther King. Hawkins Wilson was not, and challenged the chaplain's beliefs at every opportunity. Chaplain Charles took it all in stride, quietly believing that Hawkins Wilson was put on the Prairie to test him, and the chaplain was not afraid of tests. "My name is Hawkins Wilson," he said, sitting down next to Linc and picking up a song book. "And you are Lincoln Jones...of the Frank Knox." He held out his hand.

Linc looked at it pensively for a second, shook it, and returned to looking through his song book. "You done introduced us both," he observed, a small smile on his lips.

"I figure you got southern roots,' Hawk said, smiling brightly. "Otherwise a brother from the motor city would be a Methodist or somethin', am I right?"

Linc put down his song book and turned to face the Hawk. "Every brother has southern roots," he said flatly. "I don't remember hearin' about slave plantations up in New York or Vermont."

Hawk grinned. He liked brothers who had a little fire in their souls. "So which white-controlled, oppressive slave society did your kinfolk hail from?"

"Tennessee," Linc replied.

"Mississippi," Hawk said, pointing a thumb at his chest. "That's where all the really bad shit went down." He sounded proud to be from Mississippi for that very reason.

"Way I heard it," Linc retorted, "really bad shit was goin' down everywhere."

"That be true," Hawk replied. "You ever go back there? Back home I mean? Seek your roots?"

"In Tennessee?" Linc asked, a comical grin on his face.

"You right, brother. Only real pilgrimage a black man can make is to Africa. That's where I'm goin'. Talk about roots!"

Linc looked into Hawk's eyes, nodding slowly, and a small, ironic smile creased his lips. "I mean no offense Bro," he said quietly, "but a light-skinned brother like you would stick out like a nigger at a Klan rally in darkest Africa. Hell, those people so black, they blue!"

Hawk looked startled, then a flash of anger flared in his eyes. Linc thought for a moment he had just started a fight, but Hawk seemed to get control of himself, and he started laughing. He laughed loud and hard, bent over, holding his stomach. Chaplain Charles glared at him from the pulpit.

"Well," he said, struggling to catch his breath. "It ain't about color, anyway."

"It damn shore is!" Linc replied, a little louder than he meant to. "It's always been about color. Shit, man, even with us. Some sisters don't wanna truck with no dark-skinned brother. Or am I wrong?"

Hawk studied Linc's face for a long moment. This was a brother he could work with. "It shouldn't be about color," he said quietly. "It shouldn't never be about color."

"But it is. That's why people are demonstrating for civil rights back home. They want equality, which is what they deserve, and they want it regardless of their color. I tell you, Hawk, I'm damn proud of those folks."

"All this marchin' and protestin' and speech makin' is bullshit!" Hawk spat. "We ain't never gonna get whitey to give us our rights. We gotta take 'em!"

Chaplain Charles stopped the service and stepped out from behind the pulpit, his laser-like stare boring a hole through Hawk. "You men take it outside. This is a church service and I won't have you knuckleheads disrupting it." His deep voice echoed through the small library and the worshipers all turned to look back on Linc and Hawk. The chaplain crossed his hands in front of him and stared at the two men patiently, expectantly, his eyes cold.

Hawk and Linc withered under the chaplain's stare, and filed out of the library, walking toward the boat deck. Hawk stopped and turned to look up at Linc, who was at least a foot taller.

"I got the duty," Hawk explained. "But you and me need to talk." He shook his head slowly. "You gotta rid yourself of that slave mentality, brother."

"I'm from Detroit, brother," Linc retorted. "Didn't have no slaves when I was growin' up."

"Are you serious?" Hawk asked, a perplexed look on his face. "You ain't never heard of GM? Chrysler? How about Ford Motor

Company? You ever hear of Ford Motor Company?" Hawk checked his watch. He only had a couple of minutes. "Those white-owned and white-operated corporations run their businesses on the backs of our black brothers and sisters who are enslaved by them."

"They ain't slaves," Linc protested, becoming exasperated with Hawk. "They're paid by the hour, they belong to a union, they have health care, dental care, pensions...and they work side-by-side with white people!"

"Yeah, yeah," Hawk interrupted. "I gotta go, but let's talk again. Soon." He waved and disappeared down the ladder to the 02 level.

Linc stood against the railing, his back to the sea, pondering the words of Hawkins Wilson and his views on the black struggle for equal rights. Linc believed that the struggle would be made more difficult by the use of violence, and that black people had to battle against themselves, overcome these militants, before they could move forward in any significant way. *Maybe Hawk's right,* he thought, *and whitey ain't gonna just give it up, but gettin' him pissed off about the violence ain't gonna help us one bit! Side-by-side with whites, that's how it has to happen, side-by-side. That's equality, and that's what we want. We are Americans, too.*

Day 17

Admiral Wilson was satisfied. Everything that could be done, had been done, and Task Force 73 was ready for the UDT boys. Once the frogmen went down and inspected the reef, their conclusions would be reviewed, and a plan to plant the explosives would be formulated. Hopefully, they could then pull the Frank Knox to safety, and they wouldn't need the foam. Admiral Wilson was a little suspicious of the liquid Styrofoam approach. It was purely experimental, never having been used in an actual salvage operation. For the tenth time he glanced over the pile of reports on his desk. He snapped off the desk light and leaned back in his chair, confident that he had every detail covered.

"Gotta go back home tomorrow," Linc said. He and Pea were leaning against the port side flag bag, looking out across the reef at the Frank Knox. The sun had set, and an eerie silence swept over the reef and Task Force 73; an expectant, fearful silence, like the nerve-fraying lull before a battle at sea.

"That ain't home," Pea protested bitterly. "Not anymore, she's not."

R.J. came up behind them and looked out at the Knox. Ricky was sitting in the shack, air-strumming the absent Peggy Sue. Charlie

Mayweather and Chief Benson were due to take over the watch, right after the first round of the pinochle tournament ended in the bunting locker.

"Y'know, Pea," R.J. said, putting his arm around his friend's shoulder. "I bet if you talk to Chief O'Malley about it, he'll okay a transfer for you."

"Might do that," Pea said quietly. "Think you could live with that, you skivvy-wavin' flag-fags?"

Linc and R.J. laughed. "We'd miss you if you weren't here, little buddy," R.J. assured him, and for a moment, he thought Pea was going to cry. Ricky came out of the shack and readily agreed that Pea would be a great addition to the Prairie's deck force.

Another sailor started up the ladder to the signal bridge. He was short, stocky, muscular and black, and he wore his white hat down low over his eyebrows. His insignia described him as third class boatswain's mate. He grinned when he saw Pea.

"Hey, Pea," he called. "Wha's happenin'?"

"Chopper!" Pea exclaimed. "Get your big butt up here, I want you to meet some people." He waved to his friends. "Hey, fellas, meet Chopper. Tell 'em who you are, Chopper."

Clarence 'Chopper' Adams grinned broadly. "I'm a street-walker, a shit-talker, a heart-breaker and a baby-maker," he announced to the delight of the signal gang. "I'm a lover supreme and a poor ho's dream, and I'm lookin' for Lincoln Jones." He spotted Linc leaning on the flag bag, looking back at him whimsically. "Linc," Chopper called, "Hawk wanna know if you comin' to the meeting."

"What, the Black Summit?" Pea asked eagerly. "Can I come?"

Chopper frowned, looking at Pea, and for a brief moment, thought Pea might be serious. Then, realizing he was being ribbed, he started laughing, and his booming voice sounded like three men laughing. Soon, everyone on the signal bridge was infected and laughing.

"WHAT'S GOING ON UP THERE?"

The group stopped laughing, held their collective breath for a moment, and then Linc nodded toward the wing-bridge, cupped his hand behind his ear and whispered, "The plaintive call of the indigenous gooney-bird." The laughter erupted again, renewed, unbridled, and bounced along the decks, against the bulkheads and into the night air.

"WHAT THE HELL'S GOING ON UP THERE?"

R.J. tried to stop laughing, but it was impossible. He stumbled over to the railing to answer the OOD, and forced himself to put on a straight face, but laughter was bubbling up inside him like hot lava in a volcano, and he didn't think he could pull it off. Thankfully, he was rescued by Chief Benson, who was coming up to relieve the watch.

"I'll take care of it sir," Chief Benson said soothingly to the OOD. "I'm sorry for the noise. I'll make sure they keep quiet up there."

The OOD stared at the chief and up at the signal bridge. He seemed satisfied, nodded, and returned to the pilot house.

The chief came up the ladder with a frown on his face and glared at the group gathered there. "Okay," the chief demanded. "What the hell is so funny?" The laughter started up again, but Chief Benson did not join in it, and it died down quickly.

The chief looked at Chopper. "Who are you?"

"I came up to see Linc..." Chopper started.

"Tell him no," Linc interrupted. "But if he wanna come up to the bunting locker, I got some fine-soundin' jazz records." He looked at R.J., who nodded, smiling.

Chopper stared at Linc for a moment, and shrugged. "Okay, you got it." He slapped Pea on the back. "See ya, Pea." He grinned broadly and slid down the ladder to the wing bridge.

Charlie Mayweather came up the ladder slowly, nodded to the group, and settled into his usual spot in the signal shack, lounged in the chair, worrying over a half-completed crossword puzzle. Chief Benson was putting on a fresh pot of coffee and seemed not to notice Charlie. R.J. watched the two of them settling into the familiar routine of another watch, and couldn't help but notice they resembled an old married couple who know each others' moods and tendencies so well that very little verbal communication between them is necessary. R.J. smiled warmly, thinking of his grandparents, remembering the tender, comfortable way they had with each other.

Pea stared thoughtfully down the ladder where Chopper had disappeared. He turned and looked at Linc. "You gettin' all chummy with the Hawk, huh?" he asked.

"Naw, he wanna talk me into that militant shit, and I don't play that," Linc replied. He looked over at R.J. "What you think, R.J.?"

"Like I said before, that ain't the way to go about it, but..."

"But what?" Linc encouraged.

"I'm obviously not black," R.J. said, his voice growing serious. "But if I was, I think I'd be as mad as Hawk, and maybe I'd be militant, too."

"Even if you know it can't help the cause?"

"Yeah, it's a difference between thinkin' about it and feelin' about it," R.J. explained. "It's easy to talk about how you'd react in a situation until you are in that situation."

"I'm in that situation," Linc said softly, and the others immediately knew it was true.

"But you are mad, right?" Pea asked. "I mean, how can you not be mad?"

"Well, bein' mad and being militant ain't necessarily one and the same," Linc countered. "See, brother Hawk and I agree on more than he knows. I'm mad, too, but all this black power stuff is gonna backfire on our asses, you watch and see."

"I think I'd be more like the Hawk, too," Ricky chimed in.

Linc decided to lighten the mood. "Hell, I thought you were a southern boy, Ricky. Southern white boys don't like us colored folk too much."

Ricky grinned widely. "I'm a Cajun, baby, them coon-asses don't like us too much, neither."

CHAPTER TWENTY SEVEN

August 4, 1965

Day 18

Ricky stuck his head in the door of the signal shack, where R.J. pecked away at a typewriter, working on his communications traffic report. "Hey, R.J.," Ricky hollered. "Them UDT boys're here!" He pointed a thumb over his shoulder. "They comin' up the ladder. They wanna do they exercises up here on the signal bridge. Guess it's 'cause it's so dang big, huh?"

"Ricky, it's brilliant the way you put that together." R.J. knew they were coming. He'd been alerted by Chief Benson who had told him to give them anything they wanted.

Ricky smiled his sheepish, aw-shucks grin, as if he'd just been complimented. "Anyways, come out here and talk to 'em, okay?"

R.J. got up from the desk slowly, still reading the report in the typewriter, and pulled on his white hat. He stepped out of the signal shack and into the presence of six of the biggest men he had ever seen. Muscles bulged beneath their shirt sleeves, and each of them demonstrated a calm, relaxed and confident demeanor, looking right at him with cold eyes.

"You must be the UDT guys," R.J. said, holding his hand out to the officer in charge, a lieutenant.

The lieutenant took it firmly, and R.J. had a feeling the man could easily break all the bones in his hand, but the lieutenant shook R.J.'s hand and smiled a friendly smile. "You're right," he said confidently, "but they don't call us that anymore. We are SEALS."

"Seals?" R.J. asked.

"No, SEALS. It stands for Sea, Air and Land." The lieutenant grinned back at his men. "We go anywhere in the world to wreak havoc and destruction upon America's enemies." The men grinned back. "I'm Lieutenant Jablonsky, and don't bother telling me any Polack jokes, 'cause I've heard 'em all." He was smiling pleasantly, but R.J. couldn't imagine that anyone would have the guts to tell a Polish joke in front of Lieutenant Jablonsky. He was tall, about six-three, and looked like he weighed about two twenty five. He was in the best shape of anyone R.J. had ever seen.

"Well, sir, the signal deck is yours for whenever you need it." R.J. waved an arm around the deck, which was very large. The signal shack sat forward of the flag bags, and behind them a large, open deck sprawled for several feet. The rolling signal light was tied to a stanchion.

"We get together every morning at zero five hundred and do calisthenics," the lieutenant explained, "for about an hour." He looked R.J. over. "You're welcome to join us," he offered.

"Thanks, sir," R.J. replied. "Maybe I'll do that."

The lieutenant led his SEALS down the ladder after having inspected the signal bridge and finding it satisfactory for their purposes. Lieutenant Jablonsky wanted to get his men settled in, and then himself. They were attending a salvage operations meeting that Friday afternoon, and Friday morning they'd get their first look at the submerged portion of the reef, selecting locations for the explosive charges they would plant in a few days.

"Them boys are big 'uns, huh?" Ricky had come up behind R.J. and they both watched the SEALS leave.

"Yeah," R.J. agreed. "I'm sure glad they're on our side."

It hadn't taken R.J. long at all to go through the Knox personnel files one more time, and discover no link to Andrew Tompkins or any Tompkins for that matter. Disappointed, he returned the files to Deavers, apologizing for his failure.

"Don't let it bug you, R.J.," Deavers said soothingly. "Many times our best leads come from unexpected sources. When that happens, we call it serendipity."

R.J. smiled, shook the investigator's hand and returned to the bunting locker, where he located his dictionary and looked up 'serendipity.' He smiled knowingly at the definition and headed for the signal bridge, thinking about how to work serendipity into a conversation.

Chief Billings was very disappointed. He had not found a connection to Andrew Tompkins either, though he felt strongly that dental tech J.I. Parker had something to do with all this, and the connection was there, but eluding him. At least that was his fervent hope: find the connection, wrap it up, arrest Parker and get back to ship's business, simple and neat.

The chief returned all the files to Deavers except two. He retained the files on Parker and Green, though neither file revealed much, almost as if they had been...*what?...edited?* He thought about that for a moment, frowning. He decided to keep looking for something that would connect Tompkins and Green and Parker. He already had one piece of the connection: Tompkins and Green in boot camp. He only needed to connect Tompkins to Parker or Parker to Green. The connection was there, he was certain of it. It had to be.

CHAPTER TWENTY EIGHT

Aground on Pratas Reef

Day 20

Pea stood on the fantail of the Frank Knox, helping to off-load the water pumps lent to them by the Mars and Iwo Jima. Working 24 hours a day for the first week or so, the salvage team had managed to repair or shore up almost all damaged internal bulkheads. The water pumps sucked up most of the water, and sailors with large mops and buckets got the rest. Those compartments below decks which could not be pumped out were sealed off to provide watertight integrity to the adjacent compartments.

"There goes the last water pump!" Pea announced to no one in particular.

Chief Billings stepped up next to the diminutive boatswain's mate. "They did their job," the chief said. "Let's hope they don't have to send them back."

"Whatta you mean?" Pea asked.

"Depends on the kind of job we did shoring up below decks," the chief explained. "I guess we'll find out when they blow the reef."

Since the SEALS had arrived and inspected the reef, the Knox salvage crew hurried around, making preparations in case they were able to get underway. They had high hopes the tugs could pull them off the reef as soon as the ship was no longer impaled on the outcropping. They only had a few days to wait.

The salvage ops meeting was being conducted in the Prairie wardroom.

"According to Lieutenant Jablonsky," the admiral began, nodding toward the SEAL leader, "they must blow away the outcropping on which the Knox is impaled in order to allow her to move off the reef. Lieutenant?"

Jablonsky stood. "Thank you, sir. As the admiral has said, the ship is impaled on an outcropping of the reef which has lodged itself in the empty sonar dome. We inspected the area extensively when we were down there, and I believe if we place a small C-3 charge carefully, it will destroy the base of the outcropping. When she's no longer impaled, we should be able to pull her off at high tide, if we're careful."

The admiral took over the meeting. "We are going to try to get this ship off the reef without having to resort to the foam," he said. Everyone in the meeting knew Admiral Wilson didn't trust the unproven liquid Styrofoam approach. He nodded back to the SEAL leader.

"We plan to detonate the charge on the reef on Monday, the ninth," Lieutenant Jablonsky continued. He looked around the room. "That's three days from now," he added unnecessarily.

"How do you blow away the reef without damaging the ship further?" The question came from one of the salvage experts from the Conserver.

"Let me answer that," the admiral cut in. "I've been in touch with our salvage people in Pearl Harbor," he explained. "They have examined the situation carefully and have recommended the type of charge to be used." He handed Jablonsky a message slip. "Lieutenant Jablonsky's team will go down an hour or so before high tide on the ninth and place the charge. Any questions? Good. You are dismissed."

Chairs scooted back and most of the officers filed out of the wardroom. A few lingered, talking about different aspects of the operation.

Lieutenant Jablonsky stared at the recommended C-3 charge the Admiral had just handed him. The plan was to blow the outcropping, inspect the ship for leaks, then gently ease her off the flattened reef. The reef would be reduced, and at high tide, the tugs ought to be able to pull her free without too much trouble. Lieutenant Jablonsky's concern had to do with the C-3 charge.

"Excuse me, sir," the SEAL leader said hesitantly.

"Yes, Lieutenant?" the admiral asked, preoccupied with several messages.

"Well, sir, this recommended charge seems to be excessive. I mean, we use this much C-3 and we might blow up more than the reef, if you know what I mean." He smiled at the admiral, who was not smiling back.

The few remaining officers stopped talking and looked over at the admiral and the SEAL leader.

"Lieutenant Jablonsky," the admiral began in an officious, impatient manner. "In communications with salvage experts in Pearl, they recommend that size of C-3 charge, so just plant the stuff, okay?" He turned and walked out of the wardroom without waiting for an answer.

Okay, the SEAL leader thought, looking around at the other officers. *If this goes badly, I got witnesses!* He shook his head slowly and set off to prepare his team.

Sunday, August 8, 1965

Day 22

Back on the Knox, Linc had little to do but read. There was no signal traffic, since there was nothing further to discuss. The reef was going to be blown on Monday, and, hopefully, the Knox would be free. Somewhere, in the recesses of Linc's mind, where logic and reason resided, he knew that after all their calculations, all their preparation, after the explosion they so carefully planned and planted, after all that...the ship would still be stuck on the reef. It was a depressing thought, and Linc got permission to attend the Prairie's Baptist church services, where he knew his spirits would be lifted by Chaplain Charles' inspiring sermon, and the beautiful hymns sung by the Prairie's choir.

He had not seen Hawk since the previous Sunday's services. Linc did not particularly look forward to seeing him again, but he knew he couldn't avoid the Hawk any more than any of them could avoid the inevitable internal confrontation now brewing within the civil rights movement between the angry militant faction and the more moderate, more patient non-violent followers of Dr. King. He was not surprised when Hawk suddenly appeared from nowhere and sat down beside him.

"Don't gotta shuffle 'round no mo," Hawk whispered, keeping a wary eye on Chaplain Charles. "Don't gotta beg whitey to vote no more."

Linc found himself irritated by Hawk's use of black street slang. The man was obviously very well educated, yet he dropped into the jive talk too easily. Linc considered it to be a lazy trait. The chaplain swept his eyes over them to let them know he was watching.

"What you talkin' 'bout?" Linc said out of the side of his mouth.

"Lyndon Johnson signed the Voting Rights Act, my uninformed brother." Hawk was enjoying himself. "Can't keep niggers from the polls no more."

"That's a good step forward," Linc said, pleased with the news.

The chaplain wrapped up the service and the choir broke into an up-beat version of 'Go Tell it on the Mountain.' Parishioners filed out past Linc and Hawk, who were engaged closely in discussion. Chaplain Charles leaned on the pulpit and listened to them, smiling patiently.

"Well, what you think got us there?" Hawk asked. "You 'member Bloody Sunday? They beat up on a lotta peace-marchin' fools that day. Then shit started happenin', brothers quit takin' that bullshit and started fightin' back. We quit marchin' and singin', and we started kickin' and swingin'. Now they pass this here Voting Rights Act." Hawk spread his hands out, palms up. "That's all the power structure understands, Brother Lincoln. Force! Need I say more?"

Linc shook his head slowly. "Things don't happen like that," he said softly. "Not in America."

"Not in America? You serious? You talkin' 'bout the same America chained us up and dragged our black asses over here against our will? Then worked us to death for nothin' more than a handful of corn mush, THAT America?"

"You know," Linc started slowly. "Last couple of days I been reading Plutarch's Lives of the Noble Greeks, and I got to thinking..."

"Thinkin' what?"

"Slavery has existed for thousands of years on this Earth."

"That don't make it right!"

"What I mean is, it was never right, just accepted as the norm. For thousands of years."

"So?"

"So, slavery came to America, just like it did every country in the history of the world, but this time it was different."

"Yeah, more civilized, right, brother?"

"American slavery died," Linc said quietly. He looked over into Hawk's eyes. "In America, the disgrace of slavery was finally recognized for what it was, despicable, contrary to the tenets of mankind, and you know what? A whole lot of northern white boys died to help abolish it." Linc had deliberately avoided the street patois of the urban black man, and Hawk stopped for a moment, studying this black man from Detroit with renewed interest.

Chaplain Charles smiled to himself, gathered up his notes and walked out through the hatch, nodding politely to Hawk and Linc as he passed.

Hawk scoffed at Linc. "Look how white you talkin'. Next, I guess you be chasin' little Eliza 'cross the icy river, huh Tom?"

Linc ignored the insult. "I read that book, what you got against old Uncle Tom?" He turned to look at Hawk.

"He was a house nigger," Hawk replied, bitterness in his voice. "You gonna be a house nigger, Lincoln Jones?" He stared at Linc, who stared back unflinchingly. "See, ol' Tom, he just kept goin' along to get along."

Linc shook his head slowly. "The old man was beaten and died instead of rattin' out his people, ain't that enough?"

"How come he didn't run north like Eliza?"

"Maybe he was tired, Hawk, ever think maybe the old man was

just tired?"

"Or maybe he was just a weak-assed nigger," Hawk was becoming frustrated. "We got a lot of foolish old Toms who don't wanna cause no trouble with the man. Foolish!" He eyed Linc. "Your momma raise you to be foolish?"

Linc glared at him. "You wanna talk or you wanna play the dozens, brother, whatta you wanna do?"

"You ain't never gonna convince me to keep tuggin' on the man's sleeve," Hawk stated. "Ol' Tom, maybe he was broken and beat-up and tired, but I ain't none o'that."

"So you ain't gonna run like Eliza did neither, right?"

Hawk shook his head slowly. "Time for runnin' is over. Time for appeasement is over. The time of the white man keepin' us under his boot is OVER." He stood up and neatly placed his song book on the seat of his chair. "You my brother," he said to Linc without looking at him. "And you need to understand that I'm your brother." He pulled his white hat down on his head and stepped out the hatch. He looked back at Linc briefly. "Summit meeting tonight in the mess decks at nineteen hundred. You welcome to come if y'like." He headed down the passageway.

Linc sat staring at the closed hatch for a long time, then went down to the boat deck and caught a lift to the Knox. Riding across the water to the stranded destroyer, Linc couldn't get Hawk out of his mind. Hawk was smart, almost brilliant in many ways, but he allowed his anger to precede him everywhere he went, and as a result, was looked upon with suspicion and skepticism by the officers and most of the crew of the Prairie. Still, Hawk was right about so many things...

CHAPTER TWENTY NINE

USS Prairie
Monday, August 9, 1965

Day 23

The Navy SEALS, having surveyed the reef once more the day before, made short work of planting the C-3 explosives, and were popping up above the surface in less than 45 minutes. All gave the 'thumbs up' sign and the Prairie's motor whale boat swept in to pick them up.

There was nothing to do but wait. The timer on the C-3 was set for one hour, and sailors from all the gathered ships lined the sides, watching the Knox and waiting for the explosion with a heightened sense of optimism. They were certain that the operation would soon be over. Spirits were high.

Unfortunately, that renewed optimism didn't last long. Lieutenant Jablonsky was right about the C-3 charge.

R.J. and Ricky stood at the aft railing of the signal bridge, waiting for the explosives to detonate on the reef. Chief Benson and Charley had the watch, but R.J. and Ricky hung around in case they were needed. Signal traffic had been heavy for two days, and an extra signalman or two were always welcome. The signal bridge was one of the best vantage points on the ship. From there, a complete three hundred and sixty degree view of Operation Maximum Effort presented itself.

Technically, all ship's personnel could come up to the signal bridge and look around any time they wanted, but tradition dictated that signalmen discourage unwanted guests by making them feel uncomfortable...very uncomfortable. This tradition did not apply to officers, however, so R.J. and Ricky made room for Lieutenant Deavers when he came up the ladder and joined them.

"Morning, Mr. Deavers," R.J. greeted him. "Would you like a cup of coffee?"

"No, thanks, R.J. I just came up to watch the reef blow."

"Oughta be a good show," Ricky interjected. "I never seen an underwater explosion before."

"Me neither," R.J. said.

"Me neither," Deavers said quietly. He stared at the Frank Knox and sighed deeply. He was conflicted. As a US Navy sailor he wanted the Knox to be rescued and salvaged, but he knew that the longer she was stuck on the reef, the more time he had to piece together the puzzle. Once the ship was salvaged, everyone would be scattered to other duty stations. Gone would be his potential witnesses, and perhaps his potential suspects, if he were ever able to identify any.

"Wow!" Ricky pointed at the reef. On both sides of the Frank Knox huge brown-green geysers of sea water and coral reef erupted into the air, a split second before the sound of the booming blast reached the Prairie. The Knox's bow was lifted ten feet into the air by the blast, and came crashing back down on the reef, releasing a horrible wrenching and grinding sound that made everyone within earshot wince.

Chief Billings had moved the salvage crew to the fantail and had them don life vests, just in case. The chief believed there was a good chance the Knox would start to sink once the reef was blown, and he wanted his men to be prepared. The ship's officers remained on the bridge, where they could watch and monitor the operation. So did Lincoln Jones, figuring he would be needed for flashing light signals. J.I. Parker stayed on the fantail, and Chief Billings couldn't help notice how the dental tech stood off to the side, away from the other men. He was pondering dental tech Parker when the C-3 blew, shaking the ship violently and knocking the salvage crew around the deck like scattering bowling pins. The bow came up, crashed down on the reef and the salvage crew was thrown around again. They scrambled around the deck, trying to get a foothold, looking at each other with frightened expressions.

Captain Lamb picked himself up from the deck of the bridge and looked around quickly at Mr. Holliday and Mr. Darby. "Everyone okay?" he asked with nods in return. They stared at each other for a few seconds, seemingly waiting for the other shoe to drop. The ship rocked gently from side to side, and slid down on the reef, sending loud snapping and scraping noises as rivets popped out all over the ship. "Geoff," the captain called to his engineering officer. "Go below and give me a report on damage to any engineering spaces." The engineer hurried down the ladder to the 02 level. "Bill," Captain Lamb turned to his second in command. "Please make sure the members of the crew are okay, and let's find out what kind of hull damage was done." He looked down at the reef. The ship was stuck worse than before, and she seemed to sigh plaintively as the reef, aided by the high surf, slowly tightened its grip on the hull of the Frank Knox. Captain Lamb took a deep breath. *Too much damn C-3,* he thought unhappily. He watched the bow of his ship scraping and settling on the reef. *Just when I thought things couldn't be worse, they get worse.* When Mr. Darby and Mr. Holliday made their preliminary reports to him, the captain was even more unhappy.

Linc had been knocked to the deck and lost his white hat. He picked himself up slowly, testing his arms and legs, making certain nothing was broken. He had been knocked over backwards, and had landed on his rear end. He felt his buttocks carefully. They were sore. *Well,* he thought philosophically, *it coulda been worse. I coulda fell on my head!*

"Damn!" R.J. exclaimed, staring at the Knox. "I think they blew her up!"

Deavers and Ricky were looking through binoculars at the scene. "She's settled back down," Deavers reported. "I don't know if they did any good or not."

The dramatic ripple effect caused by the explosion created a trough around the ship as angry waves were blown out and away in all directions. Those waves were now returning, angrier than before, to fill in the trough. Deavers watched through his binoculars as the foaming water returned irritably to the reef, crashing frantically against the ship. Slowly, as the ocean's energy cycled down, the force of the expanding, then retracting waves gradually lessened. The once-proud destroyer stopped rolling port to starboard, and the violent crunching sounds came to a welcome stop. An eerie silence spread across the entire task force. The men and ships of Task Force 73 stopped and watched, waiting for something to happen.

Deavers watched through his binoculars and sadly shook his head. *Ripple effect,* he thought. *Always that damned ripple effect.*

After a few minutes, a signal light flashed from the Knox, and Charley spun his light around and answered it. Ricky and R.J. read Linc's message.

"Oh, crap!" R.J. exclaimed.

"What?" Deavers asked.

"That ain't good," Ricky said, shaking his head.

"What?" Deavers was becoming impatient.

"The blast blew off most of the hull patches," R.J. explained. "The flooding is worse than before, and they need more water pumps, like right now."

Down on the wing bridge, Admiral Wilson and Captain Marshall huddled together, talking softly. They nodded and followed each other to the admiral's cabin, where they would review damage reports before the salvage ops meeting later in the day. They urgently needed the liquid Styrofoam now, and Admiral Wilson, having relented and agreed to the procedure, was determined to put a rush on it, even if he had to chew some ass to get it done.

Deavers dropped the binoculars and let them hang around his neck. He breathed a sigh of relief for two reasons. The Knox was not coming off the reef today, which gave him more time with the investigation, and the ship was not destroyed by the blast, which he just now realized had been a distinct possibility.

"Well," R.J. said resignedly, "I guess they gotta start over."

Yeah, Deavers thought, *me too.* He turned to R.J. "Thanks for your help with the files, R.J."

"Yes, sir," R.J. replied. "I'm sorry I couldn't find anyone named Tompkins in them."

"Well, we had to start moving in some direction, even if only to find out we were going in the wrong direction. One potential piece to the puzzle has been eliminated, and now we have to have more information." He rubbed his face wearily with one hand. "I'm asking Captain Peterson to send me the autopsy on Andrew Tompkins. How did he die? What evidence, if any, did they have on Green?" He sighed deeply. "Too many missing pieces, R.J., see what I mean?"

"I guess we could use some serendipity, huh sir?"

Deavers smiled warmly. "That would be good," he understated.

"Let me know if I can do anything else, Mr. Deavers."

"I definitely will, lad. You've got the nose of an investigator. Ever think about being one?"

R.J. grinned. Deavers was okay. The man treated him as an equal, and didn't hesitate to ask his opinion. "I think it would be interesting," he said cautiously.

Deavers turned to leave. "Think it over, and I'll be in touch." He slid down the ladder.

CHAPTER THIRTY

Chief Billings

Chief Billings took a quick inventory on the fantail and discovered none of his crew had been injured. The Knox did not slide off the reef and sink, as he had worried, but had become even further grounded. The water was rushing back into the shored-up compartments.

"Guess we gotta start over, huh Chief?" Pea asked sadly.

The chief nodded absently, watching dental tech Parker helping other men to their feet. "We're gonna have to get those pumps back," he said calmly.

It was estimated by the salvage experts that it would take a solid week, maybe ten days to re-patch the hull and begin to get the upper hand on the flooding. The salvage crews knew they would have to work through the days and most of the nights to stem the water flow. They had twice as many pumps as before, with almost every spare pump in the task force employed, and slowly, day by day, they believed they would reduce the water level enough so that they could apply the foam. The foam would push out the remaining water.

SEALS had examined the reef and the hull of the ship, and determined that the explosives did, indeed blow away a significant portion of the coral out-cropping on which the ship was impaled. With that information in hand, Navy engineers were optimistic that they could make the ship more buoyant with the liquid Styrofoam, and she would slip off the reef.

Aboard the Knox, optimism was not that high. After almost a month on the reef, sweating through twenty seven days of short rations, very little fresh water, no showers and no air conditioning, the salvage crew was dejected, and began to express their doubts that the ship would ever be recovered. Chief Billings did all he could to shore up their spirits, assuring them they would be off the reef soon.

"There is a possibility this ship will never sail again," he told them. "It could very well be decommissioned, which means all of us will have our picks of duty stations. You can go anywhere in the world you want. Me? I'm picking shore duty in San Diego."

"You gonna leave the fleet?" Pea asked, astonished at the chief boatswain.

"Hey, I've been at sea longer than you've been playing with your little pud, my boy." The chief laughed and patted Pea on the back good-naturedly. "Now it's time for you young renegades to take over the Navy."

"So you really think they'll decommission her, Chief?" Jimmy Dole asked.

Chief Billings looked around the ship. She had been so beautiful, so powerful, and now she was rusting away, stuck forlornly on this damned reef. "Yeah, Jimmy. This old gal is just about done, I'm afraid."

The chief stayed on the fantail half the night, answering questions from his men, encouraging them, keeping their spirits up. He was proud of this crew. They all could be asleep in soft, warm bunks aboard the Mars, the Iwo Jima, or the Prairie, but they had volunteered to stay, to watch over their ship. Chief Billings figured the least he could do was stay and watch over them. Sitting around on the fantail with them, shooting the breeze, enlisted man to enlisted man, he felt bonded with them, and he knew these sessions would help to forge them into the sailors they aspired to be; sailors who would eventually become the caretakers of the Navy's traditions. They would be charged with perpetuating the ancient ceremonies and the mostly-true myths. They would hold in their hearts the honor and proud history of the United States Navy, and, when their time was over, they would pass the lessons proudly to those who came after. Chief Billings felt a deep pride, sharing these moments with his men. It was a warm, tender feeling, and the chief cherished it.

That same night, Admiral Wilson informed Task Force 73 that there would be another 'maximum effort' the next morning to pull the ship off Pratas Reef. It was the fifteenth such 'maximum effort' operation, none of which had been successful...so far. There was always that hope, that unbounded American optimism that obliged everyone to believe everything will work out fine.

The killer snapped off the light above his bunk and lay back on the pillow, hands behind his neck, staring into the dark and musing about recent events. He was becoming much more visible than he had intended. He had hoped to make his contribution to the salvage efforts in relative anonymity; doing his job quietly and with minimal notice. It would have been easier with three hundred men aboard, but with only seventy, everyone stuck out in one way or another. His conscience convinced him that the senior officers were eying him suspiciously. It was textbook paranoia, he knew, but he was more comfortable around the enlisted men anyway. They seemed concerned about things on a more basic, fundamental level, such as, 'what's for chow?' He could blend in with those men, regardless of the obvious differences, and feel like one of them. He could never feel comfortable in the company of officers. Besides, he didn't feel guilty about killing Green, the rat deserved it. He had, however, taken the life of another human and he felt the weight of that reality. But guilty? Hell no!

He had kept a surreptitious eye on Lieutenant (jg) Deavers. The man was certainly busy. He seemed to have everyone involved in the investigation. Maybe he was just covering all his bases. Maybe he was stumped.

There was no firm evidence of any connection between the killer and C.C. Green. They had met only a couple of months before. He doubted Green knew much about him. But he knew of Green. Oh, yes, he knew all about C.C. Green.

The Knox's volunteer salvage crew went back to work with renewed energy. Bolstered by sailors from the Prairie and the Iwo Jima, they swarmed over and through the ship like frantic ants, pumping out water, shoring up bulkheads, getting the ship ready for the foam. The LCM and motor whale boat traffic increased as scores of relief workers and equipment swarmed toward the Knox. Under the watchful eye of Chief Billings, the men worked tirelessly, somehow knowing they might only have one more chance to save the ship. Every day became another 'Maximum Effort' to prepare the ship for the foam, which many believed would finally free her. Many others thought she was already dead, but they labored away, harboring slight hope. Most of the rest of Task Force 73 settled back into a numbing routine, where one day was indistinguishable from another. Their morale was dipping; their optimism dimmed by the long hours under the oppressive humidity, and all that 'Maximum Effort' shit was getting on their nerves.

Admiral Wilson was sure that morale would improve, at least on the Prairie and the Frank Knox. He had decreed that all Knox sailors be invited to celebrate the Prairie's silver anniversary on board the tender. Also invited were officers from the many ships in Task Force 73. Admiral Wilson congratulated himself on having the foresight to prepare for the anniversary, and he was convinced the party would have an impact on the morale of his officers and men. Unfortunately, he could not have anticipated just how much of an impact the anniversary party would have on the ship and her crew.

August 12, 1965
Day 26

Happy Anniversary

Captain Marshall looked at the message slip, then up at the radioman who had delivered it. "Who else has seen this?" he asked, glancing down at his watch. It was 1600 hours.

RM-3 Ray "Kelly" Gysler squirmed uncomfortably in the captain's presence. "Nobody 'cept the radiomen on duty..." he gulped when Captain Marshall glared at him, "... and me...sir."

The captain frowned and read the message again. "Tell your chief and Mr. Lindsay to report to me at once, and Kelly..." The radioman had started to leave. "Keep this under your hat, understand?"

Gysler understood. "Yes, sir," he answered smartly. He hurried back to the radio shack, eager to share the news with whomever was in residence there.

Operations department head Lieutenant Lindsay, accompanied by Chief Radioman Tom Lyons, reported dutifully to the captain's cabin.

"Perhaps I'm being a bit over-cautious," he began. "But we may have a problem brewing, considering the prevailing social climate."

"Sir?" Lieutenant Lindsay asked. Chief Lyons stood at parade rest, eyes straight ahead, jaw set.

"A race riot has broken out in South Central Los Angeles," the captain explained, handing the message slip to the lieutenant. "In Watts, and it looks pretty bad."

Los Angeles, California
Wednesday, August 11, 1965
7:00 P.M.

Lee

California Highway Patrolman Lee Minikus, astride his motorcycle, cruised down 122nd Street in south central Los Angeles, glad the sun was going down, and happy his shift seemed to be settling into a lazy-hazy-days-of-summer kind of evening. Everything was quiet, but Patrolman Minikus knew, from experience, that the street could change in a heartbeat in this neighborhood, especially when it was hot and humid like tonight. Still, he wasn't really expecting any action until much later in the evening.

"Officer! Hey, Officer!"

Lee slowed until he located the source of the urgent call. A motorist, going the opposite way on 122nd, waved to him. Patrolman Minikus stopped. "Yes, sir?" he asked, hesitantly, looking around in all directions.

"They's a boy drivin' crazy down there!" the motorist exclaimed. He pointed toward Avalon Avenue. "Fool gonna kill somebody, fo shore!"

"I'll look into it, sir," Lee replied, and headed east on 122nd, turning north on Avalon. He spotted the car, two blocks ahead. Patrolman Minikus sped up to intercept what he assumed was a drunk driver. The sun was setting harshly to his left, and he held his hand to his left eye to block the glare. The evening was cooling down, bringing with it a soothing breeze, and the residents of the neighborhood began drifting out of their homes to where it was more comfortable...outside in the street.

Lee Minikus watched the car, an old clunker, weaving in and out of traffic a few blocks ahead. He hit his flashers and his siren, and moved carefully around the traffic to intercept the meandering vehicle. Technically, Lee was now in LAPD territory, but he was in pursuit, and so was within policy. He pulled up behind the car and saw the driver, a young black male, look at him in the rear view mirror. The driver pulled over at 116th Street and killed the engine. Lee called it into dispatch, got off his motorcycle, and approached the driver's side door, ticket book in hand. So far it was just a routine traffic stop.

USS Prairie
Thursday, August 12

Admiral Wilson read the dispatch, took off his glasses, and tossed the message slip on the desk in front of him. "Gentlemen," he began slowly, his eyes scanning over the faces of his staff. "I don't give a hoot's ass about what's going on in Los Angeles, and I don't give a hoot's ass about anything that does not affect this operation directly. What I *do* care about," he scanned their faces again, "is this anniversary party, which I'm convinced will help to bolster the morale of this task force. Do I make myself clear, gentlemen?"

A chorus of "Yes, sirs" answered him.

The admiral looked at the chronometer on his wall and did some mental calculations. "It's going on midnight last night in Los Angeles, and from the reports, the excrement is hitting the proverbial fan in that city. It's up to the officers and chief petty officers to keep a lid on this, so get the word out."

"Yes, sir!" The staff scrambled out the hatch.

The admiral frowned down at the message slip. "Nothing is going to interfere with this celebration," he muttered to himself. "These men deserve some leisure time."

Captain Marshall held a department heads meeting in the wardroom. He, too, warned against any conflict arising from the news of the riot. "The racial tensions being felt back home are also being felt on this ship," he told them, "and on every ship in the fleet. We have had no incidents, and I will not tolerate any." He looked at them sternly. "You department heads get the word to everyone aboard. Any sailor crosses the line on this, insults or starts a fight with another sailor, there will be no liberty when we return to Hong Kong. For anybody."

The department heads left quickly and hurried to pass the word to the crew. Captain Marshall looked out the porthole of the wardroom, satisfied that there would be no racial problems aboard the Prairie.

Los Angeles, California
Wednesday, August 11, 1965
7:10 P.M.

While Lee Minikus approached the vehicle, more people began gathering. Mostly, they were peaceful curiosity seekers, but a few comments from the crowd made Lee a bit uneasy. He knew how quickly things could change when a crowd gathered, especially on these streets, where suspicion and distrust of the police were a way of life. The damp air hung hot and heavy in the early evening. *Damn,* he thought, *you can smell the heat!*

Marquette Frye, the twenty-one-year old driver of the car, kept his hands on the steering wheel and his passenger and stepbrother Ronald Price sat staring straight ahead. *Good,* Lee thought to himself. *They know the drill and they are cooperating.* He couldn't miss the heavy smell of alcohol coming from the car.

Marquette Frye politely handed over his driver's license and Lee attached it to his ticket book. "The reason I stopped you, sir," he said calmly, "is because you were weaving in and out of traffic back there. Have you been drinking?"

Marquette smiled back at him, unfocused.

"Please step out of the car, both of you."

Lee administered the standard sobriety test, informed Marquette he had failed it and would be placed under arrest. Marquette nodded slowly and turned around, his hands behind his back. *He's been through this before,* Lee thought. He handcuffed Marquette and had him sit on the curb while he searched the car for contraband. Ronald sat down on the curb next to Marquette and waited patiently.

"Let that boy go!" A woman in the crowd hollered. "He ain't done nothin'!" The crowd murmured its agreement and began moving around the scene. Soon, Lee realized he was surrounded by about two hundred people, all becoming restless.

Finished with the car, Lee called his partner, patrolman Bob Lewis, who hurried toward the scene. Lee then called for a patrol car to take Marquette to the station, and a tow truck to retrieve his car. Ronald Price objected to having the car towed away.

"Lemme drive it home, officer," he pleaded. "Our momma's house is only a coupla blocks away."

Lee turned him down, pointing out that Ronald had also been drinking. Ronald asked permission to go get his mother so she could claim the car, and before Lee could respond, Ronald sprinted off toward his mother's house. *Maybe having their mother there would be a good thing,* Lee reasoned. *Maybe she can help diffuse this situation.* The crowd had grown to almost four hundred people, and their mood was becoming surly. Lee looked around, hoping to spot his partner and the cruiser he had called for minutes earlier.

Rena Price, mother of Ronald Price and Marquette Frye, arrived on the scene at about the same time the patrol cruiser pulled up. Bob Lewis arrived on his motorcycle a few moments later. Rena Price stalked up to Marquette and slapped him.

"I tol' you 'bout that drinkin!" she yelled at him. "You don' never listen to me, boy!"

Up to that point, Marquette Frye had been calm and cooperative, but the stinging rebuke his mother had dealt him in front of all those people embarrassed him. The humiliation was clear on his face, and the snickering of the crowd did not make him feel any better. Marquette lost it. He jumped up and backed away from Lee Minikus, toward the crowd.

"I ain't goin' to jail," he yelled. "Y'all gonna have to kill me before I go to jail!"

Lee quickly followed and subdued the struggling Marquette just as two LAPD cruisers and three more CHP cars arrived to assist. Ronald became belligerent, took a swing at Lee Minikus, and Bob Lewis placed him under arrest, handcuffing his hands behind his back. This infuriated Rena and she jumped on Officer Lewis' back, tearing his shirt. Another patrolman placed Rena under arrest, and the crowd began yelling and throwing things.

More police cars arrived as the crowd swelled to almost eight hundred people and continued to grow. Rena, Marquette and Ronald were put into the back seat of a patrol car and headed toward the station, followed by Lee Minikus and Bob Lewis on their motorcycles. Several police cars were pelted with rocks, glass and chunks of concrete as they retreated from the scene. Almost a thousand people were massing in the street, and the melee, started by an innocuous and routine traffic stop, quickly blossomed into a full scale riot that would last for six terrifying days.

Aboard the Prairie
Thursday, August 12, 1965

The celebration began peacefully enough. Steaks were grilled, soft drinks were distributed, and sailors of all departments sat on the decks together, celebrating the ship's anniversary, enjoying the food, the camaraderie and the cool calm of the evening. The trouble in Watts was far away, and most of the men couldn't care less about Los Angeles and its problems. The Knox sailors mingled easily with the Prairie crew, and very little ribbing or hazing of the Knox men took place.

After dinner, their bellies full, the happy crew moved to the mess decks for the much anticipated bingo game. They were in unusually good cheer, but when they arrived in the mess decks, the atmosphere changed quickly. Hawkins Wilson was very vocal, standing on a table with black sailors circling him, egging him on. Most of the black crewmen gravitated to one side of the mess decks, whites gathered on the opposite side. Some words were exchanged, insults thrown back and forth, and the tension began to mount.

Linc sat at a table with R.J., Pea and Ricky, slowly shaking his head at the black sailors. Hawk spotted him and called out, "Hey, there's my uncle!" The other blacks turned and looked toward Linc. Hawk showed an exaggerated grin and waved his arm. "Hey, Tom!" he called to Linc, "how ya doin,' Uncle?"

Pea looked at Linc quizzically. His friend was clearly embarrassed, angry, or maybe both. "What's he mean, Linc?"

"He's insulting me," Linc said between his teeth. "That's what he mean." Linc stood and moved to the front, where he could glare directly at Hawk. A few other blacks who were sitting with whites got up and stood behind Linc. R.J., Ricky and Pea joined them. Linc looked at the group gathering behind him and smiled softly.

"You on the wrong side of the aisle, m'man," Hawk said, loudly enough for everyone to hear. "And you got a coupla more Toms with you."

"Fuck you Hawk," came a deep, gruff voice. It came from one of the blacks behind Linc. Chopper Adams pushed his way to the front and sneered at Hawk, who instinctively took a step back. Chopper was an impressive man, built like a bank safe. He had a reputation as a very nice guy, but one who would put up with zero bullshit.

"Well, Chopper, my brother," Hawk said, his eyebrows raised in mock surprise. "It would appear that you on the wrong side of the aisle, also."

"I'm up in here to play bingo, Hawk, what 'bout you?" The deep, bass voice resonated through the mess decks. "I ain't heard of no Summit meeting scheduled. So tell me," he leaned forward. Hawk pulled back, almost imperceptibly this time. "What are you doin' here?"

"Celebratin,'" Hawk replied with a proud grin.

"Celebrating what?" Linc stood next to Chopper. "The riot in L.A.?" Linc's stare swept over the blacks. "That ain't the way to get things done, brothers."

"RIOT?" Hawk yelled, playing to the blacks. "That ain't no riot, brother! A coupla cops get rocks thrown at 'em, some fires are set, black folks millin' 'round in the street? Sheeeit, that ain't no riot, baby, that's more like a Saturday night ghetto fish fry!" Many of the blacks began applauding. "A riot is when niggers get to shoot back and all those honky-owned businesses are burned to the mudda-fuckin' ground! That's a riot, baby!"

The blacks were laughing and slapping each other on the backs. Many encouraged Hawk with comments like, "you tell it, brother!" "Right on the mark, baby!" "Testify, brother, testify!"

Hawkins held a fist in the air and began chanting, very slowly, in a whisper, "Burn baby, burn! Burn, baby, burn!" His voice became a little louder with each chant, and soon it was picked up by the rest of the blacks behind him.

"BURN, BABY, BURN!
BURN, BABY, BURN!
BURN, BABY BURN!"

Some bingo cards came sailing through the air from the white sailors and rained down on the blacks. The two groups surged toward each other. A few punches were thrown, but mostly the sailors grabbed hold of each other and hit the deck, the way they learned to survive bar fights in foreign ports. The name calling and heckling continued until someone yelled, "Attention on deck!"

Chief Boatswain's Mate and Master-at-Arms Charles O'Malley stepped into the mess-decks and took in the scene, frowning angrily. Two more masters-at-arms, Marine lance corporals, stood behind him, billy clubs hanging from scabbards on their duty belts. The blacks were chanting louder and louder and the whites were answering with cat-calls and insults. Chief O'Malley stared at the black group, and the men began to quiet down and back away. Hawk sat down on the table, his arms folded, glaring back at the chief.

"You people serving on this ship?" Chief O'Malley asked. The chief stood with his feet apart and his hands on his hips. "Reason I ask is because you all are sitting over here, away from the rest of the crew."

"That's okay with us, Chief," a voice called out from the white sailors. "They'd probably just try to burn the place down, anyway!" Snickering laughter rippled through the white group, but died off when the chief's glare was directed at them. The two groups began moving slowly toward one another again. Chief O'Malley reached out his hand and one of the Marines put a billy club in it. The chief strode confidently between the two groups, swinging the billy club. "First one of you dick-heads says another word, black or white, I'm gonna crack his skull." He gave them one more menacing glare. "Now, everybody back in his seat." The two groups hesitated. "NOW!"

Once the situation had been calmed down, and the bingo cards redistributed, the chief made an announcement. "The admiral is coming down here to call the first bingo game. He is very proud of this ship and this crew, because you...WE have performed in an exemplary manner throughout this operation." He looked around the mess decks and into the eyes of every man there. "When the admiral gets here, he's gonna see a united crew, a crew who works together and plays together. Now, everyone get up off your asses. This is what we're gonna do."

Admiral Wilson was pleased with the way the dinner had gone. The officers hung around the wardroom after the ceremony and congratulated him, toasted him and congratulated him again. The admiral, true to his promise, then headed to the mess decks to call the first bingo game, kicking off the evening's festivities. He marched down ladders and across the decks happily, a man at peace, a contented man. When he reached the mess decks and saw what awaited him there, he could only wonder at how this crew managed to work so well together.

The admiral strode into the mess decks with Captain Marshall and a few other officers in his wake. He looked around the tables and smiled. The blacks and whites were sitting together, alternating black, white, black, white, quietly awaiting the start of the bingo game. As the admiral took the podium and began rolling the bingo basket full of numbered balls, he looked out again at the mixed faces and smiled to himself. *Almost like someone staged them*, he thought. *It's great to see a crew that is as together as this one is.* Still smiling, he reached into the basket and extracted a numbered ball.

"All right, men," he called out. "Here's your first number: Under the G...14!"

The truce lasted until the bingo game broke up and the sailors were filing out of the mess decks. R.J. and his friends made their way to the bunting locker to listen to some jazz and discuss the evening's events. The admiral had returned to officer country, and Hawk and a few other blacks hung around the 03 level, taunting the white sailors as they came out on deck.

"BURN, BABY, BURN!
BURN, BABY, BURN!"

"Hey Hawk!" a white sailor called. Hawkins turned to look at him. The sailor grabbed his crotch and challenged, "Burn this, Rochester!"

Hawk stepped forward and looked up at the taller sailor. The blacks gathered behind him, and the white group gathered behind the tall sailor. The white sailor stared down into Hawk's eyes, and Hawk glared back up at him. "You gotta problem, Ofay?"

"You're the problem, Sambo. You and all your BROTHERS." He spat out the last word. "Hell, all y'all might well be brothers, none of y'all knows who your daddy was."

The two groups surged toward each other, throwing punches and cursing. There were about twenty men involved, and several punches were landed before Chief O'Malley and his Marines arrived and broke it up. They used their billy clubs to push the combatants away from each other.

Chief O'Malley began taking down the names of those involved. There were twelve whites and eight blacks. No one was injured beyond a few bruises and bloodied lips.

"You people know I'm gonna have to report this to the captain," the chief advised them, holding up the list of names. "He ain't gonna be too happy about this."

"Well, hell," Hawk replied. 'We ain't none too happy about some shit, neither."

"Tell 'im, bro!"

"Lay it out, Hawk!"

Hawk took comfort and drew courage from the men backing him up. He grinned at them and looked at Chief O'Malley. "You can also tell the captain that I demand an audience with him." He grinned again at his supporters. "To present a list of grievances from the Black Summit on behalf of all the brothers serving aboard this ship."

Chief O'Malley looked at Hawk as if he had just asked to marry his daughter. He stared at him for a moment, and then nodded. "I'll be sure and tell him that, Wilson. Meantime, you guys head aft, and you guys," he nodded to the whites and jerked his thumb in the direction of the forecastle. "Head forward."

The two groups drifted away from each other slowly, glancing back over their shoulders. O'Malley and his two Marines leaned on the railing and lit cigarettes. The moon was huge and glowing in the night sky, sending brilliant moonlight splashing over Pratas Reef.

"Well, it figures. It's a full moon, boys," the chief observed, looking up at the bright orb. "People do act weird during a full moon."

"You gonna turn that list in to the captain?" one of the Marines asked.

"Yep, and I'm gonna tell him about Hawkins Wilson's demand for an audience." The chief chuckled to himself. "Can't wait to see the skipper's face when I tell him that."

Chief O'Malley followed the chain of command. He reported the incident and turned the list of names into his department head, who called the executive officer. The exec spoke to the captain and the captain summoned O'Malley, his department head and the exec to his cabin. The captain learned of the incident only an hour after it happened. The word spread through the crew in less than half that time.

"What you guys wanna hear?" Linc stood by the record player, going through some albums.

"Let's hear some Jimmy Smith," Ricky replied, settling in a corner with Peggy Sue. "Play that 'Slaughter on Tenth Avenue'. I dig that one."

Linc put the needle in the groove and the sweet sounds of Jimmy Smith's jazz organ filled the air with 'Slaughter on Tenth Avenue'. He straddled a stool and leaned against the counter, looking around at his friends. R.J. was fiddling around with the sewing machine, and Pea was shuffling and reshuffling the pinochle cards.

No one said anything for a few minutes, and then Linc broke the silence. "That shit in the mess decks was unnecessary."

Pea and R.J. shared a look.

Ricky looked up from Peggy Sue. "I understand what Hawk is talkin' 'bout," he said softly. "Black folks where I come from ain't made much progress. Many still livin' like they did a hunnerd years ago." He looked pensive for a moment, then added, "Lots of white folks, too."

"Change is coming," Linc went on. "Like a runaway freight train, it's comin'. But lots of folks, black and white, ain't happy with change."

"Lots of white folks don' want things to change," Pea observed.

"And lots of black folks ain't happy with how long it's taking to change," Linc said. He shook his head sadly. "If men like Hawkins Wilson would channel their strong feelings toward building rather than tearing down, black people would see that change a lot faster." He pulled himself up on the counter and sighed deeply. "It's been eighteen years since Jackie Robinson broke the color line in baseball. He put up with a whole lot of terrible shit, first from some of his teammates, then by opposing teams whose pitchers threw at him, ballplayers who spiked him every time they slid into second base, and fans in every city who yelled 'nigger' and threw garbage at him. Lots of times he couldn't eat in the same restaurants as his teammates or stay in the same hotel, but he turned it around, little by little. He was eventually accepted by his teammates, his opponents, and now he's respected by all of baseball. He's a legend, and you wanna know how he did it?"

"By being non-violent?" R.J. asked. "Just takin' all that shit? I dunno if I could do that."

"By being an example," Linc replied. "By competing at a high level, and EARNING the respect he got. He never threatened nobody; he never called for riots or black power. He spoke very softly, and he was a better ballplayer than ninety percent of the white players. Soon they came to realize that. See, this is America. You want proper respect from the white establishment, you compete for it, and you become the best you can be. Respect then naturally follow." The song ended and the record played out. Linc put the Jimmy Smith album back in its jacket and replaced it on the turntable with the Cannonball Adderly quintet. Linc sat back on the counter as the mellow sounds of the Cannonball's sax swept through the compartment. "Lemme tell you a story," Linc went on. "I grew up in Detroit, in a black neighborhood. Our city officials pretty much ignored us, swept us under the rug so to speak, except during election time. The aldermen would come into the neighborhood and distribute turkeys just before election day, and with those turkeys we got a dose of how much these people were doing for us, how they were representing our needs, and how they depended on our people's votes." Linc shook his head sadly. "Most black folks were so grateful for the turkeys they wanted to believe their needs were being championed by these white politicians, so they voted their way. What they didn't want was for the turkeys to stop coming. After election day, those fat cats would disappear for another year or two. They got their votes, and we got a bunch of empty promises and a pile of turkey bones. That happened every election, for years and years, and black folks still didn't get it. They always remembered those turkeys, though."

"So, maybe Hawk is starting to make sense with his yellin' and bitchin'?" Pea asked.

"That's not my point." Linc hopped down from the counter and began pacing. "See, if we don't compete for our place in this country, we gonna end up with a lot of turkey bones and not much else."

"I don't understand what you mean, Linc," R.J. said softly. "Aren't you just arguing Hawk's point?"

"It's not his point I disagree with," Linc said gently. "It's his idea of how to prove it."

R.J. nodded slowly. "But you agree with him when he says blacks are still treated like slaves?"

Linc nodded. "President Johnson," he said firmly, "is a white Texan who been in politics his whole life. I bet he handed out a whole lot of turkeys to black folks in Texas. Now, he's president. He signed the Civil Rights Act last year and the Voting Rights Act this year. His so-called 'War on Poverty' has put millions of black folks on welfare. As far as I'm concerned, it's just the old turkey hand-out on a bigger scale. He's showin' everybody how to keep the coons in line. Remember he a white Texan. Black folks are in danger of lovin' those turkeys more than we love ourselves."

"At least folks are gettin' a little help," Pea offered.

"Yeah," Linc replied. "A little help. We gonna get used to that check every month, and every month we don't do anything to better ourselves, to compete for the dream, we gonna get lazier, more complacent, and in a few years, we ain't gonna wanna do nothin' for it." Linc stopped pacing and looked around at his friends. They were listening intently. "That's a whole different kind of racism right there," he explained. "Keepin' people down by convincing them they can't do anything for themselves.

"There are lots of strong black people who made a difference by competing successfully in this country. We need to emulate them. If we let the white government come around and hand out turkeys just to keep us quiet..." He let the thought drift off. "Hawkins Wilson and guys like him are creating resentment, and they don't care. We need to be less militant and more educated. We need to yell less and work more, otherwise we might as well just keep linin' up for those government turkeys."

R.J. stood and started exaggerated applauding. He was soon joined by the others. "Gentlemen, I give you the next senator from the state of Michigan, the honorable Lincoln Jones!" They all applauded again. Linc looked a little embarrassed and grinned sheepishly.

"You need to run for office, Linc," Pea encouraged. "You already a great speaker, probably 'cause you got that big mouth." He giggled and ducked as Linc pretended to throw a record album at him.

"Don't think I haven't thought about it," Linc said. "From WITHIN the establishment is where we gonna make the most progress. We gotta get good at handing out those turkeys, too." He sighed and added, "And people like Hawkins Wilson will mess that up for us."

The bunting locker grew silent. The men sat and listened to the music, each alone in his thoughts. Linc made a lot of sense to them. He could see the understanding creeping onto their faces, as they looked around at each other and nodded. When Charlie came down from the bridge to remind R.J. and Ricky of their watch, he startled the men in the locker by throwing the hatch open loudly and stepping in noisily.

"Hey, whatchoo doin' in here," he asked, eyebrows up. "Polishing each other's apples?" Charlie stepped in and pulled the hatch closed behind him. He looked around at the other sailors and asked, "You guys hear about the fight on the 03 level?"

"I'm going to hold on to this list of names," Captain Marshall explained calmly to the exec and Chief O'Malley. "I'm going to consider this an isolated incident brought on by the strong feelings over the disturbance in L.A., but gentlemen," he looked sternly at the other two. "If anything like this happens again, I'll bust every man involved, and I'll bust them two pay grades."

"Hawkins Wilson wants a meeting with you, sir," the chief said hesitantly.

The captain looked at Chief O'Malley and the executive officer with an expression of utter incredulity. "He wants a what?"

"He wants a meeting with you to discuss black sailors' grievances," the chief said, struggling to maintain a straight face. It wasn't easy. "That's what he told me, sir."

Captain Marshall stared at the chief for a few moments. "Please tell E-4 Hawkins Wilson that if he would like to meet me at captain's mast and become E-*2* Hawkins Wilson, I will be happy to oblige him." The captain stood, indicating the meeting was over. "And inform E-4 Hawkins Wilson that this is a US Navy warship. It's not a democracy and was never intended to be."

The chief and exec grinned at each other and left the captain's cabin.

"Boy," the chief said, "am I looking forward to this conversation."

The exec laughed. "Keep a handle on the situation, Chief."

"Yes sir."

When Hawk was advised of the captain's response, he dropped the demand for a meeting and never brought it up again.

Los Angeles, California
Thursday, August 12, 1965

An eerie silence hung over South Central Los Angeles. The anger of the evening before was still there, but seethed under the surface.

Many of the rioters of Wednesday night were still asleep, and many of them were waiting eagerly for the night, when the weather would cool down and the riot would heat up. So it was quiet. City officials and black leaders worked together to quell the violence and soothe the angry feelings of their citizens. They held a public meeting, urged calm, and truly believed the riot would not reignite. After all, it was so quiet that hot, humid day.

The day wore down, and hopes were high, but a crowd of over a thousand blacks was gathering at 116th and Avalon to reenact the events of Wednesday night. As soon as the sun went down, the rioters exploded. They turned over cars and set them on fire, they set fire to businesses and shot at the firemen who tried to put the fires out. They pelted police cars with rocks and bottles, and attacked officers openly. Gradually, the police gained control, and the rioters were pushed back. It was almost 5 A.M. before the quiet returned. Many public figures sighed deeply and thanked God for ending the riot. The rioters had left the scene, had gone back to their homes, hopefully for good.

Most of the police, however, knew they were just resting up for the weekend.

USS Prairie
Saturday, August 14, 1965

Saturday dawned hopeful for Task Force 73. The foam would arrive the next day, and the SEALS would pump it into the keel of the Knox on Monday. If everything went right, and there was no reason to expect it would because nothing so far had gone entirely right, the ship's buoyancy should improve to the point where the tugs could pull her off. As a back up measure, Admiral Wilson advised the USS Cogswell to prepare to steam past the reef at a very high speed. The ensuing rooster-tail effect would send a good-sized wave over the reef, hopefully lifting the Knox up just enough to free her.

The news from the States announced prematurely that the Los Angeles civil disturbance, as it was being referred to, was over. On the Prairie, black/white tensions cooled a bit, although Hawk and his Black Summit kept the pot stirred, albeit with more restraint. Hawk had come to the realization that social protest would not be tolerated in the Navy, and, not wanting to be busted to E-2, he chose to limit his rhetoric, displaying it only at Summit meetings, among his friends. It was generally quiet and peaceful, but almost everyone aboard the ship, and certainly everyone in South Central Los Angeles felt the underlying tension, like a volcano building up, seeking an avenue through which to explode. As it turned out, that avenue was Central Avenue in Watts.

Los Angeles, California
Friday, August 13, 1965

By Friday morning, everyone began to realize the riot was gaining new momentum, and that night, Friday in Los Angeles, would be the worst night so far. The first black man was shot dead that night, a fireman was crushed by a falling wall, and a sheriff's deputy was accidentally killed by another officer's shotgun which went off in a struggle with rioters. By midnight, the riot raged to envelop neighboring communities. Thousands of angry blacks filled the streets, throwing rocks, bottles and chunks of cement. Businesses were set on fire, cars overturned, people beaten. The fire department refused to enter certain areas, and as a result many buildings and businesses were burned to the ground.

Pawn shops and sporting goods stores were raided for guns and ammunition, and a constant barrage of gunfire filled the night air. Lieutenant Governor Anderson, in Governor Pat Brown's absence, decided to call in the National Guard. By 3 A.M. Saturday, the streets were being swept by over three thousand National Guardsmen.

The looting and fires continued on Saturday, but the presence of the Guard, its numbers increasing constantly, began to bring things under some semblance of control. Lieutenant Governor Anderson declared a curfew to begin Saturday night at 8 P.M. Any unauthorized person on the streets after that time would be arrested. Those who resisted would be shot by the National Guard. The Guard set up roadblocks around the area and soon established their authority. One sign on Central Avenue said simply, 'Turn Left or Get Shot.' The California National Guard was not in a negotiating mood.

USS Prairie
Sunday, August 15, 1965

Chaplain Charles stood at the lectern in front of the altar and waited for the sailors, predominantly black, to file in and find their seats. The mood was subdued because of the news that the L.A. riot had re-ignited, and some deaths had occurred. Even Hawk, usually quite vocal at these services, was unusually silent. Linc sat toward the back, wanting to avoid Hawk and the members of the Summit. The Prairie's small choir stood in the rear silently, waiting for the chaplain to begin the service.

The chaplain signaled for the hatch to be closed, and looked around at his charges, a deep frown etched on his face. "People are dying in Los Angeles," he said, his strong voice echoing though the compartment. "Black people, white people, brown people, death don't pay color any mind." His eyes swept the room and came to rest on Hawk. "No matter how much importance WE put on it, Old Man Death, he don't pay it any mind." He paused and took a deep breath, letting it out very slowly before he continued. "Those of you who think civil disobedience, civil disturbance, violence and anger are the way to gaining civil rights, be advised. Death don't care who you are or what side of the issue you on. He don't care if you right or you wrong, if you black or you white, if you man or woman, he just reaches down and SNATCHES you up!" He slammed his hand hard on the lectern and the men jumped, startled out of their thoughts. "And then...THEN he drops you at the feet of GOD!" Chaplain Charles stepped around the lectern, his Bible in one hand while he pointed with the other at his audience, glaring angrily down at them.

"You gonna look up into God's face," he said in a low voice. "And you gonna say, 'God, please let me into Heaven.' And God's gonna ask, 'What good have you done in your life?'" He dropped his hands to his side. "What're you gonna say then? Are you gonna say, 'I lived during the great civil rights era, Lord, and I done nothin' to help advance the cause of civil rights, 'cept I burned some cars and some buildings and threw some rocks at white policemen, and oh, yes, I almost forgot...some of my brothers got killed.'" The chaplain shook his head slowly. "What do you think God is going to say to you then? Do you think God will forgive you? Well, he probably will, but he ain't gonna invite you inside."

Many of the men laughed in spite of themselves, some at themselves. Hawk sat stoically in the front row, meeting Chaplain Charles' glare with a face devoid of any expression. He had no doubt the chaplain's remarks were directed at him and his group.

"We, and I mean all of us, black and white, need to pause and think this over. Which is the best way to go? Do we resort to violence and terror to gain our rights, do we segregate ourselves from the rest of society and hope they'll leave us alone? Or do we find a way to work together, as we do on this ship?" He smiled paternally and the men took it as a sign to relax.

"We proved that we are an outstanding team when we work together." He put his hands together and interlaced his fingers. "Together we are going to get the USS Frank Knox free of that reef. Look at the scale of this operation. Look at the many ships in Task

Force 73. Look at what we've done, thousands of men, black, white, brown, heck, we probably got some blue ones!" More laughter. Chaplain Charles walked among the men, holding his interlaced hands up for them to see. "Just look at what we have done...together. In a few more days, with God's help, the Knox will be free, and this task force, this amazing, incredible, hard-working task force, will break up and all these ships will go their own way." He stopped and smiled paternally again at the men. "In thirty years, when you're trying to find a way to entertain your grandbabies," the men laughed nervously, "you can tell them this story, the story of Pratas Reef, the one about men from different ships, different races, different religions, all coming together to accomplish an almost impossible task. You will take pride in telling the story, I promise you. And I also promise you this: when you tell the story of Pratas Reef you will naturally think of the Watts riots, and the struggle for civil rights. You must tell your grandbabies that story, too."

Chaplain Charles stood at the hatch and shook the hand of every man as he left the services, except for Lincoln Jones, who managed to slip out before the chaplain could reach him. Hawk hung back, making certain he was the last to leave.

"I appreciated your sermon, Preacher," he said, shaking the offered hand.

"But...?" The chaplain squeezed Hawk's hand warmly, and smiled softly. "See, always a but. Even when you don't say it, you say it."

"No, sir, no buts this time." Hawk looked up into the chaplain's eyes. "I agree, there is no reason for folks to die, but Preacher, we can't let up on 'em, you understand what I mean, don't you?"

"I understand you're young and impatient," the chaplain said soothingly. He put a hand on Hawk's shoulder and gave it an affectionate squeeze. "From the little acorn, the mighty oak tree grows, but it takes a long time, my son. It takes a long time because even though the little acorn can't know how great the oak tree is gonna be, it is gonna BE." He smiled his paternal smile and patted Hawk's shoulder. "The best of life takes a long time, but is always worth it. Remember what Thomas Paine said, 'What we obtain too cheap, we esteem too lightly.'"

"Thomas Paine?" Hawk asked. "Who's he?"

"He was a revolutionary, full of pee and vinegar, much like you. He lived in another time of dramatic social change. Look him up, you'll appreciate his writings."

"I will, Preacher, but we ain't just gonna sit back and be patient."

The chaplain chuckled, a deep rumbling sound. "You have the

right to free speech, son, but be careful what you say. Sometimes the most effective of your constitutional rights is the one you don't exercise."

"Keep it clean, huh?" Hawk smiled up at Chaplain Charles. He loved and respected the man, as did the entire crew of the Prairie.

"Just keep it non-violent, son." The chaplain got a twinkle in his eye. "You can holler and yell, so long as you're marching for peace." His expression grew serious, and his face took on an older, wearier appearance. "The promised land is within our reach," he said softly, his brow furrowed. "We will find it, I know we will. I believe in this country and everything it stands for. Boy, we are so lucky to live in America at this time in history, because of all the good things this country stands for, right now, for black people America stands for opportunity."

Hawk smiled warmly. "Thank you again, preacher."

"Be militant, young Hawkins, but don't be violent."

When Chaplain Charles left the library, Hawk looked through the bookshelves until he found a volume of Thomas Paine's essays, 'The Crisis.' The book described Thomas Paine as a firebrand, an American revolutionary, a patriot who stirred the budding nation with his controversial writings. Hawk opened the book to an essay dated December 23, 1776 and began reading:

> *"These are the times that try men's souls. The summer soldier and the sunshine patriot will, in this crisis, shrink from the service of their country; but he that stands by it now deserves the love and thanks of man and woman. Tyranny, like hell, is not easily conquered; yet we have this consolation with us, that the harder the conflict, the more glorious the triumph. What we obtain too cheap, we esteem too lightly: It is dearness only that gives every thing its value..."*

Hawk looked up from the book, a curious expression on his face. He was alone in the library. He tucked the volume under his arm and headed aft to his compartment. He wanted to read more of this Thomas Paine.

Later that evening, at the heavily attended Black Summit meeting, Hawk spoke more quietly and reservedly than usual. Clearly, the Los Angeles deaths were heavy on his mind. He had not thought of people dying except in the most abstract of terms. He had supported the riot, hell, even encouraged it, but that was before black people were killed for speaking out, for fighting back. *Maybe the Preacher and Linc are right,* he thought to himself. *Maybe all we doin' is gettin' our own hurt and killed.*

Hawk had never had the opportunity to be militant growing up in central Mississippi. During the fifties in the South, black folks kept their mouths shut except around other black folks. They would complain about their lives and threaten to take action among themselves, but would never vocalize those feelings in the presence of white people, whom they were raised to accept were somehow superior to blacks. By the time he was old enough to read, Hawk realized that this cultural attitude was just part of the tragic residue that was the institution of slavery. For slavery *was* an institution, a very large, widespread institution, and blacks who grew up under its yoke had became institutionalized, and often inured to its pain. They lived only to exist another day and all their thoughts and energy had to be concentrated upon that single goal. It was no wonder they lost sight of the future. When there is no hope, there is no future.

In the mess decks, standing in front of dozens of blacks, staring into the faces of his brothers, Hawk realized the most important thing any of them could do was pass on the concept of hope. Everything sprang from hope.

"There is a time for anger," he began slowly. "And there is time for grief. Now is the time for grief. We grieve for the people who died in Los Angeles, and we are sorry for the loss. But that grief must not fuel our anger, because this is not the time for anger." He looked down at the deck for a few moments, then raised his eyes to meet those of the men. "This is the time for reflection, my brothers." Most of the men looked around at each other, confused. "Let's take a step back, like the preacher said, and let things cool down." He grinned at their expressions. "I know, you thought I'd be yellin' and screamin.' Well, more of that's comin', I promise you that!" He grinned again at their applause. "The struggle for our civil rights is going to be difficult, brothers, very difficult. But those rights are dear to us, therefore valuable to us. We will gain our rights through our struggle, and the struggle must be difficult, must be hard on us, otherwise we will not appreciate the victory. The harder the conflict, the more glorious the triumph. What we obtain too cheap, we esteem too lightly." Heads were bobbing up and down in agreement. "When black folks die, we grieve, but these deaths, in this current conflict, will mark a monument in history, my brothers. Future generations will look back on this time in history and say, 'That's when they turned the corner in the struggle for equality!'"

Hawk smiled benevolently. "Keep the faith, brothers. I'll advise you about the next meeting." He left the mess decks, ignoring the curious looks of his followers.

Later that afternoon, the liquid Styrofoam was delivered to Task Force 73. The next morning the SEALS would go down and inject it into the hull of the Frank Knox. Allowing seven full days for it to dry and work its magic, the tugs should be able to pull her off Pratas Reef on Tuesday, August 24th at high tide.

CHAPTER THIRTY ONE

Pratas Reef
Monday, August 16, 1965
Day 30 on the Reef

An LCM ferried the SEALS and their equipment to Frank Knox. The liquid Styrofoam was in containers that looked too small to hold all the foam they would need, but once it was released and fully expanded, it would be enough.

The SEALS took the high-pressure hoses down into the hull of the Knox. The crew on the LCM fed out the hose steadily, and on a signal from the SEALS, started up the high-pressure pumps. The hoses twitched and snaked around the deck as the liquid Styrofoam was pumped through them. The task force watched intently, waiting for the SEALS to return to the surface. They were doing a dangerous and hazardous job under the keel of the Knox. One little miscalculation and the ship could shift or a hose could get caught, and one or more Navy SEALS could be trapped.

Under water, everything was calm and peaceful. The SEALS communicated with one another through hand signals as they poked and snaked the hoses into the flooded compartments, one by one, and shot the foam in, forcing the water out. It was a long and tiring process, but their training took over and the SEALS concentrated professionally on the job, performing their task with high energy and efficiency.

The admiral and his staff stood on the wing bridge of the Prairie and watched the surface of the water on Pratas Reef with nervous anticipation. It seemed to be taking a very long time. The admiral glanced down at his watch, looked through his binoculars at the reef, and back down at his watch. Just as he was beginning to think something was wrong, the SEALS' heads popped through the surface, one by one, until all six were treading aqua water just aft of the Frank Knox. An audible sigh of relief could be heard throughout the task force.

"Well, the foam's in, gentlemen," Admiral Wilson declared. "Nothing to do now but wait."

•

The news from Los Angeles was that the National Guard had restored peace to the embattled south central neighborhoods. The damage had been significant, and the death toll kept rising, creating an atmosphere of sadness and introspection among the crews of Task Force 73, particularly on the Prairie. A dose of reality, in the form of dead black people in Los Angeles, hit the black crewmen hard. The whites felt it, too, but the riot had taken place in black neighborhoods, and ultimately, black people would suffer the most because of it. Linc was more than happy to point this out to Hawk at dinner that Monday evening. Hawk was taking his tray to the scullery when he encountered Linc coming through the chow line. They stopped and stared at each other for a moment, then Hawk broke the awkward silence.

"Lincoln Jones, my brother," he said, offering his hand. "Where you been? I ain't seen you around much lately."

Linc took the offered hand, and noticed a book under Hawk's arm. "Been busy on the Knox," he answered. He nodded toward the book. "What you reading?"

Hawk ignored him. "Things are quiet in L.A., my brother."

"You sound like you're happy to hear that."

"Yeah, I'm happy to hear it. Don't like brothers gettin' killed."

"But that's just what you've been advocating, my brother," Linc spat out. "Now you got what you wanted. All them white-owned businesses are burnt to the ground, and mama and grandma got to ride a city bus for hours just to go grocery shoppin'." Linc shook his head slowly. "Don't you see, it ain't the way to go."

"Maybe," Hawk mused. "But, now you gonna see some action in Los Angeles, my brother. You gonna see all kinds of money come pourin' in there, trying to rush to rebuild, all them white people scramblin' around, tryin' to show who the most liberal." Hawk smiled, but his smile was wan and sad. "But, no, I don't want any brothers to die." He stared up at Linc with a curious expression on his face, and Linc felt something pass between them. "Later, bro." Hawk stepped around Linc, put his tray in the scullery and left the mess decks.

Linc stood there staring at the hatch through which Hawk had exited, then shrugged and looked around for somewhere to sit.

CHAPTER THIRTY TWO

Aboard the Prairie
Tuesday Night, August 17, 1965

Day 31

"Well, tomorrow is 'Maximum Effort Day', fellas!" Charlie burst into the signal shack to accompanying laughter from R.J., Ricky, Chief Benson and Linc. Tommy Blanchard had come up from the radio shack and was making coffee in the corner, anxious to show off his new card tricks to the signal gang.

"Another Maximum Effort ought to do it," he said encouragingly.

It was going on midnight and the last pinochle game of the evening had broken up. R.J. was waiting for Charlie to relieve him for the mid watch, and the others had gathered to drink coffee and shoot the breeze. The signal shack had become the pot-bellied stove in an old corner store where sailors of the Operations Department gathered, at all times of the day and night, to discuss women, the Navy and the world...in that order.

"We is settin' the record for Maximum Effort days," Ricky chimed in, gently strumming Peggy Sue. "Tomorrow gonna be number eleventeen."

R.J. chuckled and changed the subject. "They still don't know who killed that BM-One."

"That dude," Linc declared, "was a C.C. in boot camp."

"Well no wonder he got hisself kilt!" Ricky exclaimed. They all laughed knowingly. Boot camp was one of the things all sailors had in common. Most of them had gone through basic training in San Diego, and all had developed an intense dislike for their company commanders.

"I went through long before you guys," Chief Benson proclaimed. "Right after the Korean War. Camp Nimitz wasn't around yet."

"Oh, shit!" Charlie yelped. "I forgot about Camp Nimitz. Man, what a fucked up four weeks."

"Yeah," R.J. agreed. "The first four weeks in boot camp, being isolated on that cold, gray island in those cold cement barracks." He shuddered. "And everything and everybody smellin' like mothballs! Remember how sick you got?"

"Man, I was sicker'n a dog," Ricky replied. "Fact is I was sicker'n three dogs!"

"To this day," Tommy Blanchard cut in, "I get a sick feeling every time I smell mothballs!"

R.J. shook his head and reminisced. "I remember marching to breakfast, all the companies...there must have been thousands of guys. We all lined up on that grinder, each company in three ranks, moving very slowly, a few paces at a time, toward your turn in the chow hall."

Tom Blanchard began barking orders. "Company one-eighty-eight, three paces forward, hut!"

Ricky joined in, "Company three-seventy-two, five paces forward, hut!"

"Little by little," Charlie said, laughing. "Step by step, inch by inch we made it to chow."

Linc joined the laughter. "And thousands of recruits, all sick," he said, wrinkling his nose. "Spitting up gunk all over the grinder..."

"Everybody got sick," Charlie interrupted. "Hell, remember all the damn shots we got? Made everybody sick. That's why they quarantined our asses for four weeks."

"Boy, all them damn shots," Ricky reminisced. "They lined us up and shot us with those air guns. The only thing REALLY scared me in Nimitz was when they told us our last vaccination would be a square needle in the left nut." Ricky looked around at his audience. "'Member that lil' number?" Nods and smiles all around. Everyone had sweated out that boot camp myth. Ricky shook his head disgustedly and mused, "What the hell kinda coon-ass shit was that?"

"After the four weeks are up," R.J. said, smiling, "you get to pack your sea bag and march over that bridge and join the regular boot camp. That was a good feeling."

"Damn shore was," Ricky agreed. "But I kept thinkin' 'bout that square needle..."

"Thing that REALLY scared me the most," Tommy Blanchard piped in, "was jumpin' off the high dive in the big swimming pool with a pair of white trousers on." He looked around for encouragement. Everyone was there in the pool with him, knowing exactly what he was talking about. "We had to hit the water, take off the trousers, tie knots in the bottom of the legs..." The other sailors were laughing and pantomiming Tommy's narrative. Another thing they had all been through. "Then we take the trousers back behind our head," Blanchard was enjoying himself, holding his hands back behind his head, then pulling them forward to illustrate the survival technique he was describing. "Then whoosh! Pull them forward fast and catch air in the trouser legs. Makes a neat flotation device until you can be rescued." He grinned proudly.

"Guys have drowned behind that nonsense," Charlie observed wryly. "In fact, I was almost one of them." More laughter echoed in the signal shack.

"Yeah," Ricky agreed, "They was always pullin' some sorry coon-ass outta that pool!"

"You ain't afraid of the water, Rick?" Linc chided him.

"Hell, no! Y'all come down to Looseyana someday, and I'll take ya out huntin' alligators. After you rassled 'round in a swamp with one o'them gators, you ain't never gonna be afraid of no little old swimmin' pool."

Linc shook his head emphatically. "Thanks for the invite, Ricky," he said, grinning broadly. "But even in Detroit, we know alligators and our kind don't get along." He paused dramatically, stroking his chin. "Must be one o' those African cultural things," he mused, "collective imbedded memories of alligators eatin' our black asses."

Ricky cracked everybody up by looking wide-eyed at Linc and declaring, "Well, shit, Linc, what'd y'all think I was gonna use for bait?"

"The pool wasn't the thing that REALLY scared me," R.J. volunteered. "I was a good swimmer. Lots of hours swimming at Sunset Park in Longmont. Shit, we used to swim eight hours a day. Our parents would get off work and come pick us up at the swimming hole."

"Well, thank you for that little trip down memory lane, Mr. Davis, but, up yours," Charlie declared, accompanied by laughter from the others. "Now, you wanna tell us what REALLY scared you in boot camp?"

R.J. stopped smiling and looked around seriously at his friends. "The smoke pit," he said quietly.

For the first time that evening, the signal shack became silent. The sailors shuffled their feet and glanced at one another sheepishly. Collectively, they were all back in boot camp in the smoke pit. THE SMOKE PIT! *Oh, yeah. It was in the last two weeks of boot camp. You thought you had it licked, only ten days to go, you were cocky and confident...then...The Smoke P*it.

It was a dramatic demonstration of what could happen if a fire broke out onboard ship. Recruits were ushered into a large enclosed building, meant to simulate a ship's compartment. They were instructed on survival procedures, and then the compartment was filled with thick, black smoke from a diesel engine. The recruits had to stay in the compartment following survival procedures for three minutes. Three minutes that seemed like one hell of a lot longer when you're fighting for air. The smoke immediately penetrated their inadequate defenses and stung the eyes, noses and lungs of the recruits. It was a panicky situation, and some guys couldn't take it. They tried to bolt out the door and were pulled out of the pit, coughing and choking. Then they were shamed and humiliated by the company commander and his petty officers. They were called faggots and pussies and many other names. Some recruits went back in; some did not and were sent home.

"I thought I was gonna die," Tommy admitted. "Man, I really thought I was gonna..."

"Yeah, we all did!" Charlie said. "Damn, I remember how they tried to make us believe that some guys had died in there 'cause they didn't follow instructions. You fellas remember that?" Heads nodded. "I guarantee you I followed instructions!"

"Me, too," R.J. said. "Crouch down low, put your head between your knees, pull your watch cap down over your face and tuck it under your chin, put your hands behind your neck, breath normally, don't panic..." R.J. stopped and stared at the deck. *What was that? Watch cap?*

"R.J.!" Ricky yelled at him.

R.J. flinched back to the present. "Wha?"

"You looked like you was gonna choke, partner," Linc said. He studied R.J.'s face. "You okay?"

"I'm okay." R.J. laughed it off. The feeling, however, didn't laugh off. R.J. knew he had discovered something important about the case, but how did it tie into the investigation and what would it mean to Deavers? Where was the investigator? If he were on board the Prairie, R.J. could seek him out and share his revelation with him. If he were on the Knox, R.J. had a problem. Linc was aboard the Prairie, but even if he weren't, R.J. couldn't just flash him and ask him to deliver a personal message to Deavers. In port he could do that. In the middle of a multi-ship salvage operation, headed by a rear admiral, all signal traffic had to be strictly official.

R.J. stepped out of the shack and lit a cigarette. He leaned forward on the railing and looked out across the water at the Frank Knox, straddled dejectedly on Pratas Reef. All her pride was gone, she was disappointed and deflated, her mast sagging like the sorrowful slump in the shoulders of a lady whose lover has betrayed her.

R.J. decided to look for Deavers aboard the Prairie first. He found him in the officers' lounge, sipping coffee and studying his case file. The table in front of him was strewn with crime-scene photos and various reports. Deavers listened carefully to what R.J. said, and a grin began to creep across his face.

"That's it, of course!" he slammed his hand on the table. "The smoke pit, that's what I couldn't remember, being in that damn smoke pit with the watch cap pulled over my face!" He sorted through the pictures, found the one he wanted and stared at it.

"Did officers have to go through that, too, sir?" R.J. asked.

Deavers didn't answer. His gaze was off in space, his face blank, his mind somewhere else. "Now I know that recruit Tompkins' death has nothing to do with this case." He stood and began pacing in the small officer's lounge. "The watch cap proves it."

"It does, sir?" R.J. looked confused.

"Andrew Tompkins drowned, R.J." Deavers held up the autopsy file. "I got this today from Captain Peterson."

"What does that mean, sir?"

"It means we are missing one less piece of the puzzle, my young friend." He resumed pacing. "Maybe more than one piece." He stopped and stared at R.J. "Forget Tompkins, the smoke pit is the key."

R.J. frowned, deep in thought. "So, did Green kill someone else?" he asked absently. "Someone in the smoke pit?"

"Hmm. No, I think if there were two deaths, Captain Peterson would have informed me." He rubbed his temples with his fingertips. "What about injured? Could it be someone he injured?"

"That sounds possible, Mr. Deavers," R.J. replied. "When I was in boot camp, some guys got hurt and sent home. A few of them were pretty unhappy about it."

"That's got to be it," Deavers mused, nodding thoughtfully. The investigator suddenly felt renewed, his energy restored. A new direction had presented itself, and Deavers' well-trained nose indicated he was right to follow it. They were closing in on the solution; he felt it in his bones. *Perhaps it was serendipity.* "I'll get a confidential message off to Captain Peterson, and I'll ask him to forward the files on any recruits injured in the smoke pit during Green's tenure. We'll have the information in a couple of days." He put his hand on R.J.'s shoulder and gave him a fatherly squeeze. "You did *great,* R.J. You stumbled on something that redirected the investigation. Many times, that's how these things are solved. You're going to be a good detective some day."

"Thanks, sir. Can I ask you something?"

"Fire away."

"Do officers have to go through the smoke pit?"

"Well, if they don't, they should," Deavers replied, smiling. "I started my career as an enlisted man, remember? Then I became a warrant officer before getting my silver bar."

R.J. nodded, smiled, stepped out the door, and put on his steaming cap. "G'night, sir," he said.

"Good night, R.J. Think about what I said about being a detective." He returned to studying his photos.

R.J. closed the door behind him and headed to the signal bridge.

He was becoming quite fond of Deavers, and liked working with him. R.J. thought of the first time he'd met Deavers and chuckled. That was a long time ago. Maybe he'd go to school and study criminology. In a little over a month he'd be discharged, and become a civilian again. Then he could do whatever he wished. He smiled to himself. He knew the next thirty days would seem like months before he got out.

The next day, an order came through extending all Navy enlistments by four to nine months because of the Viet Nam conflict. R.J.'s was extended to January, 1966. Great, thought R.J. *It will be months before I get out, alright. FIVE months!*

Deavers sat on his bunk and composed a message to Captain Peterson. He complained once again about the paucity of information coming out of San Diego, and lamented the lack of cooperation between the investigative divisions. He opined that the paperwork he had received so far had obviously been sanitized prior to his getting it. *It's not going to do any good,* the investigator thought, *but I'm going to keep trying.*

The confidential file from Captain Peterson arrived two days later with a brief note attached:

Deavers,

Re your request for files on any recruit injuries in the smoke pit during the time C.C. Green served at NTC, be advised there was only one, but it was a bad one. File enclosed. It's ALL I could get.
Nobody is getting any intel on a timely basis. We're on a war footing here and cooperation is rare, so quit complaining.
Please adv how much longer to wrap this up.

Peterson

Deavers frowned at the cryptic nature of the note. He sat down on his bunk, opened the file and began going through it. When he was finished reading it, he sat, shoulders slumped, in a state of shock and stared at the deck for a solid ten minutes. He shook his head sadly. He had to admit he never saw it coming, and it sickened him. The last person he would have suspected! He stared at the deck intently and asked himself over and over why he hadn't just retired last year when he wanted to instead of staying in and having to deal with this matter. *I was so gung-ho for this case when I first heard about it,* Deavers thought. *Now I wish I hadn't taken the damn thing.*

The investigator allowed himself a few brief moments of philosophical reflection on the unfairness of life. That was all he needed to get it out of his system. It was his defense mechanism against the depression that could be brought on by the job and all the unpleasant things that came with it. Deavers went through the process, put his personal feelings aside, and began to list in his mind all the things he needed to do. The pieces were falling together, and the solution was visible, but there were still many questions to be answered, many loose ends. Deavers felt energized. This was the most exciting stage of an investigation, where everything was coming together and had to be neatly wrapped up and logically explained. He was again the professional investigator. He knew the motive, he had the murder weapon, he was already putting together the scenario, and in his heart he knew the man was guilty. The problem was, except for circumstantial evidence, he had no proof. If he couldn't find any proof, he would have to build a compelling case from what he had. *Circumstantial? Sure, but believable because it made sense. After you get over the surprise,* Deavers thought, *it makes perfect sense.*

He pulled out his pad of legal paper and began making a list of people who needed to be contacted. He was going to ask the authorities in San Diego to interview a few people there, and he needed Captain Peterson to pull some strings in the interest of speed. Who knew how much longer the Knox would be stuck on the reef? As soon as she was pulled free, the crew, including the murderer, would be released to the far corners of the earth. Deavers was confident, however, that this particular individual would stay with the Knox, wherever she went. *He had to.* Deavers sighed. This was going to be a difficult case to wrap up. He needed a break.

CHAPTER THIRTY THREE

Friday, August 20, 1965

Dear Millie

R.J. was alone in the bunting locker as he read Millie's latest missive. He folded it up and replaced it in the envelope. She had berated him for not writing, as usual. She also accused him (again) of fathering her imaginary pregnancy, causing her subsequent imaginary miscarriage, and not really giving a shit about any of it. That was in the first paragraph. The ensuing nine pages rambled on about the corruption of the uptight establishment, the war in Viet Nam, the boring town of Longmont and being snubbed by her so-called friends. She ended the letter by threatening to have it out with him when he returned to Longmont and to top it all off: '*...Penelope agrees with me!*' It was obvious Millie was slipping farther and farther into la-la land, and he had already made his decision. Longmont was not an option for him. Too small and too cold. He was going to stay in California when he got out of the Navy, just like he had originally planned. California was the land of opportunity, and R.J. was certain he would find a good job. Eventually, he would go back to school and study English, and one day he would write that novel he had been thinking about. Nowhere in those plans was a place for Millie. He took out his stationery and began writing.

Dear Millie,

Sorry, I'm not coming back to Longmont, but I'm sure the both of you will get along fine without me. You and Penelope are so close, it would be a shame to break up the set.
Have a great life, and if you ever think of me...don't!

R.J.

P.S. Tell Penelope she can kiss my ass!

He was sealing the envelope with a warm feeling of finality when Linc came into the compartment.

"Wha's happenin' Slick?" Linc headed toward the record player. "Wanna hear some tunes?"

"Absolutely," R.J. answered with a big grin. "Whatever you want to hear." He reached behind him and picked up his book of Poe poetry. He turned to 'The Raven' and began to read. A few of the pages had come loose and were sticking out the sides of the book.

"Man, looks like you done read the shit outta that book," Linc laughed. "Pages fallin' out all over the place."

"This bird," R.J. said, tapping the book with an index finger, "this Raven, is supposed to be the harbinger of death or insanity."

"That's the way I heard it," Linc replied, nodding to the music while he studied an album cover.

"Personally," R.J. said, without looking up from the book, "I think this bird is just messin' with my man."

"Jus' keep hittin' him with all that NEVERMORE shit, huh?"

"Well, it's like Poe wants us to think the raven is a symbol or the messenger of death and everlasting sorrow, but maybe..."

Linc put on Dizzy Gillespie's "Swing Low, Sweet Cadillac" and turned to listen to R.J. "You developing a new theory on that poem, Slick?"

"I think the bird is just a friggin' bird!" R.J. exclaimed, slamming the book shut. "Nobody sent him in there to drive this dude nuts, he just happened to fly up to his window." He held up the book and nodded emphatically. "Everything else is just happenin' in this poor sucker's mind."

"Go on," Linc encouraged. This was getting interesting. He pulled himself up onto the counter and got comfortable.

R.J. grinned and warmed to the task. "Like this passage right here," he said. He opened the book and began reciting slowly: "...doubtless," said I,"what it utters is its only stock and store, caught from some unhappy master whom unmerciful disaster followed fast and followed faster till his song one burden bore; till the dirges of his hope that melancholy burden bore of, nevermore...nevermore."

R.J. looked up. "See what I mean?" he asked seriously.

Linc cocked his head to one side and nodded appreciatively. "You definitely done read the shit out of that book," he said with a wide smile. He nodded his head to the beat and snapped his fingers to the melody of Mr. Dizzy's horn, eyes half-closed, a small smile on his lips. "So what do the Raven mean to you, Slick?"

R.J. closed his eyes and tried to bring a picture into his mind of the lonely, grieving narrator of 'The Raven.' In his mind he ran through the first few stanzas of the poem, and opened his eyes, staring intently into Linc's face. The big man softened, shifted his perch on the counter and nodded respectfully. R.J. closed his eyes and recited, "Once upon a midnight dreary, as I pondered, weak and weary, over many a quaint and curious volume of forgotten lore..."

Linc leaned back against the counter, listening to Dizzy's horn and R.J.'s recital of 'The Raven.' It was obvious that R.J. knew this poem well. His pace was smooth and easy, his pronunciations perfect, and it was easy to drift off in a dream-like state. Linc believed Poe was the perfect accompaniment to Dizzy Gillespie and vice versa. When R.J. was finished he looked at Linc expectantly.

"Poetry is the purest form of human expression," he said. "Besides sex, of course."

"Of course."

"Then it's poetry."

"I'll tell you, Slick, I always thought music was the purest form of human expression, except sex, but I really like that poem. It says a whole lot, doesn't it?"

"The Raven speaks only one word throughout the entire poem," R.J. said. "The narrator takes that word and makes it mean many different things, all pointing to his grief for his lost love. But it's that word, that one word, that I believe is the key to the entire poem."

"How so?" Linc encouraged. He was enjoying this.

"It's what the bird means that matters. Not what the poor old narrator thinks the bird means. He can read anything he wants into that one word, but it doesn't matter what *he* thinks it means. It only matters what the bird means when he says NEVERMORE." R.J. looked down at the book. "I think the bird is there to give the narrator something to relate to, and in doing so, he finds..." R.J. stopped and looked up at Linc.

"He finds what?"

"He finds comfort... no, that's not it..." R.J. frowned, frustrated with the poem. "This guy lost his lover, and the Raven visits him with only one word to say...nevermore. The narrator peppers the Raven with questions, and the Raven responds with the only word he knows, and the guy, he knows what the Raven is going to say, yet he still asks these painful questions, like will he ever see his love again, and the answer is still the same. At the end, he seems to accept the Raven and his one word vocabulary, maybe all his questions have been answered, maybe he's content."

"Maybe the Raven really is the messenger of Death," Linc offered.

"I...don't think so."

"Insanity? Eternal grief?"

R.J. chewed at his thumbnail. "No..." he said pensively.

"So you got an opinion on that, Slick?"

"Yeah, well, I'm working on it." R.J. closed the book and set it on the counter. "It's the last stanza, that's where the solution is, but I haven't figured it out yet."

"Well," Linc said encouragingly. "Let's hear the last stanza again."

R.J. closed his eyes.

"And the Raven, never flitting, still is sitting, still is sitting,
on that placid bust of Pallas just above my chamber door;
and his eyes have all the seeming of a demon that is dreaming,
and the lamplight o'er him streaming, throws his shadow on the
floor; and my soul, from out that shadow that lies floating on the
floor, shall be lifted--nevermore."

Chaplain Charles

The weekend arrived in an atmosphere of hope for Task Force 73. The foam would be dry in a few days, and the final 'Maximum Effort' could take place. Everyone from the admiral to the lowliest seaman believed the end was near, and the men started looking forward again; forward to the time the Knox would be free and they could go about their familiar routines. Most of the ships in Task Force 73 would be sailing directly to liberty ports such as Yokosuka, Subic Bay, and for the crew of the Prairie, back to Hong Kong.

While the black and white sailors kept to themselves for the most part, tensions between the two groups had eased. The Los Angeles riot was over. The California National Guard had put a stop to it, but the cost was staggering. Over thirty people had been killed, mostly black, and the commercial areas, where all the stores and businesses were located, were destroyed to the point that many experts thought South Central Los Angeles would never recover.

The specter of the civil rights movement still loomed large on the horizon, but the mood had changed to become more introspective, more thoughtful, as the men of the Prairie took a step back and tried to make sense out of the riot.

Chaplain Charles left the captain's cabin early Saturday morning and set off to pursue his mission, a mission the captain had wholeheartedly endorsed. The chaplain was determined to demonstrate his togetherness theme in a practical manner. He liked to have breakfast in the mess decks with the crew, and he noticed with despair the widening rift between black and white sailors. They sat apart from each other, blacks on one end of the mess decks, whites on the other, almost no interaction between them. Chaplain Charles was determined to change that.

With the captain's blessing, the chaplain spoke with every department head on the ship, urging participation in Sunday's

Baptist church services, especially among white sailors. The chaplain was extremely popular with the crew, and as a result, more than three hundred sailors packed into the ship's small library the following morning.

CHAPTER THIRTY FOUR

Sunday, August 22, 1965

Day 36

The small choir was arrayed behind the altar, and softly sang 'Rock of Ages' as the churchgoers filed into the library and quickly filled up the available seats. The rest of them lined the walls. Chaplain Charles ordered the hatch to be left open, so anyone who wanted to attend but couldn't squeeze in could hear everything from outside.

The crowd grew quiet when the chaplain took his place at the pulpit. He looked around at his audience appreciatively. There were almost as many white faces in the crowd as black, and they seemed to be comfortable with each other, at least for now. It was a start; a beginning to be sure.

"I want to thank you men for coming today," he began in his strong voice. "And attending what I hope, what we all hope, will be the last church service held at Pratas Reef." The audience cheered and laughed good-naturedly, obviously sharing the sentiment. Chaplain Charles continued. "I think I can safely say we are all together on that one." More cheers. "And that's what we are all about today, my friends, TOGETHERNESS. I look out on all your faces, black and white, standing and sitting TOGETHER, worshiping TOGETHER, sharing experiences TOGETHER, the black and the white tend to blend TOGETHER in my vision, so that I no longer see color, I no longer recognize the difference between black sailors and white sailors," he held his arms out to them, palms up, "because to me you look like you belong... TOGETHER!"

"Right on, Preacher!" Linc called from the rear.

The chaplain smiled softly. "The times we live in are pivotal for all of us, and I mean everyone on board this ship. Very soon, this operation will be over and we will return to Hong Kong." More cheers from the men, who were warming to the sermon. "Thirty six days we've been out here. For thirty six days we have worked tirelessly as a crew, as a team, sharing the joys and the sorrows, the successes and the failures, the good and the bad of this operation. But isn't that what we are SUPPOSED to be doing?" The chaplain's voice rose an octave and he began to hit his rhythm. "We are trained Navy sailors who know our jobs and how they are supposed to be done, and isn't that what we are SUPPOSED to be doing? Isn't that what GOD would expect of us? ONE ship, ONE crew, ONE goal, ONE mission!"

Chaplain Charles walked to the front of the lectern and folded his hands in front of him. "If we can work together on this ship, can we not work together as a people? Can we not recognize the things we have in common and try to ignore our differences? Can we not work together for the betterment of our society as Americans, dismissing skin color in the process?" The chaplain deliberately made no mention of the Watts riot, but it was on everyone's mind as they glanced around sheepishly at each other.

Hawk caught Linc's eye and nodded to him. Linc nodded back. Men all across the library were nodding, some to each other, some to themselves. The chaplain walked among them, pressing hands and whispering God-bless-you to each of them in turn. The choir began humming 'When the Saints Come Marching In,' low and soft, providing a background for the chaplain as he made his way through the compartment, shaking hands. The choir raised its volume a little as Chaplain Charles returned to the lectern and smiled paternally at his audience.

"Let's start here!" he called to them. "Please join me in prayer." The choir's humming got softer. "Almighty God, we stand here before you and ask for your guidance as we make our way through our lives. We stand here together, Lord, a single crew, a united crew, and we ask for your blessing. We ask this in the name of Jesus Christ our Lord. Amen."

"Amen!" chorused through the library.

The chaplain glanced back at the choir and they began humming again, this time a more up-beat version of 'When the Saints Come Marching In.' The chaplain raised his arms high. "Stand now and take the hand of your brother!" the chaplain directed, pointing to his audience. "If you're white, shake hands with every black man, and if you're black, shake the hand of every white man!" The men began milling around, shaking hands, blending together as they snaked around each other to reach other hands. Most of them were smiling. The choir raised the volume and began clapping their hands to the music and swaying back and forth. Soon, the men were all clapping and marching around the library. They began filing out, still clapping and singing. Men on all decks were leaning over the railing, looking up or down at the source of the music. The chaplain stood next to the lectern, clapping his hands, smiling benevolently as the men melded together, shaking hands. *Yes, indeed,* he thought to himself, *This is a good start.*

"Oh, when the Saints, come marching in,

When the Saints come marching in,
Oh, yes I want to be in that number..."

Linc shook hands with Hawk and they looked into each other's eyes. Linc felt a change in Hawkins Wilson. In that one little look, he sensed a softening in those intelligent eyes. Then he, R.J., Ricky and Pea headed to the signal bridge. It was a beautiful Sunday morning and they wanted to experience it from the top decks of the ship.

Sunday Night 2200 Hours

The Mule and the Wagon

The bunting locker was crowded, but relatively quiet. The semi-final round of the pinochle tournament was down to four teams, each team vying to play in the final. The two games were taking place at opposite ends of the big cutting table, and Tommy Blanchard, agreeing to referee the semi-finals and then the championship, stood resolutely between the two games, keeping a wary eye on the participants. Tommy's reputation for card tricks and sleight of hand made him the unanimous choice for referee, especially since he was barred from playing in the tournament.

Chief Benson and Charlie were on watch on the signal bridge, so R.J. and Ricky hung around the bunting locker, listening to Linc's albums. R.J. busied himself with sorting the colorful reams of bunting and waited for midnight, when he and Ricky would assume the watch. Linc had stayed aboard after the morning church services, but was uncharacteristically quiet. He preferred to sit by the record player and nod along with the soothing music of Cannonball Adderly and Oscar Peterson. The events of the morning's Baptist services dominated his thoughts. Pea sat next to him, eyes closed, smoking a cigarette and swaying with the music. Ricky sat in a corner, softly strumming Peggy Sue.

Everyone was a little startled to hear a knock on the bunting room hatch. R.J. and Ricky looked at each other curiously. "Who the hell knocks on the damn hatch?" R.J. asked no one in particular,

"Maybe it's the mailman," Ricky offered.

"Maybe it's my pizza!" Pea suggested.

R.J. shrugged. "Enter!" he called out.

The hatch swung open and Hawk stuck his head in, squinting at the brightness of the well-lighted compartment.

"Mr. Hawkins Wilson," Ricky greeted him. "C'mon in and make

y'self at home."

Hawk grinned. Like most sailors aboard the Prairie, he genuinely liked Ricky. "Thank you kindly, Ricky." He looked around until he spotted Linc, sitting alongside the record player, reading an album cover. "Hey, Linc."

"Hey Hawk,' Linc replied. "What brings you out of the snipe pit?"

"Got a minute?"

"Yeah, sure." Linc stood, followed Hawk out and closed the hatch behind him. Hawk leaned on the railing and looked out at the blue Pacific. The moon was gone, but the dark night twinkled under a canopy of bright stars. Linc leaned on the rail next to Hawk and waited for him to say what he came to say. Linc was sure he could sense a softening in Hawk's voice and manner, as if he'd come to a conclusion he wasn't quite comfortable with.

Without taking his eyes off the sea, Hawk said quietly, "That was a good church meetin' today."

Linc nodded agreement. "It was, like my grandma used to say, 'a real down home, bible-thumpin' revival."

"The Preacher really makes me think."

"Me, too."

"It's different when folks get killed."

"Yeah," Linc replied with a sigh. "Brings it all home, huh?"

Hawk nodded and looked up at Linc with a serious expression. "I ever tell you 'bout my granddaddy?"

"No," Linc answered, knowing Hawk had a story to tell. He was anxious to hear it. "Tell me."

"My mama, she was not a strong woman when she was young, and she had me out of wedlock. My daddy...seems funny to call him that 'cause he weren't never around...just took off and split. Rumor had it he was keepin' one step ahead o' the law. He was what they called a 'high yellow,' half white and half Negro. I wasn't even named after him, I was named after my granddaddy. I was born in my grandparents' house. It wasn't really a house, more like a sharecroppers shack, but it was home." He looked at Linc with a deep sadness in his eyes. "You dig?"

"I dig. Be it ever so humble, right?"

Hawk smiled and nodded. "My grandma was a sweet old woman, and she liked to spoil me. Now, my granddaddy, he didn't go for spoilin' a kid, but he was a good man who taught me a lot of very important lessons." Hawk's eyes were moistening, glistening in the pale starlight. "Like the one about the mule and the wagon." He turned and leaned back on the railing. "I think it's a story you should hear."

"Okay." Linc turned to face Hawk. Despite their different views on the civil rights movement, Linc was becoming very fond of Hawk. It was obvious the feeling was mutual. "Tell me about the mule and the wagon."

"I was screwin' up in school, had a short attention span and a wise-assed attitude, even when I was ten years old. My grandma preached patience and understanding and my granddaddy preached with a razor strap and his proverbial 'life lessons.' One would always accompany the other." A small smile of remembrance appeared, then quickly disappeared from Hawk's lips. The more he told the story, the more his accent became deep south. "Anyways, he takes me out back, and I figure I'm fixin' to get a whuppin,' but instead, he lights up his smelly pipe and points out across the meadow to his old sway-back mule, grazin' down there, and to an old beat-up wagon weren't any good for nothin' 'cept us kids playin' on it. He tells me 'boy, you gotta start usin' your head for more than a hat rack. See that ol' mule out there? Time was I would hook him up to that wagon, take our produce into town to sell, then I'd buy everything we needed to live through another month, and haul it back. But sometimes that ol' mule, he so stubborn he don' wanna pull no wagon. But fact is, boy, he jus' a mule, and that there's jus' a wagon. They ain't really good for nothin' til they hooked up to one another.'

"He puffed on his stinky pipe and pointed it my chest. He say, 'The wagon cain't go nowhere without the mule, and the mule ain't worth nothin' 'less he pull that wagon. So's I kept a two-by-four in that wagon, 'cause, see, you cain't reason with the mule 'less you get his attention first. So, I takes that two-by-four and shows it to Mr. Mule, then I hauls off and whacks him with it real hard, right there, between his eyes...jus' to get his attention. Then he pull the wagon.'" Hawk chuckled at the memory. "So I figure, now I'm gonna get whupped, because I am obviously the mule and my granddaddy is obviously the two-by-four."

"He needed to get your attention, so you'd quit screwin' up in school?"

"Well," Hawk went on, his enthusiasm for the story building, "that's what I thought, but my granddaddy, while he was a simple man, he wasn't a stupid man. He understood more than I ever gave him credit for. He looked down at me and smiled so kindly I knew then I wasn't gonna get whupped. He said, 'You, boy, are the mule. I am the two-by-four, and that school you goin' to is the wagon. If I can get your attention, and hook you up to that wagon, when you pull away with it, it gonna have in it everythin' you need for this here life you 'bout to live. That wagon gonna be full of knowledge.

You gonna learn to read and write and do your numbers. And history, Lord, that wagon gotta have a shit-load of history, 'cause black folks cain't afford to forget history.'"

Linc smiled. *Good story.* "So did your granddaddy get your attention?"

"He shorely did. I started reading and I ain't never stopped. I got my wagon full of what I needed from school, and he never had to hit me with that two-by-four. He said, 'sooner or later, the mule, he gonna recognize the two-by-four, so you gots to keep it in the wagon, but if you do it right,' and he smiled at me in a way I never seen before, 'then, boy, all you gots to do is show it to him. The mule's stubborn, but he ain't stupid. All you gots to do is use that two-by-four sparingly, unnerstan? You don't whup on the mule any more than you gots to.'"

"Your granddaddy sounds like a very smart man, Hawk."

"My granddaddy was the first Hawkins Wilson," Hawk said softly, his voice full of emotion. "But he never let anyone call him Hawk. Know why?"

"Why?"

Hawk took a deep breath and choked back a sob. "'Cause he always said he saw himself more like an EAGLE than a hawk."

Linc smiled, happy that Hawkins Wilson thought enough of him to share the story with him, but Hawk wasn't finished.

"We been debatin' on a lot of things, Lincoln Jones. I see you as a brother, and a friend."

"I consider you a friend, too, Hawk, I just think the violent, militant way isn't the way to get to where we gotta go."

Hawk reached up and grasped Link's shoulder affectionately. "My granddaddy said, 'It ain't about the mule; it ain't about the two-by-four. It be about the wagon.'" He stared out at the ocean for a long moment, then said quietly, "We need both the mule AND the wagon. You are the wagon, my brother. I am the two-by-four, and the white establishment is the mule. I'll get the mule's attention, and you fill the wagon, dig?" He squeezed Linc's shoulder again. "Fill it with everything we gonna need, and I'll keep wavin' that two-by-four in the mule's face." Hawk put his hands together and interlaced his fingers. "We need both," he said. "The mule AND the wagon." Tears welled up in his eyes. "I been reading Thomas Paine," he said softly. "You dig Thomas Paine?"

Linc nodded. "I surely do."

"I feel like I know him," Hawk continued. "I mean, even though he lived a long time ago, his essays on the American Revolution are brilliant. And the things he says, they make as much sense today as they did back then." He held his interlaced hands up to Linc. "Gotta have the mule and the wagon, but you still need that two-by-four, in case the mule forgets."

Linc stared at Hawk for several quiet moments. He always knew that Hawk was very intelligent, but until this moment, he had no idea the depth of his intelligence. He wasn't as much softening his militant stance as he was looking to blend it in with the peace movement, like a two-by-four that doesn't have to be wielded too often to be effective! He wrapped his big hands around Hawk's interlaced fingers and looked deeply into his eyes. "Mule and wagon," he said earnestly.

Hawkins stared at Linc for a long time, searching his eyes, smiling in a kindly way.

After a few awkward moments, Linc grinned and nodded toward the bunting locker. "Wanna go listen to some jazz?"

"Hell, yes," Hawk replied, grinning wide. "You got any King Pleasure?"

Linc looked at him with mocked surprise, eyebrows raised and eyes twinkling. "Do a cat got a ass?"

CHAPTER THIRTY FIVE

2330 Hours

The Dental Tech

Deavers looked at his watch. It was 2330 on Sunday night and he was weary. He thought he could get his mind off the case by reading a novel, but it wasn't working. He needed sleep, but during an investigation he slept very little, and fitfully at best. He knew if he could sleep, his mind would stop churning. He wanted tomorrow to come. He would feel better in the morning.

Tuesday would be the final 'Maximum Effort' day, and everyone was certain the Knox would be freed from the reef. He knew who the killer was, knew why he did it, knew how he did it, but the physical evidence was weak, speculative at best. He needed one more piece to complete the puzzle.

Deavers was frustrated that he had not received any answer to his several requests for information. The only thing he had received was a short, curt note from Captain Peterson: Working on it. Will advise. He was asking himself again why he hadn't put in his retirement papers when he heard a soft knocking. *Hmmm*, he thought. *Must be some late visitor at the door.* He stood and opened the door, but no one was there. Only the darkness stared back at him.

Deavers turned back into his cabin, frowning, when he heard another soft knocking, this time coming from the porthole. He opened the porthole and stared at the face of Dental Tech J.I. Parker.

"What the hell are you doing out there, sailor?" Deavers demanded.

"I wanted to make sure you were alone...sir."

"Well, I'm alone," Deavers said irritably. "Come around to the front if you want to talk with me."

Deavers held open the door, and Parker slipped in, looked around to make sure he wasn't seen, then closed the door quickly behind him. He nodded to Deavers and put a file folder on his desk. It had been delivered to Parker in the official mail pouch from San Diego, and it had stamps all over it that warned: SECRET. Deavers was cleared for SECRET. In fact, he was cleared for TOP SECRET. So was J.I. Parker, apparently.

"Something I can do for you, sailor?" Deavers asked, eyeing the file folder suspiciously. He sat down behind the desk.

"Actually, Lieutenant," Parker replied, nodding toward the file. "There is something I can do for you."

Deavers glared at him. "What?" he demanded.

Parker reached into his pocket and pulled out an ID card, which he put down on top of the file. Deavers picked up the card and examined it closely. It identified the owner as Ensign William Dall, criminal investigator from San Diego.

Deavers looked up from the ID card. "I repeat, what is this all about?"

"As you can see," the ensign replied, nodding toward the ID card, "I'm also a criminal investigator, and I've heard of you. You have a great reputation." Dall smiled, but his smile faded when Deavers did not return it. "Anyway, I think you deserve an explanation."

Deavers handed the ID back to the ensign and motioned to a chair. "Sit down, Ensign Dall," he announced resignedly, as if nothing ever surprised him. "To tell you the truth, I've been expecting you."

Dall sat and looked at Deavers curiously. "You've been expecting me?" he asked, unable to conceal his surprise.

"Not you, personally," Deavers explained, smiling slyly. "But someone like you."

"And why...how is that, sir?"

"I'll make you a deal, Ensign Dall. I'll show you mine if you show me yours."

"That's what I'm here for," Dall said, hands out, palms up. "I've been told to cooperate with you completely. So how did you know I or someone like me was coming?"

Deavers leaned forward in his chair and began explaining. He couldn't help the didactic tone of his voice. "The file on C.C. Green indicated the Tompkins investigation was on-going, but the last notation in the file was Green's transfer to the Knox. The investigation, for some reason, was never officially closed. If the investigation had not been closed, then it was logical that someone was charged with keeping an eye on him. Someone aboard the Knox. You were one of a few possibilities I had in mind." Deavers smiled, pleased with himself. Dall squirmed. Deavers continued. "Anyway, if the investigation was not closed, it had to be active. Unless, of course it was a Navy documentation SNAFU, but I doubt that. Meaning," he tapped his finger on the file folder, "the investigation was proceeding in San Diego, so there had to be a file on the case somewhere containing all the pertinent facts that were turned up." He leaned back in his chair and put his hands behind his head and smiled affably. "I figured if I could get Captain Peterson to put on enough pressure, the file would show up, presented to me by the man sent to watch C.C. Green."

Dall sat and stared at the investigator. "Well," he cleared his throat nervously. "Now I know why you've got that great reputation." He straightened up in his chair. "You are fundamentally correct in all your conclusions. Let me just add that we have hit a brick wall in our investigation. The unexpected death of our suspect has rendered our investigation superfluous. However," he said quickly, "in the conduct of that investigation, primarily in the interviewing of witnesses and concerned persons, we have uncovered certain facts and documentation which may augment your case nicely." Dall leaned back in his chair, put his hands behind his neck, and smiled pleasantly. "There's more if you care to hear it."

Deavers broke into a wide smile. "By all means," he said eagerly. "I'm dying to hear this story."

Chief Billings leaned against the bulkhead on the 02 level and stroked his chin thoughtfully. He knew something was up with that kid, Parker. His instincts told him that Parker was not who he seemed. Chief Billings had tried, but could not uncover any information about Jude Parker. The file on him was remarkable only in its brevity. *Now the dental tech was sneaking into Deavers' cabin. Were they working together on the case?* Chief Billings snorted. *Hell, everyone else on board is working on the case, Parker might as well! Or maybe he's confessing.* The chief laughed out loud and headed toward his quarters. He was tired, and tomorrow was going to be another tough day. He was confident that tomorrow would bring some answers to the Jude Parker mystery.

In the captain's cabin, Roger Lamb slowly packed up his belongings. He wouldn't be there much longer. His first command had not lasted long. The desk now held a picture of his beautiful wife Julie and their son, Eric, a cadet at Annapolis. His files filled the filing cabinet and his uniforms hung in the small closet. His Bachelor of Science degree from the Academy hung on the bulkhead, and the small name sign on his desk said, Roger Lamb, Lieutenant, USN. Still, he felt like an interloper. For several years this cabin had belonged to Commander Gerald Pizzonovich, whom Lieutenant Lamb considered to be a fine Naval officer. Now, Captain Pizzonovich was gone, ousted from his command by a gross, almost laughable mistake. Roger felt the weight of command and understood its responsibilities, its pressures, and its loneliness. He also understood that it could vanish in the blink of an eye. All it would take was one ghastly mistake, and it didn't matter who the commanding officer was. He felt a familiar rush of bitter anger and fought it off. He had to think of his command. They would probably never solve the murder of C.C. Green, but Captain Lamb could not be concerned about that.

Deavers had promised to keep the new captain current on the investigation. *So the best approach is to let him do his job,* Roger thought. *We need to concentrate on our ship.*

Deavers sat and stared at Ensign Dall. He struggled to process all the information Dall had pelted him with for the last half hour. "That is a remarkable story," Deavers said, smiling wanly. "So you people have been investigating C.C. Green for quite some time?"

"That's affirmative." Dall pulled a pack of cigarettes out of his pocket. "May I smoke?"

Deavers nodded. "And this file contains..."

"Everything you need to force a confession." Dall lit a cigarette and blew the smoke up into the air. "After the smoke pit incident, we dumped Green into the transit barracks so we would know where to find him and so he couldn't endanger any other recruits. When he suddenly ended up on the Knox, we wanted to know why and how that happened." He pointed at the file with his cigarette. "It's all in there."

"So, you guys figured out how C.C. Green ended up on the Frank Knox?"

"We had our suspicions. Again," he pointed at the file, "it's all in there."

Deavers sat drumming his fingers on Dall's file. If the San Diego investigation had stalled because of the suspect's death, why didn't they begin investigating who killed him? Deavers smiled slightly. It began to dawn on him. *It's because of my investigation into the murder! They need my file!*

"And I am the blessed recipient of all this...because?" Deavers couldn't help smirking.

Dall smiled his most disarming smile, but there was no humor in his eyes. "Because?" he said, eyebrows raised in mock surprise. "Well, I guess it's because you got this hot-shot reputation." He said it lightly, but the sarcasm came through.

Deavers felt a chilly anger come over him. His ears perked up. "Are you trying to be a wise ass, Dall?" he challenged, frostily. "'Cause if you are, I'm just in the fucking mood!"

"No...no sir," Dall said soothingly.

"Good. So you got handed the assignment to keep him under surveillance?"

"That's right."

"And you saw my investigation generating momentum, so you reported to your superiors and they instructed you to fold your investigation into mine..." Dall started to say something, but Deavers held up his hand. "Because you already suspect someone, based on what's in your file, and you believe that what's in my file will corroborate what's in your file and together we solve the case and skip down the Yellow Brick Road, hand in hand. Right, Ensign?"

Ensign Dall smiled. He was beginning to like Deavers. "Well, sir, to tell you the truth, I didn't imagine we'd be holding hands."

Deavers tried to keep a straight face, but couldn't quite pull it off. After sharing a long, stress-relieving laugh with Ensign Dall, Deavers wiped his eyes and got serious again. "I lead this investigation," he warned.

"Absolutely."

"Everything comes and goes through me."

"One hundred per cent."

"We report to our respective superiors that we are combining our efforts and will communicate progress as events occur."

"Sounds good to me."

"Then we concentrate on building a compelling case quickly, utilizing all the combined resources at our disposal, before they pull the ship off the reef. Deal?" Deavers offered his hand.

"You've got a deal," Dall said, grinning. He took Deavers' hand and added, "Boss."

Deavers pulled the file on his investigation from his desk drawer, handed it to Dall, and picked up the San Diego file. They both sat back, slowly and carefully reviewing each page of the files. They sat for two hours, reading and rereading the documentation. No words were spoken, only the occasional grunt or sigh to express their reactions to the revelations in each other's file.

Deavers finished reviewing Dall's file and looked up thoughtfully. "We've got less than two days to wrap this up," he said, almost to himself. He yawned and shook his head quickly to wake up. "Let's sleep on this, and meet early in the morning."

Dall looked at his watch and started to remark that it was already early morning, but thought better of it. "Then we confront him?"

Deavers' face took on a sad, sorrowful look. It was not going to be a pleasant task. "Yes," he said softly, "then we confront him."

CHAPTER THIRTY SIX

Monday, August 23, 1965

Day 37

Chaplain Charles made his way to the mess decks to have breakfast with the crew, as was his custom. As he neared the mess decks, he could hear the buzzing of animated conversations. At first he thought another confrontation had broken out, but when he stepped into the mess decks he stopped short and stared open-mouthed at the scene. Blacks and whites were sitting with each other, laughing and joking! He was a little confused by the fact that all the trays were full. No one was eating breakfast. The conversations died down when the men noticed Chaplain Charles standing there. One of the cooks came around the counter with a breakfast tray, piled with scrambled eggs and potatoes, just the way the chaplain liked it.

"Sir?" the cook asked. "Would you like some breakfast?"

Chaplain Charles looked at the cook with a slightly confused expression. "Why, yes," he replied, still taking in the scene. "Yes, I would." He accepted the tray. "Thank you."

"Hey Preacher!" Hawk stood and waved to the chaplain. "Sit over here, sir!"

The chaplain walked toward Hawk's table, looking left and right at the smiling faces, white and black, breakfasting together. There were no segregated tables with only black or white sailors sitting at them. Everyone mingled together, apparently randomly, and they seemed happy! The chaplain felt a little lump form in his throat as he sat down with Hawk, Linc, R.J., Pea and Ricky at their table.

"Welcome, sir," Linc greeted him. "You know these fellas, don't you?" He indicated the signal gang.

"I do indeed. Good morning, men."

"Morning, sir," came the reply.

"We were hoping you would join us for breakfast," Linc said, looking around the mess decks.

"Thank you, young Lincoln," the chaplain replied. He looked around curiously at the men. "Why isn't anyone eating breakfast?" he asked.

"We've been waiting for you, Preacher," Hawk replied. "Would you be kind enough to offer a prayer this morning?"

Chaplain Charles nodded, stood, and looked around almost in awe at the integrated mess decks. The men grew silent, all eyes on him. "Let us pray," he said softly, and lowered his head. A single tear rolled down his face and splashed down on the deck. Hawk and Linc noticed it, looked at each other and smiled.

"Almighty God," the chaplain began in a voice full of emotion. "We come together this morning to thank you for this wonderful new day, and for this bounty we are about to receive. We realize this morning, more than ever the power and wisdom of your Word. All things are possible in the light of your love, our faith tells us that. Today, we come before you as a crew, each man dependent upon the other, each man trusting the faith and love of the other, each man knowing in his heart that together we can accomplish great things. We thank you for showing us the way to salvation, and we ask your blessing on this ship and all the men who serve her. We ask this in Jesus Christ's name...Amen."

"Amen," came the chorus, and then the men stood, faced the chaplain, and began applauding. They clapped louder and louder and their applause quickly became cheers. Chaplain Charles felt another tear roll down his cheek, but he didn't care. He smiled warmly at the men, accepted their applause and beamed proudly.

The cheering subsided when the chaplain sat down. The men followed and soon sounds of silverware on trays and good-natured conversation rippled through the mess decks.

"This is wonderful," he said appreciatively, looking around at the tables filled with happy sailors.

"It's a start, sir," Linc replied to the nods of his tablemates. "A good start."

"We have a plan, Preacher," Hawk explained. He and Linc shared a look. "We know what we're supposed to do." He held out his hand and the chaplain squeezed it. "No more violence, but much more militance."

"Now, you're talking, young Hawkins, though I don't think there's any such word."

"They is now, sir."

Chaplain Charles chuckled and looked around again at the crowded mess decks. Another tear fell from his eye. "It's a miracle, isn't it?" he whispered to himself. He looked up toward the heavens and closed his eyes. "Thank you, Lord. Thank you."

Mirror Image

He decided to shave before dinner, so while the water warmed up in the small sink, Deavers inspected his face in the mirror. *I look older than I used to*, he mused, and ran his hand across the thickening stubble of his beard. His eyes were still sharp, even if his face was wrinkling, his jaws beginning to sag, and his hair...he didn't even want to think about his hair.

He soaked a wash cloth in water as hot as he could stand, and winced when he pressed it against his face. His beard was tough, and he wanted it to be softened for the shave. Deavers always shaved with a safety razor, eschewing the popular electric shavers. He was used to the blade, comfortable with it, and besides, it took longer to shave with a blade. This was extra time Deavers could spend in discussions with his mirror image.

The man in the mirror had always been Deavers' sounding board, his muse and his biggest critic. They had laughed together, wept together, and argued over many cases, most of which were solved right here, at the sink, with just the two of them...and a blade.

The investigator carefully whipped up lather in his shaving mug. He and his image always looked each other in the eye during the shaving process and shared their perspectives on whatever case was at hand. Tonight, it was about the murder of C.C. Green, and the pending arrest of the killer.

The case had been a tough one. The killing couldn't have happened under more undesirable conditions. Not only was the scene of the crime trampled over by the salvage team, the ship was aground, unsteady, inhospitable. And there were too many suspects, since there was no obvious motive. Hardly anyone on board the Knox even knew C.C. Green, who had wisely kept his head down, trying to remain inconspicuous. Now, Deavers knew who the killer was, for the incomplete information from Captain Peterson was augmented nicely by Ensign Dall's file.

It's still circumstantial! His image seemed to snap at him. "I know, I know," he protested. "He did it, I know he did it, and I'm going to put him away for it." *Knowing it and proving it are two different things, Deavers,* his image reminded him. *What you got is a circumstantial case, pure and simple. Nothing more.*

"What I got is a strong circumstantial case for premeditated murder!" *Yeah, but it's still circumstantial, and you won't get a conviction.*

Deavers pulled the razor across his face in short, quick strokes. "Then I have to force a confession, don't I?" He stopped to rinse off the razor and stared intently at his image. "You don't believe I can do it." *I believe, do you?* Deavers finished shaving and leaned forward on the sink, his nose almost touching the mirror. "He'll confess," the investigator insisted calmly. "And I'll see you tomorrow." He rinsed the razor, patted his face with a warm wash cloth, and rinsed out the sink. *You've got to give him an out,* the image said. *If he's truly the kind of a man you say he is, and his life has come to this, then you have to give him an out.* "I don't know what you're talking about, I've got to get dressed." *You know what I'm talking about, Deavers...*He ignored his image, which was still trying to get his attention, turned off the light in the small head and closed the door. "To hell with that!" He picked out his cleanest uniform and got dressed. He wanted to look as professional as possible for the interrogation.

The Admiral

Admiral Wilson went over the operational plan for the next day, Tuesday, August 24 for about the twentieth time. He studied every aspect of the plan, from the exact time of high tide, to the extra beach gear, to the ships designated to pull the Knox off the reef, to the Cogswell, the destroyer that would speed past the reef at over thirty knots, kicking up a swell which would wash over the reef and add to the effort to free the Frank Knox. If all worked out as planned...The admiral threw the file on the desk and sat down on his bunk. He decided a good nap before dinner would refresh him.

The Captain

In his cabin on the Prairie, Captain Marshall also reviewed the operational plan. He was confident everything would work this time. The engineers reported a dramatic increase in the Knox's buoyancy and with four ships hooked up to her and pulling steady, she should come free at high tide. The captain nodded, satisfied that everything that could be done, was done. He put the file away and decided to take a brisk walk around the decks before dinner. He found it always refreshed him.

The Investigators

After dinner, Deavers and Dall huddled together in the wardroom, preparing the arrest warrant and going over, for the umpteenth time, their plan of action. The actual arrest would be made at midnight, when the subject was tired and off-guard. Two masters-at-arms had flown in from Subic Bay to handle the security and transportation of the prisoner.

Since Deavers would be leaving after briefing Captain Lamb and his staff, it was decided his quarters would serve to confine the prisoner. Deavers began packing his bag. He tossed in his shaving kit, extra underwear and socks, the two spare uniforms he brought with him, and his case file. *Now,* he thought, *do I have everything I need?* He looked at the desk drawer, and a strange feeling overcame him, as if someone had walked on his grave. He shook his head, looked again at the desk drawer, and decided, for no reason he could explain, to leave it alone. He set the bag in the corner and turned to Dall.

"Let's get some air," he told the ensign. He looked at his watch. It was 2300 hours. "Then we'll wait until midnight and make the arrest."

Dall nodded acknowledgment. "Roger," he replied.

Bob Harp

Close to midnight, after a long, exhausting day in the engine room, EM-3 Bob Harp slumped heavily on his bunk, a towel wrapped around his waist. The shower had been short, cold and less than satisfying, but at least he felt clean. He sighed and took out his personal stationery and pen. He thought for a moment, and then began writing the last letter he would write from Pratas Reef:

Dear Mom and Dad,
Guess where I am? Yep, same damn place!

PART FOUR:

THE SOLUTION

CHAPTER THIRTY SEVEN

Tuesday, August 24, 1965
0700 Hours

The Final Day

Captain Roger Lamb and new executive officer Lieutenant Bill Holliday joined the group in the officers' wardroom. Captain Lamb looked around and frowned at the unusual gathering. Present were weapons officer McCarthy, Engineering Lieutenant Geoff Darby, Dental Tech J.I. Parker, and two officers neither Roger nor Bill Holliday knew, who turned out to be masters at arms from Subic Bay. They all came to attention when Captain Lamb entered.

"Alright," Captain Lamb demanded of no one in particular. "Where's Deavers? He asked for this meeting."

"He'll be here any minute now, Captain." Dental Tech Parker was speaking soothingly to Captain Lamb, and Roger didn't like the feeling he was being patronized. He was about to lash into Parker when the door opened and Deavers walked in carrying a file. He took off his sunglasses and strode, without looking at anyone, to the head of the wardroom table. He put down the file and looked up.

"Please be seated," Deavers said softly. He leaned on the table and stared at the file in front of him. Chairs were pulled out and everyone settled in.

Captain Lamb looked around the room with an irritated expression on his face, thinking, *Why isn't Chief Billings here?* Aloud he said, "What is the meaning of this meeting, Deavers?" The strain of the last month was etched on his face. "We are at a critical point in the salvaging of this ship, and you call us away to a...what did you call it? A very important meeting? You want to tell me what all the drama is about?"

Deavers cleared his throat. "I regret to inform you that early this morning Chief Boatswains Mate Frederick Billings surrendered to authorities," Deavers nodded toward the two unknown officers, "and is confined to quarters, under arrest for the murder of Boatswains Mate First Class C.C. Green."

Captain Lamb stared, astonished, at Deavers. His mind completely rejected what he had just heard. "That is absolutely absurd!" he shouted. He started to rise, but Bill Holliday put a gentle hand on his arm, and the captain sat back down.

"Deavers." Mr. Holliday turned to the investigator. The exec's teeth were clenched and he was struggling to contain his anger.

"Chief Billings was...is the best sailor aboard this ship. This is unbelievable. Are you certain you haven't made some terrible mistake?"

"Yes, sir," Deavers replied firmly. "I'm certain."

Roger Lamb looked around the room, anger and frustration in his eyes. He focused on Dental Tech Parker, and barked, "Just who the hell ARE you?"

"I'm Ensign William Dall, Captain," he replied, presenting his ID card. "I'm a Navy criminal investigator from San Diego. I've been aboard to keep C.C. Green under surveillance." Dall smiled weakly. "I'm sorry if Captain Pizzonovich didn't inform you when you took command, sir. I'm sure he had a lot on his mind."

Roger Lamb looked at the ID, scowled, then focused his attention on the two unfamiliar officers. "You men investigators, too?"

"These officers are from the Master at Arms office in Subic Bay. They will escort Chief Billings to Subic this afternoon." Deavers shuffled some papers. He was uncomfortable bringing news like this to men like these, after what they had been through. "Chief Billings is in his quarters, under guard. He is cooperating."

"And when the hell was I going to be advised of all this?" Roger leaned forward on the table and glared at Deavers. "You agreed to keep me informed of any developments."

"We only pooled our resources day before yesterday, Captain," Deavers replied soothingly. "The case came together late last night. We are sharing all the information with you, first, before we report to our superiors." He smiled as reassuringly as he could manage. "You are the first people to hear the complete story." It was true, although the report was on its way to Captain Peterson and Admiral Wilson.

That seemed to mollify the captain. He looked at Mr. Holliday who nodded solemnly. "Very well," Captain Lamb instructed, leaning back in his seat. "Tell us what you've got."

Deavers nodded respectfully and sat down in his chair. He opened the file in front of him and began. "Ensign Dall's office has been investigating C.C. Green because of an accidental death of one of Green's recruits in basic training at San Diego. The boy's name was Andrew Tompkins. While the investigation was moving forward, another recruit was seriously injured while Green was in charge. That prompted the authorities in San Diego to place Green in the transit barracks, where they thought they left him languishing so they would know where to find him. But, as I'll explain later, Green got assigned to the Knox, which surprised the people in San Diego, and they had to dispatch someone to keep an eye on him. Ensign Dall actually attended dental school, so they made him a dental tech because he could speak the lingo." Deavers glanced at Dall. "And, because he was the only investigator available. When Green died, the San Diego investigation ran out of steam. Why investigate someone who's dead? But they didn't close their investigation. They began an inquiry into how Green got shipped out, and they asked Ensign Dall to keep them advised of my investigation into the apparent murder."

"What does this Andrew Tompkins have to do with Chief Billings?" Captain Lamb asked.

"Nothing, Captain."

"Then why would Chief Billings kill Green?" Lieutenant Holliday asked. "Don't you think maybe it could have been some relative or friend of this Andrew Tompkins who killed Green for revenge?"

"We thought so at first, naturally, but as with most investigations, it turned out not to be that simple." Deavers looked around the room. Everyone was listening attentively. "It wasn't the death of Tompkins that served as a motive, and yes, Mr. Holliday, it was definitely a revenge killing. C.C. Green was murdered because he caused a severe, life-altering injury which put a young man into a coma, effectively rendering him a vegetable for the rest of his life."

"This injured recruit was related to Chief Billings?" Captain Lamb asked, his face furrowed in a frown.

"Yes, sir, he was." Deavers folded his hands on the desk and a sad look passed over his face. "The recruit, James Conklin, was...is the younger brother of Chief Billings' wife, Janice." Deavers looked over at Dall and nodded.

Dall stood and began pacing. "Janice Billings was devoted to her little brother. He lived with her and the chief since he was about twelve, and the chief looked after him as his own son. The boy, as Deavers has told you, is in a coma and will be for the rest of his life. Janice Billings had a nervous breakdown when the accident happened, you may remember Chief Billings' emergency leave last March." Roger Lamb and Bill Holliday looked at each other and nodded. "She has never really recovered. She's moved James' bed and all the equipment keeping him alive into their home. She spends all her time in the room with James. She sleeps there; she even takes her meals there. She's slowly descending into despair. I'm sorry to say the Billings' marriage is collapsing under the strain."

"And all of that is in these files?" Captain Lamb asked.

"Yes, sir."

"I knew the chief had a wife and son, but he was very private. He never spoke of his family," Lieutenant Holliday mused. "He kept all that to himself?"

"Yes, sir," Deavers replied. "It must have been a heavy burden."

Captain Lamb and Lieutenant Holliday shook their heads sadly. "How did you figure it out?" the captain asked.

"We were stumped by the way the body was staged," Deavers continued the narrative. "The watch cap pulled over the face almost cried out as a clue, but we couldn't make the connection. R.J. Davis, a sailor on the Prairie discovered an important piece of the puzzle," Deavers said. "At least he came up with the explanation for the clue."

"Watch cap?" Bill Holliday asked.

"In the smoke pit," Deavers replied, nodding. "The simulation of a fire at sea, teaching survival techniques in a compartment filled with black smoke."

Mr. Holliday and Mr. Lamb looked at each other knowingly. They'd had to go through that training at Annapolis.

United States Naval Training Center
Boot Camp
San Diego, California

March, 1965

The rumors began at morning chow, when James and his friends talked to some soon-to-graduate recruits who had been through the smoke pit and were more than happy to perpetuate several boot camp myths about the experience: Three or four guys will get injured, maybe one will die. It happens all the time. You won't be able to breathe. It's the scariest thing you ever experienced. Today is the worst day of your life. If you can, put in a chit to go to sick bay, anything to stay out of the pit.

James Conklin and his buddies made fun of the myths, but privately, they were afraid, especially James, who was claustrophobic. The idea of being trapped in a tight space created nightmares for him. What would happen when they pumped the tight space full of smoke? James felt a twinge of panic and he shuddered. He was determined, however, to make it through the smoke pit and anything else C.C. Green had up his sleeve. He'd made it through ten weeks of everything that prick could think up, another ten days wouldn't stop him.

USS Frank Knox
Pratas Reef

"James Conklin was a small, thin young man who looked almost anemic," Ensign Dall explained. "But he was bright, articulate and funny. The very traits someone like C.C. Green would envy, and try to ridicule in order to shore up his own private feelings of self-contempt."

"So, now you're a psychologist, Ensign Dall?" Captain Lamb made a point of not disguising his sarcasm. He glared at the young ensign until Deavers broke in.

"Captain, we are here, as a matter of respect for you and your command, to inform you of the findings and conclusions of our investigation into a murder committed on board your ship. If this is an inconvenient time for you, perhaps I could speak to Admiral Wilson about re-convening this meeting aboard the Prairie. He is very anxious to see our report, and I don't believe the admiral will approach these findings and conclusions with your cavalier attitude." Deavers stared, stone-faced at Captain Lamb.

The wardroom air grew thick. Mr. McCarthy and Mr. Darby took advantage of the pregnant pause to carefully inspect their shoelaces. Mr. Holliday glanced between Dall, Deavers and Roger Lamb. Deavers and Captain Lamb stared intently at each other. Again, Deavers broke the silence.

"The past few weeks have been hard on all of us," the investigator said in a conciliatory tone. "Mostly, it's been hard on the good crew of the Knox." He smiled affably. "We are, all of us, trying to do difficult jobs under less than optimum circumstances, but we are all on the same side, Captain. We're all in the same Navy, and we all want the same things." Deavers stood and pulled the curtains away from the porthole. He pointed out toward Task Force 73. "The United States Navy is here for the Frank Knox," he declared, motioning at the assembled rescue and salvage ships dotting the horizon. "We are here to take care of one of our own, and Captain," Deavers dropped the curtain and turned to face Roger Lamb. "With all due respect, James Conklin is one of our own, Andrew Tompkins was one of our own...and C.C. Green was one of our own, too."

Captain Lamb stared at Deavers for a few moments. He realized that the investigator was right, of course. He cleared his throat to speak, but Bill Holliday beat him to it.

"We realize all that, Deavers," the lieutenant explained, somewhat impatiently. "But you must understand that today, of all days, the Captain's three main concerns are one, the Frank Knox, two, the Frank Knox, and three, the Frank Knox."

"Yes, sir, I do."

Captain Lamb took a deep breath, let it out slowly, and looked around the wardroom. "Do we have any coffee?" he asked. "If not, I suggest we make some. We might be here a while."

USNTC
March, 1965

The Smoke Pit

By week ten of Navy boot camp, morning inspections, greatly feared in the first few weeks, were becoming routine. James Conklin sat on his bunk and carefully tightened the laces on his leggings. His boondockers gleamed with a carefully-applied spit-shine. His white hat and leggings, scrubbed for an hour on the wash table with bleach and powdered toothpaste, would glare hot-white in the bright morning sun as Company 132 fell out for inspection. He had learned the secret for keeping his trousers straight and sharp, with no blousy bulges. Before pulling his trousers up to his waist and buckling them, he would leave them around his thighs until the legs were tucked into his boondockers, and tied around his ankles with a clothes stop. Then he would tighten the leggings around his boots and stand, pulling the trousers up hard, stretching them before securing them with the belt, insuring a tight surface, taut enough for the inspector to bounce a quarter off, *should the sadistic bastard want to,* he thought.

After inspection, instructional classes were scheduled for the rest of the morning. Then lunch. Then back to the barracks to change into dungarees and watch caps. That afternoon they would encounter the smoke pit.

Company 132, in rows of three, marched toward the choppy channel that flowed through the Naval Training Center and into the bay. They followed the narrow, paved-over path traveled by so many others, leaving the brightly painted barracks of the Navy boot camp behind. Soon, the gray, concrete pillbox known as the 'smoke-pit' came into view a half mile away, its foreboding features tucked neatly into the side of a hill, seeming to beckon to the recruits, as if the pit could smell their fear. Off into the distance, beyond the channel, beyond the recruits' vision and far into the bay, proud Navy ships moved in and out, announcing their departures and arrivals with bells, whistles and stack horns.

"Hear that?" Rudy Cobb asked, holding his hand cupped to his ear as he marched in perfect step.

"Hear what?" James chided, smiling and marching along.

"That's the fleet out there, baby!" Rudy announced. He looked around at his squad mates. "I mean, right? That's the fleet out there?"

James chuckled at his friend. "No, Rudy," he announced. "That's the NAVY out there!"

Company commander C.C. Green stepped to the front of the formation and barked, "Company, HALT!" He stalked up and down the ranks, glaring at his charges. He stopped when he reached James Conklin.

"You the pussy doing all the jawin' in ranks?"

"No, sir."

"You a lyin' sumbitch!" Green's face was only about a half-inch away from James Conklin's, and the young recruit recoiled at the breath of the company commander. "I don't like you, maggot," Green seethed. "I'm gonna be on your ass twenty four hours a day until you graduate...IF you graduate." Green put his mouth up next to James' ear and barked, "You got that recruit?"

"Yes, sir!" James retorted smartly.

Green nodded, still staring wide-eyed at James. He looked around at the rest of the company as if he had just discovered they were there. He turned and marched to the head of the column. "All right! Let's move, forward...HUT!"

Rudy whispered under his breath, "Man, I hate that nigger."

James shook his head quickly as a warning. The formation marched around a bend in the road and suddenly found themselves staring at the foreboding concrete pillbox known as 'The Pit.' Three Navy petty officers in dungarees stood beside the entrance to the pit, reviewing some paperwork on a clipboard. James could see a jeep off to one side, its doors open.

"Corpsmen!" Rudy whispered. "Whadda they need those guys for?"

C.C. Green halted the company and stood before them, glaring. "These three men," he motioned toward the corpsmen, "are going to walk you through the procedures for this training. Listen to them, follow their instructions to the letter and you will get through this. If you don't listen, one or more of you may panic and try to escape." He stepped up closer to the ranks and hissed, "No recruit of mine has ever failed this training." He looked over at James Conklin, who stared straight ahead. "And none of you will fail today, that I promise you. Now, pay attention to these men!" Green walked off to the side and leaned casually against the concrete pillbox. He folded his arms and glowered at his recruits.

The first corpsman, obviously the team leader, stepped forward. The other two took places behind him. "Good afternoon, men," the lead corpsman said cheerfully. "My name is Donovan, I'm a corpsman first class. behind me are Johnson and Greggs, both corpsmen second class. Today you are going to experience what can happen on board ship during a fire. I am going to instruct you in how to survive a fire like that. This building..." he pointed to the concrete monolith. Most of the recruits didn't look at it as he continued with his instructions. "...Simulates a ship's compartment, below decks, where easy access to egress is blocked. When we put you in that compartment, you will sit down against the bulkheads, pull your watch caps over your faces and tuck them under your chins, duck your heads down between your legs, and clasp your hands behind your heads." Johnson and Greggs demonstrated. "Breathe normally, don't panic. It's all over in three minutes. Believe me, you're gonna want to bolt for the door, but follow instructions and you will be fine." He smiled to show them they would be fine, then said seriously, "I know you guys have heard all the boot camp rumors about guys dying in this smoke pit. Well, I'm here to tell you that never happened. It's just a story some of the 'old salts' tell to scare you. Don't believe it."

James Conklin stared straight ahead. His knees were trembling slightly, and he was becoming flushed. His chest felt tight, as if someone were sitting on it, he felt faint and he was having trouble breathing. He hoped no one noticed.

C.C. Green noticed. He stood leaning against the building, arms crossed, a sadistic sneer on his face, staring at recruit Conklin.

"One more thing," Donovan cautioned. "If I hear any banging on this door from the inside, regardless of who is doing the banging, I will open it immediately to allow the exit of any man who can't take it." He made it sound like banging on the door would be a despicable thing to do. "Any questions? None? Okay, then, let's get started." The three corpsmen took up stations at the entrance to the smoke pit. Donovan pulled open the big iron door and motioned to the recruits, "Single file, men! Step into the compartment and take your places against the bulkhead."

James tried to maneuver his way into a position near the door, but sailors streaming into the compartment forced him to the rear. Inside, the compartment was built into a large, circular area with an overhead so low many of the recruits had to duck down to enter. Heavy, black smoke stains painted the circular bulkhead and covered the overhead with billowing memories of black soot. James sat down next to Rudy and pulled his knees up as close to his chest as he could. He looked around furtively and licked his lips frantically. The thick, stale-smoke smell in the pit almost gagged him. He shut his eyes and tried not to think of what it was going to be like when the smoke pouring came in.

"Take it easy, buddy," Rudy whispered. "This is gonna be a piece of cake, right?" He nudged James in the ribs and repeated more urgently, "RIGHT?"

"Yeah, yeah, right." James gulped the air, and nodded his head up and down. "I'm good. I'm good. I'm good." He struggled to control the trembling in his limbs. He breathed deeply and let the air out slowly. He closed his eyes and imagined himself outside, the exercise over, breathing the fresh salt air. It didn't help much.

"Three minutes," Rudy whispered. "That's all."

James rocked back and forth, his head pressing on his knees. He had been instructed to lace his fingers behind the back of his head and pull his head down, between his knees. He rocked and mumbled trance-like, "Three minutes. Three minutes. Three minutes." Sweat poured down his face and a wide stain darkened his shirt, spreading out from under his arms. His breath was coming in short gasps.

C.C. Green stood in the hatchway, shifting a large flashlight from hand to hand, staring at James as if he were enjoying the recruit's dilemma. He did a quick roster check and nodded that he was satisfied all the recruits were present. He grinned at his charges and pulled a gas-mask over his face, adjusted the straps and checked the air flow. He ducked into the compartment and nodded to Donovan, who called to the recruits, "Your three minutes starts now!" He swung the big iron door closed and dogged it off, effectively sealing off the compartment. The deep, resounding CLUNK of the slammed door echoed throughout the compartment long after the smoke had begun to seep in. The horrible clunking sound lingered in James' mind long after that. It roared loudly in his ears, morphing into a frantic voice that screamed at him, *"Get Out! Get Out! Get Out!"*

2:59----

Green swung the big flashlight left and right, peering into the smoke from his position at the door. The beam flowed over the recruits, illuminating them. They hunkered down, fingers laced behind their heads, watch caps pulled over their faces, scrambling to get closer to the deck or the bulkhead. They were getting their first dose of the black, oily smoke. The beginning was the worst. If someone was going to lose it, it usually happened in the first minute.

2:45----

James tried to slow his breathing, but he was starting to taste the bitter fear that always signaled the beginning of a panic attack. The smoke was already unbearable. It was soup-thick, and the damn watch cap did him no good, it seemed to absorb the smoke. He reached up to pull it off, but thought better of it, and squeezed his eyes shut tight, willing himself to settle down and fight his fear. He prayed to God for strength.

2:30----

Green checked his watch. It was time for someone to bolt for the door, if it was going to happen. He scanned the compartment, seeking out potential candidates. They all seemed calm, even the company wimp. Well, it was early. The smoke billowed into the compartment with more force, and the recruits shuffled around, trying to find safety. Green grinned at the hazy sight. He'd keep an eye on recruit Conklin. He was the one most likely to fall apart.

2:15----

James Conklin began to gag. *My God,* he thought, *it's almost been three minutes, hasn't it?* The heavy, black smoke swirled and flowed, rushing around the compartment and slapping up against the recruits like the Furies unleashed. James gagged again and choked down a cough. *If I start coughing,* he reasoned, *I'll die.* He swallowed hard several times to keep from coughing. He lifted his head just enough to locate the door, then dropped it back down on his knees.

2:00----

It was becoming unbearable. The smoke crashed down on the recruits like a collapsing circus tent. Some of the recruits swore, others yelled, most just kept their heads down. James' throat was almost closed, and his lungs seemed full of smoke. He couldn't catch a breath, and his head began spinning. *I'm gonna pass out...* He lifted up the edge of his watch cap to try and get some air, but smoke rushed into his lungs. *I can't...I can't brea...*

1:45----

James peeled off his watch cap and scrambled desperately toward the door. Green anticipated the move and was waiting for him. He grabbed James around the waist and wrestled him to the floor before he could pound on the door. Most of the other recruits had no idea what was going on, their attention focused on surviving the three minutes.

"No! No!" James pleaded. "Let me go! Let me..." he started coughing and choking again, and fell to his knees.

1:30----

"No you don't, recruit!" Green yelled through his mask. He had James in a hammerlock, holding him down on the deck. "Get your stupid face down!" he yelled. "If there's any air left, it'll be down low." He pushed James' face down and felt around for the watch cap.

Green recovered James' watch cap and glanced around. The smoke was very thick. He couldn't see anything with his gas mask on, surely no one else was going to see anything.

1:15----

Green pressed a knee into James' back and pulled the watch cap back over his face. "You ain't screwing up my record!" He tied James' wrists behind his back with a short rope. "You gonna go through this like everybody else!"

James gagged, scrambling toward the bulkhead. His heart pumped wildly, and he had trouble holding a thought in his head. He tried to breathe slowly, but the smoke got into his lungs anyway. He feared he would throw up.

1:00----

"One minute to go!" Green called out. "One minute!" He held up his index finger as if the recruits could see it. They had their heads down, whispering softly to themselves,"...59..58..57.."

Green sat back near the door and swept his light around the compartment. The recruits were all toughing it out. They squirmed and shifted, many attempting to maintain the countdown, whispering, "...25...24...23..." Time slowed to a merciless crawl. Each tick of the clock came later than the one before.

0:45----

He didn't expect it to be this easy. Green waved his flashlight over the recruits and snorted. *Even that weakling calmed down,* he thought, his light resting on Conklin. *The kid must have learned his lesson, he hasn't moved since I tossed his ass back in there. Nobody is gonna screw up my record! They stay in the Pit because they follow instructions or because they're afraid of me. I don't give a shit which, long as they stay.*

0:30----

A quiet calm came over the Smoke Pit. The recruits had followed Rudy Cobb's steady countdown and were certain the end was near. Most of them had barely held on, and some of them had almost run for the door, but only one had run. Everyone in the Pit thought he knew who it was. Rudy counted carefully, and felt next to him, where James had been sitting, but his hand touched only the bulkhead. *It was James I saw!*

0:15----

"...3...2...1..." Rudy counted down to zero. Nothing happened. The door didn't open. Some of the recruits glanced around like frantic monkeys. It was eerily quiet inside the smoke pit as the last agonizing seconds ticked away. No one seemed to breathe. In the smoke-filtered glow of C.C. Green's flashlight, the recruits looked like people who had been frozen in time. They were soot-covered and huddled together tightly, motionlessly, like people in Pompeii who were trapped by the eruption of Vesuvius.

0:00----

The big door creaked open and exhaust fans sprang into life, sucking the smoke out of the compartment. The recruits of Company 132 staggered out into the fresh air, their faces blackened, many coughing and choking, their eyes stinging with smoke. Green lingered behind.

"Don't rub your eyes!" Donovan yelled, walking up and down in front of them. "We'll give you wet towels and water." He motioned to Johnson and Greggs who began distributing towels and water, and checking the recruits for injuries. There were none.

Rudy Cobb took a long pull on the water, soaked his towel and rinsed his eyes. He looked around happily, relieved the Smoke Pit was finally behind him, and tried to locate James. "Hey," he called out to the rest of the company. "Where's Conklin?"

USS Frank Knox

"By the time they pulled recruit Conklin out of the Pit, he had stopped breathing." Dall leafed through his notes and continued. "They laid him out on the pathway while one of the corpsmen called for an ambulance. By all accounts, he suffered severe cerebral hypoxia."

"Severe what, Ensign?" Bill Holliday interrupted the investigator.

Deavers cut in. "His brain was deprived of oxygen for several minutes," he explained matter-of-factly. "He is in a coma, and will be for the rest of his life." Deavers nodded to Dall to take over.

"The smoke damage to his lungs was extensive," the ensign continued. "While his body continued to pump blood into his brain, the blood carried no oxygen to speak of. The brain can suffer severe damage if the oxygen deprivation lasts longer than five or six minutes."

"You've gathered a great deal of information about what happened in the Smoke Pit, Deavers," the captain said. "I trust you can prove it."

"Yes, sir, we can."

"You have witnesses?"

"Just one, sir," Deavers opened the file and extracted a sheaf of papers. "Seaman Rudy Cobb, a recruit in Green's company and a friend of James Conklin." Deavers leafed through the papers before continuing. "Right after boot camp he was assigned to Radar 'A' school in San Diego. This is his statement." The investigator slid the papers across the table to the captain.

Roger glanced through the statement report. He looked down at his watch. "Bill," he turned to his executive officer. "High tide is at what time?"

"Eleven twenty-six, sir." Bill Holliday looked down at his watch, nodding. "We've got about three hours before conditions are optimal, but I'd really like to get everything in place early, because..."

Captain Lamb held up his hand. "I know, Bill, and you are

absolutely right. We have to be ready." He pointed at his wrist watch and looked over at Deavers. "This entire task force is poised for one massive maximum effort to pull this ship off the reef this morning at eleven twenty-six. It is now zero-eight-thirty. I can only give you another hour, Deavers, so please sum this up as quickly as possible."

Deavers nodded, a small smile lifting the corners of his mouth. *Just like the Navy,* he thought. *Wrap it up and let's get going! The salvage operation and the murder investigation had run along parallel lines. We can safely estimate that C.C. Green died about the same time the Knox hit the reef, and so the two incidents will forever be intertwined. One story cannot be told without the other as background, and vice versa. Now, after thirty-seven days of maximum effort, both sagas are ending almost simultaneously, and that's as it should be. The USS Frank Knox will be freed from the reef, and this time they were sure. Conditions will be perfect. The investigation has come to an end, too. A very sad end.* Deavers sighed as he prepared to sum things up as quickly as possible. *I don't want to remember this case. I don't ever want to think about it again. I'm just glad it's finally over.* It wasn't, but at that moment, Deavers did not know it.

"Recruit Conklin was revived on the way to the Naval hospital, but never regained consciousness." Deavers felt tired all of a sudden, and he looked it. His eyes were bloodshot, and his face seemed to sag, as if some internal force were pulling it down. He stood and began pacing, trying to force some life into his limbs.

"Everyone on the scene was interviewed in the following days, and while no evidence of fault could be found, C.C. Green was suspected of doing something. Andrew Tompkins had died only a month prior to Conklin's injury, and the Tompkins incident was still fresh in everyone's mind."

"In the Smoke Pit, again?" Mr. Holliday asked.

"No, sir. Andrew Tompkins drowned in the swimming pool during survival training." Deavers flipped through San Diego's report until he found the page he was looking for. "By some accounts, recruit Tompkins told Green he couldn't swim and was terrified of the water, but Green humiliated him in front of the rest of the company. Tompkins got angry and jumped into the pool with all the other recruits. With all the splashing and kicking going on, no one noticed that recruit Tompkins had sunk to the bottom of the pool and drowned." He put the report down and shrugged. "It never got beyond the suspicion stage. There were no witnesses to any wrongdoing on Green's part."

"But you had a witness to the Smoke Pit incident. Why wasn't Green promptly court-martialed?" Captain Lamb demanded.

"Because the witness never came forward." Ensign Dall stood and took over the narrative. "He was afraid of Green. All the recruits were interviewed at the time, each swore he neither saw nor heard anything out of the ordinary. In fact, everyone agreed it was C.C. Green who pulled Conklin out of the smoke pit. When Green got killed, and the focus of the investigation was redirected, those witnesses were re-interviewed as a matter of routine procedure. It was the re-interview with Rudy Cobb that began to fill in some of the gaps for us."

USNTC
San Diego

Rudy had been one of the last recruits interviewed by the Navy investigators about the smoke pit incident. By the time they got around to him, he was nervous and on edge. The recruits who had preceded him described the questions he would be asked. He sat ramrod straight in the chair in front of the investigator's desk and declined the offer of a cigarette, just as the others had done. He answered all questions with a polite, "Yes, sir, no, sir, I don't know, sir."

The interviewer, already bored with the process, made perfunctory notes on a legal pad. After the last recruit had been interviewed, and the last perfunctory notes recorded, one investigator turned to the other and said, "Maybe Green had something to do with this accident, and maybe not. But we ain't gonna find out from these boys."

Rudy Cobb got hit with a strong dose of regret as soon as he got back to the barracks. James Conklin's bunk had been stripped, the bare mattress folded in half, exposing the naked bed springs, which looked like a picked over carcass.

Late that night, lying awake in his bunk, Rudy struggled with the guilt that would haunt him for several months. He should have told what he had seen in the Smoke Pit. It was dark, smoke was swirling around wildly, but Rudy stole a quick look around. James was not next to him anymore and Rudy wanted to try to locate his friend. He saw the image of C.C. Green, bending over someone (James?). It looked like he was tying up a calf in a rodeo, because when he was finished he stood up quickly and looked around. Green did not notice Rudy Cobb.

Later, when he couldn't find James outside the pit, he suddenly remembered the images, and he spotted Green stepping out of the door to the pit, wrapping something around his hand. A short length of rope? After boot camp, when he was assigned to Radar "A" school in San Diego, he had thought about going to the investigator and telling him what he had seen, but Rudy was never able to muster the courage to do it. He was privately relieved when Chief Billings showed up in his barracks one afternoon, and he gladly poured out everything he could remember. It was a cathartic experience for his conscience, and he promised the chief he wouldn't repeat the tale to anyone else. But when Green died, and a criminal investigator came to re-interview him, Rudy broke down and unburdened his soul.

USS Frank Knox

"I was one of the investigators who interviewed the recruits initially," Dall explained. "And I always felt that Rudy Cobb knew more than he admitted, but I couldn't shake him. When Green was killed, Cobb was re-interviewed by our office. As it turned out, he was the only one who saw anything, but what he said he saw, and what he told Chief Billings he saw, fits the scenario as reconstructed by Mr. Deavers."

All heads turned to Deavers. "In the incidents of Conklin and Green we found common denominators. The watch cap over the faces of both men and hands tied behind both their backs. When we finally connected James Conklin to Chief Billings, all the pieces fell neatly into place. You see, San Diego investigators were looking into the Smoke Pit accident and the drowning of recruit Tompkins, with C.C. Green their top suspect. But Green got transferred to the fleet, and was no longer within easy reach. They wanted to know why, so they began questioning people at the transit barracks. They got nowhere with them until Green was murdered, then they drove the Golden Spike."

"The Golden Spike?" Mr. Holliday asked.

"Yes, sir. The Golden Spike that connected the two lines of the investigation and made them one."

Mr. Holliday looked thoughtful. Captain Lamb was clearly impatient and irritated.

"Like the joining of the trans-continental railroad at Promontory, Utah?" Deavers prodded.

Dall lowered his eyes and smiled. *Boy, Deavers can sure come up with some weird shit!*

"Anyway," Deavers continued, unabashed. "They discovered how Green got assigned to the Knox, and the whole case pivoted in the direction of Chief Billings."

"And how did Green get sent to us?" Captain Lamb asked, glancing down impatiently at his watch.

"He was assigned by the chief petty officer in charge of transit personnel."

"Who?" Mr. Holliday asked.

Deavers smiled. "The Golden Spike," he explained. "Master Chief Boatswains' Mate Marty McGarry."

U.S. Navy Transit Barracks
32nd Street, San Diego
April, 1965

King Neptune

Chief McGarry jumped up and hurried around his desk to throw his arms around the younger chief boatswains' mate who had just stepped into the office.

"Freddy, boy, how the hell are ya?"

Frederick Billings gasped for breath in the big man's bear hug. "Damn, Marty! You like ta kill me!"

Marty McGarry let go the hug and held his friend at arms' length, looking him up and down. "You still a pretty-boy, ain't ya, Freddy?" He walked behind his desk and plopped down into a worn, leather chair. The chair seemed to sigh heavily with the chief's weight, but was obviously accustomed to the big man, and bore its burden in silence, emitting neither a creak nor a groan. "Sit yer butt down." Chief McGarry indicated an equally worn wooden chair opposite the desk. It was piled with paper and files, but Chief Billings lifted up the pile and dropped it unceremoniously on the deck, where it joined several other similar piles.

Looking around the Transit Personnel office, Chief Billings had to smile. Marty McGarry was one of the most disorganized administrators he had ever seen. Paperwork was piled everywhere, on every surface. It scattered across the desk, along with a half-eaten sandwich, a half bottle of stale beer, and a large ashtray half filled with ashes and half-smoked cigar butts. One of the butts smoldered in the ashtray, and another, newer one smoldered in McGarry's mouth.

"You ain't here for a Kearsarge reunion, so what's on your mind?" Marty leaned back and grinned at his former protégé from the big aircraft carrier. *That was years ago, and the kid done good. Real good.*

Fred Billings gestured around the cluttered office. "Do you actually know where any..."

"My boy," McGarry interrupted. He leaned across the desk and grinned slyly. "I am the master of this here domain. I, and only I, know where everything and everybody is at." He leaned back and blew cigar smoke into the air. "At all times," he added, confidently punctuating the air with his cigar.

"Well, then," Billings replied, looking around the room doubtfully. "You are, indeed, the evil genius I always suspected you to be."

"So, what you doin' here, Freddy?"

"I'm on leave, thought I'd stop by to say hello."

McGarry chewed on his cigar and eyed his friend suspiciously. "Yeah? How's Janice and the family?"

"Everything's aces, Marty," he lied. "Everything is going great."

McGarry nodded knowingly. "You're lookin' for bodies, aren't you, Freddy?"

Billings chuckled. "You could always see through me, Marty."

"You can't throw that shit past me, Freddy. Why don't you just come out and say you need to fill a billet or two? You know I'll always help you guys out. Hell, yesterday," he leaned forward conspiratorially and lowered his voice, "I put a deck ape on a tin can an hour before she got underway." Marty chewed his cigar and grinned broadly. "He had a pissed-off papa on his ass. Something about a dishonored daughter and a shotgun. Anyways, like I said, why you gotta create all this drama?" The fat chief smiled smugly and leaned back in his chair, hands laced behind his head. The chair sighed quietly, adjusting to the big man's shifting heft.

"We've got a billet for a BM-one," Fred explained. "But, really, I wanted to say hello to you. Just make a note of it, and maybe locate someone." He looked around the cluttered office and frowned. "IF you can locate anyone in this place," he added, doubtfully.

McGarry took it as a challenge. "Wait one!" He reached behind his chair and plucked one of several clipboards off the bulkhead. He leafed through a few pages and turned around, that smug smile on his face. "Well, my boy, it looks like we got two--count 'em-TWO first class anchor-clankers. We got a guy named Brown, and we got a guy named Green." Chief McGarry looked up and his smile was even more smug. "What color you want?"

Billings laughed out loud. "I don't know how you do it, Marty, but I'll take the Green one because it reminds me of money."

"Yeah, Green's better," Marty agreed, scribbling some notes on the clipboard. "Brown always reminds me of somebody's puckered ass."

Fred Billings laughed again and reached out to shake his friend's hand. "You are the master of your domain, Marty McGarry. You are the King Neptune of the under-sea world of paperwork."

"I am the master of all that you see before you," Marty

announced grandly, waving his arm around the room. "Never again doubt the Wizard, Dorothy or I'll zap your ass back to Kansas." Marty was clearly enjoying himself and Fred Billings laughed right along with him.

Chief Billings drove away and Marty McGarry leaned against the doorway of his office, watching Freddy's car disappear down the street toward the main gate. *King Neptune, my salty ass!* he thought. *Hell, come to think of it, I actually was King Neptune on several occasions.* He chuckled as he remembered the many equator crossings and coinciding initiation ceremonies he had presided over. *Yep, I converted many slimy young Pollywogs into trusty Shellbacks.* He chuckled again, his big belly bouncing in perfect rhythm. *I can't get over Fred Billings coming in here and trying to maneuver me. He made it a challenge, and I fell for it. If he just asked, I woulda helped him. I wonder why he came at me from the side. Hmmm.*

The chief thought about it for a moment, grunted and inspected the end of his cigar. It had gone out. He returned to his desk and dropped the butt into the ashtray. He put the Billings encounter out of his mind and unpeeled the wrapper off a fresh cigar.

USS Frank Knox
August 24, 1965

"The first time I interviewed Chief McGarry," Dall continued, "he, 'didn't know nothing about Green or Billings or nobody else.' That's a direct quote. The chief is an interesting man," Dall chuckled to himself. "Upon hearing about C.C. Green's murder, it didn't take him long to add it up. McGarry is an old hand. He's been in the Navy for almost thirty years, and he knows how the bureaucracy works. He's been successful at manipulating it from time to time to suit his own purposes. Concerned that Billings would break down and confess everything, and knowing he would eventually wind up in the investigation's cross-hairs, Chief McGarry did what any competent Navy wheeler-dealer would do: he came to us and proposed a deal." Dall selected a few pages from the case file and handed them to Captain Lamb. "That's his statement, and the report on the meeting with him."

Roger Lamb glanced through the file and looked up sharply at Dall. "This statement was taken ten days ago! You held this report up?"

"No, sir," Dall replied patiently. "I received the report from San Diego two days ago, and I immediately turned it over to Mr. Deavers. Since that time we've been formulating our strategy..." he held a hand in the air to stop Mr. Holliday from interrupting. "...bear with me. We pooled our information, requested the arrest warrant from Subic Bay, confronted Chief Billings, learned the entire story, and put it down in a logical, organized, comprehensive narrative."

Deavers stepped in. "It took San Diego a few days to close the deal with McGarry, document it all, and get it to us. We've acted with incredible alacrity, I believe." He smiled affably, hoping to soften the mood. Judging from the look on Captain Lamb's face, he was not succeeding.

Naval Investigation Offices
San Diego, CA

August 14, 1965

Navy investigator Ensign Mary Lou Lavigne stared at the big chief boatswains' mate with a mixture of mirth and curiosity. *Too bad Dall isn't here,* she mused, *he'd get a charge out of this.*

Master Chief Marty McGarry sat sprawled casually across the small leather couch in the investigator's office. He chewed aggressively on a large, black, un-lit cigar, having been told by the LADY ensign that smoking was not permitted in her office. *Fuckin' women in the Navy!* He chewed and glared, waiting for her to digest all he had just told her. His uniform jacket strained to cover his ample belly, and his once-pressed trousers wrinkled at his waist and knees, the legs two inches too short, revealing the chief's sagging socks, one brown, one blue.

"Would you like some coffee while we wait?" Ensign Lavigne was trying to be gracious.

"Sure," the big chief replied. *Maybe she ain't all that bad.*

"It's down the hall to the left," she pointed out the door helpfully.

Chief McGarry grunted. *Figures. Fuckin' split-tails don't belong in uniform, damn it! Won't get a guy a cup!* He pulled himself up and tried in vain to smooth the wrinkles out of his trousers. He grunted again and waddled out the door, turning right. A moment later, he came steaming back the other direction.

Mary Lou had wisely phoned her boss, Commander Talley, outlining what the chief had told her. The commander asked her if the chief was drunk. Mary Lou admitted she couldn't tell. He told her to hold on, he was going to get a legal opinion and he would be right down. In the meantime, keep him there. Try to be gracious to him. Mary Lou smiled and replied, "Yes, sir!" before hanging up the phone. She sat at her desk and drummed her fingers nervously. *I wonder what's keeping the commander?*

Chief McGarry returned clasping a cup of coffee and glared down at the lady ensign. "So, where's your boss, honey? Out playing golf?"

Mary Lou looked past the chief, toward the door. "Good morning, Commander Talley," she exclaimed.

Chief McGarry winced and turned around slowly to face the commander. No one was there. He looked back at Mary Lou with a sneer. She held a middle finger in the air.

"That's for calling me honey, chief," she declared.

Marty started to reply, but shut up when Commander Talley appeared in the doorway. He was red-faced and a little out of breath, but he stalked into the office and assumed command.

"Chief McGarry?" He stared directly into the chief's eyes. "Have a seat." The commander pulled a small chair up to face the chief while he settled his big body into the couch. "Let me get a few things straight, Chief." The commander leafed through some papers on a clipboard. "You claim to have information that will help us close the investigation of the murder of Boatswains' Mate First Class C.C. Green?"

"That's correct."

The commander looked up at McGarry, one eyebrow arched.

"Sir," the big chief relented.

"You informed Lieutenant Lavigne that you know who killed Green and why. You also said you could provide the 'Golden Spike.' What does that mean, chief?" The commander tried to take a hard, bullying tone, but it didn't work on Marty McGarry. He'd been kicked around that block more than a few times.

"It means, sir," Marty said sharply. He could also be a bully. "That I can connect, link up the two investigations for you." He smiled, but his eyes were cold. "So you can close your file. Plus, the Navy can keep this whole thing indoors, if you know what I mean." He smiled coldly. "The civilian newspapers don't need to hear anything about it." He leaned forward and looked directly into the eyes of the commander. "But I gotta have some assurances, if you know what I mean...sir."

Commander Talley turned and looked at Mary Lou, who raised her eyebrows. They both understood the underlying implication. Chief McGarry would keep his mouth shut and go away quietly...as long as he was absolved of any possible wrongdoing. The chief wanted what amounted to immunity. Commander Talley nodded and turned back to the perspiring chief. "And, in return," the commander continued, "you want to take your thirty year retirement early, with no interference from the Navy, and you want what amounts to 'gangway liberty' on this entire incident."

The chief chuckled. "If that means I get to spend my days fishing off the Florida Keys and not worrying about finding myself complicit in this little affair," he replied, "then, yeah, gimme my liberty card."

Commander Talley studied the fat chief carefully. *He has the lingo down pat,* he thought to himself. *Complicit in this affair. Just like a sea lawyer.* "Well, I talked with legal and there is no reason we can't agree to that. You have what you want." The commander put out his hand, and the chief grudgingly took it. He knew when to back off. He was going to insist on something in writing, but he decided not to push it.

"Good." The commander smiled and leaned back in his chair. "Tell me exactly what happened, and take your time. Don't leave anything out."

Chief McGarry laid it all out. He explained his curious meeting with Fred Billings and the apparently random way he'd selected C.C. Green. He glossed over the fact that Fred Billings had presented him with a challenge, hinting that Chief McGarry couldn't find anything in his own office. He didn't tell the commander that he had produced the list of available BM-1's as a matter of pride, just to show off to his former student.

Commander Talley asked several questions, and the chief answered each one patiently and fully. When the commander was finished he stood and once again held out his hand. "I'm going to put all this information together and get it to the people investigating the murder," he declared. "In the meantime, you talk to no one about this." He stepped closer to the chief and glared at him. "Understand? No one."

"Yes, sir," the chief replied impatiently. He started toward the door.

"Chief?" Mary Lou called to him.

He turned and glared at her. "Yes, ma'am?"

"Why didn't you tell the investigators about your meeting with Chief Billings when they talked to you last spring?"

"I didn't appreciate the relevance that meeting had to this investigation," he explained. He turned and headed down the hall.

Commander Talley shook his head slowly. *More sea lawyer lingo.*

"Commander?"

He turned to face Ensign Lavigne. "Yes?"

"Can we do that?" She nibbled on her thumbnail. "I mean...can we guarantee he gets a free pass on this?"

"Hell, I don't know," the commander replied, smiling wearily. "At least we can get this info out to Dall and close the files on both cases."

Mary Lou nodded absently and munched on her thumbnail. She didn't notice when Commander Talley left her office.

Marty McGarry shrugged out of his jacket and piled into his pick-up truck. He piloted the truck out the main gate of the base and pulled into the parking lot of his favorite, and closest to the base, watering hole. The Rusty Anchor sat hunched in the center of a trash-strewn, weeded-over parking lot. The lot was covered with gravel, which sent dust swirling every time a car pulled into the lot or out of it. On a busy night, you couldn't see the road. The drive-way circled all the way around the bar, which created many late night challenge races around the dusty and worn track. All these contests were performed by men too drunk to acknowledge they missed their chance at the Indianapolis 500. It was said that on a particularly busy Saturday night a few years back, two San Diego motorcycle cops wrote over fifty traffic tickets in less than two hours in the parking lot of the Rusty Anchor. The place was legendary.

The chief loosened his tie and threw it onto the floor of the truck. He sat for a moment and thought about the exchange with Commander Talley. *Got what I want, huh? Hell, I don't know if the Navy can or will gimme what I want, but I took my best shot. I got my papers in, and I'm gone, regardless of what they decide. I just needed to cover my ass.* He sighed, stepped out of the truck and strode up to the front doors of the Rusty Anchor. From inside, the sounds of pool balls glancing off one another, the muted conversations, and the juke box wailing out a Hank Williams tune drifted out to greet him. He put on his biggest grin, pushed through the double doors and strutted in. He was immediately greeted by the dozen denizens of the bar.

"Hey McGarry!"

"Boats! C'mon over!"

"Pour this man some whiskey, barkeep, he looks like he had a bad day." Marty's best friend, Buddy Nixon, pulled another stool up to the bar as Marty gratefully accepted the drink and plopped down. The stool wavered slightly, but bore up.

"Gimme another, Jimmy," the chief said, downing his whiskey and setting the shot glass down on the bar. He turned to Buddy. "I'm gonna miss this man's Navy." He picked up the refilled shot glass and held it in the air. "Yay, Navy!"

A chorus of "Yay Navys!" answered him from around the dingy bar.

"So," Buddy asked. "You get what you wanted?"

"Yeah, I guess so," Marty replied. "I told them I was gonna retire to the Florida Keys and go fishing." He grunted and held up the empty shot glass for the bartender to see.

"That don't sound half bad, Marty," Buddy said, sipping at a bottle of beer. "Layin' back on your boat in the Keys, sippin' cold ones, fishin' line in the water."

"It's too fuckin' humid down there," Marty replied. "Hell, I'd rather tend bar in Vegas than get stuck on a boat in the fuckin' Keys!"

"I'll drink to that," Buddy gulped down his beer.

"Whatta you drinking to?" Marty demanded, beginning to feel the whiskey. "The boat in the Keys or tending bar in Vegas?"

"You damn right!" Buddy declared. He saluted Marty with his beer bottle and chug-a-lugged it down.

Marty grinned fondly at his friend, and looked around the dingy barroom. A few barflies straddled the stools at the bar, content to drink and stare into their glasses. Two pool games were being contested in the back, and judging from the language being employed, the participants were most assuredly Navy men, probably retirees. There were quite a few retirees among the denizens of The Rusty Anchor, and McGarry knew them all. He smiled, sighed and turned back to his drink. He caught a glimpse of a tired, worn-looking old man in the mirror behind the bar, and was about to look away when he recognized it as his own reflection. He stared at the reflection for a few moments, thinking back on the meeting with the investigators and on his thirty years in the Navy. He smiled sadly, saluted the reflection with his shot glass and drank it down. *Time to go,* he thought wearily. *Time to fuckin' go.*

USS Frank Knox

"Like I said," Deavers spoke gently, aware of the weary tone of his voice, and aware that Captain Lamb and Mr. Holliday were growing more and more impatient. "Everything fell into place with the interviews of Rudy Cobb, and especially Marty McGarry."

"Deavers," Bill Holliday sounded equally weary. "Do you have fingerprints on the murder weapon, an eyewitness to the crime, any physical evidence connecting Chief Billings to the murder?"

"No, sir," Deavers admitted. "We don't."

"Well," Mr. Holliday went on, his voice strained. "I'm no lawyer, Deavers, but what you have here is a case which is purely circumstantial."

Captain Lamb let his frustration show. "It's crap is what it is." He looked at Deavers harshly. "You're willing to ruin a good man's career because you SUSPECT him strongly? That's all you've got?"

"No, sir," Deavers replied quietly. "We have this." He pulled a sheet of paper from the file and laid it on the table between Captain Lamb and Lieutenant Holliday. "Chief Billings confessed."

The two officers sat stunned, staring blankly at the handwritten document on the table in front of them. They looked at each other sadly, communicating through the pain in their eyes. Roger Lamb slid the papers over closer, and Bill Holliday leaned in. Together, they read Chief Billings' confession.

August 23, 1965

On 18 July, 1965 I stalked Boatswains' Mate First Class C.C. Green, knowing it was his custom to get up in the middle of the night, usually around 0200, and go to the head. I waited for him to appear, and when he did, I pushed him into the shower stall and hit him once in the back of the head with a chipping hammer. I hit him with all the strength I could muster. I was going to hit him again and again, but the chipping hammer got stuck in the back of his head and I had to work to get it out.

Then the ship hit the reef and as fast as I could, I pulled the watch cap over his face, just as he had done to James, and I tied his hands behind his back, just as he had done to James. Then I hurried out of the head and got back to the chief's quarters before anyone missed me. It was total chaos, so no one even noticed me sneaking back in. All that time I hoped Green wasn't yet dead. I hoped and prayed that he lay there suffering before he died.

I have absolutely no regrets or remorse for what I did.

I would do it again.

I would do it again today.

Okay, so you want the whole story, here it is in a nutshell: C. C. Green was an ignorant bully and a disgrace to the Navy uniform. He destroyed my life. He put James in a coma and drove my wife into despair. I arranged for his transfer to the Knox so I could kill him. I was going to throw him over the side, but the ship hit the reef, so I couldn't.

Thinking back on it, everything worked out because now everyone knows about him and what he did and no one is going to care that he's dead.

I would do it again.

I would do it again today.

(signed) Frederick Billings, BMC

"And that's the sequence of events," Deavers concluded and set the file down in front of Captain Lamb, who ignored it.

"This is unbelievable," Mr. Holliday said, picking up the file and shaking his head sadly while he leafed through it. "A man like Billings..." He looked up beseechingly at Deavers. "But there are mitigating circumstances here," he pleaded. "Aren't there?"

"It was premeditated murder," Deavers stated wearily.

"But a case can be made that he had provocation..."

"He devised a plan to murder another human being," Deavers retorted, letting his impatience show. "He carried out that plan and committed murder." The investigator made a show of gathering up his papers. "And he confessed." He tucked the file under his arm in what he hoped was a gesture of finality, and looked sympathetically at Captain Lamb and Lieutenant Holliday. "Case closed," he said softly.

"Can't you put in a good word for him, Deavers?" Mr. Holliday asked.

"We can't worry about that right now, Bill," Captain Lamb cautioned. "High tide is in less than two hours, and we must be ready for one last maximum effort." Roger Lamb clenched his teeth. *Chief Billings a murderer!* He couldn't quite digest what it all meant, but one important element still vexed him and that was getting the ship off the reef. That was all that occupied his mind at the present. He could sympathize with Chief Billings later, now he had to concentrate on the Knox.

The meeting broke up and the attendees were filing out the wardroom door when one of the Marine guards assigned to keep an eye on Chief Billings came running up the deck toward them. He stopped, out of breath, and saluted the captain.

"Sir, it's Chief Billings..." The Marine swallowed hard and looked around at the others nervously.

"What?" Roger Lamb asked, grabbing the Marine's arm. "Settle down. What's wrong?"

"It's the chief," the Marine gasped, pointing behind him. "Chief Billings just shot himself."

Captain Lamb opened his mouth to say something, but just stared at the nervous young Marine. "How..." He looked over at Lieutenant Holliday, who stared back, his face white. "Let's go!"

Captain Lamb, followed by Mr. Holliday, the Marine guard, Deavers, both masters-at-arms, Ensign Dall, Lieutenants McCarthy and Darby hurried aft toward the junior officers' quarters where Billings had been isolated.

The other Marine standing guard at the cabin door snapped to attention nervously when the group arrived. Captain Lamb and

Lieutenant Holliday stepped into the small cabin and the captain motioned for the others to stay where they were. Deavers ignored the gesture and followed them in.

Chief Boatswains' Mate Frederick Billings lay on his back on his bunk. His ankles were crossed and he stared blankly at the overhead. His left hand was resting on his chest, and his right hand reached out toward the officers, palm up, fingers open. He looked as if he were taking a nap, except for the bullet hole in his temple, which slowly leaked blood, and the large, red bloodstain on the bulkhead next to his head. He had literally blown his brains out. On the deck below his outstretched hand lay a Smith & Wesson snub nose .38 caliber revolver. All cylinders were loaded; only one shell had been fired.

Deavers stared sadly at the gun. "Christ!" he murmured to himself, "he did it!"

"What is it, Deavers?" Captain Lamb asked. He and Lieutenant Holliday were staring down at the body in a mixture of anger and sorrow. They turned when they noticed Deavers in the compartment.

"Nothing, sir. I was looking at the gun."

"I gave orders to collect all the firearms with the exception of the shark watch. What the hell happened?"

"I don't know, sir..." the Marine stammered. "The chief wasn't armed when we put him in here." The Marine chewed his lip nervously. "We searched him, sir," he said reassuringly.

"Then how the hell..."

"That's not a Navy pistol," Deavers interjected. "That must be the chief's personal gun."

"Personal firearms are not permitted aboard ship!" the captain barked. He realized the emptiness of his statement and snorted derisively through his nose. The snort was directed at himself. He couldn't very well put the man on report, could he?

The captain leaned back against the bulkhead and shook his head sadly. They were finally going to get the ship off the reef after thirty seven days of unbelievably hard work under incredibly difficult circumstances. Surely, they had a right to be optimistic, hopeful, look forward to better times. They had no reason to think something bad like this would happen. *Something else bad.* How much could this ship and crew endure? Then Roger Lamb stood up straight and gathered his wits. *We will endure whatever it takes,* he thought resolutely. "Deavers, please go get your camera. Bill, let's get a detail to move the chief to the Iwo Jima as soon as Deavers is finished in here. You men," he pointed at the masters-at-arms. "Secure this passageway.

Close it off completely, and I want these Marines to continue guarding the door." He turned to the investigator. "Deavers..." he began.

"I'll handle the official report, sir," Deavers assured him.

Roger nodded absent-mindedly, stepped out the hatch and leaned against the life-line, breathing deeply. Bill Holliday leaned against the life-line next to him and asked, "You okay, Captain?"

"Yeah, yeah, just needed some air." Captain Lamb turned to his executive officer. "Have someone go up to the signal bridge and ask Lincoln Jones to lower our flag to half-mast." He glanced back into the cabin at the body of Chief Billings. "I think this man deserves that tribute."

"Aye, sir," Mr. Holliday agreed.

"I'll be in my cabin. We've got a lot of work to do." The captain walked up the deck toward his quarters.

Mr. Holliday watched his friend go. He seemed to have aged in the past few weeks, since he assumed command. *This kind of situation puts a strain on all of us*, he thought, *the commanding officer especially. God, I'm glad it's almost over!*

Mr. Holliday went aft to organize a working party, and the captain returned to his quarters to file his preliminary report with Admiral Wilson. The two Marines took positions on either side of the door to Billings' quarters, and the masters-at-arms began roping off the passageway.

Deavers picked up the pistol and casually dropped it into his pocket. Then he produced his camera and took pictures from many angles. He got as close to the body as possible without touching it and examined the stain on the opposite bulkhead. He was focusing his camera on the large stain when something caught his eye. Under Chief Billings' left hand, resting on his chest was the corner of a piece of paper. Deavers very gently took hold of the corner with thumb and forefinger, and pulled. The paper came out easily. It was a priority message to Chief Billings from a Navy chaplain in San Diego. Deavers held it up by its corners and read the message. His face took on a weary sadness, and he nodded his head slowly, knowingly, as if he had come to a startling understanding. Tears welled up in his eyes. He folded the message and put it into his pocket. He took a last look at Chief Billings, dabbed at his eyes with his handkerchief, and set out to find Captain Lamb.

Pea was instructed to tell the signal bridge to lower the ensign to half mast, and he ran forward and scurried up the ladder. "Linc!" he yelled. "Linc, where are you?"

"What's the big hurry, little man?" Linc stepped out of the pilot house, munching on an apple.

"Chief Billings is dead!" Pea had tears running down his cheeks. "He shot himself!"

Linc stared down at Pea as if he wasn't sure he heard him correctly. "Wha?"

"Mr. Holliday just told us. They say the chief killed C.C. Green!"

Linc still didn't fully comprehend. "Wha?"

Pea began sobbing. "The chief was a good man," he sputtered. "He was the best man on this ship."

"How did it happen?" Linc was beginning to understand, but his mind fought the realization.

"They arrested him and put him in his quarters and he had a gun and he just shot himself."

"Dear God," Linc lowered his head and whispered a short prayer. "Chief Billings, I...I just can't believe it."

Pea regained his composure. "Captain wants the flag at half-mast for the chief," he said, sniffling and wiping his nose on the back of his sleeve. "Can I do it, Linc? Can I lower the flag?"

"Yes, Pea," Linc agreed, his mind fighting through the shock. "Please do."

Pea and Linc made their way to the mainmast, where the American ensign still fluttered proudly over the Frank Knox. Pea untied the lanyard and lowered the flag very slowly to half mast, fighting back tears. When it was done, he and Linc stepped back and saluted.

"That's for Chief Billings," Pea sniffed.

"For Chief Billings," Linc agreed.

"We gotta tell R.J. about this," Pea said softly.

Linc and Pea returned to the signal bridge. Linc knew that if he signaled the news to R.J. Davis on the Prairie, every signal bridge on every ship in the task force would see it and the word would spread quickly. He could get into trouble for sending unauthorized traffic. "Screw it!" he spat. He turned the signal light on, spun it around and flashed the Prairie.

Deavers made his way slowly to the captain's cabin, his feet shuffling as if under a heavy burden. There was no way for him to feel the satisfaction he usually felt when wrapping up a case. He had conducted dozens of investigations in his twenty three years in the Navy, but *this* one, this one had to be the most emotional of his entire career. He was exhausted, not so much from lack of sleep, though it was a contributing factor. He was exhausted because this case took a great deal out of him. *I should have retired when I wanted to,* he thought. *A year and a half and I'll have my twenty five. A year and a half.* It seemed to Deavers to be a very long time. He sighed and knocked gently on the captain's door.

"My God, it just keeps getting worse!" Captain Lamb threw the message slip on the desk and shook his head sadly. The message informed Chief Billings of the death of his wife, Janice. She had taken an overdose of sleeping pills and lay down next to James Conklin's bed, where she died during the night. She had never recovered from the shock of the tragedy, slipping further and further into depression and despair until she could only see one solution, one way out of her pain. Told by the doctors that James was technically dead, that his body just didn't know it, she knew she had to stay with him. In her diminished capacity, numbed by the tragedy, she felt she had no choice but to follow him into death

"This is as bad as it gets, sir," Deavers agreed. He watched Roger Lamb as the captain looked out his porthole at the task force. The captain was tired, and his shoulders slumped. He stared out the porthole for several moments, then his shoulders seemed to straighten, and he stood a little taller. When he turned, his face had taken on the professional look of a Naval officer who had a big job ahead of him.

"We go on," he stated strongly. "We've got a ship to save."

"Yes, sir," Deavers acknowledged. "Chief Billings would agree, I'm sure."

The captain took a deep breath. "He was the best of us," he said softly. "And the Frank Knox was the best ship in the Seventh Fleet, largely because of his efforts." He looked out the porthole again. "Now, they are both lost to us." He sighed and put on his cap, readying himself for the task at hand. "Maybe that's the way it should be," he said wearily. "I think that's the way Chief Billings wanted it."

"Yes, sir," Deavers said softly.

Captain Lamb opened the cabin door and motioned for Deavers to precede him. "I want you to know I appreciate all your efforts, Deavers. I've been tough on you because of the situation, but you did a hell of a job under the circumstances."

"Thank you, Captain," Deavers replied, but he didn't feel any satisfaction with the captain's words.

"You're welcome to stay aboard while we pull off the reef," the captain offered.

"Thank you, sir, but all my gear is on its way to the Prairie. I'm going to watch the operation from there."

"Very well." Captain Lamb put out his hand and Deavers shook it. They looked into each others' eyes with a mutual respect. Captain

Lamb nodded and strode toward the pilot house where Mr. Holliday and Mr. McCarthy awaited him. He wasn't looking forward to telling them about Chief Billings' wife.

R.J. turned off the signal light and leaned against the flag bag, slowly shaking his head. He didn't know Chief Billings, but Pea talked about him all the time. He had a reputation as a good man, a top-notch boatswain. Deavers had talked about how the chief was helping him with some of the files, just as R.J. had done, and that bonded them, even if they didn't know each other. For reasons he couldn't understand, R.J. felt depressed about the chief's death.

"Man, what a shame," Chief Benson had been reading the flashing light from the Knox and he came up behind R.J. "I didn't know the man, but from what I heard, he was a helluva sailor."

"I heard that, too, Chief," R.J. replied.

"I guess we'll learn the whole story one of these days."

"I guess so," R.J. said absently. He stared out at the Knox, alone in his thoughts until he was interrupted by Ricky's noisy arrival on the signal bridge.

"Hoowee!" Ricky yelled as he bounded up the ladder, Peggy Sue held lovingly at his side. "Today gonna be the day, by God. Today's the day we drag that coon-ass ship off that coon-ass reef!"

R.J. and Chief Benson looked at each other and smiled.

CHAPTER THIRTY EIGHT

Salvation

Deavers stood on the Prairie's signal bridge, empty coffee cup in hand. He was waiting for R.J. to make fresh coffee. He had explained the entire case to R.J., using him as a kind of sounding board for the report which Deavers would submit. R.J. had listened intently, quietly, and Deavers noticed the young signalman's eyes tearing up when he told him about James Conklin and Janice Billings. R.J. found himself empathizing with Chief Billings and despising C.C. Green. When Deavers was finished, R.J. excused himself to make more coffee. Deavers watched through the window of the signal shack as R.J. wiped away tears and blew his nose with a handkerchief.

Now, along with several other sailors lining the port side of the big tender, R.J. and the investigator waited to watch one more 'Maximum Effort' to free the Knox from Pratas Reef. Today was the day, they assured everyone. Admiral Wilson had issued a message to the fleet, confidently promising everyone involved that, "...on the Prairie's fiftieth anniversary, we will all be talking about this day, the day we got the Frank Knox off the reef."

Almost all the salvage crew had been moved off the Frank Knox in anticipation of towing her to Yokosuka. Linc had asked for, and was granted a transfer to the Prairie's signal bridge. Chief Benson and the entire signal gang wholeheartedly approved the transfer. Linc would make an outstanding addition to Chief Benson's crew.

Pea had also asked to be assigned to the Prairie. Chief O'Malley welcomed him, saying, "Hell, we can always use another deck ape!"

The USS Frank Knox squatted wearily on Pratas Reef, a hopeful tilt to her bow, which was lifted gently by the rising tide. She looked more buoyant, almost eager as waves splashed white foam over the reef and up against her sides. She wriggled, almost floating, just for a few seconds, and her stern bobbed up and down in the deepening water.

"Light!"

R.J. heard the call and dashed to the mobile signal light. He flipped it on, spun the circular platform to the right, and rolled the entire apparatus up next to the port railing. The signal was coming from the USS Cogswell DD-651. R.J. sent "K" for 'go ahead', and held the light open. He accepted the message by sending "R" for 'receipt' and leaned over the rail, calling to the captain on the port wing, "The Cogswell is ready to make her run, sir!"

The captain nodded and put his binoculars to his eyes. Several junior officers on the wing-bridge did the same. "Execute!" Captain Marshall ordered.

R.J. sent the message and signed off. The Cogswell receipted for the message and immediately began speeding up. The Grapple, Conserver, Sioux, Greenlet and Cocopa took a slow, tight strain on the cables attached to the stern of the Knox. The grounded DDR seemed to move, just slightly. R.J. and Deavers looked at each other questioningly. R.J. raised his eyebrows, and Deavers shrugged. It was high tide.

Ricky was watching the ship through the big-eyes binoculars. "C'mon, baby," he urged, "C'mon, now."

The rooster-tail behind the Cogswell was growing in height and volume, creating a small swell from the sharp bow, and it slowly became a rolling wave. The faster the destroyer went, the bigger the rooster-tail and following wave. By the time the Cogswell reached its maximum position behind the reef, she was doing close to thirty five knots, her rooster-tail sprouting high in the air like a Yellowstone geyser. The subsequent wave crashed into the reef, pushing the Knox up just a little. It was enough. The salvage ships and tugs took a tighter strain on their cables as the Cogswell's wave hit the reef. They pulled harder, screws churning up boiling, white foam from under their sterns. Everyone in Task Force 73 held his breath. Some prayed, some crossed their fingers, some crossed themselves. Then, suddenly, almost as if she had never run aground, the Frank Knox drifted easily off the reef and bobbed, afloat again in the welcome blue refuge of deep water.

For a few moments, there was complete silence. Sailors on all the ships of Task Force 73 stopped and stared, not quite believing it was really over. Only the steady sound of insistent waves crashing on Pratas Reef interrupted the silence. The reef was already beginning to heal itself, returning to claim its own. The US Seventh Fleet had gathered to claim its own, too. Pratas Reef and Task Force 73 had spent over a month locked in mortal combat, and now it was over. The reef and the fleet would recover, each would return to some semblance of normality. It seemed appropriate for the battle to end in a draw.

The eerie silence was broken when the Knox blew her whistle and blasted her horn, announcing to the world that she was once again underway! Task Force 73 erupted in cheers. Every ship blew its horn in return, and on every ship in the task force men stood and cheered, waving their shirts, hats, bed sheets, anything they could find. Thirty seven days of 'Maximum Effort' had finally freed the

Knox. The best-case scenario had played out. The cheering roared across the reef and echoed back to the fleet, building force and power. It was a glorious sound, fueled by released frustration and the collective relief of thousands of sailors, yet tempered by the humility the grounding had forced upon them all. The Frank Knox seemed embarrassed by the ovation. She slipped off the reef and into deep water cautiously, like a prodigal daughter who was returning home hesitantly after a long absence.

"Well, I guess that's it, then," Deavers sighed, turning toward R.J. "For one, I'm glad all this is over. This has not been an easy case." He shook his head sadly. "Too many bad things happened."

"At least one good thing happened, sir," R.J. offered, pointing at the Knox. "At least we finally got the ship off the reef. That's a good thing, right?"

"It sure is, R.J.," Deavers said, smiling.

R.J. grew serious. "People dead, lives ruined, all 'cause of one guy."

"It's a sad story. Very sad."

"It's tragic, sir."

"Yes, tragic," Deavers agreed. "Like a Russian novel."

"Like Dostoevsky, huh Mr. Deavers?"

Deavers turned to look at the younger man and nodded, impressed with R.J.'s comment.

"You've read Dostoevsky, R.J.?"

"Yes, sir." R.J. chuckled. "But it wasn't easy."

Deavers looked out at the reef, a sad look in his eyes. He nodded, but he didn't reply.

R.J. cleared his throat self consciously, and asked softly, "What about James Conklin, sir?"

Deavers took a deep breath and let it out slowly. "James Conklin continues to linger in a coma. For how long, no one knows." His face suddenly grew very sad and he frowned deeply. "This hasn't been the toughest case I've ever worked, but it certainly is the most heart-wrenching." He took off his cap and smoothed his hair back, replacing the cap on his head. "I don't know, maybe I'm just tired, but it feels like maybe James is the lucky one in all this." Deavers stared out across the water. "At least he's beyond feeling."

R.J. turned and looked into the investigator's sad face. "You're right, sir," he said softly, "you're just tired."

Deavers smiled wanly. "There's a life lesson here for you, R.J.," he said sadly. "Tragedy always has a ripple effect. Just like tossing a pebble into a pool, it spreads out three hundred and sixty degrees and engulfs people, many times innocent people, in its ever-expanding circle of carnage." He leaned back against the railing and took off his hat, gesturing with it. "A bomb goes off and the blast blows outward three hundred and sixty degrees. Same thing with a typhoon, a tornado, or an earthquake. All disasters occur in that manner. You can't predict it, and often you can't avoid it. Just be in the path of the ripple at the wrong time."

R.J. stared out at the sky, the sea, the reef and the Frank Knox, trying to comprehend the lesson Deavers was illustrating. *So, life is being in the wrong place at the wrong time; no one can control his own destiny, Fate is a crapshoot? What does it mean?*

He turned to face the investigator. "Why do you think Chief Billings shot himself, sir?"

Deavers sighed and adjusted his sunglasses. "It was his salvation, R.J.," he said quietly.

"Salvation, sir?"

"Look around you." The lieutenant swept his arm wide across the ship-dotted horizon. "That's what all this is about, R.J., salvation." R.J. looked doubtful so Deavers continued. "We salvaged the Knox, and by doing so salvaged her well-earned reputation. We salvaged a little justice for James Conklin by proving the culpability of C.C. Green. Hell, in a way, you might say Green found salvation, too."

"We couldn't salvage Chief Billings, though."

"No, R.J., you're right, we couldn't." He smiled at the younger man like a proud and patient teacher. "Chief Billings was the instrument of his own salvation."

"What if he didn't have that gun?" R.J. countered. "He wouldn't have been able to kill himself."

"That's correct." Deavers sounded very tired, like he had something heavy to carry. "And then he would have lived a life of despair, wouldn't he?"

"Yes, sir, I'm just sayin', it's lucky he had that gun."

"Lucky," Deavers murmured, staring off across the reef. He turned slowly and stared into R.J.'s eyes. His face took on an older, wiser, almost fatherly look, and his eyes gleamed sadly, seeming to stare into R.J.'s soul. "It was the only way...to salvation, I mean," he said in a near whisper.

Suddenly, R.J. got it. *Billings had no gun. Deavers had given him the gun. Why? Out of what? Respect for what the chief had been through? Pity? Both?* Whatever the reason or reasons, R.J. knew in his heart that Deavers had provided Chief Billings with the gun. He tried to feel shock and scorn for the lieutenant, but R.J. couldn't help admiring him, and he thought he had a better understanding of what it all meant. *Salvation, Mr. Deavers had said. It was all about salvation.* He stared back into the investigator's eyes.

Deavers saw the look in the younger man's eyes, and they shared a silent understanding. "Our answers lie not in the ripples of our lives, R.J., but in the shadows. Learn to read between the lines; learn to recognize varying shades of gray, and remember that not all salvation is pretty."

Yeah, R.J. thought. *Like the narrator of The Raven, trying to understand, really understand what the bird meant, what message it brought.* R.J. felt like a light bulb went off in his head. *Shadows? Look to the shadows, Mr. Deavers said. Aha!* Then he knew he had it. He had solved the conundrum that was 'The Raven.' He had figured out the poem. He nodded to himself and sighed deeply. "Did you find salvation, Mr. Deavers?"

A slow smile crept onto Deavers' face, and his eyes took on a kindly light, a warm inner light, like someone had returned home to a cold, dark cottage and relit the fireplace. "You could say that, my young friend," he said, his proud smile growing larger. "And you, did you find salvation?"

R.J. frowned as he thought about it. He was free of Millie, that was salvation enough, and he believed he had discovered the key to 'The Raven'. He believed he knew what the black bird represented. He believed he understood the meaning of the clues imbedded in the last stanza. *The Raven was all about salvation, not death or insanity or eternal despair. Salvation! And salvation is not represented in the form of the Raven. It lies within the Raven's shadow!'...and my soul from out that shadow that lies floating on the floor, shall be lifted...nevermore!* "Yes, sir," he grinned up at Deavers, "I think I did."

Deavers nodded knowingly and put out his hand. "It's good to see you again, R.J., and thanks for helping with the case."

R.J. shook his hand. "Thank you, sir, but I didn't do anything. You're the one who solved it."

"Pieces, R.J.," Deavers replied, holding his index finger in the air. "It's always a puzzle and you need to put together the pieces, one by one. You provided an important piece to the puzzle. Like I said before, you'd make a good detective."

"So long, Mr. Deavers," R.J. said seriously. "For what it's worth, I think you did the right thing."

Deavers raised an eyebrow, then let it down slowly. *Yeah, the right thing,* he thought, *who the hell knows?* "Just Deavers, R.J. To you it's just Deavers!" He scooted down the ladder to the wing and disappeared down the deck toward the helicopter pad. R.J. turned back to the signal shack. His sound powered phone was ringing. It was the captain who wanted to dictate a message from the admiral to be flag-hoisted to Task Force 73.

The Marine helicopter lifted off the Prairie and headed toward the Iwo Jima. Deavers stared out the window at the point in the reef where the Knox had been grounded. From where he sat, there was no visible evidence of the destroyer's presence. The surf subsided slightly, and the tide, having reached its zenith, began to ebb. *All the physical ripples are gone*, he thought, staring sadly out the window. *The emotional ones will linger on, as James Conklin lingers on. The ripples will continue to torment Gerald Pizzonovich, Roger Lamb, Bill Holliday, and most of the men of the Knox. And me...the ripples seem to hang around longer for me than they used to. Or maybe I'm just tired. Maybe leaving the pistol where Chief Billings could easily find it was not the right thing to do, but the man was in such terrible pain, it seemed the humane thing.*

Deavers had helped escort the chief to the cabin he would be confined to until they could arrange transportation to the Iwo Jima. The cabin had been Deavers' quarters while he was on board, but now that the case was over, and the investigator would be leaving, he gladly turned the cabin over to Chief Billings. Despite what the chief had done, Deavers liked Billings, even admired him, and had stayed behind to talk to Fred Billings, to offer understanding, compassion. The chief had received the message about his wife just before Deavers left. He had held it tightly against his chest, and his body seemed to deflate, as if everything that had happened in the last few weeks hit him at once. He looked up at Deavers with an expression of pain so deep, the investigator felt his eyes tearing up. Deavers didn't know what was in the message, all he knew was it was bad news, probably tragic news, judging from the look of abject defeat on the face of Chief Billings. Deavers had realized then that for Chief Billings, life was over. His wife in terrible mental anguish, her younger brother in a coma, and Chief Billings under arrest for murder, which meant the end of his Navy career. Everything the man ever cared about, everything that mattered in his life was snatched from him in a matter of a few months.

Deavers had quietly packed all his belongings except his personal pistol, which was in the drawer of the desk next to the bunk. He bid farewell to Billings and offered his hand, but the chief didn't notice. He lay on his back on his bunk, staring blankly at the overhead. The message slip was held tightly in his hands, which were folded on his chest. Deavers had closed the door quietly and proceeded to the meeting with the captain and exec, where he would explain the solution of the case for them.

Now, staring down at the reef from the Marine helicopter,

Deavers searched his heart. *Did I leave the gun on purpose, or did I forget it was there in all the confusion*? After the chief's suicide, Deavers had read the message from San Diego, and he had felt then that he had done the right thing. A man like Billings would rather die than spend the rest of his life in a federal penitentiary. The gun wouldn't be traced to Deavers because he was the one who would write the report. It would be easy to bury the gun in all that official paperwork. No one would look too hard at his report. Deavers knew his superiors. They would want to forget the incident as soon as possible.

Salvation? he thought. *Bullshit!*

He sighed again and put his mind on the days ahead. He would steam with the Mars to Subic, and catch a flight back to Pearl. He was looking forward to getting home, back to familiar surroundings, and Maggie. Don't forget Maggie. He smiled and wondered if the ops officer on the Mars still had that bottle of scotch he had been bragging about.

R.J. pulled in the starboard flag hoist, while Ricky did the same on the port side, and began replacing the flags into their slots in the flag bag. The Knox was free, and the flag hoist he was storing away had advised all ships that the USS Frank Knox salvage operation had concluded. 'Operation Maximum Effort' had been a great success for the Navy. Now, the ships and men of Task Force 73 were scattering in various directions, off to new duty stations and new adventures, justifiably proud of a job well done. Many lessons had been learned, lessons that could be applied in future operations, and each man on each ship had a brand new inventory of stories to tell.

Deavers and Dall were returning to Pearl Harbor and San Diego respectively, each having developed a good contact for future operations. Only a few men were staying with the Knox. The rest of her crew were being transferred to various duty stations around the world.

The bodies of C.C. Green and Frederick Billings were being transported to San Diego for burial. Billings would be buried next to his wife, Janice. No one knew or cared about the disposal of Green's remains. The Navy would see to him.

In a short time, Pratas Reef would heal its wounds, smooth the scars left by the Frank Knox, and return to what it was in the days before the grounding. The reef, having a very short memory, would quickly forget the incident. The men of the Knox, however, and the families and friends of Green and Billings, would forever be haunted by the incident. Those wounds and scars would take a great deal longer to heal.

CHAPTER THIRTY NINE

A Sad Farewell

Captain Roger Lamb stood on the 02 level of the Frank Knox and looked aft sadly as the USS Munsee towed her toward Taiwan. She would go from there to Yokosuka. Roger was tired, completely exhausted, and doubted he could hold his eyes open much longer.

On either side of the captain, Bill Holliday and Geoff Darby stood watching the same scene. It seemed undignified for a United States warship, especially one like the Knox, to be towed away by her stern, and they could feel their captain's sorrow.

"I can't imagine her coming back," Captain Lamb said. "I just don't see how they can repair her."

"Let's hope they can," Lieutenant Darby said. "The power plant is in pretty good shape."

"Remember what they did with the Yorktown after the battle of Coral Sea," Bill Holliday reminded them. "I think these Navy engineers can do anything."

"From your lips to God's ear," Captain Lamb said softly.

"Amen," Geoff Darby agreed.

R.J. leaned on the flag bag and stared down at the many multicolored flags, all neatly arranged in their designated slots, waiting to be snapped in and pulled up the lanyard to form a flag hoist. The flags seemed to look up at R.J. with anticipation. *Are we going up?* They seemed to whisper anxiously. *How comfortable they are in their flag bag, waiting for the moment when I or some other signalman reaches in and frees them to do the only job they know how to do.* R.J. smiled down at the flags and ran his hand lovingly across the rows. *When their job is done, they know I will pull them in and tuck them back into their warm nest, which is their salvation. No wonder they see the world in such a bright and happy light. Why can't life be this organized,* he thought, *why can't life be this predictable? There should be clues to life,* he thought, *like the clues Poe planted in the last verses of The Raven. Clues that would explain life the way those clues explain that poem; clues that would lead us to enlightenment.* R.J. grinned to himself, knowing no such road map existed for his life. *At least I figured out the poem. That's a kind of salvation, right?*

A little depressed and very tired, R.J. sat on the rung of the flag bag and pulled Chuck's letter out of his back pocket. If he ever needed to be cheered up, now was the time. He unfolded the letter and began reading his favorite part:

...we were already in the hotel room when you and Millie came in next door. We were already partying. And I'll tell you this, but you have to swear you will never tell Renee about it. Ok, here goes. Renee's mom had this muscle massager, you know, it vibrates and loosens your muscles. We found another use for it, but I have to tell you, that sum bitch was loud. Sounded like an airplane coming in for a landing. Renee called the thing 'Mr. Buzzy.' We were laughing like crazy and playing with it when Millie started banging on the wall. She thought we were maids vacuuming the room! Isn't that a riot? We turned it off, but we were laughing so hard we almost peed the bed. Millie probably still thinks it was the maids. HA HA!

R.J. chuckled to himself. *I'm glad the honeymoon went good,* he thought. *The wedding and the reception were wild as hell!* He laughed out loud, thinking of Millie banging on the hotel room wall and yelling at the maids.

R.J. heard Pea and Linc stomping up the port ladder and he turned to meet his friends.

"Can you believe it R.J.?" Pea came up on the signal bridge with tears rolling down his face. Linc was patting him on the back affectionately, trying to calm the little guy.

R.J. nodded sadly. "It's terrible news, fellas. I'm sorry. I know the chief was your friend."

"It ain't fuckin' right!" Pea stormed. "It just ain't right!"

"Bad things happen to good people," R.J. said soothingly, repeating one of his grandfather's favorite sayings.

"That fuckin' Green deserved to die! The chief didn't." Pea pounded on the side of the flag bag, tears of frustration rolling down his face. "How could he do that? How could he kill himself?"

"Everyone says he was a good man," R.J. said.

"He was one o' the best I ever met," Linc said sadly. "Why did he kill Green, R.J., do you know?"

"And why did he kill himself, R.J.?" Pea pleaded. "Do you know why he did that?"

R.J. nodded solemnly. "Mr. Deavers told me a couple of hours ago." He sighed and looked into the sad eyes of his friends. Deavers had cautioned him that the information was confidential, but R.J. didn't give a shit. He motioned Pea and Linc closer and told them the entire story. He told them about C.C. Green and James Conklin, and about Janice Billings' suicide. He did not tell him about his belief that Deavers left the gun for Billings.

"I woulda just fuckin' let him go, you know?" Pea pulled out a handkerchief and blew his nose loudly. "Who cares if guys like Green wind up dead?

"It's a sad story," Linc agreed. "Somebody oughta write a book about it."

R.J. grinned to himself. *Yeah, someone oughta.*

"And our ship." Pea began sobbing again. "Just look at her!"

R.J. and Linc stood on either side of Pea, watching the USS Frank Knox being towed slowly away from the reef and toward the horizon. She seemed to groan wearily, and she rolled slightly, still listing to starboard.

"Towed away by her ass-end," Pea said sadly, wiping his eyes, his head shaking back and forth.

"She was such a beautiful ship," Linc said.

"Not the most dignified way to go," R.J. agreed. He tried to imagine how his friends must feel; their ship, their home was being towed away as if for scrap and a man they greatly admired and respected was dead by his own hand.

The Knox began moving northeast behind the USS Munsee, the fleet tug charged with towing her to Taiwan, then to Yokosuka. There, engineers believed, they could repair her and make her operational again. The once proud warship was being towed away by her stern. Her decks were covered with grease and grime. Rust patches appeared on her bulkheads, and she looked exhausted, beaten, as she was being dragged away unceremoniously. Her bow dipped under the stern tow, as if she were lowering her head in shame and humiliation at her unladylike appearance.

"She got beat up real bad on that fuckin' reef," Pea complained. "Look at how messed up she looks." He blew his nose again. "She was a good ship," he said, his voice breaking.

"One of the Navy's best," Linc agreed, watching the sad ship slip slowly away.

"She didn't deserve this," Pea complained.

"No, she sure as hell didn't," R.J. agreed.

"I hope they can make her seaworthy again," Pea said, sniffling.

R.J. and Linc looked down sympathetically at their friend. Each put an arm around Pea's shoulder and gave him an affectionate squeeze. "Me, too, little buddy," Linc said, fighting back tears of his own.

R.J. watched the mast of the USS Frank Knox ebb away, growing smaller and smaller, and the events of the past thirty seven days flooded his mind. The Frank Knox had brought them all together. New friendships were formed, memories were created, a mystery was solved, and the Navy had a successful salvage operation to point to with pride, and all because the Frank Knox, that proud, beautiful jewel in the crown, had sacrificed herself on the altar of Pratas Reef. *Could they make her seaworthy again?* His friends certainly hoped they could. He watched as the Knox disappeared over the horizon, and he smiled sadly. "Me, too, fellas," he said almost to himself. "Me, too."

CHAPTER FORTY

San Diego, California

James

James Conklin lies peacefully on his back, motionless in his hospital bed. Curtains drawn across the small, single window assure a perpetual look of gray to his room. His eyes stare blankly off to one side, his facial muscles slack and unresponsive. Drool rolls down from the corner of his mouth and drips onto his shoulder, but he doesn't notice. His voice and mind have been quieted by forces beyond his control. The steady *huffing-in* and *puffing-out* of the artificial respirator competes harshly with the Mozart violin concertos drifting melodically from the record player in the corner of his room.

"Huuuufff--Puuuufff!

All the nurses believe James can hear the music and it soothes him. They bring in classical music albums and debate the virtues of each submission. They argue incessantly about how much James can hear or see or feel. No one really knows for sure, but occasionally a tiny fragment of light or the briefest note of music will seep into the recesses of his damaged brain, and he will twitch slightly, a small hint of a smile appearing, then quickly disappearing, from his lips. They have all noticed and commented on it. They all believe James is aware of them. In the afternoon, a nurse will slip in and pull back the curtains from the window, allowing a little sunlight into the room. The slanting sun streams over James, casting his shadow lengthwise across the floor. James lives as much in that shadow as he does in his bed.

"Huuuufff--Puuuufff!
"Huuuufff--Puuuufff!

So, for twenty-four hours a day, seven days a week, the nurses assigned to James and the other comatose patients take turns going into James' room every half-hour or so, when the Mozart record is finished. They plump up his pillow, check his IV and bed sheets, record his vital-sign functions, and turn the record over, gently placing the needle in the groove to start the music again. The evening schedule, including James' intravenous meal, is reviewed and any necessary notations dutifully written down. Each nurse then stands quietly at the foot of James' bed, speaking softly to him the phrase they all agreed upon. "James, honey, if you can hear me, we love you, and we pray for the day you will return to us." They wait, patiently, for a response. "James, honey, if you can hear me, we love you, and we pray for the day you will return to us." They pause for a few moments, hesitating, hoping for some distant response, but it never comes. Then they go back to their card games and relax, for a little while, comforted by the steady rhythm of the *huffing-in* and *puffing-out* of the breathing machine down the hall.

"Huuufff--Puuufff!
"Huuufff---Puuufff!
"Huuufff---Puuufff!

Day after day, night after night, the dedicated Navy nurses minister to James Conklin. While he doesn't know it, they are his friends, and they feel a close connection to him, though he never talks to them, never answers them, never acknowledges them. "James, honey, if you can hear me, we love you, and we pray for the day you will return to us." James drifts through eternity in a subliminal fog, kept alive by machinery and modern medicine, unaware of the kindnesses the nurses perform on his behalf, ignorant of the tragic events surrounding his life, oblivious to the ghastly pain and suffering that followed the circumstances of his near-death. Navy Boot Camp Class 132 graduated without him; his fellow recruits strewn to the winds, reporting to duty stations all over the globe, pursuing their Navy careers. And still James drifts, unseeing, unfeeling and unknowing. The Frank Knox incident and subsequent salvage operation is beyond his awareness and comprehension. He does not know of the death of his loving sister or that of his brother-in-law, Chief Billings, or that of C.C. Green. He is completely unaware, his mind a blank page, his thoughts non-existent. "James, honey, if you can hear me, we love you, and we pray for the day you will return to us." Eventually, his body will waste away, and he will die alone in the dark, never seeing, never feeling, never knowing, accompanied only by a little Mozart and the raspy, labored breathing of his respirator.

"Huuufff--Puuufff!
"Huuufff---Puuufff!
"Huuufff---Puuufff!
"Huuufff...

The End

EPILOGUE:

The Wedding
Longmont, Colorado
Late August, 1964

The Rehearsal Dinner

It was Renee's parents' fault she was late to her own wedding. Not that it would have mattered much, considering the cast of characters involved, but had she been on time, Renee might have provided a calming influence on the wedding party. It had all started the night before, at the rehearsal dinner.

Benny Ortega was best man, and having been thus designated, took it upon himself to reinterpret the traditional tasks and responsibilities customary to that position. He took possession of the ring, which was traditional, but he delegated it to his girlfriend Karen for safe-keeping, which was not. He wrote a toast for the reception, which was traditional, but later tore it up, deciding to wing it, which, as it turned out, was ill-advised. Benny hired a hooker for the stag party, but decided to retain her services for his own personal use, which was why he didn't show up to the rehearsal dinner, incurring the wrath of Karen and almost every other female in Longmont, mostly on Karen's behalf. Benny couldn't fathom what all the fuss was about.

Chuck took on the role of nervous bridegroom with a zeal rarely seen in north-central Colorado. When Benny failed to appear for the rehearsal dinner, Chuck was forced to stand and make his own toast to his bride and wedding. He blew it badly, having nervously drunk a half-dozen glasses of white wine while waiting for his best man. Renee was not pleased, and blamed Chuck for Benny's transgressions, which made Chuck even more nervous.

The bridesmaids, led and agitated by Millie, were angry on behalf of their sister bridesmaid, Karen, and the ushers all sided with Benny, though they too thought he was wrong. The two groups sat across the table from each other, arms folded, ushers frowning, bridesmaids glaring. Renee's mother and father, Miriam and Roland, were not on the best of terms when they arrived for the rehearsal dinner. In fact, R.J. had learned that they had been on bad terms for quite some time. R.J. truly liked Renee's father, Roland. He was a personable guy with a great sense of humor. R.J. figured that came in handy for a municipal court judge. R.J. had never cared for Miriam. The feeling was mutual.

Miriam, small and painfully thin, chain-smoked cigarettes to relieve her stress, and talked in a wheezing, gasping voice, the tone of which obviously drove Roland nuts. Roland, tall, elegant, well groomed and the very picture of a distinguished judge, sipped bourbon from a silver flask to numb himself. Halfway through dinner, when it became obvious that Benny was not going to show, Miriam decided to take it out on Roland, who had sipped enough bourbon to catch an attitude. She and he ducked into a small alcove of the restaurant, where they believed they couldn't be heard, and unleashed upon one another vile and vicious streams of invective which included grievances covering the past twenty two years. Miriam and Roland had been married twenty three years.

The loud yelling and name-calling continued, the angry voices echoing off the walls in the small alcove. Renee fumed and her guests winced and covered their eyes. Chuck looked around helplessly, sweating profusely. He reached for a bottle of wine, but shrank back meekly under Renee's disapproving glare. Finally, she got up, smoothed her skirt and marched, head held high, into the alcove. After a few urgent and muffled words, all three came out and took their places at the table. Miriam sat and stared straight ahead, her face flushed. Roland made a gracious and happily short toast, and everything seemed back to normal.

R.J. sat back and watched the scenario play out, as if by script. He knew things were not back to normal, they were simply swept under the rug, contained, until a new opportunity to burst onto the surface presented itself. All the elements for a disaster were at hand: the bridesmaids and the ushers were at each others' throats, the father and mother of the bride were battling like the Bickersons, Renee and Chuck were stressing out, and Millie was behaving more and more strangely. *Who knows what tomorrow will bring,,* R.J. thought. *It should be an interesting wedding.*

The Nuptials

It was hot and humid inside the church. R.J. was sorry he had worn his dress blues. He had worn them just to show off, and to please Millie. He sat in a rear pew and fanned himself with a hymn book. *Feels like Guam,* he thought. The wedding guests were beginning to squirm in their seats, looking back toward the rear of the church, hoping to see Renee and her father ready to come down the aisle. The invitation said, "...ceremony at one, reception at two..." It was now one-thirty!

R.J. looked toward the front of the church. To the right of the altar, tucked away in a corner, was the little anteroom hosting the groom and his ushers. The door was open just a crack, and R.J. could see Benny's eyes peeking out, darting around nervously. Benny had a lot to be nervous about. The bridesmaids had heard about the hooker, and were, at that very moment, discussing Benny's ancestry in their little anteroom in the rear of the church. The more they talked, of course, the madder they got, and their anger for Benny soon grew to include anyone who was unfortunate enough to be born with a penis. Renee was late, so the bridesmaids had some spare time on their hands, which they happily dedicated to bashing men...all men, and feeding off one another's anger.

The ushers weren't all that happy with Benny, either. First, he'd pissed off all the women so all the men were made to suffer. He should have come to the rehearsal dinner, they argued. And he should have shared the hooker. Right is right.

R.J. heard a "pssst!" behind him and he turned to see Millie peering around the corner, hooking a finger and summoning him. He sighed, got up and made his way to the rear of the church.

"Wha?" he asked irritably, resentful at being called out like that.

"Renee isn't here, yet," she whispered.

"Well, why're you whispering? Everybody knows that."

"C'mere," she whined, crooking that finger again.

He let her lead him around the corner where they couldn't be seen. "I'm glad you're not back there with those creeps," she sneered, motioning with her head toward the ushers' room.

"Millie, why don't you just cool it?" he asked. "And tell the other girls to do the same."

"Because we're not going to take this shit anymore!" she said loudly. Several guests turned in their pews to look toward the back of the church.

"Shhh!" He held a finger to his lips and looked around uneasily. "This is a wedding, dammit, and you are in it. Act like it, and tell the rest of them to stop pouting. This ain't the time for it."

"Why don't you go hang out with your friends, Big Shot?" Millie said too loudly. "That's where you belong, anyway." She started to turn and leave, but he caught her by the arm and pulled her up close to him.

"If you screw this wedding up for Chuck and Renee," he snarled, his lip curled, "I swear to God you will never see me again." She pouted and he tightened his grip on her arm. "You go tell the rest of those girls to quit acting like babies for just a few hours." He glared at her, hoping he was expressing the anger he felt. "You're the maid of honor, so go do your job. How would you feel if you were the bride?" That seemed to get her attention. He pushed her away roughly, ignored her open-mouthed look of shock as she rubbed her arm where he had gripped it, and made his way back to the pew. He was about to sit down when he heard a "Pssst!"

R.J. looked up. The ushers' anteroom door was open, and Benny Ortega was standing in the doorway, taking a long pull on a flask. He was in plain view of the wedding guests, many of whom frowned disapprovingly. He waved R.J. over.

"Hey, R.J.!" he yelled, oblivious to the wedding guests. "Screw them bitches! C'mon in here with us!"

Oh, crap! Resigning himself to the task, R.J. made his way hurriedly to the ushers' room, slipped inside and pulled the door closed behind him. Chuck was sitting in the corner, alone on a chair, wiping his sweating brow with a handkerchief. Benny and Dino were passing the flask back and forth, laughing like grade-schoolers, and Jim Wallace was leaning against the back wall, bow tie hanging loose, his cummerbund bunched up around his waist. He was drunk, and grinned foolishly at nothing in particular. He kept glancing up at the ceiling and cocking his head, as if he could hear something no one else could.

Great, R.J. thought, looking around the room disgustedly. *These guys are drunk, the bridesmaids are all pissed off, and Renee and her parents have not yet arrived.* He sighed and shook his head at the scene.

"Have a swig of this, buddy!" Benny Ortega stuck the flask under R.J.'s nose. It was tequila and R.J. declined the offer. *This can only get worse,* he thought. He decided to do something about it.

R.J. took the flask away from Benny, looked around at his friends and scolded them for being drunk. "This is Chuck's wedding, and you fuckin' guys are gonna mess it up for him!"

"It ain't us, R.J.," Dino said slowly. "Them broads are causing all this shit!"

"Just be cool, you guys!" R.J. warned. "Lookit poor Chuck."

They all turned and looked at poor Chuck. He slumped on the chair, mopping his brow, glancing at his watch and looking frightened. His face came up and he pleaded with his friends, "What if she doesn't show? What do I do then?"

They all stood quietly, looking at poor Chuck. Each tried to put himself in poor Chuck's place and they glanced around at each other with shamed looks on their faces.

"Keep it together for a couple of hours, fellas," R.J. insisted. "Go nuts after Chuck and Renee leave for their honeymoon, okay?" He looked around at his friends angrily. "OKAY?"

Benny looked at the floor with an expression he hoped communicated contrition. R.J. was not impressed. The others nodded slowly, sheepishly and began straightening out their tuxedoes. Dino stood next to poor Chuck, patting him on the shoulder, frowning down at him with exaggerated pity and sympathy.

A commotion began at the rear of the church. Renee and her parents had arrived. Roland, who had been sipping bourbon all morning, was blaming Miriam, who had had a three-Bloody Mary-breakfast, for the delay and vice versa. R.J. pulled open the door to the anteroom just in time to hear Miriam shriek, "You are full of S-H-I-T, mister, you hear me? S-T-H-...S-H-T...SHIT! You hear me? YOU ARE FULL OF SHIT!"

"Oh, crap," R.J. muttered. He hurried down the side aisle to see what was going on. As he turned the corner, he saw Renee and Millie holding Miriam up between them. She was struggling against them, kicking her stockinged feet wildly in Roland's direction. Roland stood safely out of range, calmly sipping from his flask and frowning at Miriam as if she were a convicted felon appearing before his bench for sentencing.

"Mother *please*!" Renee pleaded. Miriam seemed to settle down.

"Places, everyone!" the organist warned and broke into a soft melody. Millie led the bridesmaids to their places in line and nodded curtly to them, conveying a warning with her eyes.

The cute little flower girl began walking down the aisle, self-consciously looking down at the carpeting, wildly tossing flower petals out in all directions. The mild snickering from the guests made her blush red.

The bridesmaids began walking down the aisle, one by one, in carefully spaced intervals, and Millie put on her sweetest smile and began walking slowly down the aisle behind them.

Renee took her place and looked back at her parents, beseeching them with her eyes. Her hands shook nervously, and her bouquet of white roses and baby's breath trembled in her clutch.

Her mother was carrying on a long harangue at Roland, who leaned against the wall, sipping and glaring. He put the flask into his breast pocket, straightened his cummerbund, and reached out, grabbing Miriam by both arms. She started to protest, but he stuffed her into a coat closet and leaned back against the door, grinning devilishly at his daughter. Renee rolled her eyes but couldn't hide the little smile that crept across her lips. Miriam banged on the door and threw her skinny little body against it, which had no effect at all.

Roland smirked self-satisfactorily, pushed the coat closet door shut and locked it, dropping the key into his pocket. He ignored the muffled and frantic cries coming from inside the closet, and took a quick swig of bourbon from his silver flask. He smoothed his perfect gray hair, ran a finger across his immaculately trimmed moustache, and adjusted his tuxedo jacket. He looked up and saw Renee, radiantly beautiful in her wedding gown, waiting for him at the rear of the church. He smiled with paternal pride and adjusted the white rose boutonnière on his lapel. It was going to be a lovely wedding, he decided. He walked, straight and steadily toward his daughter, took her arm, and winked at the organist. He proudly led his daughter down the aisle to the strains of 'Here comes the bride.' The guests all stood, relieved that the wedding was finally underway. No one could hear the muffled pounding and swearing coming from inside the coat closet. They had made it all the way to the altar, and were almost to the point in the ceremony where the father gives away the bride, when Miriam broke out of the closet and stumbled, somewhat disarrayed and very angry, down the aisle.

"...and who giveth this woman to be married to this man?" The minister's voice boomed throughout the small chapel.

Roland pulled himself up to his full height and declared proudly in his deep judicial voice, "I giveth this woman to this man." He lifted her veil, gave her a peck on the cheek, took her hand and put it into Chuck's hand. The father of the bride stepped back and smiled proudly and paternally. Chuck smiled back meekly and wiped the sweat off his forehead with an already sopping handkerchief.

"What about me? Don't forget the bride's mother!" Miriam shrieked and stumbled down the aisle toward the altar, panting heavily as she took her place next to the father of the bride.

Roland looked around at the minister, at Renee, at Chuck and at Miriam. "Very well," he declared grandly, "I giveth THIS woman, too!" He pushed Miriam in the back and she stumbled into Chuck's arms. Miriam looked a little disheveled. Renee looked a little confused. Chuck looked frightened out of his wits. R.J. covered his eyes with his hand and slowly shook his head.

Roland brushed his hands together in a gesture of finality, nodded politely to the minister, and walked resolutely down the aisle toward the door, smiling graciously to the wedding guests as he went by. When he passed R.J. he grinned and gave the 'thumbs up' sign.

R.J. grinned and gave it back. Roland walked out of the church, down the front steps, climbed into his big Buick and drove away.

Miriam stared blankly at the open church door, not fully grasping what had just happened. She could not have known that everything had been pre-ordained, that the moment had been long in the planning, and that she would never see Roland again. She made her way slowly to her spot in the front pew and sat down, smoothing her hair and fussing with her dress. She folded her hands lady-like across her knees in an attempt to regain her dignity, and nodded to the minister, who nodded back nervously and continued the ceremony.

The guests sat back down and watched the ceremony politely, but no one could ignore the soft but insistent buzzing as the wedding guests whispered back and forth. The minister made it official, accepting the 'I do's' and announcing the union. He turned the bride and groom around to face the audience and introduced them to the guests:

"Ladies and gentlemen, Mr. and Mrs. Charles Phipps!"

Everyone applauded. The women all wept into their hankies, and the men all checked their watches and pulled at their collars, relieved that they could finally get out of that church! Renee and Chuck started down the aisle to lead the procession out, when Miriam shrieked and darted in front of the bride and groom. She held a hanky to her face and sobbed into it as she led the procession slowly, painfully slowly, down the aisle to the back of the church and to much-needed fresh air. The guests didn't know whether to applaud the newlyweds or laugh at Miriam, so they applauded and laughed.

Renee seemed to be in shock as she and Chuck stood on the church steps and accepted congratulations from the people filing past them. The entire weekend seemed like a strange dream, but today...today was a nightmare! And it wasn't over! The ushers and bridesmaids stood in a circle at the bottom of the stairs, pointing, accusing, and pelting each other with insults.

R.J. was one of the last in line. He shook Chuck's hand and gave Renee a peck on the cheek. Then he hugged them both together. "Now, on to the reception, huh, kids?" R.J. tried to sound as light and happy as possible. "It's almost over."

Renee and Chuck looked at the arguing wedding party doubtfully. Renee smiled up at her husband. "The reception can't be as bad as the wedding, honey. Think positive." She pinched his cheek and kissed him.

Chuck grinned self-consciously. "Yeah," he agreed. "The reception can't be as crazy as the wedding."

The Reception

Miriam left the newlyweds and well-wishers at the church and hurried to the reception to make certain everything met with her satisfaction. No one was surprised when it didn't. She stood in the middle of the VFW dance floor, hip cocked to one side, hair teased a bit too high, slowly peeling off her white gloves while she glared threateningly at the caterer and her staff. The mother of the bride stepped behind the bar and poured herself a glass of champagne, drank it down and poured another. Maybe her daughter hated her, maybe her tight-assed husband ran out on her, but she knew how to throw a catered affair, by God, and she was going to do it right!

"All right, everybody," she barked, clapping her hands sharply. She refilled her glass once again, and waved for them to gather around. "Let's get this show started!"

When the first wedding guests arrived at the VFW hall, they found Miriam standing at the speaker's podium. She had discovered a microphone, much to her glee, and much to the dismay of the caterers. She was beginning to feel the wine, and had decided to be in a festive mood. Nothing was going to tarnish her daughter's wedding reception. She spotted a white-jacketed server fussing at the centerpiece on one of the tables.

"NO, SWEETIE, PUT IT IN THE CENTER," she called into the microphone. The white-clad server almost jumped out of his skin. The mike, on high volume, blared loudly through the room. Miriam looked down at the mike and shrugged. She pointed a crooked finger at the nervous server. "LIKE THE OTHERS, DEAR!" The microphone boomed and Miriam sloshed champagne on the front of her dress. She didn't seem to notice. She leaned unsteadily on the podium and waved to the arriving guests.

"C'MON IN DARLINGS!" Her voice echoed loudly in the near-empty hall. Miriam tried to adjust the volume, but only succeeded in dropping the microphone, which bounced on the floor and thumped its way down two stairs until its cord ran out and stopped. The mike swung back and forth, bumping up against the carpeted stair, making a loud *THWUMP-THWUMP-THWUMP* sound throughout the hall.

Miriam looked down at the swinging microphone and giggled. "Oh, poop! Did I do that?" She laughed more uproariously than the situation warranted, stumbled down the stairs in pursuit of the wayward mike, misjudged the distance and fell, landing hard on her skinny little ass. She giggled, leaned back against the stairs, recovered the microphone, and decided to share her Ella Fitzgerald impression with the arriving guests. When Chuck and Renee came into the reception hall, they were shocked to find her mother lounging against the stairs in front of the podium, warbling 'Won't You Come Home, Bill Bailey' into the microphone. Her skirt had crept up, showing one skinny white leg encased in a nylon stocking with runs spreading from her toes to her garter belt. A small crowd surrounded her, cheering her on.

"Chuck!" Renee gasped. "My God, look at my mother!"

"Well, what do you want me to do?" Chuck asked.

"Stop her!"

"Stop her? How the hell am I supposed to stop her?"

R.J. arrived at the scene, already pissed off at pouting Millie, found a table near the dais where the wedding party would sit, and deposited Millie in a chair. "Stay!" he ordered. She looked up at him and snarled. R.J. snarled back. He looked around for Chuck and Renee and spotted Miriam. One look at Renee's mother and he hurried up to the podium and disconnected the microphone. The crowd lost interest and left Miriam on the stairs, squinting suspiciously at the mike, pounding it on the floor, trying to get it to work.

The bridesmaids arrived before the ushers and positioned themselves on one side of the dais, creating a no-man's-land in the area of the podium. When the ushers arrived they had to sit on the other side of the podium where they would be without the company of women, which they didn't deserve anyway, being that they were disgusting pigs.

Chuck led Miriam to her place at the head table and got her settled in between him and Renee, where everyone hoped she would settle down. The pouting bridesmaids and glaring ushers pledged to behave, smiled patiently for the photographer, reluctantly posed next to each other, and joined in toasting the bride and groom. Only the occasional dirty look, sneer or raised middle finger marred the picture of wedding bliss. Meanwhile, several bottles of champagne were consumed, and the level of animosity in the atmosphere slowly began to rise.

Benny stood and ad-libbed a rambling, incomprehensible, tequila-fueled toast to the bride and groom. After the third reference to a mole on Renee's left breast (which didn't exist), the best man was finally hooted away from the microphone, much to the relief of a blushing bride and embarrassed groom.

The bridesmaids looked at Benny as if he were something the neighbor's dog had deposited in their yards, especially Karen, who looked like she wanted to kill him.

R.J. tried to steer Millie away from the dais by dancing with her and showering her with attention. She seemed to enjoy it, and the more champagne she drank, the more fun she had. R.J. thought they might actually get through the cutting of the cake without a fight breaking out. They almost made it.

As soon as the huge wedding cake was wheeled into the room, R.J. experienced a feeling of dread. He couldn't help but notice that the bridesmaids and ushers were looking at the cake, then at each other, and back at the cake. It didn't take a mind reader to figure out what they were thinking.

The picture-taking went well during the cake cutting. Chuck and Renee held pieces of cake up to each other's mouths and nibbled away, ignoring the pleas from their friends to push the cake into each other's faces. Miriam, unsteady but resolute, cut the rest of the cake and pieces were handed out. The mother of the bride sat at the table and stared down drunkenly at the remains of her daughter's wedding cake, now half-gone. She sobbed quietly, sniffled, and dabbed at her eyes with a hanky.

The ushers and bridesmaids glared at each other. Millie hefted her piece of cake, balanced precariously on a paper plate, and grinned at R.J. She made a motion like she was going to push the cake into his face, and the other bridesmaids began cheering her on. Millie grinned, but hesitated at the look on R.J.'s face. The ushers were coming up behind him with their pieces of cake in hand. R.J. glared at Millie, his lip curled. She knew not to push her luck when he did that thing with his lip, and she wisely backed off. Chuck and Renee were mingling with the guests, saying their goodbyes. The ushers' coats had come off, and ties were loosened or discarded. The bridesmaids took off their shoes. Battle lines were forming. The scene was set for a major confrontation.

Miriam suddenly became alert and realized her daughter and new husband were leaving for their honeymoon. "BWAAAA!" She screamed, pointing a crooked finger toward the departing newlyweds.

Everyone in the hall stopped and turned toward Miriam. Tears were pouring down her sallow cheeks, and her makeup was smeared all over her face. "BWAAAA!" she screamed again, and passed out, her face plopping down into the remaining cake where it sent a loud, resounding 'SCHLAAAAP' echoing through the hall.

Everyone froze for a moment, hesitantly looking around at each other, then the cake hit the fan. No one knows who threw the first piece, but it caught Millie squarely in the back of the head, sending her hair poofing into the air. She turned around slowly; shoulders hunched, and threw her cake at Chuck, who ducked. The cake hit Renee in the side of the face and the air quickly became filled with flying cake. Renee and Chuck were pelted as they made their escape. R.J. and Millie came running through the cake gauntlet and burst out of the hall behind the newlyweds. The four of them leaned against the building, out of breath, laughing uncontrollably. Inside, the confrontation had escalated into full melee status. Most of the wedding party and several of the guests had slipped on the cake-covered floor and were scrambling to get up, slipping and sliding and falling back down. Miriam, face down and forgotten by the wedding party and guests, snored softly into the remains of the wedding cake.

"Let's get out of here," Chuck suggested. He and Renee started toward their car.

"Take it easy, you guys!" R.J. called to them. "Don't do anything I wouldn't do."

"Yeah, Big Shot?" Millie had come up behind him and slipped her arms around his waist. "What wouldn't you do?"

R.J. turned and took her into his arms. Her eyes were a little unfocused. She had downed more than her share of champagne, and she was a little unsteady. "You feeling okay?" he asked.

"Sure," she said, smiling sweetly. "Let's go see Penelope, then we can go to the hotel."

Run!

That little voice again. R.J. hesitated. He looked back at the entrance to the VFW hall. Loud screeching laughter, accompanied by louder music and the sound of breaking glass filtered out and up the street. He glanced up and down Main Street, almost deserted at that time of night. The door to the VFW swung open and a couple of escaping wedding guests, their clothing splattered with cake, scurried toward the parking lot. The noise in the hall was getting louder. "Okay," he said, blocking out the persistent little voice. "Let's go."

Roland

The sun slanted harshly across the wind-swept landscape, dipping grandly into the western horizon. Roland shielded his eyes and groped around for his sunglasses, all the time holding the big Buick steady at seventy-five. He had passed Grand Junction and was headed for the Utah state line. He slipped the sunglasses on and smiled at his reflection in the rear view mirror. Where he was going he would need to get used to wearing sunglasses.

He chuckled at the thought of his daughter's wedding. *Oh, well,* he reasoned. *She'll get over it. Maybe one day she'll learn to laugh about it.* He frowned. *Maybe not.*

Roland had looked forward to his daughter's wedding day with gleeful anticipation. It was to be, after all, his Independence Day. After twenty three years of marriage to Miriam, he was ready for a change. Really ready. He recognized a budding young woman in his daughter when Renee was twelve, and it had occurred to him then that she would be getting married before he knew it. That's when the germ of the idea first took root in his mind. The more he thought about it, the more he liked the idea. He'd wanted to get away from that shrew Miriam for years, but he promised himself he wouldn't leave until Renee, his only child, was married. Renee's wedding day would be his Day of Emancipation. He could plan on that, concentrate on it; something to take his mind off that hideous bitch he was married to all of these years.

Miriam might have been a bitch, but at least she had the good grace to be an ignorant bitch. She knew nothing of finances or investments, which made his plan all the more easy to implement. Seven years ago he began planning finances for Renee's wedding. As he made contributions to her wedding fund, he also made contributions to his 'Into-the-Sunset Fund' as he called it. When Renee and Chuck said their 'I do's' they had a tidy little sum to get them started. Miriam also had a tidy little sum to take care of her, plus the house, the cabin near Estes Park, and two of the three cars. He kept the big Buick for himself, along with his tidy little sum, which just happened to be more than Renee's and Miriam's tidy little sums combined. Roland considered it just compensation for all those years of marriage to that harridan.

His 'Into-the-Sunset Fund' plan had lacked one important component: a destination. He had not put a great deal of thought into where he was going, California, Florida, Hawaii...certainly someplace warm. Then, one evening a few years back, Renee dragged him to the movie theater to watch a film starring one of her teenage heart throbs. That night he decided what his destination would be. It was perfect, of course. The more he thought about it, the more excited he became, until he could hardly contain himself. He thought of Miriam, her skinny arms and legs, her frizzy hair, her painted-on eyebrows. *What a disgusting...*He shook his head hard and rolled down the window. The cooling evening breeze swept in and calmed him. *That's all behind me now,* he thought, and twisted the rear-view mirror until it pointed straight down. He was never going to look back again.

Roland sighed happily. Everything had worked out according to plan, and now he was free! He would continue west on Interstate 70, turn south on Interstate 15 and cruise into town in the wee hours of the morning, when things were just beginning to rock! He smiled self-satisfactorily, tapped a beat against the steering wheel, and sang loudly into the fresh evening air:

"...there's a thousand pretty women waitin' out there,
and they're all livin' devil may care,
and I'm just the devil with love to spare!
Viva Las Vegas!
Viva Las Vegas!
Viva! Viva! Las Vegas!"

Author's note:

After the salvage operation, the USS Frank Knox was towed to Yokosuka, Japan, for an extensive overhaul, and after over a year of repairs and rehabilitation, she returned to active duty with the US Seventh Fleet, re-designated as a DD, (destroyer) shedding her designation as a DDR (Destroyer, Radar Picket Ship). It would appear that the crazy Navy engineers knew more than we gave them credit for. She participated in several more combat missions in Viet Nam, was decommissioned in January, 1971, and sold to the Greek Navy soon thereafter.

She served the Greek Navy under the name Themistocles for over two decades, and was taken out of service in the early 1990's.

The ship added September 11, 2001 to her resume when she was sunk as target practice by a Greek submarine on that fateful day. Her life thus ended, she now resides where she finally rested, at the bottom of the Sea.

May she forever rest in peace.

Rick Ainsworth
August, 2006

ACKNOWLEDGMENTS

Thanks again to the aforementioned men of the Knox for sharing generously their anecdotes and personal memories. Bill Dall, Bob Harp, Gary Johnson, Gary Platou, Harry Abbott, Jim Lewis, K.C. Troise and Richard Huehn, who was the first to solve the mystery.

Many thanks to my friend and editor, Debbie Hall for always holding the banner high and for always believing in the dream.

A novel such as this one cannot be written without the love and encouragement of a wonderful mate. So every day, with every breath I take, I thank God for Therese.

And thank you, Jack Janss, wherever you are!